MAGIC SPELL

"Do you always have an answer for everything?" Splashing through the water, Alexandra halted when she reached the sun-warmed sand.

Suddenly, strong arms caught her and turned her around.

"Not always." Matt lifted a hand to brush the hair from her temple.

Though his expression didn't change, she saw the sudden hunger in his eyes. "For instance, why can't I figure out what sort of spell kept me here all night? Whatever your magic is, woman, I've fallen for it."

He brushed his lips over hers.

"I don't think . . ." She shrank back, eyes wide.

"Don't think. Just feel."

———

ALL THAT GLITTERS

Ruth Ryan Langan

HarperPaperbacks
A Division of HarperCollinsPublishers

This is a work of fiction. The characters, incidents, and dialogues are products of the author's imagination and are not to be construed as real. Any resemblance to actual events or persons, living or dead, is entirely coincidental.

HarperPaperbacks *A Division of* HarperCollins*Publishers*
10 East 53rd Street, New York, N.Y. 10022

Copyright © 1994 by Ruth Ryan Langan
All rights reserved. No part of this book may be used or reproduced in any manner whatsoever without written permission of the publisher, except in the case of brief quotations embodied in critical articles and reviews. For information address HarperCollins*Publishers*,
10 East 53rd Street, New York, N.Y. 10022.

Cover illustration by Pino Daeni

First printing: June 1994

Printed in the United States of America

HarperPaperbacks, HarperMonogram, and colophon are trademarks of HarperCollins*Publishers*

❖ 10 9 8 7 6 5 4 3 2 1

To my family,
the only true treasure.

And, of course, to Tom,
whose love made me rich beyond measure.

ALL THAT GLITTERS

1

"*Hey, kid.* Nice singing. Sorry about the smoke. If you can make it again next Friday, I'll have a fan on, okay?"

Alexandra Corday blinked against the pall of smoke assaulting her eyes and nodded. "Sure, Will."

"How much did you make?"

She pulled a handful of crumpled bills from the pocket of her jeans and counted. "Seventeen dollars."

He shrugged. "Not so hot. But some nights are better, you know?"

She nodded. "Yeah. Got to run, Will. See you next Friday."

"Okay, kid. Take it easy."

As she walked out of the smoke-filled coffeehouse, Alexandra breathed in the fresh, clean air. The early evening sky was a clear, cloudless blue.

What had her father always said about such days? "Give me a rainstorm any day. At least then you expect a little thunder and lightning. But watch out for the days that look perfect, Alex," Wild Bill Corday used to warn her. "They're the ones that rear back and sucker-punch you."

Her dad had been right. All the really terrible things had happened to her on beautiful days.

Funny. Even though her father had been dead all these years, she could still remember everything about him. The way he looked and smelled. The deep timbre of his voice, especially when he laughed, which was most of the time. Always joking and teasing, he didn't have a serious bone in his body.

Alexandra could recall whole conversations they'd had. He had been the most handsome, charming, exciting father any girl could ever hope for. He'd faced each day of his life with enthusiasm and a sense of adventure that was contagious. Everyone around him had been affected by his zest for life.

In most respects, Alex was her father's daughter. She'd inherited his free spirit, and his friendly, outgoing nature, even though the events of her young life should have taught her to be more cautious.

Tossing her guitar in the back seat, she got into her old Chevy, turned on the ignition, and backed out of the parking space. As usual, she was late. It had become a way of life for her. With classes at UCLA and a job as a waitress for a posh catering firm, she never seemed to have enough hours in the day. On Fridays and alternate weekends she sang at a campus coffee-house, but she couldn't really consider it a job, since she didn't get paid, except for the occasional tip.

No one ever saw her walk. She ran through her days—and half her nights.

At the age when most girls were still playing with dolls, Alex had discovered just how fragile life can be. Maybe it was then that she'd leapt onto that treadmill, running and running, like the white mice in the science lab, who spent their days frantically going nowhere, hoping for their reward. Too exhausted at the end of the day to do more than fall into bed, only to awaken and begin the endless cycle again.

It never occurred to her that she could jump off. If she did, would she find a reward waiting for her? Or would she find herself, as Wild Bill had, dropping through endless space . . . ?

She pulled her mind back from such dark thoughts. Threading the Chevy through the Hollywood Freeway traffic, she turned into the neighborhood where she and her little brother, Kip, had lived for the past eight years with their grandmother.

Once the neighborhood had been considered a cut above middle-class; Now the houses and yards bore signs of neglect, but Nanna persistently groomed her immaculate little yard and tended her flowers, while the places around her decayed.

Parking at the curb, Alex bolted out of the car and raced up the front porch steps two at a time.

"Dinner, honey," her grandmother called from the kitchen.

"No time. Got to run." Tossing her books on a chair, she flew up the stairs.

She stripped off her jeans and sweater in the little bedroom and rushed into the small bathroom. A few minutes later, draped in a towel, she hurried from the steamy bathroom back to the bedroom, where she rummaged through the closet until she found her crisp black uniform and white ruffled apron. Alex dressed without even glancing in the mirror. Running a brush through her waist-length hair she secured it with a comb on either side, leaving it to stream down her back in a riot of damp russet curls. Then she grabbed a makeup bag and stuffed it into her purse. She'd attend to makeup later; right now, she had to get to the Montrose mansion before the catering truck.

"Alex. You have to eat something."

"Can't, Nanna. I'm late."

"Look at you," her grandmother scolded from the kitchen doorway, pointing a wooden spoon. "You're so thin, you'd blow away in a good wind."

"Look who's talking." Planting a kiss on the old woman's cheek, Alex tugged at her cheerful print housedress. "This old thing used to be snug at the waist, Nanna. Now it's practically falling off you."

A gleam lit the old woman's blue eyes. "You can't be too thin or too rich."

"You'll have to settle for one out of two."

"So will you, honey, so will you. But I still think rich would be better."

At that, they shared a laugh.

Alex went to the little boy who sat at the table listening to their banter and gave him a quick kiss. "Sorry I can't hear about your day, Kip. We'll talk in the morning."

He couldn't wait until morning. He was bursting at the seams with the news he was carrying inside. "I won the school art contest," he blurted out.

"You did? Oh Kip!" She gave her little brother a warm hug and kissed the tip of his nose. His hair was more copper-colored than red, and a parade of freckles dusted his nose.

"That's wonderful." Turning to her grandmother she said, "Don't make dinner tomorrow night. I don't have to work, so I'll take all of us to McDonald's to celebrate."

"Wow." The little boy's eyes lit up. "That's great, Alex."

"See you in the morning, Squirt." She opened the front door. "I'll be late, Nanna. Don't wait up."

"Where're you working tonight?"

"Didn't I tell you?" Alex paused with her hand on the doorknob. "Sidney Montrose, the director, is having a party. He lives in the old DeVine mansion."

"Harold DeVine." Nanna's voice held a trace of awe. "I used to think he was the handsomest actor in Hollywood. I've passed that mansion a hundred times. Be sure and notice everything so you can tell me all about it tomorrow."

"I will." Alex grinned at the look on her grandmother's face. "Maybe I'll even get to meet old Harold's ghost. They say he still haunts the place."

"If you do, give him a kiss for me."

Alex was already running toward her car, her bag flung carelessly over her shoulder.

The Montrose house was a blaze of lights. It had been built in the twenties for the silent screen star and had been remodeled and enlarged several times to include tennis courts, an Olympic-size pool, and a guest cottage. It was a distinctly California structure, with terracotta roof tiles and stucco walls that had weathered to a pale buff. Wide stone steps were lined with clay pots brimming with vines and bright splashes of azaleas, petunias, and cool fragrant gardenias. The caterer's trucks were already parked in the circular driveway, and several uniformed men were unloading them.

Using the car mirror, Alex put on blush and lip gloss and applied mascara to her gold-tipped lashes. She thought about adding a touch of color to her eyelids, but there wasn't time. When a young man approached and asked if he could park her car, she got out, tossing him the keys, and hurried inside.

Remnants of something her father had once said rang in her mind: "Regardless of what the rest of the world thinks, insiders know that Hollywood is just a small town—filled with very big egos."

Alex stifled a grin. The more she worked these parties, the more she realized how right her father had been. Not that she was an insider. But in his day, Wild Bill had been, and she had grown up on the fringes, aware of what went on, if not part of it.

After the heat of the day, the interior of the house was refreshingly cool. Alex's gym shoes made soft squishing sounds on the gleaming marble floor of the foyer. As she entered the kitchen, the manager of the catering firm looked up with a frown.

"You're late."

"Traffic. Where do you want me to work?"

Ignoring her question, he glanced down at her shoes. "I told you to wear high heels. You know the image."

She rummaged in her shoulder bag and produced black sandals. The manager looked relieved.

"Okay, Alex. You handle drinks in the pool and patio

area." He handed her a tray and turned away to give the other young women their orders.

Pulling out a kitchen chair, Alex slipped out of her comfortable shoes and buckled the straps of the spike-heeled sandals. She picked up her tray and headed for the open French doors that led to the pool.

Within the hour the crowd had swelled to over a hundred. An hour after that Alex had overheard so much Hollywood gossip, the words had begun to blur together: Annie Martinson, the soap queen, was pregnant by her director; Vicky Donlon, the comedienne, was suing her manager; hot young actor Tom Brennan, who lived with an actress almost twice his age, had just signed to star in Jerry Conrad's new film. Every juicy piece of information whispered tonight would be repeated in tomorrow's papers. There were as many reporters present as stars.

"Just look at that face-lift," a brunette said, helping herself to a drink from Alexandra's tray. "Her skin wasn't that firm when she was sixteen."

"And that was more than fifty years ago," the man beside her said.

"Don, you beast. You know her bio lists her age as forty-five."

They both chuckled.

". . . said if I don't see the color of your money by the end of the day, you won't see me back on that stage. And if you think that little stand-in can do eight shows a week on empty promises, go right ahead and let her try." The dancer who'd been speaking paused only long enough to set her empty glass on Alex's tray and take a fresh drink. She turned to her companion and added, "He managed to come up with a cashier's check before the bank closed. And from now on he's going to pay me—in cash—every week. I don't trust the bastard. And I'll never sign another contract with him either."

". . . her third husband, Harry. The one over there with the toothy blonde. And when I passed the dining room, her second husband was here with his latest. But she doesn't mind, because she's introducing that jerk hanging on her arm as her 'fiancé.' Where the hell does she find them?"

"Did you see the girl with David Ashcroft? This one looks about fifteen. Wearing leather and a lot of flesh. God, they just keep getting younger and younger. Pretty soon, I swear, he'll show up at one of these parties with a dimpled little darling sucking a pacifier."

As the man speaking reached for a drink, Alex had a hard time keeping a straight face. She'd just seen the couple he described. The man, close to seventy, was wearing a tuxedo, though the affair was far from formal. The girl with him could have been his granddaughter. She appeared to be barely in her teens—except for her eyes. There was a hardness about the eyes that gave her a world-weary look.

". . . want to see the contract. I absolutely will not work with animals. No dogs, no horses, no birds. Ever again." The woman peeled back the sleeve of her dress and showed her arm to the cluster of people gathered around her. There were gasps and murmurs of sympathy as she displayed her scars. "Goddamn hawk sank his talons in and tore clear through my jacket. By the time they got him off me, I was hysterical."

Alex returned to the bar, unloaded the empty glasses, and began giving the bartender another order.

During the lull she wriggled her foot from side to side, willing the feeling back into her toes. She'd been on her feet all day, and she had at least four more hours to go.

When the tray was once again filled, she lifted it and moved purposefully through the crowd.

Matt Montrose stepped down from his Bronco and gave the keys to a parking attendant. "Be sure and lock it," he said. "There's a fortune in photographic equipment in the back."

"Insured, I hope," the attendant shot back.

"Yeah. But I've grown fond of several of those cameras. They've been around the world and back with me. I'd hate to have to replace them."

Matt rubbed his shoulder, which had begun throbbing again. He walked with a slow, steady gait that revealed only a hint of a limp. As he climbed the stairs he studied the house. A familiar figure emerged from the front door.

"Matt. How good to see you."

"Hubert." He embraced the white-haired houseman affectionately. "How are you?"

"Fine, Matt." The old man held him at arm's length and gave him an appraising look. "And from what I've been reading, so are you. Thank God. When we heard about that land mine in the Middle East, we all feared the worst. Especially your father. If it hadn't been for Mrs. Montrose's objections, I think he'd have flown there and stayed by your side until you were back on your feet."

"I wish I could have spared him the anxiety. I've

mended nicely, thanks to a lot of physical therapy. Things are going well for me, Hubert."

"I never doubted that they would, Matt. From the time you were just a lad, I could see that you would go far."

The houseman studied Matt's rugged profile as he turned to look over his parents' house once more.

"I always loved this place, Hubert. Do you remember when my father bought the house?"

The old man nodded. "As if it were yesterday. You were eight when your mother, God rest her, passed on. And I remember the day, two years later, when your father married Miss Elyse and brought her and her young son, Dirk, to live with us here."

Matt smiled. "That's almost twenty years ago, Hubert."

"Right after your father had directed his first Academy Award–winning film," the old man said proudly. "And look at him today. He's still at the top of a highly competitive career."

Matt found himself smiling at the pride in the old man's tone. In a town that could boast few loyalties, the affection of all Sydney Montrose's associates was legend. And if that wasn't record enough, the popular director had an even more impressive one: he and his wife Elyse had remained married, despite the difficulties of merging two families. In Hollywood, that was cause for celebration.

"Your father will be delighted to see you, Matt." The old man squeezed his shoulder before turning away to greet another guest.

Almost reluctantly Matt went inside. He hadn't wanted to come tonight. In fact, he'd been adamant about staying away. Only Elyse's pleading could have changed his mind. She could be very persuasive. Their friends asked about him, she had said, and there would be influential people here who could benefit his career.

His career. The thought brought a frown. Until the accident, Matt Montrose had been highly regarded as a photojournalist. It was while he was doing a photo essay on the Middle East that his Jeep had hit a mine. His driver had died instantly. Matt had been luckier— or so they'd told him. At the time, with his shoulder almost severed and his leg ripped open from hip to ankle, he'd been in too much pain to be thankful that his life had been spared.

The photograph he'd managed to snap during the moment of impact had earned him the Pulitzer. Later, during his long recovery, he'd won the prestigious Raleigh Award for his portraits of street people. His pictures of the dark, seamy side of Hollywood had been featured in a sellout show for the past three months at the Avidson Gallery. It was whispered that it was only a matter of time before he turned his vision to the big screen. With his dark genius he would probably be an even finer director than his famous father.

No, it wasn't glamour or prestige that brought Matt here tonight, nor a desire to see old friends. It was his father's health. Elyse had confided that she was concerned about Sidney's heart. She wanted Matt to persuade his father to drop out of his latest project and take a much needed rest. Elyse had known that there was one appeal Matt couldn't resist, even if it meant enduring one of her parties; there wasn't anything Matt wouldn't do for his father.

Seeing him, Elyse disengaged herself from the crowd and hurried forward.

"Matt." She studied him with a critical eye, noticing that he looked tired. Of course, he'd been looking haggard since the accident. "I was afraid you wouldn't come."

"And miss one of your parties? You look wonderful, Elyse." He kissed her cheek.

At fifty-five Elyse Cochrain Montrose was still a strikingly beautiful woman who resisted all her friends' attempts to persuade her to have a face-lift. Her blonde hair had been pulled back into a chignon. On her, it didn't seem severe, but chic. Her face was carefully made up to hide the fine lines around the famous almond eyes; her dress was a swirl of black silk and lace that accentuated her slender figure.

"How is Dad?"

"Your father's in the library, talking business. Why don't you mingle and I'll drag him out to the land of the living."

Matt nodded and began threading his way through the crowd, pausing only long enough to shake hands, and exchange a few words. A few of the people were lifelong friends of his family, and Matt felt real pleasure at seeing them again, but many were simply here to be seen. They used any Hollywood party as an excuse to try to make the right contacts. And in this crowd, there were enough movers and shakers to cause an earthquake.

Stepping into the warm night air, he accepted a drink from the bartender, then turned to study the people milling around the pool.

It was then that he saw her.

Alex was standing near the edge of the pool, holding her tray while several couples helped themselves to drinks. She had long ago stopped listening to the stream of petty gossip, the litany of complaints. While she mechanically did her job, she thought about her little brother, Kip. It was obvious, even at the tender age of nine, that he had inherited their father's artistic talent. His teachers all confirmed that he was way beyond his classmates. Talent like his deserved to be nurtured. That was why he attended special classes, where he would be exposed to the masters.

She and Nanna had agreed to tighten their belts in order to send him to the art classes. The insurance money from her father's death was adequate to cover their education, but there was nothing left over for extras. Her mother, who had died of cancer shortly before her husband's tragic accident, had been on the verge of becoming a singer of some acclaim, but she'd been forced to cut back on her club dates in order to raise Kip. And then, just as her career was being revitalized, the disease had struck.

As Nanna said, they were getting by. But just barely.

Lost in thought, Alex failed to notice the man who stood studying her.

Matt itched for his camera. She was stunning. Slender, but not frail; in fact, there was such strength in her. It was there in the way she carried herself, in the way she lifted her chin slightly, meeting every look, every word, head on. She wasn't tall, no more than five feet six, yet she gave the illusion of height. Her legs were long, shapely. A dancer's legs, he knew instinctively. He could imagine her studying ballet, lifting her arms in a graceful arc, bending at the knees, spine straight, head high. The black uniform molded her body, displaying high, firm breasts and softly curving hips. The frilly white apron emphasized a tiny waist. His gaze slid downward, to the ridiculously high-heeled shoes. How did women balance in them? he wondered. Then his gaze moved to the cascade of mahogany waves that fell down her back. Fabulous hair, he thought. It gleamed red-gold in the flickering light of a hundred hurricane candles. This was how he'd like to photograph her, by candlelight.

She turned and for the first time glanced in his direction. He felt his hand tighten around his glass. God, she was more than beautiful; she was breathtaking. Not classically beautiful, he realized, but she had the sort of looks that command attention. Her face was small, oval, with high cheekbones. Her full lips were pursed into a sensual pout. As she took a step closer, the candlelight illuminated her face. Her skin was as pale and transluscent as porcelain; her eyes were green, with little flecks of gold that caught and reflected the light. Star eyes. He felt as if he'd just taken a blow to the midsection.

For the space of a single heartbeat, Alex froze. Unlike the other guests, who outdid themselves to be noticed, the man watching her stood half in shadow, as if avoiding the bright lights. Though he didn't move, she felt his touch as surely as if he'd actually reached out to her.

She heard two women discussing him. ". . . almost superhuman. Any other man would have been killed by the blast. Too bad about the limp, although I think on him it's sexy."

As the two women continued talking, Alex regarded

him. He was tall, well over six feet, with a trim, athletic build. The perfectly tailored charcoal jacket did nothing to camouflage the muscles of his shoulders and upper arms. He had the aura of a man who was comfortable with himself, yet his lean face, with its craggy, almost hawklike features, set him apart from the tanned, perfect profiles of those who earned their living from their looks. There was nothing manicured about this man. Though his jacket was cashmere and his shoes fine leather, he would look equally at home in jeans and a faded shirt. Shaggy dark hair in need of a trim curled softly at his collar. It was obvious he'd grown up in the lap of luxury and was comfortable with its trappings, but there was a spareness to him that revealed a rugged, fiercely independent nature.

Feeling the hypnotic pull of his gaze, she gave a tremulous smile and approached him.

"Would you like me to freshen your drink?"

Her voice was low, sultry. The kind of voice that would touch a man with the simplest phrase, and whisper over his senses.

"Yes. Thanks." As he handed her his glass, his fingers brushed hers. He was surprised by the rush of heat he felt. "Scotch. Rocks."

Curling his hand into a fist, Matt watched her walk away. The bow of her apron moved with each step, emphasizing the sway of her hips. He was sweating. What the hell was the matter with him? Must be the pain medication.

His ability to dissect people was both a blessing and a curse. It was what elevated his craft to the level of art and set him apart from other photographers. Still, sometimes he resented the way his mind worked. He couldn't simply enjoy the sight of a pretty woman; he had to crawl inside her mind and determine what put the look of pain or the spark of laughter in her eyes.

He'd seen her hands. Small, with long tapered fingers. A musician's hands. The nails were small ovals, without polish. But he'd noticed the cuticles as well. Bitten and worried until they were ragged. A calm surface, he decided—with a hell of a storm brewing underneath.

He forced himself to look away, to study the faces in the crowd, but within minutes he was watching her again as she began threading her way through the guests, dispensing drinks, with a smile fixed on her face. And then she was heading his way, and the only full glass left on the tray was his. He uncurled his fingers and ordered himself to relax.

"Here you are." She handed him his drink.

"Thanks."

"Enjoy." She turned away.

"Miss."

Alex half turned, waiting.

Matt could see Elyse making her way around the pool with his father in tow. Though they would no doubt be stopped several times before they reached his side, he knew that once they did they would monopolize his time.

"What's your name?"

"Alex. Alexandra Corday." She waited uneasily. The manager of the catering firm was looking her way. If he thought she was ignoring the other guests, he'd be angry

"Alexandra." He deliberately chose her full name. It suited her. He saw Elyse swooping closer. "I've been watching you, Alexandra. You do a good job."

She gave him a distracted smile while keeping an eye on the manager. "Thanks."

"In about ten minutes I'd like you to bring me another one of these," he said, just as Elyse caught his arm.

Nodding, Alex turned away, heading for the bar. She shook her head to clear her thoughts. She might be tired, but she was far from dead. She hadn't imagined the magnetism; it was real. In this whole house filled with handsome, dynamic men, he was the only one who had managed to affect her like this. He had the most compelling eyes she'd ever seen. She'd been almost unable to turn away from him.

Alex gave the bartender her order and glanced at her watch, then back at the shadowed area where the man was standing with the hosts, Sidney and Elyse Montrose.

Ten minutes. She'd remember.

2

The red Ferrari roared up the driveway and ground to a screeching halt just an inch away from the silver Rolls. A parking attendant shot to attention with a startled glance, hurrying over as the driver uncoiled himself from the car.

Dirk Montrose strolled up the steps of his parents' house feeling extremely pleased with himself. On the flight from England he'd had to make a difficult choice: the accommodating stewardess or Deedee, the leggy blonde across the aisle. He'd decided to go for the blonde, and she turned out to be a model and sometime porno actress who rented a place in Malibu. They'd been together for four days now, and he was getting a little bored with her. This party was the perfect excuse to cut loose. He hadn't bothered to leave a forwarding address. He really wasn't interested in hearing from Deedee. After all, he'd paid his dues. He'd given her as much fun as she'd given him.

Dirk knew that if he didn't bother to mention when he'd left Europe, his family would assume he'd just flown home today to be with them. That would please his mother. It never occurred to Dirk that he was being dishonest. He'd convinced himself that it was an act of kindness to allow his parents to think they were the most important people in his life. After all, wasn't he the most important person in theirs?

"Hello, Dirk." Hubert's voice held none of the affection he'd showered on Matt. "We weren't expecting you."

"Thought I'd surprise Mother."

"She'll be pleased." The old man cleared his throat. "We thought you were still in Europe."

"Did we?" Sarcasm sharpened Dirk's tone. He'd always disliked the old busybody who thought of the Montrose family as his own. All through his growing-up years, Dirk had resented the houseman, who had seen it as an obligation to report every little infraction of the rules. Old fart, Dirk thought. Ought to be pensioned off to a nursing home.

"Don't you think you'd better earn your keep and see to the guests, Hubert?" The old man took a step back, then spun on his heel, leaving Dirk alone.

He stood in the foyer for long minutes, listening to the clink of glasses, the sound of voices, the occasional trill of laughter. Home. And yet, not home. It was an odd sensation. He'd been six when his mother had married Sidney Montrose and moved into this fine big house. To cement the relationship, Sidney had adopted Dirk so that he would have the same last name as his own son, Matt. From then on, this life of luxury was the only life Dirk had known.

But four years at Berkeley and three years abroad had taught him that there was even more luxury to be had. One summer he and a group of friends had cruised the South Pacific, docking whenever they chose, picking up women with unbelievable ease. It had been an endless party. Another summer he'd lived with a somewhat older actress in her villa at Nice. She'd introduced him to more pleasures than he'd ever dreamed of. By the age of twenty-seven, Dirk Montrose had tried every liquor, every pill, every drug known to man, and a few that were still unknown. There had been so many women, he'd lost count. His personal rule: if you know where to look for it, there's a party every day of your life. There were a lot of pleasures in this world, and Dirk intended to experience them all.

Studying the faces of the people in the dining room, he made his way to the bar and quickly downed two double scotches before picking up a third drink and crossing to the French doors leading to the pool.

"Dirk. Dirk Montrose." A pretty dark-haired young woman came toward him, pressing herself close as her lips brushed his cheek. "You devil. Your mother didn't even tell me you'd be here tonight."

"She didn't know, Karen. It's a surprise."

The girl's eyes lit with a pleasure. "You mean you just got in tonight?"

Dirk nodded. "Just off the plane from London." The lie came easily to him. Hell, no one would ever be the wiser.

"I hope I'm going to see you sometime. You know where I live." She dropped a possessive hand on his arm.

Dirk bent his head, pressing his lips to her ear. "Believe me, I haven't forgotten. I'll call you."

"Promise?" She swatted at him playfully as he walked away.

Karen wasn't the only one whose eyes followed Dirk as he made his way among the clusters of old friends. Several other women watched his progress with obvious interest. With his perfect features enhanced by a deep tan and his sun-kissed hair curling softly around the collar of an open-necked shirt, he was the image of the California golden boy.

"Dirk. I don't believe it." His mother flew into his arms and hugged him, long and hard. Then she drew back to study his handsome face. "Why didn't you tell us you were coming?"

"I wanted to surprise you." With one arm around his mother's shoulders, he extended his right hand to his father.

"Looks like you've had plenty of sun." Sidney squeezed his hand.

"South of France. Had to say good-bye to some friends." He turned to Matt. "I'm surprised to see you here. I thought these Hollywood parties weren't your thing."

"They aren't." Matt shook Dirk's hand, noting the bloodshot eyes that all the eyedrops in the world couldn't make clear. "Are you home for good?"

Dirk shrugged, looking down at his mother, still snuggled against his shoulder. "That depends."

"On what?" Matt found himself wondering what had brought Dirk home this time. Money troubles, most likely. With Dirk, there were always money problems. There wasn't any amount of money that was enough to satisfy him. Most men would consider getting a job, but Dirk had always found it easier to charm the money out of his mother. When it came to her son, Elyse had a blind spot. He could do no wrong. And Sidney had given up fighting with her over it years ago. Sidney Montrose, the infamous tyrant on the set of a picture, was no match for his wife's determination where Dirk was concerned.

"On whether or not something interesting pops up."

"Such as?" Sidney asked.

Dirk shrugged. "I've been thinking of trying my hand at acting," he said to his mother.

"You'd be perfect for it. Wouldn't he, Sidney?"

"Maybe." His father studied him more carefully, seeing for the first time the lines around his mouth, the red-rimmed eyes. "The camera can be brutally honest. Why acting? And why now?"

Dirk flashed his most brilliant smile. "I've been asked so many times if I'm an actor, I got tired of saying no. Maybe I should give it a try. We know a lot of people in the business. Besides, I may have inherited my mother's genes."

"Oh, Dirk." Elyse wrapped both arms around his waist. "I'm so happy. This is like a dream come true. You're home. And this time, maybe you'll stay. Come on," she said, catching his hand. "There are some people you should meet. I heard that Frank Ellis is casting for a new film." They started to walk away, but Elysse turned back suddenly. "Matt, you will talk to your father about . . ." She smiled. "Of course you will."

Both men watched as Elyse led Dirk toward a noisy group standing beside the bar set up near the far end of the pool.

Sidney Montrose arched a brow and studied his son. "Talk to me about what?"

"Elyse thinks you're working too hard. She's worried about your health. She'd like you to take some time off and rest."

"She would, would she?" The director took a long drink of his whiskey, draining his glass. "And what do you think?"

Matt watched Alexandra approach with fresh drinks. With a smile she accepted their empty glasses and handed them full ones. As she walked away, Matt watched the sway of her hips and felt a warmth that had nothing to do with the weather.

He pulled his thoughts back to his father. "I think you're the kind of man who wouldn't know what to do with time on your hands. I think you'd probably die of boredom if you ever took more than a week off."

Sidney slapped his son on the back. "Thank God, at least one of my family understands me." Turning, he added, "I'm going inside for a while. Blake Riverton wants to talk to me about a script he's just finished."

When he walked away, Matt scanned the pool area until he located Alexandra. She stood with her back to him dispensing drinks. As she walked to the bar, Matt watched her from his vantage point in the shadows, unaware of the intense look on his face.

Dirk was charming. He smiled and nodded and stared deeply into the eyes of the woman he was talking to, as if hanging on her every word. In fact, he was already bored. The director his mother had introduced him to wouldn't be casting for another six months, and if Dirk had to live in his mother's house and wait for his big break for six months, he'd go crazy. What he needed was his own place. Preferably in Malibu. He intended to talk to Elyse about it tomorrow.

As the conversation swirled around him he happened to glance toward Matt, who was still standing at the far end of the pool. Matt was staring intently at someone. Following the direction of Matt's gaze, Dirk saw the slender waitress balancing a tray of drinks. Not bad. Matt had always had good taste. Of course, Dirk much preferred curvy blondes with a lot of cleavage, but this one was interesting, even if she didn't display much flesh.

He glanced once more at Matt, and a slow smile spread across his face. Son of a bitch. Good old Matt was staring at that girl like a lovesick teenager. Dirk's boredom was suddenly replaced by a rush of adrenaline. He'd always enjoyed the chance to burst his brother's balloon. This ought to be fun.

Excusing himself, Dirk went to the bar for a closer look. The waitress was just turning, her hands gripping a full tray. With perfectly executed casualness, Dirk managed to walk directly into her path. The tray crashed to the brick paving, sending liquid and shattered glass everywhere. The sound of breaking crystal echoed in the hushed silence that followed.

"My God. I'm so sorry." Dirk caught her by the shoulders. "Are you all right?"

The girl looked up, and Dirk found himself staring into the most beautiful eyes he'd ever seen. The face was equally impressive. And the voice, when she spoke, was a sultry surprise. "No. I'm fine. Just—shaken up. How about you?"

"No damage." He gave her a slow, lazy smile.

When she bent to retrieve the tray and began picking up shards of glass, he squatted down beside her. "Don't worry about cleaning up the mess. I'll have someone out here in a minute."

"You will?" She arched a brow at his faintly superior tone. "And how will you manage that?"

"I live here," he said with importance, and was disappointed at her lack of response. "My name's Dirk Montrose. What's yours?"

"Alex. Alexandra Corday."

"Pretty name. Pretty lady." He snapped his fingers and was rewarded by an immediate response: a maid hurried toward them, brandishing a broom and dustpan. Within minutes the mess had been cleared away.

Alex fought to calm her jumping nerves. Half the party had paused to watch her clumsy antics, and the catering manager was swooping toward her, primed for a fight. Smoothing down her apron, she licked her lips. "Well, guess I'll try again." As she gave the bartender her order, Dirk stood beside her, listening to the sound of her voice.

"Could I see you sometime?" he asked casually.

"Sorry." Alex chose her words carefully. "I'm afraid I don't have much time for socializing." She didn't want to insult the son of the man who was paying for this lavish party. But though his attention was flattering, she wasn't impressed with Dirk Montrose. In fact, there was something about him that made her uneasy. He was too smooth, too flashy.

"Need a ride home?"

"No thanks. I have a car." When the bartender set

the last glass on her tray, she lifted it and turned away, effectively dismissing Dirk.

He leaned a hip against the bar and watched her walk away. Glancing once more at his brother, he nearly laughed aloud at the frown that knit Matt's dark brows. So big brother was jealous, was he? Dirk couldn't think of anything that would please him more. Maybe he'd forget about cruising the bars and just stay a while longer.

The dark-haired man at the far end of the pool had refused any more drinks; that left Alex with no excuse to approach him. But while she worked she was achingly aware of the way he continued to stare at her. If looks could touch, she thought, he was touching her in a way that no one ever had before.

Dirk Montrose, on the other hand, had ordered so many drinks from her she was becoming alarmed. It certainly wasn't her place to tell him that he'd had too much to drink—not if she valued this job. But she had whispered to the bartender to water down Dirk's whiskey. At this point, he wouldn't know the difference. She glanced at her watch. Less than an hour to go. Already some of the guests had begun drifting away, collecting their wraps, saying their good-byes.

Dirk was heading her way again, swaying slightly. She groaned inwardly.

"One more for the road," he said, giving her his best smile.

"I thought you lived here." Alex watched as the bartender added a trace of whiskey to the water before handing Dirk the drink.

"I do. But that doesn't mean I have to sleep here."

"Why? Where will you sleep?" she asked.

"I was hoping you would have some suggestions."

Alex turned away, ignoring him. Moving around the pool area, she began collecting empty glasses and full ashtrays. Out of the corner of her eye she saw the dark-haired stranger approaching. He walked with a noticeable limp. She felt an odd flutter in the pit of her stomach.

"I guess it's time to turn out the lights," Matt said. He had stayed a good two hours longer than he'd planned, and all because of a woman whose face begged to be photographed. He just couldn't walk away.

Alex nodded. "Just a few stragglers left."

He glanced toward Dirk, who was leaning against the bar. "I hope you'll forgive my brother. I think the transcontinental flight didn't mix well with the liquor."

"Brother?" She stared at him in surprise.

Matt nodded. When she continued to stare at him he said softly, "I'm sorry. I never introduced myself, did I? I'm Matt Montrose."

He took her hand in his and again experienced a jolt. He hadn't imagined it the first time their fingers had brushed—it was happening again. Whatever the chemistry between them, it was a living thing.

"It's nice to meet you, Matt."

"The pleasure is mine." He studied her for one expectant moment, then said briskly, "We'll meet again."

As he walked away, Alex stared after him with a mixture of surprise and admiration. Matt Montrose. It all made sense now.

She'd heard of him, she realized, but not in connection with the movies. She searched her mind and was rewarded with a sudden flash of recognition: a photographer, photojournalist, who'd been nearly killed in some kind of accident. She'd taken Kip to see the exhibit of his photographs at the Avidson Gallery.

When she looked around, the pool and patio area were empty. She was relieved that Dirk had left; she was in no mood to duel with a drunk. She kicked off her shoes, and again began cleaning up the mess. As she worked, one name echoed through her mind, one face was burned into her memory: the rugged features, the dark shaggy hair, the gray, compelling eyes of Matt Montrose.

3

Matt wandered through the empty house in search of his father. With the guests gone, Sidney and Elyse had retired to the office, where Sidney was settling accounts with the caterer. As Matt strolled into his father's book-lined sanctuary, the phone rang.

Sidney pressed the button on the speakerphone and barked his usual greeting. "Sidney Montrose here."

"Sidney Montrose? The director? Are you related to Dirk?"

"I'm his father. Who is this?"

There was a moment of strained silence before the caller answered, her high-pitched voice sounding shrill in the quiet room.

"My name is Deedee. Dierdre Michael. I'm a friend of Dirk's. I found this number in the wallet he dropped beside my bed."

Hastily scrawling his signature on a check, Sidney handed it to the caterer and watched him leave the room. Then he said idly, "Are you calling all the way from London?"

"London? No. I live in Malibu."

"You must be mistaken, Miss Michael." He returned the gold pen to its holder on his desk and said almost irritably, "My son just arrived from Europe."

"We both flew in from Europe, Mr. Montrose. Four days ago. We met on the plane. We've been together at my place in Malibu ever since." In her excitement and agitation, her voice took on a piercing whine. "This isn't a social call. I just got home and found out that Dirk took off in my new Ferrari. What's more, Dirk charged over five thousand dollars' worth of food, liquor, and clothing on my credit card. Now you listen to me, Mr. Montrose. If my car isn't returned immediately and these debts paid, I'm calling the police."

Sidney looked up to find his wife and son staring at him in shocked silence. Thinking quickly he said, "Give me your number, Miss Michael. I'll get back to you." He spoke in the flat tone of a man who had been through this sort of thing before. Taking the number down on a pad, he pressed the disconnect button without another word.

Elyse's eyes flashed fire. "That girl is a liar. Why would Dirk take her car when we have a fleet of cars here at his disposal? What need would Dirk have to charge anything on this—this person's credit card? Dirk has plenty of his own credit cards. And how could he possibly have been with this tramp when he just arrived from London tonight?

"That's the trouble with being the son of a celebrity," Elyse went on before her husband could say a word. "There's always someone out there trying to take advantage of you. But this time we've caught her in her own lie: Dirk was in London when she claims he was with her."

Sidney ran a hand through his graying hair. "How do you know that? We didn't pick him up at the airport. And did you take a good look at him tonight? He looked rough. Damn rough."

"Oh, you'd look fresh and chipper if you flew all the way in from London, wouldn't you? Especially if you hurried right over from the airport to attend your parents' party." Her voice was heavy with sarcasm. "Without, I might add, even taking the time to unpack and change."

"Why are we having this discussion?" Matt asked tiredly. He sat in a leather wing chair beside the desk and studied his father with a mixture of sadness and impatience. "Dirk is old enough to do as he pleases."

"As long as he's man enough to clean up his messes," Sidney snapped. "Do you know how the press would treat us if this girl has him picked up for credit card fraud, or worse, for stealing her car?"

"Then let's settle this thing right now." Matt rose and headed toward the door. "Why don't we catch Dirk before he has a chance to leave and ask him if he has his wallet? While we're at it, we'll ask him how he got here tonight."

"I'm betting he drove a Ferrari," Sidney said.

Elyse turned on him. "Are you taking the side of that liar?"

"Elyse, be sensible. Why would she lie?"

"She has a little scheme going." Elyse began to pace. "They all have an angle—I seem to recall you saying that very thing one night, Matt, in a moment of anger many years ago. I believe it was some would-be actress who kept hounding you, begging to pose for you. She suggested you would make each other famous."

"In the end, she didn't need my help, Elyse. She's been on the cover of dozens of magazines."

"Oh yes. I've seen her," Elyse said sarcastically. "All of her. But you can't deny she wanted to use you, Matt. There are millions of women like that out there."

"Why are we fighting?" Matt said, struggling to control his anger. "I'll bring Dirk in and ask him for the truth."

"I won't have it." Elyse stormed over to her husband's desk and placed both palms flat on the desktop, meeting Sidney's dark gaze. "I won't have you hauling Dirk in here and pouncing on him. The two of you will gang up on him and make his life miserable, as you've always done. You'll accuse him in that righteous tone, and you and Matt will exchange knowing looks. Dirk will leave again, and I'll never know where he is or what he's doing. I won't have it. Do you hear me?"

Sidney glanced warily at Matt, then looked away in defeat.

"Maybe we'd all be better off not knowing where he is or what he's doing," Matt muttered. "If you'll excuse me, it's late. And I'm tired of this scene. It's become a rerun."

"It's so easy for you, Matt," Elyse cried. "You've always been sure of your father's love. But Dirk has always felt like an outsider. He's just—"

Matt closed the door after him. He stalked along the hallway past the dining room, crowded with steam tables and littered with trays of food, and through the front entrance of his father's home. He barely glanced at the workers from the catering company, who were busy loading tables and portable bars, soiled table linen, silver, and crystal into the backs of the trucks.

One of the parking attendants brought Matt's Bronco around the circular drive, leaving it idling at the curb behind the convoy of trucks. Matt climbed inside, shook a cigarette from the pack he took from his jacket pocket and lit it. In the darkness of the car he took a deep drag, filling his lungs, then exhaled a stream of smoke and stared at the blackened sky.

This was why, he told himself, he hated to come home. They'd been playing this little game for a lifetime. And he was too tired of it to play anymore.

The uniformed waitresses filed out the door and stood in a cluster while the parking attendants brought their cars. For a moment Matt was too engrossed in his thinking to even notice. Then one figure separated herself from the others, and Matt looked over to see Alexandra climbing into her little car. The line of catering trucks pulled away, and the Chevy followed. Matt glanced toward the house at the silhouettes of Sidney and Elyse, who were still arguing in Sidney's office, as the convoy rounded a curve and the red Ferrari pulled out of the shadows and slipped into line behind Alex's car.

Alex was bone tired. She drove mechanically through the sparse traffic, taking no notice of the blinking neon signs advertising the motels, all-night businesses, and fast-food places that lined the freeway. All she wanted was to get out of her clothes and fall into bed.

When she turned onto her street, she saw the headlights behind her, but her mind registered no surprise. This was a busy neighborhood. There were plenty of other people just getting home at two in the morning. She climbed out of the car and slammed the door, turning to find herself face to face with a smiling Dirk Montrose.

"What . . ." Her heart lurched, and she licked her lips and tried again. "What are you doing here?"

"Following you home. It isn't safe for a pretty girl to be out alone at this time of night."

"Thanks, but I do it all the time. I can take care of myself."

He took a step closer and reached for her bag. When she stiffened, he gave her a lopsided, boyish grin. "Hey, I wasn't going to steal it. I was just going to offer to carry it. It looks too heavy for you." As his hands closed around the strap he looked at her with a guileless smile. "What are you carrying in here? This thing weighs a ton."

"Just my shoes, makeup. I can manage." She took it from him and headed for the porch.

"Did you get to meet lots of celebrities tonight?" Dirk asked, keeping his tone casual.

Alex shrugged. "A few."

"Anybody special?" He managed to keep up with her brisk strides.

"Yuri Borov, the Russian dancer. He's even better-looking close up."

So, she liked ballet. He decided to use that knowledge.

"I wish I'd known you wanted to meet him." Dirk's manner was so sincere, Alex glanced over to study him in the dim glow that reached them from the streetlamps. "He and I are friends. I would have been glad to introduce you."

"You know Yuri Borov?"

Digging his hands into his pockets, Dirk assumed a shy, almost embarrassed pose. "I guess I know just about everyone in Hollywood. Or my parents do."

"That's nice." Alex paused at the bottom step. "Well, good night, Dirk. I have to get in."

He caught her hand and stared into her eyes. "I'd like to introduce you to everyone I know. Wouldn't that be fun, to meet every celebrity in Hollywood?"

She grinned. It was obvious that he was still slightly drunk and trying to be on his best behavior. Away from his Hollywood crowd, he seemed younger, almost boyish.

"Yes. That would be fun. Now good night."

"Alex." He said her name in a quick rush of panic, as though afraid he'd lose his nerve any moment. "Don't go in just yet. Stay and talk to me awhile."

"Can't. It's late, and I'm very tired. I went to classes all day, then worked all night. Now let go of my hand."

"No one ever wants to just talk to me." His voice rose in pitch, like a petulant child's, and he threw back his head and shouted, "I meet the most beautiful girl in the world tonight, and she doesn't even want to talk to me."

"Shhh." She placed her hand quickly over his mouth to silence him. "My grandmother is asleep in that room." She pointed to the window that overlooked the street. "She's old, and she doesn't sleep well. If you wake her, she'll be awake for the rest of the night."

"All right." He gave her a sweet, boyish grin that would have melted the coldest heart. "I'll be quiet if you promise to just sit and talk to me awhile."

She tried not to be flattered by his attentions, but she was weakening. "Dirk, I'm—"

"Come on." He took her by the hand. "Have you ever sat in a Ferrari before?"

By now Alex was giggling. He was charming.

"There." He led her back down the path to the street, opened the Ferrari's passenger door, and helped her inside, running around to slide into the driver's seat. "Smell it," he said, inhaling deeply. "Doesn't a new car smell fantastic?"

Alex followed his lead and grinned. "Yeah." Running her hand along the soft leather seat, she gave an admiring sigh. "Your car is beautiful."

"You ought to see how easily she handles."

"Another time. What did you want to talk about?"

But Dirk wasn't listening. God, he was a good actor. No woman had ever been able to resist him. He'd honed his skills at his mother's knee. If he wanted to, he thought smugly, he could charm the Statue of Liberty. He turned the key in the ignition and shifted the car into gear, and they shot off down the dark street.

"Dirk!" Alex shouted above the squeal of tires, but the man beside her paid no attention. Changing gears, he floored the accelerator and peeled around a corner.

Pressed against the smooth leather seat, Alex turned a terrified gaze on Dirk. He had changed before her very eyes. No longer silly or charming, or even very drunk, the look on his face was one of pure malice.

"What are you doing? You promised we'd just talk."

"You can't be that stupid. Do you think when a man looks at you the way I did tonight, he'd be willing to settle for talk? I want action, baby. But first, I want to

get out of this goddamn depressing neighborhood. I
can't believe people actually live here."

Alex felt the panic rise in her throat. What had she
done? Oh God, what had she just done? She knew
nothing at all about this man. And she'd broken just
about every rule of safety she'd ever learned: she'd
neglected to watch the rearview mirror while she drove
alone at night, she'd stepped out of her car before looking around, and worst of all, she had actually let him
persuade her to get into his car.

Calling herself every kind of fool, she looked wildly
around as the streets sped by, struggling to orient herself. She had to get out of this car, and somehow run to
safety.

Careening down a side street, Dirk pressed the
accelerator, thrilling to the surge of speed. Even the
look of fear on Alex's face gave him a thrill. This was
going to be fun. And when it was over, he'd rub Matt's
nose in it. He'd just happen to let slip how much the
little waitress had enjoyed their romp in the motel after
the party. Then he'd twist the knife a little more by
offering to introduce her to Matt, so he could have a
little fun of his own.

Turning another corner, he saw the red light ahead
and decided to beat it. As the light changed, the
Ferrari lurched forward. Too late, Dirk saw the dog
dart from between parked cars into the street. Alex
called out a warning.

With a reflex action that left him breathless, Dirk
spun the wheel and just avoided hitting the animal. He
turned a triumphant face toward the girl who sat
clutching the handle of the door beside her. Instead of
relief he saw the look of horror on her face as she

stared straight ahead. Abruptly he turned his attention back to the street.

"No. Oh my God!"

An old man, starkly illuminated in the oncoming headlights, was standing just a few feet in front of them. His eyes were wide, his hands lifted as if to ward off a blow. The vehicle hurtled forward so fast, it seemed barely to bounce as it struck him. Dirk heard a shrill, piercing sound, like a siren, and realized it was Alex's screams.

Several hundred feet beyond, he managed to bring the car to a stop. He sat gripping the wheel; his hands seemed to have lost all feeling. There were no more screams, no sirens. Only silence. A terrible, awesome silence, punctuated by a low, shuddering sound. Glancing to his right, Dirk saw Alex's body shaking uncontrollably as she sobbed into her hands.

Staring into the rearview mirror, he strained for a glimpse of the old man. It was too dark. There were no headlights, no streetlights.

Shifting into reverse, he backed up slowly, looking for anything that resembled the man he had seen in his headlights. Though she was still crying, Alex lifted her head and wiped her tears with the back of her hand.

They hadn't hit the old man, she thought desperately. They had managed to avoid him. The bump she had felt was just something on the pavement. He'd survived. Everything was fine. It had to be.

The car backed up slowly, slowly, and then stopped. Dirk stared at the dark heap in the middle of the street. Following his gaze, Alex gasped.

"You hit him." Her voice was low, choked with tears and rage.

Dirk studied the dark form for a minute longer, then seemed to come to an immediate decision. He shifted gears again. The car shot forward, engines roaring.

"You have to stop!" She was shouting at him, but Dirk acted as if he couldn't hear her.

They rounded a corner, and the little car surged ahead, faster, faster, until the houses and parked cars were a blur of color mixed with her tears.

"You have to go back and see if he's alive. If we take him to a hospital, he might live. Dirk, for God's sake, you have to stop." Catching his arm, she clawed at it. "You're acting crazy, Dirk. Let me out of here."

He blinked, forcing himself out of the stupor that held him in its grip. Turning to her he growled, "You want out, baby?"

She stared at him as if he'd gone mad, then drew in a ragged breath. "Yes. I want out of here now."

"Go on." He slammed on the brake, and the Ferrari screeched to a halt. "Get out," he said, reaching across her to throw the door open.

Alex scooped up her bag and fixed him with a look of pure hatred. "If you killed that old man, I'll see that you pay."

His hand shot out and grasped her arm, his fingers digging into her flesh. The coldest eyes she'd ever seen held her own so that she couldn't look away. "You listen to me, baby. My family is very influential in this town. My father knows every judge, every lawyer. The district attorney is a close personal friend—in fact, he was with my father tonight at the party. If you decide to get cute and go to the authorities with this, you'll be very sorry."

"You can't just run someone down and drive away. You have to—"

He swung his hand in an arc, catching her across the face with a stinging blow. "Don't ever try to tell me what I have to do! *Nobody* orders Dirk Montrose to do anything. They never did; they never will. Now get out." He gave her a shove, sending her sprawling into the street. With a screech of tires he sped away, leaving her lying on the pavement.

By the time she managed to struggle to her feet, the red Ferrari was out of sight. With blood oozing from the cuts on her hands and tears streaming down her face, Alex began running almost blindly along the street. She stumbled into a corner phone booth, trembling so violently she had to use two hands to hold the phone to her ear. When the nine-one-one operator responded, Alex could barely get the words out as she reported the time and place of the accident.

"Hurry!" she cried frantically. "Hurry!"

Tears streaming down her cheeks, she replaced the receiver and threw open the door of the phone booth, dragging cold night air into her burning lungs. She had only one thought now—home. She had to make it back. Back to Nanna and Kip. Back to where people were normal, where there was love and warmth and safety.

Safety. God, would she ever feel safe again?

Shivering, she wrapped her arms about herself and doggedly continued in the direction of home.

4

Alex studied her reflection in the mirror, wincing. Dark circles rimmed her bloodshot eyes, testimony to the sleepless night she'd spent.

"Come on, honey." Nanna's voice drifted up the stairs. "You promised to drop Kip off at school, remember?"

Alex gripped the edge of the sink and retched until she was drained. She wanted desperately to confide in her grandmother, but until she knew whether or not the old man had died from his injuries, it didn't seem right to lay such a heavy burden on Nanna. Maybe, she thought, closing her eyes, he'd survived. . . .

"Alex." She could hear Kip's childish voice from the foot of the stairs. "Come on."

She splashed water on her face before racing downstairs.

"Honey, you look awful. How late did they keep you?" Nanna said.

Alex turned away from her grandmother's scrutiny.

"Not too late. Gotta run, Nanna. See you around four."

"Alex," her grandmother said softly.

Alex paused with her hand on the door, then slowly turned.

"It's just . . . I worry about you, honey," Nanna said.

"I know." She went and gathered the older woman close for a quick kiss on the cheek. Closing her eyes she pressed her smooth forehead to the wrinkled one. "I love you, Nanna."

Dashing outside and down the path to the street, she unlocked the car door, but when she turned the key in the ignition, the battery was dead. What more could go wrong today? She fought down a wave of frustration.

As she got out of the car, a Bronco pulled up alongside her. When she caught sight of the driver, she shrank back.

"Car trouble?" Matt Montrose was already berating himself for being here, but he couldn't seem to help himself. All night he'd been haunted by the vision of Alexandra's face. He had to photograph her. At first light he'd phoned the catering company to get her address. Though at first they'd resisted, when they'd heard his name, they were only too happy to oblige. And now he was here, feeling like an intruder. To make matters worse, he'd noticed the way she shrank back from him the moment she'd caught sight of him.

"The battery is dead." Her heart was pounding, her palms sweating. Had Dirk sent his brother to convince her to keep quiet about last night?

"Where're you headed?"

She couldn't think. She had to swallow twice before saying, "Class at UCLA."

"Hop in. I'll give you a lift."

Alex glanced back at Nanna and Kip, who were standing on the front porch wearing identical expressions of concern. Thinking quickly she said, "I—I can't. I have to drop my little brother at school on the way."

"No problem. Tell him to come along." Matt leaned across the seat to open the door. Maybe the fates were smiling on him after all. This was working out better than he'd planned. All the way here he'd debated how best to approach her. Now, at least, they would have some time to talk.

Alex hurried to the front porch. "Nanna."

Her grandmother squeezed her hands. "Honey, your hands are as cold as ice. Maybe you're coming down with something."

Alex shook her head, swallowing back the fear that had her in its grip.

"Who is that young man, honey?"

"He's the son of the man who gave the party last night. His name's Matt Montrose. He's offered to give Kip and me a ride, but I'm not sure—"

Nanna swooped down from the porch and approached the vehicle, bending so she could stare at Matt through the open passenger door. "Good morning, young man. I'm Anna Corday."

"Mrs. Corday, I'm Matt Montrose."

"How is it you happen to be here?" Nanna asked, watching him closely.

"I'm not sure myself. . . ." He frowned. "That's not true. I'm a photographer. I'd like to photograph your granddaughter."

"For what purpose?" Nanna's brows drew together as she appraised him.

"I don't know yet. I only know that she has a face that begs to be on film. This may sound crazy, but ever since I saw her last night, I haven't been able to get her out of my mind."

Nanna suddenly smiled, remembering another young man, so serious, so intense, who had provoked her father's anger by announcing after one chance meeting that he had met the woman he intended to marry. He had filled her life with happiness and adventure for forty-five years.

Alex was stunned when her grandmother suddenly turned and said with a smile, "Go ahead, dear. This nice young man will see you safely to class."

"But you don't even know him," Alex said.

"That's true, honey. But I have a feeling about him. I trust him. Go ahead, both of you. You're going to be late."

Alex had never known Nanna to be wrong about people. She had a sixth sense about such things. Still, this time was different. This was Dirk Montrose's brother.

Nanna urged Kip to go ahead. Without further discussion, Alex got into the vehicle after her little brother.

"See you tonight, Nanna. Remember, Alex promised to take us to McDonald's," Kip called as they pulled away from the curb. "Hey, what's all this stuff?" he asked as he cleared a place on the back seat.

"Photography equipment."

"Why do you need so many cameras?"

"Each one does a special job. Some are better for distance, others for close-up."

"I bet I'd like photography," the little boy said, running a hand over the equipment. "I'm taking special art classes right now."

"You're an artist?" Glancing in the rearview mirror, Matt studied the solemn little boy. "I took several art classes myself before I settled on photography."

"Wow. Maybe I'll grow up to be a photographer too."

"It's something to think about. If you'd like, I'll let you try one of my cameras."

"Thanks. I'd have to ask Nanna first. Can I see your work sometime?"

"You already have," Alex said softly. "At the Avidson."

The little boy's eyes widened. "Wow! You're that guy?"

Matt grinned. "Yeah. I'm that guy."

"Here's my school," the boy said without enthusiasm. It was plain that he wished the ride could have lasted longer. "'Bye, Matt," he called as he ran up the walk.

"See you later," Matt replied.

As they pulled away, Alex grew silent. They drove for miles without speaking. Every time Matt glanced at his passenger, she had her head averted and was staring out the window. When he stopped too quickly at a light, her fingers curled around the door handle and her face took on the color of chalk.

It was the same reaction he'd had after the accident, every time he heard a loud report of any kind.

"You all right?" Matt asked.

She nodded, unable to relax in his presence. Last night she'd been so aware of him, standing among small clusters of important men and women yet somehow apart from them. Even now she felt a strange sensation curling along her spine at the thought of his eyes, dark and piercing. And then another thought intruded. It was his brother, Dirk, who had . . .

"Why were you at my house?" she finally asked. "Who sent you?"

"Sent me? Nobody sent me. I told your grand-mother the truth: I wanted to find you to ask you if you'd let me photograph you."

"I thought you would be jetting off around the world to take your photographs."

"That was before." Without realizing it, he rubbed his aching shoulder.

Alex suddenly remembered the bits and pieces of gossip she'd overheard at the party: . . . land mine . . . badly wounded . . . probably never be able to go over-seas again.

"What made you go to all those dangerous places?" she asked.

He shrugged. "The challenge, I guess. Some people just have a need to live close to the edge of danger."

His words had her jaw dropping. "That's exactly what my father once said about his job."

"Really? What did he do?"

She turned away, but not before he caught sight of her stricken look.

Hoping to get her to open up he said, "About the photographs—"

"No photographs," she said quickly. Too quickly. She didn't speak again until Matt pulled up at the cam-pus. "Thank you for the ride," she muttered as she gathered her things.

He winced at the stiff, correct words. He wasn't making any progress at all. "How are you planning on getting home?"

"I hadn't thought about it."

"What time is your last class?"

"Two."

"I'll pick you up here at three."

"No, thank you. I'll get a ride." She avoided looking at him as she rushed from his car.

Alex sat in a booth in the campus coffeeshop, scanning the L.A. *Times*. She'd had to sit through two classes back to back before she could take a break, now she began a frantic search of the newspaper.

The article she'd been seeking was buried in a back page. Her heart stopped as she read of the hit-and-run killing of an aged west Los Angeles resident named Freddy Trilby. The coroner speculated that the man had probably died shortly after having been struck by a vehicle traveling at a very high speed. Police were asking anyone with information to come forward.

Dear God! This was her worst nightmare.

With trembling hands she fumbled in her purse for a quarter, then hurried to a pay phone. It wasn't Nanna's advice she sought; she knew what her grandmother would tell her. Alex had known all along what she had to do, but she desperately needed to hear the soothing sound of Nanna's voice. In times of crises, she had always relied on the old woman's quiet strength.

The phone rang three times, four times. Closing her eyes, Alex leaned her forehead against the cold glass of the phone booth, picturing her grandmother out in her small yard, kneeling among her flower beds, pruning the vines and bushes. It gave her a measure of comfort to think of her grandmother taking pleasure in such mundane chores. Somehow it seemed to make Alex feel that the world was sane and normal.

She glanced at her watch as she hung up the phone. If she had her car she'd dash home and unburden herself right now. But she'd be home in three hours. She would share a cup of tea with Nanna, as they did every afternoon after school. Then she'd notify the authorities.

She hurried off to her next class, wondering how she would manage to concentrate on astronomy at a time like this. If she did, at least she wouldn't have time to think about having to report the hit-and-run. But as she took a seat in the lecture hall and the professor began speaking in a monotone, she found her mind returning time and again to the accident. And each time she remembered the slight bump as the Ferarri hit the old man, her stomach lurched and her heart began racing. While others around her took notes, she found herself staring into space, reliving every painful minute of her drive with Dirk Montrose. She had been, for that short time, his prisoner. And as she went back over everything he'd said and done, she had no doubt what her fate would have been at his hands had it not been for the unexpected appearance of that old man in the street.

All the charm, all the shy, sweet demeanor, had been a clever act. He'd meant to hurt her. To force her. She couldn't bring herself even to think the word *rape,* but the knowledge of what he'd planned left her trembling.

When the others filed from the lecture hall, Alex followed in a daze, fighting down a wave of nausea. These past few hours had been the longest of her life, but she'd come to a firm decision. Dirk Montrose was not just a spoiled, willful playboy. He was dangerous. And by now, with the story of the hit-and-run in the paper, he might become desperate. She had no choice but to report what had happened and let Dirk take his chances with the authorities.

Escaping the confines of the campus, Alex walked to the bus stop. Knowing what she planned to do about his brother, she could no longer accept any favors from Matt. She had no intention of seeing him again.

A car stopped alongside her. "What are you doing here? I told you I'd pick you up."

She froze at the sound of Matt's voice. "I know, but . . ." Her mind raced. She couldn't accept a ride from the brother of the man she was about to report for hit-and-run. "I don't want you to go out of your way for me."

"It isn't out of my way. Get in."

She thought of Nanna's calm assurance that she trusted this man. The simple truth was, so did Alex. Though his brother tried to hide his true self under a layer of false charm, Matt Montrose seemed genuine. She was convinced that he had no idea of his brother's dark deeds. Stiffly she climbed into the Bronco.

"What'll you do about your car?" Matt asked.

She struggled to pull her mind away from the thoughts that tormented her. "Guess I'll have to invest in a new battery. I've seen it coming. It's been harder and harder to start. Today it didn't even turn over."

"I'll give you a hand getting it started. Along with all the other junk in the back of this car, I've got jumper cables. They come in handy on some of the assignments I've been given."

"There's no need." She turned away to stare out the window once more.

Matt turned onto the freeway and mulled over how to break through the wall she seemed to have built around herself. "Will we be picking up your brother?" he asked.

She nodded.

As they pulled up in front of Kip's school, a stream of students spilled through the open doors and down the old stone steps. Kip hurried over, and Alex got out of the car and allowed her little brother to climb into the back seat.

For the rest of the ride home, she stared out the window while Matt and Kip carried on an animated conversation. Matt was grateful for the boy's presence. Without him they'd be locked in an awkward silence.

"Is Kip short for something?"

"Kipling. Nanna says my folks named me for a guy named Rudyard Kipling." The boy grinned. "Alex says I should be glad they didn't name me Rudyard."

Matt threw back his head and laughed, glancing at the woman who continued to sit silently beside him. She didn't seem even to be aware of their conversation. She looked as if she carried the weight of the world on those slender shoulders.

As they entered the quiet neighborhood, a police car raced up behind them, sirens screaming. Matt pulled to the side of the street to allow the car to pass.

"I thought he was after you," Kip said, letting out a little laugh. "Wonder where they're going?"

Matt's car rounded a curve, and they saw the fire trucks and police cars at the end of the street. Thick black smoke hung low, casting a dark cloud over the entire neighborhood. As Matt's car drew closer, Alex gripped the door handle.

"It looks like . . ." She swallowed back the words.

Alex was out of the car before it came to a complete stop, pushing her way through the line of neighbors and onlookers, with Matt and Kip trailing behind. She let out a cry when she caught sight of the pile of rubble where her grandmother's house had stood. Acrid smoke still wafted up from the ashes. The roof had collapsed, bringing the walls down with it. Only the stone fireplace remained intact, looking incongruous amid the wreckage. Alex's car was still parked at the curb, the front window shattered by a brass weathervane that had fallen from the roof of the burned-out house.

A fireman continued to direct a stream of water toward a smoldering sofa lying on its side in one corner of what had once been the living room. The microwave oven had melted, the plastic frame molding itself onto the countertop. On the sidewalk stood a small round table holding one of Nanna's favorite old figurines. In some small part of her mind Alex noted that the head was missing. She would have to try to find it later and put it back together for Nanna.

"Step back, miss," someone called.

Alex glanced around at the crowd, seeking the familiar face of her grandmother.

"Nanna!" she shouted. "Where is Nanna?"

"Step behind those lines, miss."

The fireman caught her, but she wrenched away and started to run toward the crumbled remains of the house.

"You can't go in there." Rough hands caught Alex's shoulders and spun her around.

"I live here with my grandmother," she cried. "Where is she?"

"Calm down, miss." With a worried frown the fireman recognized the warning signs of the beginnings of hysteria. He quickly signaled to a police inspector, who stepped between them. By this time, Kip and Matt were beside Alex. The little boy was clinging to his sister's arm. Her skin, Matt noted, was the color of putty, and her voice was close to breaking.

"Where is my grandmother?" Turning to the crowd Alex recognized a neighbor and wailed, "Mrs. Parsons, where is she?"

The woman looked away, refusing to meet her eyes.

Alex felt the first wave of terror wash over her, leaving her struggling to catch her breath. The inspector and two uniformed policemen formed a tight ring around her and her brother.

"Come over to the police car," one of them was saying.

"No." Alex dug in her heels, refusing to budge until she had her answer. "You tell me where you've taken my grandmother."

"I'm sorry. Really sorry." The officer kept his voice low in an attempt to soothe her. "We weren't in time to save her, miss. She . . . perished in the fire."

"Alex." Kip was tugging frantically on her sleeve. "What does 'perished' mean?"

"Kip. Oh my God, Kip." Alex was unaware of the tears that spilled from her eyes, streaming down her cheeks as she knelt in the rubble and gathered her little brother into her arms. "It means," she whispered against his temple, "that Nanna . . ." She choked and tried again. "It means that Nanna's dead."

$\overline{5}$

"*I still don't* understand why you're doing this," Elyse said. Despite the makeup and the stunning pink silk pegnoir trimmed with ostrich feathers, her appearance showed the ravages of a night spent fretting over Dirk and arguing with Sidney about her son's behavior.

"I told you, Mother." Dirk's temper was on a short fuse. He'd ditched the Ferrari outside a dingy bar and left the keys in it, practically guaranteeing that it would be stolen and stripped before it could be traced to the old man's death. But the girl, Alex, was another matter. The death of a grandmother and the loss of the family home might be enough to distract most people. Still, he'd seen the horror, and more than that, the hatred in her eyes after the car had hit the old man. If she called the authorities, it would be her word against his. But he didn't want to risk it. He'd lie low for a while in Europe, hang out with a few friends.

If luck was still with him, it would all blow over in time.

"This is the chance of a lifetime. If I get this part, who knows? Maybe I'll become the next king of the spaghetti Westerns," Dirk said.

"Spaghetti Westerns." Sidney ran a hand through his hair and shuffled over to his desk. In robe and slippers, he appeared much older than the dapper man who'd hosted the party only two nights ago. "You can't even give me the name of the director. If you would, I could make a few calls and pull some strings."

"I told you, I can't remember his name. But once I get to Paris, my friend will meet me. I'll call you when I find out."

"Yeah. Sure." Sidney glanced at his wife, then pulled out a checkbook and began scribbling. He tore a check off and handed it to Dirk, muttering, "Just a little to tide you over."

Dirk pocketed it without even bothering to thank him and turned to Matt. "Okay, let's go. I've got a plane to catch." He endured the embrace of his mother, then pulled away and walked out the door.

In the car, he pulled the check from his pocket and studied the figures. Ten thousand. Not much, but he'd make do. He leaned back and closed his eyes, but he was too agitated to rest. His mind was going a million miles an hour. What if the girl snitched? How much juice did Sidney really have in this town? He hoped he didn't have to find out.

Matt, who had been up since dawn, drove in silence. On the one hand he was relieved that Dirk was leaving; at least for a little while, his father's life would be free of stress. Though Elyse would miss her darling, she would relax, convinced that he was finally getting his act together. On the other hand, Matt knew that there was no job waiting for Dirk in Europe. Whatever scrape he'd gotten himself into this time, he was following a familiar pattern. But sooner or later, trouble always caught up with him.

With little traffic on the freeways at this time of day, it didn't take long to reach L.A. International. As they pulled up to the curb, Dirk opened his eyes and shot a lazy grin at Matt.

"Well, off to business."

"Knowing you, Dirk, it's probably dirty business."

"Son of a bitch." Dirk sat back, studying the man he'd always hated. From the time he was a little boy, Dirk had been jealous of the way Matt wore success so easily. Now he decided to leave him with a parting shot.

"You know that pretty little waitress you were eyeing at Sidney's party?"

Matt sat perfectly still, but Dirk had seen a tiny flicker of emotion. That was enough to satisfy him that he was on the right track. So, Matt remembered? Well, he'd see that he never forgot.

"What a teriffic little slut, Matt. Definitely not your type, of course, but I'm here to tell you she was one fine piece. We met after the party and had a little party of our own." He got out of the car and pressed a tip into the skycap's hand. Leaning down, he spoke through the open window. "Listen, if you'd like to try her out, let me know. I'll give you her number. I don't mind sharing."

He sauntered into the airport terminal without a backward glance. But judging from the look of fury in those dark eyes, he figured that the dart he'd just aimed at his big brother's heart had hit the bull's eye.

The sky was a clear, cloudless blue; the sun so bright it hurt the eye. A fresh breeze rippled the acres of manicured lawns. It was the kind of day, Alex thought, that always made Nanna hurry outside to tend her flowers.

Alex held her little brother's hand firmly as the minister intoned the final prayer over Nanna's casket, his voice properly sad and mournful. Alex managed to blot out most of the words—she'd heard them all before. The last time had been when she was only nine. They'd been said over her father's casket, and a year before that, her mother's.

Nanna was being laid to rest beside her husband, her son, and his wife in Forest Lawn in Glendale.

You aren't in there, Nanna, Alex thought. Remember what you always told me about my dad and mom, when we brought flowers to their graves? They aren't there, honey, you would say. They're here, in our hearts, and there, all around us. Now they've been set free, you would say. Well, Nanna, now you're free too. Your hair is no longer white; it's red again, falling to your waist. And your legs are strong and limber, the way they were when you were a young ballerina. You and Grandpa are young again, and he's cheering as you pirouette on a headstone and dance across the lawn for him.

". . . May her soul rest in peace."

Alex swallowed the lump in her throat that was threatening to choke her. Rest now, Nanna. You worked so hard to keep us all together after Dad . . .

after we found ourselves alone. You were so good to Kip and me, taking us in when we were alone and scared, going back to teaching dance to make ends meet. Now you've earned your eternal rest. Go walk with Grandpa in the gardens, and let me worry about Kip.

The minister shook hands with Aunt Bernice and Uncle Vince. Alex studied them warily. The last time she'd seen them had been almost ten years ago. Even then, Aunt Bernice had looked old and tired, though she'd been barely in her forties. Nanna had said it was because Bernice had forgotten how to laugh. Now just over fifty, she wore a perpetual frown, and her mouth tightened like a prune whenever she glanced at her niece and nephew.

Uncle Vince's middle had thickened, and his hair had gone gray. Like his wife, he seemed to wear his unhappiness like a badge of honor.

Alex tensed as the minister approached.

"You've suffered many losses in your young lives. But you've been fortunate to have family who love and care for you." He swept his hand to include Vince and Bernice. "I was happy to hear that these good people have offered to raise young Kip here as their own son."

"I'm not their son." Kip looked terrified as he turned to his sister. "Alex, tell them I'm not their son."

"Shh." She drew him close and said to the minister, "I'll take care of Kip. I've been taking care of him since he was born."

"Yes. Well . . ." The minister was not about to get caught up in a family disagreement. He avoided looking at them again, moving past them and nodding to the others.

The few neighbors and friends who had come to the funeral began to drift back to their cars.

"Come on." Relieved to be done with what he considered an unpleasant duty, Uncle Vince placed a hand under his wife's elbow, guiding her away from the grave. "Let's get back to the motel. We've got a lot of packing to do."

Kip tightened his grasp on his sister's hand. She felt a wave of compassion. So much had happened in the last few days. Their childhood home had been destroyed; in an instant they'd been cut adrift from Nanna, the only anchor they'd had. Their neighbor, Mrs. Parsons, had taken them in the first night; the next day Vince and Bernice had flown in from South Dakota, and the four of them had moved into adjoining motel rooms. With the details of the funeral arrangements, the meetings with the lawyer about her grandmother's estate, and the endless questions from the fire inspectors, there had been little time to grieve. Poor Kip must be reeling from it all.

She looked at the man who should have had her father's warmth, her father's smile. But his older brother bore no resemblance to the man she'd adored when she was little. Where her father's smile had radiated an inner light, Vince's smile never reached his eyes. Her father had been a dashing adventurer, full of wit and charm. His older brother inhabited a drab gray world of endless work and little reward, a world that had no room for the pursuit of happiness.

"I think Kip and I will stay here for a little while. We'd like to be alone with Nanna."

Bernice shot a look at her husband.

"I'm afraid not," Vince said uncomfortably. "We

only have the rental car, and I don't want to have to come all the way back here to pick you up later. Come on, girl."

He reached out to grab her arm but froze at the sight of a tall figure standing directly behind her.

Matt stood deep in thought, his hands thrust into his pockets. He still seethed with rage at the seed of mistrust Dirk had managed to plant in his mind. He was certain it was all a lie, and yet . . . Dirk had always been very good at getting under his skin.

Alex turned and, catching sight of Matt, let out a little gasp.

"Matt. I—I never thanked you for all your help the other day. I guess I didn't make too much sense after . . . after the fire."

"I wish I could have done more. But when your neighbor took you home, there wasn't anything else for me to do."

"You did more than enough."

"Matt." Kip went to grasp his hand, seeming to take strength from the familiar, friendly figure. Matt wrapped an arm around the boy's shoulders and extended his hand to Alex. He noticed that she was trembling. He had a fleeting wish to draw her into his arms. Then he remembered again what Dirk had boasted, and his frown returned.

"I'm sorry about your grandmother, Alexandra. If there's anything I can do . . ."

"You can let us get out of here. We've had enough sympathy for one day," Vince said. He caught Alex's wrist in a firm grasp, but she shook herself free.

"I haven't introduced you. Uncle Vince, Aunt Bernice, this is my friend Matt Montrose."

Vince didn't even bother to offer his hand. "I've met enough of your friends and neighbors to last a lifetime. Come on, girl," he said again. As he practically dragged her toward the car he muttered, "You're just like my kid, Vince Junior. Before he took off and joined the Marines, I always had to drag him away from his friends. Fool kid used to hang on for dear life. Never wanted to go home."

Surprised by the coldness of the act, Matt stood very still and watched as Alex got into the cramped back seat and drew her little brother close. Both of them turned toward him for a last glance as the car sped away from the quiet, spacious grounds, past the famous copy of Michelangelo's David and back to the teeming city.

"We'll come out tomorrow after school, Kip, and visit with Nanna."

Alex saw a look pass between Vince and Bernice.

"Where are we going to live?" Kip's voice trembled, and Alex knew he was fighting tears.

"We'll rent an apartment until Nanna's house can be rebuilt."

"Rebuilt?" Bernice shifted in the front seat to glare over her shoulder at her niece. "What are you talking about? Why in the world would you want to rebuild in a neighborhood like that?"

"Because Nanna loved it there. Besides, the property is still there, and it's all paid for. We can't afford to move somewhere else."

"What'll we use to build it?" Kip asked.

"Nanna had the house fully insured. There'll be

plenty of money to rebuild." Alex smoothed his fine red hair away from his forehead. "You and I don't need much. We'll have a nice little place, just like the one we had before."

"I think you should tell them." Bernice turned to her husband.

Alex felt keenly the sense of mistrust that had begun as soon as her aunt and uncle had arrived. "Tell us what, Uncle Vince?" She unconsciously closed her hand around Kip's.

"I was named beneficiary on all my mother's policies."

For a moment Alex was shocked into silence. When she found her voice she said softly, "Most of Nanna's income came from the small trust from my father's insurance. Nanna always told me that she intended to use it to see that Kip and I were taken care of."

"And you will be. After I've cleared up all my mother's debts."

"Nanna never told me about any debts."

"I'm sure she didn't tell you everything." Vince swung the wheel and turned into the motel parking lot. Turning off the ignition, he added, "But if the fire inspectors ever give their approval for the insurance to be paid, I have no intention of rebuilding my mother's house. In fact, I've already told the lawyer to list the property for sale the minute the investigation is complete. That will give us a little more money to put away for the future."

Alex knew that there were many unanswered questions about the fire. The inspectors believed it had been deliberately started with a flammable liquid, although neighbors and friends had reinforced what her grandchildren had insisted—that Nanna had no enemies. There had also been a question about why the elderly woman hadn't fled the fire in time. She'd been found lying beneath an overturned, charred chair, and the speculation was that in her panic, she had tripped and was too dazed to escape.

"Without Nanna's house, where will we live?" Kip asked again, his frightened voice breaking through his sister's thoughts.

"With us." Vince got out of the car and went around to his wife's door. When he'd helped her out, he slid back the seat and waited until Kip and Alex climbed out.

"You'll like it on the farm, boy. The air is clean. There's none of this smog and traffic congestion. You'll adjust to farm chores."

"We'll all have some adjusting to do," his wife interrupted. Bernice's lips thinned. "It won't be easy for us, after already raising a son of our own. But it's our duty. And you can repay us by taking on some of the chores that have been piling up since Vincent junior left. It will certainly be a better place for a boy to grow up than this . . ." She sniffed and looked around with a shudder. They walked in silence to their rooms.

"What about Alex? Can she still go to college? Or will she have to do farm chores, too?" asked Kip as Vince turned the key in the lock and held the door of the motel room open for his wife.

At the boy's innocent question, the man and woman exchanged a glance before going inside and busying themselves with their suitcases.

It was then that Alex knew. She had suspected as much at the cemetery, when the minister had said that her aunt and uncle wanted to raise Kip like their own son. There had been no mention of her. Now their reaction confirmed her suspicions.

"I don't think Aunt Bernice and Uncle Vince are including me in their plans, Kip."

Vince opened a dresser drawer and removed several neatly folded shirts. "Bernice and I talked it over. We both feel, after watching you and Kip, that you exert too much influence on the boy. It isn't too late for Kip. But you, Alex, you're as headstrong as your father. As Bernice pointed out, Bill was on his own at an even earlier age than you are now. He was only seventeen when he took off and joined that motorcycle gang."

"They weren't a gang, Uncle Vince. They were motorcycle stuntmen traveling with the circus."

"Mm-hm." He rocked back on his heels, regarding her. Her face wore the same defiant look he'd always remembered seeing on his younger brother's. A rebel, just like Bill. "I just think it would be best if you remained here, Alex."

"Best for me? Or best for you to leave me here?" In her effort to keep the fear out of her voice, her words were more sarcastic than she'd intended. "Alone."

"You won't be alone," Vince said in that infuriating tone of bland patience he used whenever he spoke to her. "You'll have your college classes and your job. I'm sure you'd miss your friends if you moved to South Dakota."

Kip leapt to his sister's defense. "All Alex ever had was Nanna and me, and now all she has is me. You can't take me away from her."

"Nobody's going to take you away, Kip," Alex said softly. "I won't let them."

"You won't let us?" Vince looked her directly in the eye. The hostility Alex saw in his face left her with a feeling of dread. "Let me set you straight, young lady. I've already talked to my mother's lawyer. You have no legal way to stop me from doing what I think is right for Kip." His tone hardened. "Bernice and I have talked it over. A boy needs parents, something Kip hasn't had since he was an infant. I'm not faulting my mother," he said quickly when Alex opened her mouth to argue. "You can't expect a frail old woman to be able to keep up with the needs of a normal active boy. But we both feel that life with us will do him a world of good."

"What about his special classes? He's been studying art for over a year."

"Special classes," Bernice scoffed. "A boy of nine needs discipline. He needs a firm hand." She caught Kip's hand and held it, palm up, as if to prove her point. "A boy his age needs to toughen his hands, get them around a shovel or rake, not waste his time playing with paint brushes and crayons."

"He isn't playing. Kip has real talent." Alex drew the boy close, as if to protect him from the simmering anger she could read in her aunt's eyes. "He inherited his talent from our father."

"Yes—and he probably inherited a streak of wildness from your father too. But when we're through with him he'll be a nice, normal boy, and not some Hollywood freak."

A freak. They thought Kip was a freak? Alex felt herself reeling from their open hostility. They were no longer taking the trouble to hide their true feelings.

"I can't let you take him."

"Like I said," Vince said, his words clipped, "our lawyer advised us that until you reach the age of twenty-one, we are within our legal rights."

"Come on, Kip." Alex caught her brother by the hand.

"Where do you think you're going?" Her uncle took a menacing step toward her, and she backed up until she felt the wall against her back.

"I thought we'd take a walk and let you pack."

He glanced over his shoulder toward his wife, who nodded her assent, looking as if she would be only too glad to be rid of them for a while.

"Okay. But first, let's take care of this little matter." He produced two documents and handed Alex a pen.

She glanced at them, then up at her uncle. "What are these?"

"The lawyer said you had to sign two copies of this, to show you understand that I'm executor of my mother's will."

She read carefully, while Vince stood over her growling, "Hurry up and sign."

After she scratched her name at the bottom of the first form, he lifted the corner, barely giving her time to sign the second before snatching it away. Pulling open the door he cautioned, "I expect you back within the hour. The boy needs to get some sleep. We'll be leaving for the airport at dawn. And Alex," he added quietly, "remember this. Until you're twenty-one, you have no rights in this matter. So you can make this easy for the boy, or you can make it hard. Do you get my drift?"

She knew he was right—and hated him for it. Never before had she felt so powerless.

Her uncle was enjoying her misery. It was there in

his eyes, in the way he watched her. He was drunk with his sense of power. She swallowed back the words she wanted to hurl at him and merely nodded.

Alex awoke to the sound of voices. A worried glance at her brother, lying in the bed next to hers, assured her that his sleep wasn't disturbed. She was relieved. She'd had to do some fancy talking to calm him before they'd returned to face her aunt and uncle. She prayed that some of the things she'd said to Kip earlier tonight would give him a measure of comfort in the years to come.

"Just remember," she'd whispered, "I promise that as soon as I turn twenty-one, I'll send for you."

"What if Uncle Vince won't let me go?"

"Then I'll go to court and force him to."

Kip's eyes had widened in surprise. "You'd do that?"

"I'll do anything I have to, Kip, to get you back where you belong. You're my brother. Nobody can change that."

"What'll you do all alone, Alex?"

She swallowed, her heart aching. The empty days and nights seemed to loom ahead of her. But she wouldn't allow herself to think about that now. Kip needed to hear something hopeful. Much as she hated to admit it, Uncle Vince had been right about that too. If Kip had to leave her, it would be best to keep her fears to herself and send him on his way with words of hope.

"I'll go to classes, get a job. And then . . . buy a house." To keep his mind off what was coming in the morning, she'd asked, "Where would you like to live when we get back together?"

He had shrugged. "I don't know. Maybe near the ocean."

"The ocean. Okay." Hoping to make it a game, she'd said, "Malibu. We'll share a great big house, with glass walls looking out over the water. And you'll have your own studio up on the roof, with perfect light, where you can paint all the changing moods of the sea."

"I'd like that, Alex." His voice had been so sad, so wistful. "Is there an ocean in South Dakota?"

"No. But that will just make it all the nicer when you and I get back together."

He had finally drifted off to sleep with a smile on his face. She hoped he was dreaming about a bright, happy future when he and his beloved sister would be reunited; she prayed it wasn't just a pipe dream. As she'd already learned in her nineteen years, a lot could happen in the real world.

Alex realized her aunt and uncle were arguing next door. The walls between their adjoining bedrooms were thin enough to allow her to overhear everything they said when they raised their voices.

". . . girl could be trouble." Bernice's voice was shrill. "I don't want any further contact with her."

"You mean just cut her off without a cent? It could get pretty rough for a kid alone in this town."

"What about us, Vince? What about all the hard years we went through? I'm not some ignorant hick. I've watched *Lifestyles of the Rich and Famous.* I know how much money it takes to shop on Rodeo Drive. I've seen the mansions in Beverly Hills. I ask you, did your brother ever send you a dime all those years that he was living so high on the hog?"

"I think Bill and Marney had some rough times too. He just never talked about them. And I know it was a struggle for my mother after he died and left two little ones. And don't forget, it's not like any of *them* ever shopped on Rodeo Drive or lived in a mansion."

"Am I hearing right? Is this the same man who told me at least a million times how much he disapproved of the crazy life-style of his younger brother and his wife?"

"Yeah. Well, it was crazy. I mean, how many men do you know who make a living driving over cliffs and jumping off buildings, and painting nudes while the little wife sings in sleazy bars?" Vince's voice ebbed and flowed, and Alex realized he was pacing.

"Well the shoe is on the other foot now," Bernice said. "This time we'll get to control the money for as long as the boy is with us. As for the girl, every time I look at her I see your brother."

Alex strained to hear her uncle's response. After a long silence, she heard him say, "Yeah. I see it too, in her eyes. She's got that same streak of wildness, or defiance or something, that Bill had when we were kids. It always bugged me the way he would try anything, regardless of the consequences. And no matter how much I tried to knock some sense into him, he always came back for more. He was . . . I don't know. Fearless."

"Or crazy."

There was another silence. Then, "He'd rise up out of his grave if he knew Ma had signed over everything to me."

"Well, Bill isn't here now, so stop worrying. And remember, we're the victims in all this. We've already raised one family; now we have to start all over. But at least this time we'll be amply rewarded." Bernice's voice lowered. "Now come to bed."

In the darkness Alex heard the creak of bedsprings, and then the soft, muted sounds of the night. Traffic rolled past the motel, cars, trucks, buses, all hurrying on to their destinations. Occasionally a pounding thrum of rap music blasted from an open car window. In the distance she heard the mournful call of a train. Home, she thought. They were all heading home.

Deeply troubled, she lay awake struggling to swallow back the tears that threatened. Shouldn't everyone have a home?

She clenched her fists. She would—for Kip. Because it wasn't her own future that worried her; no matter what, she knew she'd survive. But what about her little brother?

"Oh Nanna," she whispered into her pillow. "How can I let Kip go? Especially to people who feel such hostility toward him?"

She couldn't remember when she'd ever felt so alone, or so helpless. At least before when her world had fallen apart, after the death of her parents, there had been Nanna. But now there was no one.

When the tears were finally spent, she got out of bed, drawing a blanket around her shoulders, and went to the window. By the time dawn light streaked the horizon, she had decided on a course of action. For Kip's sake she would keep her feelings carefully hidden; if it killed her, their good-byes would be as hopeful as she could manage. But as soon as she could, she would claim her little brother.

6

"I've paid for this motel room for the rest of the month," Uncle Vince was saying as he loaded luggage into the trunk of the rental car. "Set me back a pretty penny, too. But that'll give you time to find a place to stay." He slammed the trunk lid and turned to Alex. "I suppose you'll need some spending money, too."

Alex hated accepting money from him, but she was desperate. "All I have are the clothes on my back," she said.

"Yeah. Well this ought to keep you in jeans for a while."

He made a big show of peeling three one-hundred-dollar bills from a roll in his wallet and presenting them to her. Silently, she shoved them into her pocket. Kip was clinging to her hand so hard it hurt. He hadn't said a word for the past hour. He just kept staring up at her with that trusting look in his eyes that gave her a sick feeling in the pit of her stomach.

"We'd better go," Bernice called. "You have to turn in the car before we catch that plane." Vince went around to the front of the car.

A look of panic leapt into Kip's eyes. "I don't want to leave you, Alex."

She drew him close and stroked his hair. "I know, Kip. I know. I don't want to see you go. But we both know what we have to do." She leaned close, whispering into his ear, "If we can hang on for just a little while, we'll be together for always."

A big tear rolled down his cheek. "Promise?"

"Promise." She wiped the tears away, then pressed her lips to his temple and hugged him fiercely. "And nobody will ever separate us again."

"Come on." Uncle Vince's tone was rougher than he'd intended, but his wife was glaring at him from the front seat, and he knew she was eager to get away. "We've got a plane to catch." He held the back door open and waited until Kip had climbed in. "Well," he said, clearing his throat. "Take care of yourself, girl."

Alex nodded, fighting back the tears.

"Say good-bye to your aunt," he said, as he settled himself behind the wheel and fastened his seat belt.

"Good-bye, Aunt Bernice."

The car idled.

Her aunt stared past her husband and right through her. "Good-bye, Alex."

"I'll write, Kip," Alex told her brother.

The little boy's face crumpled, and the tears streamed down his cheeks as the car began to roll forward. Turning, he stared out the back window.

Alex stood very still, waving until they rounded a curve and disappeared. She wasn't certain just how long she continued standing there. It could have been only minutes, but it felt like hours. At last, weighted down by the enormity of her loss, she could no longer hold back her own tears. Seeking sanctuary in the shabby motel room, she collapsed onto the bed, her body wracked by sobs.

At least, she consoled herself, she had maintained her composure until they were safely away. She had kept her feelings safely hidden from her aunt and uncle, and especially from her little brother, who needed more than ever to be strong. Now she allowed the tears to run their course, until there were none left.

Drained, she sat up and vowed that there would be no more displays of weakness. She would keep all her fears buried so deep, no one would ever guess just how badly broken her heart really was.

Somehow, she had to find a way to gain control of her life again. And when she did, nobody would ever again harm her or the people she loved.

"I came about the apartment you advertised."

Alex glanced around the gloomy interior of the high rise's foyer. It had once been a hotel but since falling on hard times had become a low-income apartment building.

The man behind the desk lowered the newspaper he was reading to peer at her over the rim of his bifocals. He reached for a ring of keys and came out from behind the desk, heading toward the elevator with a terse, "Follow me."

As Alex stepped into the elevator, she braced herself for the inevitable sick feeling in her stomach. "What floor is it on?"

"Sixteenth." He sized her up and figured he'd have been better off staying downstairs with the racing form. A girl like that didn't stay in a dump like this.

For a moment Alex closed her eyes, fighting the nausea that always plagued her when she was forced to confront her fear of heights. She opened her eyes to find the man watching her and looked away to stare at the floor numbers as they flashed by. Sixteen. Why did it have to be up so high?

She'd begun with student housing, but nothing would be available until the start of a new semester. Now she was reduced to drab, dreary apartments. Those she could afford had been so depressing, she'd fled before even hearing the sales pitch. Others, cleaner, offering little more than a room with a bed, would have cost twice what she earned with the catering firm. The elevator came to a shuddering halt and the door opened.

"Emergency stairs are over there." He pointed to a door with a red exit sign over it as he led the way down a hallway that reeked of cigarettes and stale beer. Stopping at the door of an apartment a little way beyond the stairs, he turned a key in the lock.

Alex stepped inside warily. It was no better or worse than the others she'd looked at. There was a narrow bed along one wall, and a chipped dresser along the other. And the rent was within her budget, if she was careful. Maybe, if she didn't think about where she was . . .

The man crossed the room, pulled up the shade, and opened the window.

"That's better." He breathed deeply as exhaust fumes from a nearby rooftop generator replaced the musty stench of mildew.

Alex glanced at him and then at the weathered wall of the building across the street. She went to the window to look down at pavement far below. Too late, she realized her mistake. The nausea swelled; bile rose in her throat. A combination of panic and shame washed over her. Oh, God, she was going to be sick. She turned and fled.

She made it down three flights of stairs before she was forced to stop and retch. When she had made her way outside, she leaned against the wall of the building, relieved to be back on solid ground.

Coward, she berated herself. She'd allowed her fear of heights to rear its ugly head once more. God, how she hated this weakness.

On trembling legs she turned away. No more high rises, she vowed. No matter what the condition of the apartment she finally took, there was one thing she was certain of: it would be on the first floor.

She started walking toward the campus. She had one more class to get through, and two more apartments to look at after school.

Outside the lecture hall she heard someone call her name. Alex turned to see Matt Montrose walking toward her. She felt a flutter in the pit of her stomach.

"Hello, Matt."

"I didn't know how else to locate you, so I inquired at the university registry. I was afraid maybe you'd left town with your relatives."

"No. I . . . had a lot of things to take care of." She didn't bother to add that it had taken her three days to work up the courage to go back to class. For three days she'd hidden inside the motel room, terrified at the thought of facing the enormity of her situation. But now, by dealing with one thing at a time, she was gradually gaining confidence. Not that all her fears had magically disappeared. She still felt adrift, returning each night to the motel, dreading the arrival of each new day—and wondering if she would ever again find a place that felt like home. But at least by returning to class she had taken a first step.

"Did your uncle tell you about your car?"

Alex nodded. "He said it wasn't worth repairing. He told me he'd had to pay to have it hauled to a scrapyard."

A hint of laughter danced in Matt's eyes. "If he paid a scrap dealer, he paid him for nothing."

"What do you mean?"

"I mean the scrap dealer didn't find your car at the curb."

"What are you talking about?"

"I paid a visit to your grandmother's neighborhood right after the fire, and I happened to run into your uncle. I told him that your car could be fixed. He said he wasn't interested. So I found a young neighbor of yours who was willing to jump the battery and take it to his house. He phoned me to say it's ready to be picked up."

"Are you serious?" Alex's eyes widened as she grabbed his hand.

Matt struggled to show no reaction to her touch. "It's not exactly as good as new, but at least you'll have wheels. I can take you there after class and you can see for yourself."

"I'd like that." A smile sprang to her lips. "Where will I meet you?"

She was still holding his hand and she felt the warmth, the strength that seemed to emanate from him. Something about this man made her feel both cautious and excited at the same time.

"I'll be right here."

Alex floated into the lecture hall. For the first time in days, the sun wasn't shining through the big windows. She should have known something good would come of the clouds.

Though she'd been gone only scant weeks, it seemed strange riding through the old neighborhood. Alex stared hungrily, devouring familiar landmarks. When they neared the vacant lot where her grandmother's house had been, she let out a gasp. The rubble had been removed. A bulldozer had filled in the basement and leveled the property. A sign offered the property for sale and listed a realtor's name and number. There was nothing left of the house and yard she'd loved since she was a little girl.

Though Matt had anticipated some of her pain, he hadn't known that this would be her first glimpse of the place since the fire. He could tell by the look on her face that she was on the verge of tears. Without a word he stopped the car. Alex got out and moved slowly, tentatively, around the yard. She felt the lump growing in her throat, bigger even than the one that had formed at the cemetery. This little plot of land had been part of Nanna's heart and soul. And Uncle Vince was selling it, without any regard for what it had meant to his mother.

"Oh, Nanna." Alex studied the freshly raked soil where only days ago flowers and vines had tangled in a riot of color. "I feel so lost. You were always here for me. Even when my whole world fell apart, and I was forced to live out my worst nightmare, I always knew I could count on you to be here. But where will I find you now?"

She walked around the perimeter of the yard, stopping every so often to glance at the empty space where the house had been, as if expecting it to magically reappear. She could close her eyes and see every wall, every window, every brick. In Nanna's bedroom wall there had been a crack, where the house had settled. A bird had built a nest under the front porch railing. The back door had begun to stick, and Nanna had vowed to replace it. But she never would have, Alex thought.

She smiled at the thought of the curtains she and Nanna had made for Kip's room from yards of Ninja Turtle fabric. A year later he had given his fickle heart to another, and she and her grandmother had dutifully replaced them with Batman curtains.

This had been her home. Here, surrounded by love, she and Kip and Nanna had been a family.

From the car, Matt saw Alex bend and retrieve something. Straightening, she stared around for long minutes, as if picturing the way it had been.

When she got back in the car, she was clutching a single wilted red rose in her hand. "I can't imagine how this survived the fire trucks and the bulldozer," she said, breathing in its fragrance. She felt her spirits begin to climb. How could she do less than this single, fragile flower? Despite the devastation, it had survived. She would do the same.

Matt was careful not to intrude on her privacy. He drove in silence, occasionally glancing at her as she stared out the window.

Maybe I've just discovered where you are, Nanna, Alex thought. Not walking in your old yard, and not dancing on those headstones. You're in a place where you will live forever. You're in every beautiful flower, every sweet breeze. And every haunting note of music. She swallowed the lump in her throat and touched a hand to her heart.

Matt pulled up at the neighbor's garage, where two boys were darting up and down the driveway in a rough-and-tumble game of basketball. Their shrieks and cries filled the air.

A sandy-haired youth came out of the side door of the garage and walked around to the front, wiping his hands on a rag. "Want to hold it down for a couple of minutes?" he shouted to his brothers as he shoved the garage door up.

"Hey!" one of the boys shouted. "Where'd you find her?"

Alex grinned as she got out of Matt's car. The boy had sandy hair like his older brother, and the same warm smile. He was older than Kip by a few years, but something about his openness reminded her of her own brother.

"He found me at school." She caught the basketball and drove in close for an easy lay-up. The ball swished through the net, and the second boy, taller and with the lean, rangy build of a high school athlete, caught it.

"Nice move. For a girl."

"Sexist!" she shouted. "Let's see you do better."

As she came toward him he sidestepped and tossed the ball to his little brother. When she went after the younger boy he tried to pass it back, but Alex stole it and went in for another basket.

"Okay, so you can handle a basketball. But you can't deny you're a girl. If I wanted to play as rough as I do against the guys, you wouldn't stand a chance."

"Hey, lay off, Jason," the mechanic shouted.

"He's right," Alex admitted. "I'm not much of a basketball player."

"Like I said, you're not bad for a girl," Jason said.

"Don't mind him," the mechanic said. "Ever since he made varsity, his head's been too big to fit through the door. He'll pick up some manners in a couple of years."

She laughed. "I understand. I have a little brother."

"Mike Wilton," Matt said, "this is Alexandra Corday. She owns the car you've been working on."

"I know Alex," the mechanic said. "That is, I know who you are. I used to see you around the neighborhood. I'm sorry about your grandmother." He carefully wiped his hand before accepting hers.

"Thank you," she murmured awkwardly.

He gestured them inside the garage, where they found Alex's little Chevy, freshly washed and sporting a new windshield.

"It looks beautiful."

Handing her the keys Mike said, "Give it a try."

She got in and turned the key, and the engine started right away. "Sounds wonderful." She looked at him with wide eyes. "I can't believe it. I'd already resigned myself to losing my car along with everything else. What do I owe you."

"I've already been paid," Mike said. Just then the phone rang, and he excused himself.

Alex turned to Matt. "How much was it?"

He shook his head. "Don't worry about it."

"But I can't let you pay for my car. What did it cost?"

He leaned down and said through the open window, "Tell you what. Have dinner with me tonight and we'll call it even."

Now it was her turn to shake her head. "Sorry. I've still got two apartments to look at and a paper to write. Just tell me what it cost, Matt. I can't pay you all of it at one time, but I can pay a little each week."

"No deal. I'll go with you to look at the apartments, and then we'll stop somewhere for dinner. That'll still leave you time to work on your paper afterward."

Alex was aware of the way he was watching her. Though Nanna had said she trusted him, Alex felt she couldn't be certain of anything anymore. She turned off the ignition and climbed out of her car. "Okay. Deal. But only if I get to pick the place."

Matt caught her hand and stared down into her upturned face. He was still drawn to her beauty, but it was impossible to forget what Dirk had hinted at. God knew, he'd tried to stay away from her. But the argument within him continued.

"Come on," he said, more gruffly than he'd intended. "Let's get out of here before you change your mind."

"I can't believe you picked this place. The manager is an old college buddy of mine."

Kisses was a huge, noisy bar in a converted cosmetics factory, frequented mainly by students from the nearby campus. The overhead pipes had been painted lipstick red, to match the graffiti scrawled thickly on the walls in lipstick and eye liner. The waitresses wore skin-tight black jeans and white T-shirts with bright red lip prints on them. The tables were scarred, the chairs mismatched, but they had the best nachos in town, and the pizza had a thin crust and oozed sloppy cheese and every topping known to man—and a few that only the most adventuresome would sample.

A waitress led Matt and Alex to a table tucked in a small alcove, where they could observe the crowd without being crushed by it.

"So? What do you do now?" Matt sipped his beer and watched Alex stare dejectedly into her Pepsi.

It was plain that her spirits were low after inspecting the two apartments. It would take more than Kisses' pizza to cheer her. The first apartment, a neat, clean lower walkout in a private residence with its own entrance, had seemed too good to be true. It was. The price listed in the paper had been an error; the amount being asked was more than Alex could afford. The second had been another disappointment, offering nothing more than a bed and dresser in a seedy building that had been new in the days of silent movies.

"I think I'll take the second one." She moved her index finger around and around the rim of her glass. "At least it was on the ground floor."

"You're crazy." Matt slumped back in his chair. "I wouldn't let a dog live there."

"That bad, huh?"

"Yeah." He sat up and reached out to take her hand,

causing her to look at him. "There are hundreds of better places to live."

"But not in my price range."

"Didn't you get any insurance money from the fire?"

She shook her head. "They're still investigating. And when they do settle, my uncle will be the one to collect. He was named beneficiary."

"Then why don't you go live with your uncle?"

"He . . ." She was avoiding Matt's eyes, and he felt her hand tense in his. She pulled it away, squaring her shoulders. "He thought I should stay here and finish school."

Matt felt a flash of anger. Now he knew why he'd mistrusted Vince on sight. Alexandra wasn't fooling him; her uncle didn't want her. Matt had been disgusted when Vince had refused to even consider having her car repaired. It had been obvious that the man had only one concern—to settle with the insurance company, grab the money, and run. Now Matt had an even better reason for hating her uncle.

"Are you telling me you're not going to get any help from him?" he asked.

"He's got the added expense of my little brother now. I'm just glad Kip's got a place to stay."

"That doesn't solve your problem. How about a job?"

She shrugged. "I work some nights and most weekends for the catering firm that handled your father's party. I don't see how I can carry another job on top of that."

"What happens if the catering firm doesn't have a job scheduled?"

Their waitress appeared and served their pizza. Matt ordered another beer.

Alex took a bite. "That's the problem," she said when the waitress had left. "If there's no catering job, I don't work. And if I don't work, I definitely don't get paid."

"You'll never pay the rent that way. How about a job here?"

Alex stared at him.

"The pay is just average," Matt said, thinking aloud. "But the tips are great. On weekends you can't find a table in this joint. According to Jeff, you're exactly what they're looking for: young, fresh, experienced as a waitress. And definitely easy on the eyes."

Alex glanced around at the busy, bustling staff. They were all young and seemed friendly and energetic.

"And best of all, the manager owes me a big favor," Matt added with a laugh. "Excuse me. I'll be back in a minute."

Before Alex could protest, he was gone. A short time later he returned with the smiling manager.

"Matt says you're experienced and looking for a job."

Alex swallowed a bite of her pizza and nodded.

"I need another waitress. But I'd need you more than just a couple of evenings a week. Can you give me some afternoons too?"

"I guess so. As long as I can work them into my class schedule."

"Good. We'll sit down and figure out the hours. Can you start tomorrow?"

"My last class is over at four."

"How about working from five until closing?"

Alex nodded.

"Good. Drop by my office on your way out and fill out the forms."

One of the waitresses approached and asked Jeff to approve a check. Before turning away he said briskly, "I'll see you tomorrow at five, Alex."

Matt sipped his beer and grinned at her over the rim of his mug. "I think you should go look at that first apartment again."

7

"*Charlie, get your butt* over here and clear this table." The harried busboy jumped in response to the bellowed order.

Christina Theopholis stood only five foot two, but she worked circles around the other waitresses at Kisses. After a week of working with Alex, Tina liked what she saw. Alex was the only employee who could keep up with her frantic pace.

"You want me to take table five for you?" Tina asked as they stood side by side at the bar, waiting for the bartender to fill their orders.

"I can handle it. You've got enough to deal with."

"I don't mind." Tina glanced over at the raucous crowd. "Those guys are in here every weekend. Bunch of smart-asses."

"I can handle them."

"Yeah." Tina gave her familiar cackling laugh, so infectious it made everyone who heard it smile. "You sure can. I've seen you charm a bunch of jerks with just a smile. But remember, if they get out of line with you, let me know. I'll put them in their place."

"Thanks," Alex said, laughing. She picked up her tray and headed out onto the floor. Alex had no doubt that Tina could put an ax murderer in his place.

A few minutes later, just as she was about to take another order, she looked up to see Mike Wilton, the mechanic who'd repaired her car, standing beside her.

"Hi, Mike. Where are you sitting?"

"Across the room. I was hoping you'd notice, but I guess you're too busy. I tried to get a table in your section but the place is too crowded."

The couple at the table glared at her, then at Mike. "You going to take our order?" the man asked.

"Yeah." She shifted her attention to the job. "What'll you have?"

They gave their order, and she started toward the bar with Mike trailing.

"How about stopping by my table later?" he said.

"Sorry, Mike, I can't leave my station. Jeff would fire me on the spot if he saw me goofing off." She paused and turned to look at him. "I can't afford to lose this job."

With a blast of amplified guitar that seemed to shake the foundations, the band started playing.

"I haven't seen you since I repaired your car," Mike shouted at the top of his lungs.

"How can you say that? Last night I waited on your table."

"Yeah, well that's not what I meant. How about having a drink with me later?"

"I'm really sorry, Mike. By the time I finish here, I can hardly make it home to bed." She shouted her order to the bartender, then waited while he filled her tray.

Tina shoved in beside her, easing Mike out of the way. Sulking, he turned away and returned to his table to nurse a beer.

"Who's that?"

"Mike Wilton. A friend of mine."

Even though they were both shouting, half their words were drowned out by the band.

"Didn't look like he wanted to be your friend, honey. He looks more like a lovesick little boy."

Alex picked up her tray and shook her head. "We've never even been on a date. We're just friends."

"I still say he wants more than friendship."

"You've got a wild imagination, Tina."

"That's what my last boyfriend said." She cackled. "But he certainly wasn't complaining."

Giggling, they went their separate ways with the heavy trays. Tina was good for her, Alex thought. She had a way of making her laugh, making her forget all her troubles.

For the next two hours, the noisy weekend crowd kept Alex scrambling through her section, shouting orders to the bartender. It wasn't until after midnight that the crowd began to thin. The band took a break before their last set of the night.

"You don't even look wilted."

At the sound of Mike's voice, Alex turned to him with a smile. "Makeup tricks. Every woman learns them. Underneath all this makeup, I'm really asleep on my feet."

"You don't look it. I've been watching you. I don't know how you do it."

"It's going to catch up with me tomorrow. I intend to sleep until noon."

"I was hoping I could come over and see your new apartment tomorrow," Mike said, unable to hide his disappointment.

"Call first. And if you call before noon, I'll put arsenic in your beer."

He playfully tugged a lock of her hair before heading for the door. On the bandstand, the lead guitar player fiddled with the amplifier and watched as Alex cleared a table and headed back to the bar with another order. He jumped down and threaded his way among the tables, reaching the bar as she did, and chose a stool beside the waitress station.

He enjoyed the view as she stood on tiptoe to reach across the bar for a wedge of lime, which she dropped into a drink on her tray.

"I've been watching you running all night. Do your batteries ever wear out?"

At the sound of the deep voice beside her, Alex turned.

"Gary Hampstead." He stuck out his hand.

"Hi, Gary," she said, shaking hands. "Alex Corday."

He was surprised and a little unsettled by her voice. Velvet where he'd expected silk. Whiskey where he'd anticipated champagne.

She smiled. "Whispers is terrific."

He returned the smile. "You like the band? That's the highest compliment you can pay me."

"Ah, I see. A man who lives for his music."

"Is there anything else?"

At that moment the bartender handed him a beer. He took a long drink. "Unless of course," he said, sighing, "it's a cold brew after a long, hot gig."

He was an arresting presence, whether on the bandstand or face to face. Tall and lean, with a flowing mane of blond hair, a deeply tanned face, and ice blue eyes, around which, at the moment, laugh lines crinkled. He wore jeans and a denim shirt stained with sweat after the long, exhausting night performing.

Alex picked up her heavy tray and made her way to a table, while Gary continued to sit at the bar and watch her. Because of the workload at Kisses, the turnover of waitresses was high. It was not unusual to see a new waitress almost every week. But there hadn't been one so easy to look at in a long while. Gary feasted his eyes until he had to return to the bandstand for the last set of the night.

There was something satisfying about the bar after closing time. With the last customer gone, the waitresses gossiped and joked as they wiped down the tables and stacked the chairs on them for the morning cleaning crew. The band members carefully tucked away their instruments for the night. The busboys waited patiently for the waitresses to count their tips so that they could claim a portion. With another night of work behind them, there was an easy camaraderie among the staff. Alex found that she actually prolonged the work, putting off for as long as possible the time when she would have to return to her empty apartment.

"How about stopping for coffee?" Tina asked as she

pulled on a sweater. Alex nodded and followed her out the door.

"Sure. Where?"

"There's a twenty-four-hour restaurant around the corner."

The two young women walked in companionable silence. Inside the restaurant, the smell of onions on the grill had their mouths watering.

They ordered, then sat sipping hot black coffee.

"How do you feel after your first week at Kisses?" Tina asked. Her hair had been secured on top of her head with a clip, but wispy strands had come loose and clung damply to her neck. She blew the purple bangs out of her eyes. Three days ago, Alexandra remembered, that same hair had been orange.

"I like the work, and best of all, I like the people."

Tina nodded. "Most of 'em are okay. If Charlie doesn't get the lead out and start bussing my tables faster, I'm going to have a talk with Jeff about him." Their food arrived, and Tina bit into her hamburger, closing her eyes for a moment. "Mmm. That's good." She looked across the table at Alex. "You do anything except work at Kisses?"

"I'm going to UCLA."

"What're you studying?"

"A general course of studies, heavy on English. My grandmother was hoping I'd be something sensible, like a schoolteacher, but my real love is music. I've been writing songs since I was a kid. I just never decided which I liked better; dance or piano. I've studied both. My grandmother was a ballerina, and my mother was a musician."

"It shows," Tina said with a trace of envy. "You

move like a dancer. Why not keep on studying both?"

Alex gave a wry smile. "I can hardly keep up with what I'm doing now. In fact, I'm thinking about cutting back on my classes next semester. And I already gave up a little singing job I had at the campus coffeehouse. These hours are getting to me."

Tina nodded. "I know what you mean. I'm going to class four days a week to be a hairdresser. Afternoons I wash hair at the Hair Emporium, then nights I'm at Kisses. As soon as I pass the state exams, I'm out of here. Someday you'll read about me: Tina Theopholis, hairdresser to the stars. All the big-time actresses will be swarming around my shop, begging me to do their hair for the Academy Awards."

She braced herself for Alex's reaction. But instead of laughing, like the others, Alex just sipped her coffee and nodded. "I think that'd be great, Tina. I hope you make it happen."

"You don't think I'm just a crazy dreamer?"

Alex found herself grinning at the look on Tina's face. "Well of course you're crazy. And a dreamer. But why not? Isn't everybody?"

"Yeah." Tina polished off the rest of her hamburger. "You know . . ." She regarded Alex for a moment. "You really ought to let me try bleaching your hair. You'd be a knockout as a blonde."

"Uh-uh. I'll stick with this, thank you." Alex finished her coffee and dug her keys out of her purse. "Come on, Tina. My car's parked down the street. I'll drop you off on my way home."

"Thanks."

A few minutes later as Tina was climbing out of the

Chevy, she gave Alex another appraising look. "Are you sure you wouldn't like to be a blonde?" she asked.

Alex smiled. "If I change my mind, I'll let you know. After all, you are going to be the hairdresser to the stars."

"You bet I am." In the glare of the streetlight, Tina's eyes danced with unconcealed pleasure. "Thanks for believing, Alex. You're the first one who hasn't laughed at me. See you tomorrow."

Alex waved as she pulled away from the curb. Dreams, she thought, everybody has them. She kept trying to keep hers simple: stay in college, get a good job, send for Kip. Be a family again.

She bit her lip and prayed that dream would one day come true.

*   *   *

Dear Kip,

Wait until you meet my new roommate, Tina. She's so much fun. She makes me laugh whenever I start to feel sad. Our apartment is about the size of Nanna's bedroom and bathroom, but it's big enough for the two of us. I hope you're making friends at your new school. I tried phoning you Sunday night, but Aunt Bernice said you were already in bed. Sorry I missed you, but I'll try again next weekend, when the rates are cheap.

Hugs and kisses,
Alex

"Alex, you look beat," Tina rummaged through her

closet. "Why don't you take a night off?" she asked, selecting a shirt.

"Can't afford it."

"Can you afford to get sick?" Tina pulled the shirt over her head and began fussing with her hair, which was blue-black this week. "If you do you'll miss a whole lot more than one night. You could find yourself in bed for a week."

"I'm fine."

"Yeah." Tina glanced at the letter written in childish block print which Alex had hungrily ripped open just minutes before. That was why she drove herself; the little brother in South Dakota was all she talked about. Tina knew that Alex called every Sunday night, and tried to write every week.

The days and nights of endless tension had begun to take their toll. By the end of the semester, Alex had been forced to cut back on her classes, but even that wasn't enough. To pay the bills, she'd invited Tina to share her tiny apartment. The fiery little waitress was only too happy to give up the dingy room she had been renting and move in with Alex.

The two couldn't have been more dissimilar. Alex liked everything neat. Tina preferred what she called "controlled clutter," cleaning only when she could no longer find what she needed. Alex's decorating leaned to the spare look, her only furniture a bed, a dresser, a sofa, a table, and two chairs. Tina had brought a collection of hundreds of perfume bottles, and boxes of frilly satin and lace handcrafted articles to decorate lampshades, tissue boxes, even toilet tissue rolls. Alex shopped bargains in used clothing shops. Tina could look at a designer dress in a store and whip up an exact copy on her old sewing machine overnight. Tina's body was all lush curves, earthy, with a blatant sexuality. Alex, on the other hand, had a more refined, subtle look that was enhanced by the forties-style clothes she preferred.

Alex's dresser top displayed a framed picture of her parents and a photo taken of Alex and Kip with Nanna. Tina's family pictures included shots of four brothers and three sisters and assorted nieces and nephews, mounted on every square inch of wall space. She lovingly referred to the display as her rogues' gallery. Between her dressmaker dummy and the bolts of fabric on her bed and stashed in her closet, the apartment had the cluttered look of an army surplus store.

Tina had confided that she had no intention of marrying and settling down like her brothers and sisters. She wanted a career and was willing to pay any price to reach her goals. Alex had admitted that she wanted a man like her father. A man willing to take risks. A man who would love her without smothering her.

Though the two were different in so many ways, they discovered they were compatible roommates. It was a wonder that the two found any time to form a friendship. When they weren't studying, they were working. Alex always volunteered to fill in for any waitress who couldn't work a shift. Some weeks she found herself working day and night without a break.

"So what did Kip have to say?" Tina felt as if she already knew Alex's little brother. Though her roommate was reticent about anything personal, she couldn't help boasting about the nine-year-old boy whose letters she devoured as soon as they arrived.

"I'll tell you later. Come on, we're going to be late."

"One of these days," Tina muttered, following Alex out of the apartment, "we're going to kiss all this good-bye."

"Yeah. When we find fame and fortune."

"Keep dreaming."

Laughing, they hurried off to work.

Tina noticed that a lot of the rowdy crowd at Kisses had begun asking to be seated in Alex's section. If it was anyone else, she would have hated her for earning the most tips, but it was impossible to hate Alex. Tina understood. It wasn't just the fact that her roommate was by far the best-looking waitress in the place. More important, she made all her customers feel good about being there. She remembered their names and their favorite drinks. She commiserated with them over lost loves and laughed at their silly jokes.

But, Tina noted, whenever any of the men tried to get closer, Alex held them at arm's length. She'd had dozens of offers for dates and refused all of them. She had become especially suspicious of handsome, charming men who came on too strong. Tina didn't know why. When she'd tried to get her roommate to open up, Alex always claimed there wasn't any particular reason, except that the thought of going out with a stranger filled her with dread. When she saw that Tina was going to question her further, she insisted that the truth was that she was just too tired and busy to date. Besides, weren't all these guys just ordinary? She wanted a man who lived life on the edge of danger.

Jeff, the manager, was aware of the value of his new

waitress. A girl like Alex Corday was a magnet for the kind of customers he wanted; young, upwardly mobile, and eager to spend a lot of money for the privilege of being on the receiving end of a smile from a pretty face.

From the things he heard and observed, Jeff gradually became aware of the one thing that made her different from all the other waitresses. She turned down all offers of dates from the customers. That only made her more valuable, since the men were vying for her attention. It seemed odd that a girl so pretty and outgoing would seem to have so little interest in socializing, but it made her seem all the more desirable. Jeff began boasting that if he could clone Alex, he'd have the perfect staff.

He sat in his office counting the night's receipts. Out of the corner of his eye he watched the waitresses as they cleaned tables and stacked chairs. As always, Tina was doing most of the jabbering. Alex, he noted, thoroughly enjoyed Tina's jokes while she quietly went about her work.

When an argument broke out on the bandstand, heads came up.

"What do you mean, you want me to stay and rehearse again?" The singer, a lanky blonde dressed in a leather miniskirt, put her hands on her hips and shouted at the top of her lungs at the leader, Gary Hampstead, "I'm sick of all this rehearsing. I know every song by heart. I could sing them in my sleep."

"Sometimes that's how it sounds," he returned, "like you're singing in your sleep. Now let's get started."

"Do you know what time it is? It's two friggin' thirty. I've been on my feet since nine o'clock. My boyfriend's outside, and I'm not going to keep him waiting any longer. So you can just rehearse without me." She strode off the bandstand.

Gary shouted to her retreating back, "If you walk out now, sweetheart, don't bother coming back tomorrow."

"And what'll you do without me?" She swung around and shot him a wicked smile. "Sing duets with yourself?"

"You heard me." His voice had grown deceptively soft. "You walk now, you keep right on walking."

"Just watch me." Tossing her purse over her shoulder, she stormed out of the bar.

The rest of the band members looked from one to the other in uncomfortable silence.

"Let's get started," Gary announced.

"We're going to rehearse without Annie?" the drummer asked.

Gary nodded, and the musicians began shuffling around the bandstand, setting up their music.

Bear, who carried more than two hundred pounds on his stocky, five-foot-eight-inch frame, warmed up on the tenor sax. Jeremy, the bass guitarist, ran a hand over the beard he was trying to grow. He replaced a broken string and began tuning his instrument. Len, at the keyboard, adjusted his thick glasses and played a couple of riffs. His dark skin gleamed in the stage lights. His head, which he regularly shaved, was bent over the music.

"We'll run through 'Lovin'' first," Gary said, strumming the opening chords of the band's theme song. "Casey, you take the vocals."

The drummer shook his head. "It needs a woman's voice."

Gary swore, then strummed the opening chords again. As he did, his gaze swept the empty bar, coming to rest on Alex, who was wiping down the last table. The other waitresses had already disappeared to claim their sweaters and purses.

"Hey, Alex. Can you sing as good as you look?"

She gave a shrug.

"Do you know the words to 'Lovin''?"

"She ought to," Tina called as she emerged from the back room. "We've all had to hear them at least a hundred times over the past weeks."

The others laughed, and Gary struggled with the temper he was still feeling. "Come on, Alex. Give it a try."

He could see that she was considering his offer. Still, she hesitated.

"Go on," Tina shouted. "You said you love music and dance. Didn't you say you used to sing in a campus coffeehouse? Let's see you strut your stuff."

With the rest of the waitresses shouting encouragement, Alex was shoved toward the bandstand, where Gary was already adjusting the microphone. At his nod the musicians broke into the opening strains of their theme, and before she could even catch her breath, Alex was forced to begin.

For a minute Gary couldn't believe what he was hearing. Her voice was low, bluesy, like aged Irish whiskey. She stood very still, staring at a point on the far wall, letting the music wash over her. At first she was hesitant, trying the words, almost tasting them. Then, slowly, gradually, without even being aware of it, she lost the feeling of self-consciousness. As she continued to sing, the heart-wrenching words tugged at her until she became lost in them.

> "... So much pain, in lovin'
> So much heartache ..."

She felt it deep inside, the emptiness, the weariness, the fear that tomorrow would be much like today.

Her thoughts turned to Kip. She phoned him once a week, but each time she heard his voice, frightened, tearful, she felt the knife twist in her heart. In between calls she wrote long letters, reminding him about the life they would have together—someday. Always someday. Did he really believe it? Did she? God, she was scared. So scared. She loved him too much to bear the thought of losing him.

Love. That was what she felt, growing in her heart, swelling with each chord. Love for a little brother, laced with a growing fear that he was somehow drifting away from her. Would there always be pain with love? Would she always have the ones she loved wrenched away from her? Mom. Dad. Nanna. Now Kip.

Gary slowed the tempo to suit her mood. They'd always done 'Lovin'' with an up tempo, but Alex's interpretation made it sound new, different. The effect was riveting.

He glanced around. The two busboys who'd been arguing in the back of the room were now quiet, respectfully attentive; the waitresses had stopped at the door to watch and listen. Even Jeff had stepped out of his office.

Gary turned his attention to the woman at the microphone. She wasn't aware of anyone or anything except the music. Her eyes were closed; her hands, small, graceful, held out in front of her, as if in supplication. She exuded energy, so pure, so vital, she seemed to glow with it.

He glanced at his musicians, who wore matching looks of surprise laced with pleasure. Prodded on by her emotion, the bass guitar throbbed, the tenor sax wailed, the piano all but cried.

When the song ended Alex opened her eyes, looking almost dazed, as if not quite certain what she'd done, or how much she'd revealed. For a long moment there was total silence. Then, just as Alex was beginning to suspect that she had made a terrible mistake, the room erupted with shouts and applause.

Gary watched as his musicians crowded around her. She seemed genuinely surprised and touched by their compliments. The waitresses, led by Tina, raced to the bandstand to voice their approval.

"You're wasting your time as a waitress," Tina told her. "Anybody with a voice like yours ought to be earning a living with it."

Gary glanced toward the rear of the room, where Jeff stood perfectly still, watching and listening. "How about another song? Let's try 'On My Own'."

The words could have been written by her, Alex realized as she lost herself in the music once more. Again she seemed to weave a spell, holding everyone, even when they tried to turn away. Among the staff, the lateness of the hour was forgotten, the need to dash home to bed dissolved. There was only Alex and her heart-tugging voice.

Halfway through the song they all knew—knew that Jeff had just lost his best waitress, and that Gary had just found what he'd been searching for since the first time he'd picked up a guitar: a woman with a voice so perfectly matched to the music that was playing inside his head, it was as if she had a secret door to his mind. Not to mention his heart and soul.

"Alex, I'd like you to stay another couple of hours and rehearse with the band," Gary said when the song ended.

She thought of all the reasons why she shouldn't. There was her nine o'clock class in the morning—not to mention the fact that she'd already been without sleep for almost twenty hours. But the music had her adrenaline pumping, and she knew she could stay up for as long as they were willing to play.

"How much are you going to pay me?"

Gary threw back his head and roared with laughter. "I knew you were too good to be true."

She waited. When he didn't say more, she tried again. "Well? How much?"

"More than you can make waiting tables in this dump. What do you say?"

A slow smile touched her lips. "You just said the magic word. I guess I can give it a try. But I don't want to give up my waitress job. Think I can do both?"

Gary swallowed back his protest; they'd work it out later. Right now, he was satisfied. Whispers wasn't going to be just another saloon band. They'd just found the key to stardom.

8

"*Once the joint* is filled tonight, nobody else gets in until a table is vacated. You got that?" Jeff sat at his desk and leveled a look at the new bouncer he'd hired. "I got a letter from the city. It seems the fire inspector paid a visit last weekend and counted more bodies than our capacity allows. If he finds us over-crowded again this weekend, we'll get a violation."

When his employee left, Jeff sat back with a smile. He'd take a violation any time, in return for this. No one had been prepared for such success. Alex had only been singing for four weeks, but she already had people eagerly waiting in line at the door. Suddenly, Kisses was the hottest spot in town. And Jeff had received a substantial raise from a grateful owner.

As the band members began assembling their instruments on stage, Alex walked in. Jeff got to his feet, watching her make her way through the crowd.

As Gary had predicted, she'd been forced to give up waitressing after only a week. It wasn't possible to wait tables and rush to the bandstand too. Besides, a singer in a Kisses T-shirt didn't present the image he wanted.

Tonight she wore a red dress made of a sheer gauzy fabric. The fitted bodice emphasized the swell of her breasts and her tiny waist, and the skirt fell in loose folds almost to her ankles. On anyone else, Jeff thought, it would look dowdy, like a grandmother's dress; on Alex it was stunning. He saw the way the men turned to watch her as she approached the stand. Oddly enough, she seemed completely unaware of their stares. Or else, he thought, she was very good at hiding her reaction.

Len reached out a hand to help her up.

"I've been working on a new song," she muttered, placing the music in front of him.

She took a seat beside him at the piano, and the two bent their heads over the music. They remained that way until it was time to begin.

Matt pushed his way through the crowd and took a seat at the bar. His camera hung around his neck. He'd been prowling the streets in search of candidates for his latest project. *Life* magazine had hired him to capture the face of young America at play. It was his first assignment since the accident.

He'd left the beaches and ski resorts to others; he preferred the night scene.

The crowd outside Kisses had piqued his interest. What had suddenly increased the place's popularity among young executives and law clerks?

He craned his neck, unconsciously searching the faces of the waitresses, but Alexandra was nowhere to be seen. Onstage a black piano player traded riffs with a guitarist who looked more like a surfer, with his mane of flowing blond hair and dark glasses. The rest of the musicians followed the drummer's slow rhythm.

And then he heard the voice. It was low, soft, vibrating with emotion. Like the others around him, Matt strained to see the singer, though he already knew. The voice touched something, some basic chord inside him. He shivered as the song washed over him.

The crowd was strangely silent, caught up in the drama. The words, the voice, the haunting music created a tension that was almost palpable. The song was driving to its conclusion, and still the singer was shrouded in darkness somewhere behind the band.

She held the note; held it until it sounded more like a violin than a human voice. As it ended, three spotlights finally illuminated the singer.

Alex's reaction to the light was always the same: for that one brief moment she had a flash of memory—of headlights illuminating a ragged old man. Of a feeling of stark terror. She stopped, lifting her hands as if to hold back the glare, like an animal frozen in a car's headlights.

The crowd was electrified. As one they were on their feet, cheering, clapping, shouting.

One hour later, when Alex and the musicians had finished their set and the stage was again dark and silent, Matt sat perfectly still. The drink in his hand remained untasted. A kick in the gut by a karate expert would have been less shocking than what he'd just experienced. He couldn't remember when he'd been so moved, so excited by a singer.

But this wasn't just another singer. The sign outside had simply stated VOCALS BY ALEX. That was the name called out by the bartender and the customers as they cheered each song.

Bumming a cigarette from the man beside him, Matt held a lighter to the tip. He'd gone two whole days without a smoke. He would quit another time. Right now he needed a cigarette.

He filled his lungs and exhaled slowly. Son of a bitch. Alexandra Corday, the woman who had haunted his dreams since the first time he'd seen her, the girl who had eagerly accepted a waitress job to pay her bills. Onstage, she was so transformed he would not have recognized her had it not been for her familiar voice.

He picked up his glass and tasted the liquor. Maybe when she returned to the stage for the next set, he'd be a little better prepared for the jolt. But Matt was wrong. The cigarette and the drink hadn't helped. Nothing could fortify him against the intense emotions this woman and her music evoked.

He'd never experienced anything quite like it. It was as if she had tapped into his soul and articulated everything he'd ever thought or felt. Songs he'd heard a hundred times before took on new meaning when she sang them. She dared to slow the rhythm of an up-tempo song, lingering over every word, forcing him to listen, really listen, until he felt her pain. And his own.

Glancing around the room, he found he wasn't alone in this reaction. The bartenders and waitresses stood watching and listening, their customers forgotten for the moment; the crowd leaned forward, holding its collective breath, while she bled from their wounds, cried for their despair.

At times he could sense the strength in her, as she clenched her fists at her side and lifted her chin defiantly, a woman scorned. At other times she seemed so fragile, so vulnerable, singing of a love gone wrong and a heart broken beyond repair. She was, he realized, the consummate actress, assuming the identity of everyone. Mother, daughter, woman, child, innocent, seductress. She drew out every exquisite emotion until pleasure and pain had merged and blended, and it was impossible to distinguish one from the other.

Unable to stop himself, he quickly took his camera out of its case. With just the stage lights for effect, he framed her in his viewfinder, capturing all her moods and poses.

By the time the band played its last set of the night, Matt felt drained. Through the lens of his camera he watched the slender figure on stage accept the accolades of the crowd, her arms extended, her eyes overbright. Excitement? he wondered. Or tears? He caught the moment with his camera, freezing it for all time.

As suddenly as Alex had appeared in the blaze of spotlights, she was swallowed up by the darkness. The band continued to play, and the crowd leapt to its feet and roared for more. But though their cheering continued for a full five minutes, the object of their adulation remained in the shadows, unwilling or unable to step forward one more time.

If he was this exhausted, Matt thought, how much more drained must she be?

The waitresses gave last call, and the patrons slowly began to slip away into the night. No one had left since the music had begun hours earlier. Without people, the cavernous room more resembled the factory it had once been than the crowded bar it had become.

"Closing time, buddy," the bartender announced.

"Yeah." Matt remained where he was and glanced toward the bandstand. The piano player was seated at his instrument beside the slender figure in the red dress. The two sat, heads bent over the keys, quietly dissecting a song. They were so intent on their task they seemed oblivious of anything else.

The rest of the musicians gathered around, and the piano player began running through a series of notes.

Matt thought briefly about approaching her, then decided against it. After all, what could he possibly say about the performance he'd just witnessed? He wasn't certain he could even put his feelings into words. The images he'd captured on film would have to speak for him.

He dropped his money on the bar and strode out into the night.

On the bandstand, Alex gave up trying to ignore the eerie feeling that she was being studied under a microscope. Turning, she scanned the room. The place was empty, silent and still, except for the whisper of smoke curling toward the ceiling from an ashtray on the bar.

"Wait'll you get a load of this." Gary tossed an open magazine onto the piano stool while the others crowded around.

"Hey. That's Alex!" Bear shouted. "Look, Alex. It's you."

As Bear flipped the pages, she caught sight of several dramatic black-and-white photos, all showing a woman with an intense expression on her face, her hands uplifted, singing to a rapt audience.

"Is this how I look?" She felt as if she were seeing a stranger.

"That's you, sugar. You look real enough to leap off the pages." Len glanced toward Gary. *"Billboard?"*

"No," Gary said proudly. *"Life."*

At that, Casey, the drummer, let out a whistle. *"Life* magazine did a spread on us?"

"Just a couple of shots," Gary said. "For something called 'Young America At Play.' But my phone's been ringing off the hook ever since it hit the stands. I've had offers from some of the best clubs in California."

"Forget the clubs," Len said. "When do we get a recording contract?"

"It'll happen," Gary assured him. "All in good time. Right now, let's concentrate on playing the places where we'll get noticed. I'm meeting with the manager of Moondog in Carmel. If he decides to hire us, we're on our way."

"Why? What's so great about that place?" Jeremy asked.

"It's owned by a couple of actors who've made it a local hangout for stars when they're in town. Once they get a chance to hear us, we'll be on a fast track to fame and fortune."

"Hear that, Alex? You're going to be a superstar."

Len turned to where Alex stood staring at the pictures. But the words were lost on her. It wasn't her face she was studying so carefully; what had caught her attention was the name beneath the photos—Matt Montrose.

He'd been here, watching, listening, taking her picture.

The thought of him sitting in the dark, studying her without her knowledge, gave her the strangest feeling. She realized that hundreds of people watched her perform every night, but still, she was able to block them from her mind. She considered singing to be an intensely personal thing. Once the music started, she forgot about everything else. It was as if a door closed, shutting her away from everyone, everything. There was just her, alone with the feelings.

She felt a prickle of recognition. She knew exactly which night Matt had been there. She could still recall the feeling of having been touched.

He'd watched her—and taken pictures. Based on the various poses, he must have spent hours observing her.

And he hadn't even bothered to approach her.

She felt a flash of annoyance. Maybe he thought he was too important to reveal himself to a mere saloon singer. Her anger turned to deep disappointment: maybe he'd been turned off by what he saw and heard.

She studied the photos again, this time trying to look at them objectively. A tiny shiver passed through her. They seemed . . . intimate. As though the photographer sensed things about her that only she had a right to know.

"Did you hear me, Alex?" Jeremy picked up his bass guitar and bent to plug it in. "I said you're going to be a superstar."

"Yeah. Right after I run for president." She flashed him a wicked smile and tossed the magazine aside. She'd just had another thought, one that left her numb. Matt Montrose was the brother of Dirk. And Dirk Montrose wasn't a man; he was an animal, the worst sort of animal. A cruel, unfeeling predator. Somehow, whenever she had been around Matt, she'd forgotten that fact. But she couldn't afford to forget it again.

She shivered and turned away, determined to block all thought of him from her mind. There was only one way.

"Let's go through the California songs we've been working on," she said.

"Guess what?" Tina said as she burst into the tiny apartment.

"Okay. What?" Alex, seated on the middle of her bed, looked up from the sheet music she'd been studying. She and the band had been putting together a new list of songs. They'd rehearsed until they had them cold. "What?"

"You're looking at Christina Theopholis, state-certified hairdresser and cosmetologist." She waved the certificate in the air.

"Oh, Tina. That's wonderful." Alex leapt from the bed to hug her friend. "Now what? Are you going to look for a job in some exclusive salon?"

"It's not very exclusive, but I already found one," Tina admitted proudly. "The Hair Emporium was my first stop after collecting this little prize. I start next week—not as a shampoo girl, as an honest-to-god hairdresser."

"I guess that means you'll be quitting Kisses."

Tina picked up the phone. "That's my next order of business. I'm calling to tell Jeff I'm all through working after tonight."

"That makes two of us."

At her words Tina dropped the telephone. "What?"

"It means Gary just booked us in a club in Carmel. Tonight's our last night here. Jeff is furious that he's lost us, but he said he couldn't afford to match what the new club is offering."

Tina slumped into a chair. "What about your classes? And this apartment? What are you going to do about the rent?"

"I'll be dropping out of UCLA. I was hoping you'd stay here, maybe take in a new roommate while I'm gone."

"I don't want a new roommate."

Alex perched on the edge of the bed. "It looks like we don't have a choice."

"How long will you be in Carmel?"

"Who knows? The contract calls for two weeks, with a two-week option. If they really like us, we might be there for as much as a month more. If not. . . ."

"Why wouldn't they like you? Hell, they'd have to be nuts not to extend your contract."

Alex grinned. "Gary ought to hire you to handle our PR."

"There's only one thing I want to do." Tina's eyes glittered. "I want to be—"

"Hairdresser to the stars," Alex finished for her.

"That's right. So sit over here." Tina led her to the small dressing table. "Someday, when you're a big star, you'll be able to tell everyone that Tina Theopholis did your hair when you were a nobody."

"I am not a nobody. And neither are you. The world just hasn't heard about us yet."

"They will." Tina grabbed a handful of Alex's hair and began to comb it.

"You're not going to change the color," Alex warned, glancing at their reflections in the mirror. This week, her roommate's hair was the color of pink cotton candy.

"Wouldn't I love to. But since you're such a grouch about it, I'll just change the style."

Working quickly, she secured a jeweled comb in one side of Alex's hair and drew it all neatly over the other shoulder, leaving it to fall across her breast in a tangle of curls. "Tonight, before you go to bed, let me braid it. Tomorrow you'll have crimped hair. What do you think?"

Alex nodded. "I like it." Standing, she hugged Tina. "I wish I didn't have to work tonight. I'd take you out to celebrate."

"We'll celebrate," Tina said, "when you get back from Carmel. By then, my client list will be so long, you'll have to make an appointment a month in advance just to get in to see me. And you," she said, pointing with her comb, "will be the talk of the music world. We'll both be making so much money we won't be able to spend it."

"I hope so, Tina," Alex said, getting to her feet. "I really hope so." She picked up the small framed photo beside her bed. "Then I could send for Kip, and everything would be so perfect."

Tina gave a snort of laughter. "You and I know nothing's ever perfect. But it would be great to meet this kid I've heard so much about. Now I've got to get ready for my last night of waitress work." Tina slipped out of her clothes and yanked a lip-print-embossed T-shirt from a drawer. As she pulled it over her head she muttered, "This is one thing I'm definitely not going to miss." She touched up her hair and makeup and hurried to the door. "See you at Kisses."

Before Alex could respond, she was gone.

After their last performance at Kisses, Gary caught Alex's arm before she could step down from the band-stand. "Alex, we're all going out to celebrate. Want to come along?"

"Thanks, Gary, but I've made plans."

The leader of the band glanced around the deserted room. His eyes narrowed slightly. He'd never seen Alex accept an invitation from anyone.

"Got a date?"

She shook her head. "I have a lot to do before I leave town. Are you sure you don't mind driving me to Carmel?"

"I'm sure. No sense taking your car all that way. But I'd like to be on the road early."

"I'll be ready. What about the rest of the guys?"

"Bear'll take the instruments in his van, and the others want to go with him."

"All right. See you in the morning."

She hurried back to her apartment. Though it was too late to telephone, she would write a long, newsy letter to Kip so he wouldn't be upset about the change in her plans.

9

There wasn't much to pack. Alex had forgotten how little she had been left with after the fire. Besides two pairs of jeans and a couple of Kisses T-shirts, she'd managed to acquire a wardrobe of mostly vintage forties gowns that she'd picked up for a few dollars in a secondhand shop. Slinky, ankle-length dresses in clingy fabrics that showed off her figure to its best advantage, they had become her trademark on stage.

When she wasn't performing, she preferred jeans and a slightly frayed blazer she'd found in a resale shop, along with a battered old felt hat that had been in the inside pocket.

Tina watched silently as Alex set her single suitcase beside the door. They both looked up when they heard Gary's car stop and the car door slam.

"I guess this is it." Alex swallowed, dreading their

good-bye. Tina was the closest thing to a sister she'd ever had.

"I'm so torn," Tina whispered. "I want the owners of this new club to like you, but I know if they do, you won't be coming back."

"I'll be back."

"You'd better," Tina muttered, gathering her close. "I already told Sheila she can only live here until you need your space back. Then she'll have to find another place."

Alex hugged her fiercely. "Oh Tina, I'm going to miss you."

"No you're not." Tina squeezed her eyes shut, fighting tears. What was wrong with her? she wondered. She hadn't even cried when she'd left home. "You're not going to do anything except concentrate on becoming a famous singer. And when you do, remember your favorite hairdresser."

"Yeah." Alex kissed her cheek, then turned away, wiping her eyes with the back of her hand. At Gary's insistent knock, she opened the front door and picked up her suitcase.

"Ready?" He paused on the threshhold, feeling like an intruder. Tina was eyeing him as if he was a mass murderer.

"I'm ready." Alex squared her shoulders and took a last, long look at her friend. "I'll call you."

Tina nodded, glowering at the man who had come between them. "See that you treat her right."

"Hey, just because she has a suitcase in her hand, it doesn't mean we're running away together. I'm just driving her to Carmel."

Tina stood in the doorway watching as the two

walked out to Gary's car. But suddenly Alex dropped her bag and raced back, digging into her pocket.

"I almost forgot. I won't be needing my car for a while. I thought you could use it." Tina's mouth dropped open as Alex put the keys in her hand. "Now you won't have any excuse not to drive up to Carmel and catch our act," she said.

Before Tina could think of a thing to say, Alex went and got into the car.

As the car sped away, Alex turned in her seat and waved until Tina was out of sight. Then she settled back and watched as the City of Angels flew past.

They followed the spectacular coastal highway, U.S. 101, all the way to San Luis Obispo, where Gary's battered old car sputtered to a stop. After half an hour of tinkering, they were back on the road.

"I always thought this was the classic California city," Gary said, slowing as they passed the centuries-old Spanish mission in the heart of town, which was surrounded by a mixture of Victorian and contemporary homes. "Everything about this place shouts California."

"Were you born in California?" Alex asked.

He shook his head. "Cleveland. I didn't discover the wonders of the West until college. But I dropped out after one semester when I teamed up with the others and formed the band. How about you, Alex? Born here?"

She nodded.

"I could tell."

"How?"

He shrugged. "You have a California look about you."

"A California look?"

He glanced at her. "You just look comfortable here. Like you're not impressed with all the big names and the big homes and the big contradictions in this part of the country."

"I guess that's true." She paused, considering. "When I was a little girl, my parents brought me to the sand dunes." She turned to stare out the window. "My father surprised us with a picnic. We walked for miles along the sandy beaches, until we stopped at a secluded ocean cove."

Funny, she hadn't thought about that in years. She settled back, remembering. Her father and mother had played and laughed like two children, and after the picnic they'd walked arm-in-arm back to the car. Less than a year later her little brother had been born. Had that been when . . . ?

"Penny for your thoughts."

As she turned her head, Gary thought he detected a blush on her cheeks.

"Nothing. Just trying to take it all in. Are we going to stop and eat soon?"

"Yeah, we'll pick up something. Holler when you spot a fast-food place. I don't want to waste time at a restaurant. I'd like to make it to Carmel in time to rehearse before going on tonight."

An hour later they were devouring greasy fries and burgers and sipping soft drinks as they rolled along the highway.

"I was wondering." Gary popped some fries in his mouth. "Where'd you learn to sing like that?"

"I just sort of picked it up."

He took his gaze from the road long enough to glance at her. "Uh-uh, sweetheart. Not the way you sing. That first time, when you opened your mouth, it was like you'd been rehearsing for years."

"Maybe I have been."

"Who taught you?"

"What makes you think I had lessons?"

"It . . ." He grinned. "It's pretty obvious."

Alex sighed. "I never thought of it as having music lessons. I guess I just thought that everybody's mother sang like mine."

"Your mother's a singer? What's her name?"

"It was Marney Corday."

Was. He said nothing.

"I used to listen to her for hours," Alex added softly.

"I guess it rubbed off. Was she a songwriter too?"

Alex nodded. "She'd sit at the piano, going over and over certain notes, and spend days thinking of the perfect word or phrase."

"So it's in your blood."

That idea pleased her. She hadn't thought about it all that much. "I guess it is. How about you, Gary? How did you get into music?"

"My grandfather. He was a plumber, but he spent his nights and weekends playing in a ragtime band. My dad used to say that it was the only time his father seemed alive. Gramps bought me my first guitar when I was eleven. From then on, there was nothing else for me but music."

She could understand that. For as far back as she could remember, she'd found solace in music. "After my mother died, I found some old recordings of hers. I

played them over and over, singing along. It's funny."
Alex kept her face averted, watching fields of gold
California poppies and blue lupines drift past the win-
dow. "I felt closer to her then than when she was alive.
It was as if the music was a connection between us."

Gary didn't want to get her hopes up too much, but
the truth was, he had a feeling about her. Ever since
she'd joined the group, they'd become electrified. He
chose his words carefully.

"If this gig works out, I think the band should concentrate on our own original music until we have
enough to forget about doing other people's songs
completely."

She turned to study him. "That's pretty ambitious."

"Yeah, I know." He grinned. "But what else are we
going to do with ourselves all day?"

Alex opened the travel brochure Tina had brought
home from the beauty salon. "Let's see. There's surf-
ing, bicycling, horseback riding, tennis, golf . . ."

"Like I said, what else are we going to do with ourselves all day?"

They laughed as Gary turned the car onto Highway
1 and smoothly maneuvered the hairpin turns that
meandered up the coast.

After two more time-consuming breakdowns, they
reached Carmel. They drove slowly through the
unique seaside village, staring at the fairy-tale cottages
and fanciful houses and shops, until they came to a
glass and stone structure built on a small promontory.
The weathered inn had aged gracefully and had the
charm of a very old, very comfortable building.

"Why are we stopping here?"

"This is it, Alex. The Cypress."

"But I thought we were playing a club called Moondog."

"We are. That's the name of the nightclub here in The Cypress."

Her mouth dropped open in surprise. She'd expected something noisy, smoky, and crowded. She'd expected another Kisses.

"All the comforts of home." Gary chuckled. "Except, home was never like this." As he stepped out of the car, Gary tossed his keys to an attendant and asked, "Where will I find Zane Christy?"

"Ask at the desk," the young man called. "They'll have him paged."

"Thanks."

Gary led the way through the lobby, with Alex trailing slowly behind. Her gaze swept from the high beamed ceilings inset with skylights, to the floor of dull field-stone. Potted plants grew in profusion. Sunlight poured into every corner, giving the feeling of an atrium.

At the front desk Gary spoke with a young woman who gave him a smile.

"If you'll follow me, I'll take you to Mr. Christy's office. He's been expecting you."

They were ushered into a room crammed with three desks, computers, phones, faxes, and a copy machine. The man behind one desk was shouting into a telephone in a staccato voice. The sleeves of his gray silk shirt were rolled up to the elbows, and his suit jacket was tossed carelessly over the arm of a chair. Although his face was youthful, his dark brown hair was sprinkled with silver strands.

Finally he dropped the receiver into the cradle and came around the desk to extend his hand to Gary. "You made good time from L.A."

"Not nearly as good as I'd hoped." Gary decided not to explain about the number of breakdowns they'd suffered. "I wanted time to look over the room where we'll be working. Zane, this is Alex Corday."

Her hand was caught in a firm grasp and she was studied almost clinically.

"I've been looking forward to this, Alex. The photos of you in *Life* were intriguing, but I'd have to say they didn't do you justice. The reviews I've been getting are very impressive."

"Thank you, Mr. Christy."

"Zane. Around here, we don't believe in formality." He released her hand and turned to Gary. "The rest of your musicians are already here. They're setting up their instruments in the club. There's a four-bedroom cottage on the grounds that you and your group can use. I'll have someone take your luggage over while I show you around."

"If you don't mind," Gary said, "I'd rather get the Cook's tour later. Right now I'd like to see where we'll be playing."

"Right." All business. Zane liked that. He'd dealt with a lot of musicians through the years, and he'd decided that at least half of them thought life was one big party. Since hiring on with the Cypress, he'd learned to handle all kinds, but he preferred to deal with people who knew when to work and when to play. "Come on," he said with a smile.

They followed him through the lobby and up a staircase to an upper level, where the nightclub was.

The room had a wall of glass overlooking the most spectacular view Alex had ever seen. It was a vast seacoast panorama of blue sky meeting even bluer water. Above, seabirds wheeled and dipped, filling the air with their cries. Below, surf pounded on rocks, and rare Monterey cypress clung to tiny patches of soil, their gnarled branches shaped and twisted by wind and rain.

Casey, Bear, Jeremy, and Len looked up from the bandstand where they were adjusting their instruments.

"What kept you?" Bear asked.

"We took the scenic route."

"Didn't you know that way would add a couple of extra hours?"

"Yeah, but it was worth it. Alex is still speaking to me."

"The truth is," Bear said with a laugh, "we figured you guys would beat us here. The van broke down twice."

"We beat that record. My car broke down three times. And I've discovered that Alex has another talent besides singing."

Bear's eyes widened. "Don't tell me she can fix a car."

"No. But she sure knows how to hit an engine with a hammer when she's mad."

They all burst into laughter.

While the others continued laughing and bantering about their travels, Gary sauntered closer and ran a hand along one of the speakers. The view outside was lost on him now; the only thing he cared about was right here. The sound, the lighting, the music. That was what mattered.

"Let's get set up and test the acoustics."

"I'll leave you to it," Zane said. As he crossed the room he called, "Alex, would you like to take a look at your accommodations?"

"Yes." She knew she would have precious little time for herself. They were all so nervous, they would probably run through their music until showtime, but right now, Gary had to be satisfied with the sound. She'd watched him enough in the past to know that he would play with the speakers until he had them exactly the way he wanted.

"When will you need me?" she asked Gary.

"Take half an hour."

She nearly laughed. He acted like he was giving her the moon. Checking her watch she said, "I'll be right back."

Gary didn't even bother to look up. He plugged in his guitar and strummed a few chords, listening to the reverberation. With a wave to the others, she followed Zane from the room.

"I think you're going to like it here," he said as he led her outside and down a back stairway to a paved courtyard.

"I like it already. I've never seen anything so beautiful."

"Your first time in Carmel?"

She nodded.

"Careful," he said as he inserted a key in the lock and held the door for her. "You may never want to leave."

She stepped into a small foyer that led to a huge central living and dining area. Like the rest of the buildings, it had a vaulted ceiling with skylights that let light into every corner. A glass table and six chairs dominated one side of the room; along the other wall was a fireplace.

"There are two double bedrooms in the front, and two small single bedrooms in back. All open into this central living and dining area." Zane crossed to the jumble of suitcases and duffle bags in the middle of the room. "Show me which of these belong to you and I'll set them wherever you'd like."

"Don't bother. I can manage by myself."

"Okay. I'll leave you to settle in." He touched a finger to a button on the wall and the draperies slid silently open, revealing floor-to-ceiling windows. "Enjoy the view, Alex."

"Oh." She gave a sigh of pure pleasure and stood very still, absorbing the spectacular scenery. She didn't even hear him leave.

So this was the "cottage." To her, it was a mansion.

A short time later she carried her suitcase to one of the smaller back bedrooms. She was delighted to discover that each bedroom had its own bath. She'd been prepared to share with five messy musicians, and now the unexpected luxury of her own bathroom made her smile. Unpacking quickly, she laid out what she would need for the show that night, then hurried back to the club to rehearse.

As she made her way across the courtyard, she thought about what Zane had said. It would be easy to fall in love with this place and never leave it. A smile touched her lips. She couldn't wait to sit down and write a long letter to Kip, telling him everything about her new paradise.

10

Nerves. They were all suffering from them. Gary had spent the past hours snapping and snarling, driving them through rehearsal like some sort of crazed lion tamer. When Casey had complained that his drums had been damaged en route, producing a distortion in the sound, Gary had thrown a temper tantrum. Jeremy had stopped right in the middle of a song to tune his bass guitar, causing everyone to jump on him. Len had misplaced a stack of music and went into a tailspin until it was located in the bottom of a satchel. Even Bear, the most placid of them all, had insisted on having sandwiches brought in, or, he'd vowed, his two-hundred-plus-pound frame would collapse. In the end they'd taken a short break, and even Gary had to admit that he felt better for it.

Now they were back at the cottage, with less than an hour before their first show.

Alex stepped into the shower. When she emerged

she wrapped herself in a thick robe and, picking up a hairbrush, went out to the deck outside her bedroom. As long as she had the luxury of a few more minutes, she would spend them here. She sat cross-legged on a lounge chair, watching the surf crash against the shore, slowly brushing her hair and allowing the breeze to dry it.

This was how she would deal with her nerves. Gary had the little song he hummed while he showered and dressed. Casey, she knew, would dress quickly and watch mindless cartoons on television. Bear would fix himself something to eat. Jeremy would catch a cat nap. Len would go over his sheet music, even though they all knew that he could play everything from memory.

Alex realized that she had to have a moment of quiet time. She hadn't known it until she stepped onto the deck. Watching the seabirds, listening to the sound of the surf, she felt her spirit respond to the calming influence. She took a deep breath, filling her lungs with the fresh, clean breeze, before reluctantly turning away.

Back in her room she slipped into a dramatic long-sleeved black beaded gown that molded her body from neck to ankle. The high collar fastened at her throat, leaving her back bare. The straight skirt was slit to the thigh. She brushed her hair and left it loose, for dramatic effect.

Stepping back, Alex studied her reflection in the full-length mirror. The dress had been new in the forties, but the beading was intact, and the fabric showed no sign of fraying. She stepped into black beaded pumps and added glittering earrings that dangled just above her shoulders, then surveyed herself again. It looked as if the costume had been made just for her, though, in fact, she had bought it, as she bought almost everything, in a thrift shop.

Satisfied that she was ready for the grueling hours ahead, she picked up her makeup bag and headed out the door.

"Wow!" It was Casey, just turning off the TV, who first caught sight of her.

She was aware that the others had turned to stare. Gary looked up from the notes he was writing at the dining table. There was a smile of pure appreciation on his lips. "Alex, you're going to knock 'em dead."

"I hope so. This outfit set me back fifty-seven dollars."

Bear, who'd been known to spend that much on a pair of cashmere socks, burst into laughter.

"It looks like fifty-seven grand," he managed to say while polishing off the last of his Oreos and milk.

She shot him a grin as Len yanked open the door. When she walked outside, Gary caught up to her. "You going to be all right tonight?"

"Yeah. How about you?"

"Once we start playing, we'll all be okay."

"Did Zane tell you what kind of a crowd to expect?"

He shrugged. "It's the middle of the week. It should be slow. Especially since we're new. It'll give us a chance to break in some fresh material without having too many people witness our blunders."

She paused. "What new material?"

Gary caught her arm and winked at Len. "Those two new songs you wrote. I think it's time to try them out on an audience."

"Not yet. I'm not ready."

He forced her to keep moving. He wasn't going to engage in battle in the middle of a public courtyard. Besides, once onstage, she would have no choice but to sing what they played.

"Don't worry about it, Alex. Let's just see how the evening goes."

The evening was going better than expected.

Zane Christy stood in a dark corner of the club and surveyed the Wednesday night crowd. There were the tourists, who had come to admire the view and would stay for one drink to see if any of the celebrity-owners of Moondog would show their faces. There were the golfers, who were more interested in replaying today's game than in the musicians.

There were, of course, the guests of the Cypress, who paid no cover charge. But they were an elite group who rarely stayed beyond the first performance, unless it was an exceptional act.

So far, no one had left, and the room was better than half full. For a club of this size that was quite an accomplishment.

Zane watched the woman onstage and, like everyone else in the place, became caught up in the spell she was weaving. As she sang about broken dreams and broken lives, he felt a knife twist in his own heart. Leaning against the wall, he lingered for almost an hour, charmed by a voice unlike anything he'd ever heard. When he finally managed to glance away from her, he realized that everyone around him was reacting in the same manner. Even the golfers, for once, were silent, their game forgotten. All heads were lifted, all eyes staring intently at the woman in the black beaded gown.

Zane felt a shiver pass through him. With an effort he managed to tear himself away, but he knew that before the band played its last set he'd be back. There was something about Alex, something about the way she seemed to sing directly to him, making him forget there was anyone else in the place.

Onstage Alex heard the first chords of her new song. She felt a flash of anger. Gary wasn't being fair. She shouldn't have to test a brand new song on the first night of a new show. She wasn't ready, she'd told him so. And now he was pushing her in a direction she definitely didn't want to go.

Casey picked up the beat and Jeremy added his rhythm. Len's fingers rippled over the keys, and before she could think of a graceful way out, she found herself singing the words of the song she'd written just days ago.

To anyone listening, it spoke of lost love. To Alex, it spoke of the emptiness in her life since the death of Nanna and her long separation from Kip. Lately she had felt a nagging suspicion that her aunt and uncle were deliberately building a wall between her and Kip. So often, when she telephoned on Sunday nights, she was told that Kip was visiting a friend's house or had already gone to bed. But in his letters, he never mentioned friends. In fact, he had begun questioning why she wasn't writing and phoning as much as she had in the past. She wondered if they were withholding calls and letters from him.

Fear, love, betrayal. All the emotions she kept so carefully locked in her heart came tumbling out in the song.

She saw a sudden flurry of activity near the doorway as a group of men entered and were escorted to a table. Closing her eyes against the distraction, she caught a note, pure and clean, and held it until it seemed to shimmer in the very air. Len perfectly matched the note on the piano, then led her into the refrain. She was so lost in her music again, she wasn't aware of anyone or anything.

Matt took his seat and ordered a drink, but in fact he was too stunned to know what he was doing or saying. All his attention was focused on the vision in the spotlight.

He hadn't bothered to glance at the posters announcing the entertainment. He hadn't come here to be entertained. This meeting his father had arranged between J. T. Pearlman, the head of Pearl Pictures, and Sven Nordstrum, acclaimed cinematographer, was strictly business.

At the moment, business was forgotten.

Matt's drink sat untouched. His eyes were narrowed in concentration. When the song ended and the crowd burst into applause, he continued to study Alex with a critical photographer's eye. She seemed thinner than the first time he'd seen her. Probably not taking time to eat. Definitely more relaxed onstage. That was bound to happen, given enough exposure to crowds. And still displaying that uncanny gift for losing herself in her music. It was what set her apart from the competition.

When she finally acknowledged the audience, it was as if she were just emerging from a trance. She smiled, waved her arm to encompass the band, then stepped back into the shadows, her black gown blending into the darkness beyond the spotlight.

"There was something familiar about that singer," Sidney Montrose said.

Matt merely smiled.

"That was some voice." J.T. drained his glass and signaled for a refill. "That kid's got a great future. The face alone would sell albums. Don't you agree, Swede?"

Sven nodded and sipped his drink. "But we didn't come here to discuss singers."

"Right. Well . . ." J.T. cleared his throat and turned to Matt. "Now about this film you're planning to direct."

"What about it?" Matt was aware of the band members moving around the bandstand, checking their instruments before taking a break. He scanned the room for a glimpse of the singer, feeling a stab of disappointment when he didn't see her. He forced his attention back to the man seated across from him in the booth.

"You've signed on the best." J.T. nodded his head toward Sven. "When do you start?"

"Another month or two. We're in preproduction."

"Once you start, I'd be happy to look at the rushes."

Matt almost smiled but caught himself in time. He knew his father had gone to a lot of trouble to arrange this meeting. But now that word was out that Pearl Pictures was interested, his phone was ringing off the hook. "You'll have to get in line."

"God damn it. Who beat me to it? Richardson? Barry? Levi over at Cameo?"

"All of the above."

J.T. swore again. "I knew it. The minute word gets out about a winner in this town, they open the doors to the zoo."

"Winner?" Sidney said with a laugh. "Don't you think that's a little premature, J.T.? You don't even know if it'll be any good."

"By the time I do know, there'll be a dozen studios offering to distribute it." J.T. leaned close. "Look, Matt. Our studio needs a winner. Our last two releases were dogs." He waited until the waitress brought their drinks and walked away. Lifting his glass, he said, "Your old man and I go back a long way."

"I know. He told me you gave him his first break."

J.T. nodded, glancing across the table at Sidney. "And he paid me back a couple of years later by bringing home an Oscar." He turned to meet Matt's gaze. "I'm not trying to trade on my friendship with your father; whatever debts were between us, they were settled years ago." He gave a snort of laughter. "Hell, who am I kidding? Of course I want to use your father's friendship; I'll use anything I can. I just want your word that I'll have a chance to compete with the other studios."

"If that's all you ask, you have it."

J.T.'s mouth dropped open. "Just like that?"

Matt shrugged. "Just like that." He extended his hand. "You have my word."

J.T. shook his hand, then signaled for the waitress again. "This calls for a celebration. Order whatever you'd like." He slid out of the booth. "Excuse me. I have a phone call to make."

By the time the band had returned for their final set J.T. had downed his fifth vodka. Sven kept his hand beneath J.T.'s elbow as he helped him from the booth. To Matt he muttered, "You turning in?"

Matt shook his head. "Think I'll stay awhile. How about you, Dad?"

"I'm getting too old for this night life," his father responded. "Besides, I promised Elyse I'd be home tomorrow in time for her birthday bash. I don't dare disappoint her."

J. T. Pearlman stuck out his hand. "You won't be sorry, Matt. Pearl Pictures knows how to treat its people."

"That's what my father's always said."

J.T. nodded vigorously before being led away, and Sidney Montrose said good night to his son and followed.

Matt gave a sigh of relief. He'd made the trip to Carmel as a favor to his father and had intended to hurry back to begin work on his project. He'd planned to spend the night in his room going over the volumes of notes he'd compiled. Finding Alexandra here was like a gift from the gods. Suddenly the thought of spending the night listening to her music was too tantalizing to pass up.

As the band members made their way to the stage, he emptied his glass, feeling a sudden ripple of tension go through him.

Matt heard the first note, low and teasing, before the spotlight suddenly caught her in its blaze. As before, he had a quick impression of a wild creature startled by a predator. Just as quickly the surprise vanished from her eyes as she slipped under the spell of the music. For the next hour and a half he forgot everything except the woman onstage.

She took her audience on a roller coaster, giving them no time to recover their senses. They smiled with her; wept with her. They held their breath as she drew out a note longer then humanly possible, then released it as she swept them easily into an old familiar tune that had their toes tapping.

Along with the rest of the people in the room, Matt experienced every feeling that she poured into her music. He was amazed by her range, and even more surprised by the depth of her emotions. He had no doubt he was witnessing a rare event. It was only a matter of time until the world discovered her talent.

When she took her final bow he was as drained as if he'd been the one performing.

Although he knew he had to be on the road by dawn, he discarded any notion of going to his room. To hell with work. To hell with routine and discipline. There was only one thought in his mind: he had to see her. There was no longer any choice.

11

As the nightclub began to empty, Matt remained where he was. When a waitress made her way over he handed her a folded slip of paper and a twenty-dollar bill.

"Could you bring me a phone? And see that the young lady up on the bandstand gets this note."

The waitress pocketed the money and returned minutes later with a house phone, which she placed in front of him before going toward the front of the room.

Onstage, Gary conferred with Alex, making notations in the margins of his music. "I think we should run through your new songs again."

"Absolutely. I'd like to slow down the tempo on . . ." Alex's words trailed off as the waitress approached and handed her the note.

As she finished reading it her head came up sharply. She glanced around the room until she caught sight of Matt seated all alone in a booth. His expression was unreadable, but even from so great a distance the look in his eyes held her.

For a moment she couldn't find her voice. It was as if a fist had just squeezed her heart, making it painful to breathe.

Following the direction of her gaze, Gary's smile turned into a frown. He'd caught the look in her eyes, a mixture of surprise and something else, something he hadn't seen in her eyes before. "Somebody you know?" he asked.

"Yes. I . . ." At a loss for words, she turned to the others. "Would you mind if we postponed rehearsal until tomorrow?"

"Suits me." Len pushed away from the piano and stretched his arms over his head. "I'm starving. Where can we go for tacos in this town?"

"No, chili," Bear said, rubbing his stomach. "All night I've been thinking about a big bowl of hot, fiery chili."

"How about both?" Jeremy suggested as he snapped the case of his bass guitar closed. "And a couple of cold beers."

"Yeah. A gallon of beer." Gary felt a sudden urge to get roaring drunk. He turned to Alex, who was standing as still as a statue. "You joining us?"

"No. You guys go ahead."

"Rehearsal tomorrow morning. Nine o'clock sharp. Don't be late." With his frown deepening, Gary followed the others from the bandstand.

Matt was aware of their scrutiny as they passed him, and from the leader, a thinly veiled hostility. On the one hand, Matt felt a flash of annoyance. They had no right to such possessiveness. After all, Alexandra was one of their group, not their property. On the other hand, he was amused. They were behaving like a bunch of older brothers who were giving a new boyfriend the once-over. He decided to accept it as an odd sort of compliment. And at least they were looking out for her interests.

When they were gone, he went to the bandstand, halting at the bottom of the steps.

"I couldn't believe it when I saw you onstage. I thought my mind was playing tricks."

She swallowed. "I'm real."

He was achingly aware of that fact.

He held out his hand and she caught it as she descended the stairs. With each step closer she took, he felt the jolt. The black beaded gown she was wearing was molded to her body like a second skin. Each movement parted the slit skirt, revealing her thigh. Yet despite the blatant sensuality of her costume, the innocence he'd first sensed in her was still apparent.

She paused in front of him, releasing his hand. He breathed in the subtle fragrance of jasmine, aware of her in a way he'd never before been aware of a woman.

"I watched you perform one night in Hollywood at Kisses."

"I know." She felt a tiny shiver at the thought of him in the darkness beyond the spotlight, watching, listening. Sharing her intimate thoughts and feelings. "I saw the photos you took. Looks like you finally managed to photograph me, with or without my permission."

"Did you mind?"

She grinned. "How could I? They're the reason we got this job."

"Really?" He smiled. "Then I'm glad I was able to help."

"Did you take more photographs tonight?"

"No. I don't have my camera with me." He didn't need a camera. Her image was etched so clearly in his mind.

"Then why are you here?"

"Business."

She felt her heart plummet. For just a moment she'd allowed herself to believe that he was here to see her. She abruptly dismissed the foolish thought.

"Are you hungry?" he asked.

She struggled to regain her smile. "Starving."

"Good. I know a place that has the best seafood in town." He caught her hand once more and began to lead her from the room.

"Don't you think I'm a little overdressed?"

He shot her a dangerous grin. "Where we're going, nobody will ever notice."

She knew that this was the point where she should protest. Still, for some reason she couldn't fathom, she allowed him to usher her along the corridor toward the exit. When they stepped outside she spotted a golf cart loaded with a blanket and a picnic hamper.

"Yours?" she asked.

"It belongs to the hotel."

"And you just happened to have it parked and waiting."

"All it took was a phone call." His smile grew as he helped settle her inside before climbing in and putting the cart in gear.

In silence they drove along a deserted stretch of beach. When they came to a finger of land that jutted into the water, Matt stopped the cart.

"Might as well be comfortable," he muttered, removing his shoes and jacket. Rolling up the sleeves of his silk shirt, he climbed out of the cart and spread the blanket on the sand. Then he got the huge picnic basket and set it down on the blanket.

Alex remained where she was, watching, hesitating. After all, though there was something appealing about him, she'd once been burned by someone who'd been smooth and charming.

"Dinner is served," he announced.

When she still remained seated in the golf cart, he looked at her questioningly. "I thought you said you were hungry."

"I'm always starving after a performance. Maybe because I can't eat a thing until it's over."

"Come on, then. The lobster won't bite, and neither will I."

Shrugging aside her last hesitation, Alex slipped off her shoes and stepped into the warm sand. Though the sun had set hours ago, the sand still retained its heat.

Kneeling opposite him on the blanket, she opened the basket and removed a covered silver bowl filled with seafood on a bed of shaved ice.

"Mmm. Heavenly."

She lifted a second covered dish. This one contained delicate pastries. She plucked a piece of lobster from its icy nest and tasted it, giving a sigh of pleasure.

"How did you ever manage such a feast?"

Matt filled two plastic cups with champagne and handed one to her. If he noticed the distance she kept between them, he made no mention of it.

"The chef at the Cypress is an old friend of the family."

"You mean he did all this as a favor to you?"

With perfect deadpan Matt said, "Well, I did have to promise him absolute rights to my firstborn."

Despite her mistrust, her eyes twinkled. "Is that all?"

He began to chuckle. "No. Here's the really tough part. I also had to promise him tickets to the preview of my father's new picture next weekend."

"I knew there was a catch." For the first time they shared an easy laugh. Alex sipped her champagne and began to relax. He wasn't at all like his brother. He seemed . . . genuine.

"Your father must be excited. The rumor is that it could be one of the top movies of the year."

Matt nodded. "All the early reports are positive. We've got our fingers crossed for him. If the public agrees with me he'll have a hit on his hands."

"Then I wish him luck. And what about you? Still living the life of danger? Are you working on another photo assignment?"

He shook his head and said, "That part of my life is over. I'm about to start my first movie. As director."

Her eyes widened. "Director?"

He nodded. "It's something I've been thinking about for a long time now, especially since I won't be accepting any more overseas photo assignments." Without realizing it he rubbed a hand over his shoulder. Though the wounds had healed, there would always remain twinges of pain. And regret for the passing of a way of life he'd loved.

There was genuine enthusiasm in her tone. "Directing a movie—Matt, that's wonderful!"

"I hope so. Of course, I know firsthand how fickle

the movie business can be. If it bombs, my name will be mud in this town."

"How could a movie of yours fail? I've seen what you can do with a simple black-and-white photo essay. If you bring even half that talent to the big screen, it's bound to be a success."

Her words pleased him more than anything he could think of. "I've always been fascinated with people," he said between bites of crab and lobster. "I love seeing them through the lens of my camera."

Alex watched the way the breeze ruffled his dark hair. Here on the beach, relaxed and away from the scrutiny of others, he seemed younger, more carefree. He had, thankfully, none of the practiced charm of his brother, none of the gloss and polish. He seemed easy, natural, and unaffected by his success.

"Now," he added, "I want to take it a step further, by making the images of people live and breathe and laugh and cry, all at my direction."

"Who wrote the script?"

"I did." He drank some of his champagne. "I couldn't trust anyone else to tell my story. It's something I've been thinking about for a long time now."

"Can you tell me about it?"

"It's about two street people, desperately fighting just to survive." He stared up at the dark sky for a moment. The stars looked close enough to touch.

"In my photo assignments, I've met a lot of street people," he said, shaking his head. "Some of them have pretty incredible stories to tell. Like the two in my movie. In their struggle, they find an amazing treasure of love, not only in each other, but in the people around them."

Alex watched his eyes. As he told her about the plot, his pupils darkened with barely concealed passion. It was as if he had suddenly become infused with life. And when he met her gaze, she felt the ripple of recognition clear to her soul.

Life on the edge. Hadn't it been the only life she'd known when her father was alive? She understood his passion for his work. It was something she felt completely each time she stepped onstage.

Without thinking, she touched his hand. Then she quickly withdrew it, feeling awkward and shy. "It sounds wonderful, Matt. Do you have any stars signed to play the leads?"

He'd been much too aware of her touch. Struggling to ignore the sudden flare of heat, he deliberately kept his tone impersonal.

"No stars. In fact, no recognizable names. I'm using unknowns, as well as a few authentic street people who will play themselves."

"Isn't that risky?"

"Years ago I learned that anything worth having will require taking risks."

"My father always used to say that." She lowered her gaze and nervously pleated a corner of the blanket between her fingers.

Such long, delicate fingers, he thought. And yet so expressive. He'd seen the way she used her hands, her arms, her body, as she performed her music. He found himself wondering what those fingers would feel like on his naked flesh. Dangerous thoughts, he warned himself.

"You told me you were hungry," he said, and stared pointedly at the dish of seafood.

"I was. I am." She made a feeble attempt to eat another bite of lobster, but her appetite had fled. Needing something to do, she drained her glass. The champagne was cool and soothing to her throat which had gone suddenly dry.

"Come on." With a smile he stood and offered his hand. "Let's take a walk."

She took his hand and got to her feet, and again they both felt the current that seemed to flow between them at the simplest touch. He quickly dropped her hand, taking care that they didn't touch again.

"Tell me about the band. How did you happen to start singing with them?"

As they strolled along the beach, she told him about the fight between the singer and Gary, and how she'd been coaxed into singing at rehearsal. Soon they were laughing together, occasionally darting away from an incoming wave. When they encountered a line of cypress growing right to the water's edge, they paused awhile, watching the surf pounding against the shore.

It was so easy to talk to Matt. Alex found herself telling him all the funny little things that had happened on the drive to Carmel. She even admitted to hitting Gary's engine with a hammer when it went dead for the third time.

He loved the way the stars were reflected in her eyes as she talked and laughed, and the way the moonlight set the ends of her hair to flame.

Matt glanced at the sky. Where had the night gone? Already the distant horizon was streaked with the first ribbons of dawn light, and still there was so much he didn't know about her. So much he wanted to share.

"The story of you and the band would make a great movie," he commented.

"Only if we become superstars. Right now, we wouldn't even merit a sixty-second commercial."

They turned back toward the blanket, a distant dark square in acres of white sand.

"Do you want to become a superstar?"

"I haven't really thought about it. No, that isn't true," she quickly amended. "Of course I do. Who wouldn't? But not for the reasons you think. Right now, I'm just interested in making enough to pay the rent and for—things." Like getting Kip.

"Still no help from your uncle?"

He noted her slight hesitation. "It's enough that they're keeping Kip."

"How's your little brother doing?"

"Still living in South Dakota. But as soon as I can, I intend to send for him. That's why I have to save." A thread of steel was evident in her tone. "No one is going to keep us from being a family."

"Has somebody tried?"

She shrugged. "I get the feeling that my aunt and uncle want to make it as difficult as possible for me to communicate with Kip." Her voice roughened. "But we're family. No one has the right to come between us."

He heard the passion in her voice. After a moment's pause he said, "So until you get your little brother back, the guys in the band have become your family."

She considered his words carefully, surprised at his perception. "I guess you're right."

"Tell me about them."

"Len, the piano player, is the easiest to work with.

When I write a new song, I take it to Len. He and I work together on the arrangements before the others see it." She glanced up shyly at him. "Bear plays the sax," she said, her voice warm with affection. "He lives up to his name. He's like a cuddly old teddy bear."

Lucky Bear, Matt thought as he strolled beside her.

"Jeremy, the bass player, and Casey, the drummer, have played together the longest. They're real pros. When it's time to rehearse, they work like dogs; the rest of the time they're content to do nothing. Their idea of a good time is a day off with nothing to do but watch TV and sleep on the sofa. But they're terrific musicians."

"How about the leader?"

She shook her head. "Gary is hard to figure. He's a loner, and a workaholic. If we'd let him, he'd drive us to rehearse day and night. Not that I'm complaining," she added quickly. "If it weren't for Gary, I'd still be waiting tables. He pushes me—more than I'd like, sometimes—but at least he keeps his goals clearly in sight. Gary is driven to be the best."

"And you?"

She shrugged. "I'm doing what I always wanted to do. I grew up around music. My mom was a singer."

Was. He waited only a second or two. When no further explanation was forthcoming he asked. "How did she die?"

"Cancer. Just months after my little brother was born. After that, we went to live with Nanna, my father's mother."

"And what about your father?"

She hesitated for the briefest of moments. Her reticence wasn't lost on Matt. It was apparent that she wasn't comfortable talking about herself and her family. That only made him all the more determined to get her to reveal more.

Her voice softened almost to a whisper. "He died a year after my mother did."

Matt felt a wave of compassion. He too had lost his mother when he was young. But at least he'd always had one parent. Even when Sidney had brought Elyse home, and with her Dirk, Matt had always known his father was there for him.

"You were close to him?" Matt asked.

She nodded. "He was so proud of the fact that he'd worked his way to the top of his profession. Then one day it all came crumbling down. Maybe that's why sometimes, when we've had a really enthusiastic audience, I'm afraid I'll wake up and find it's all a dream."

"And if that happened, what would you do?"

She gave a low, throaty laugh that whispered over his senses, reminding him once again why he'd wanted so desperately to be with her tonight. He'd experienced the same reaction the first time he saw her.

"I guess I could always go back to waiting tables."

The breeze caught a strand of her hair, lifting it, then dropping it over one eye. He caught the strand and drew it through his fingers.

"I don't think there's any danger of that." His voice was gruff.

She felt her breath catch in her throat and struggled to keep her tone light. His touch was doing strange things to her nerves, but she couldn't seem to find the will to step away. "I wouldn't be so sure."

"Trust me." His gaze centered on her mouth. "I've already seen you perform. I know what effect you have on your audience. If you want it badly enough, you can have it all."

"Oh, I do want it. The more exposure I have to this life, the more I want it. It's addictive. Getting lost in the music, hearing the response from the audience." She closed her eyes a moment, as if the feelings were too intense even to talk about. "I'd be lying if I didn't admit that I do want it all."

For the space of a heartbeat he fought the temptation to draw her close and ravish her mouth. Calling on all his willpower, he clenched his fists at his sides and took a step back.

The sky had grown light. Already the birds had begun their morning chorus, and the wild creatures were greeting another day.

"Come on." He turned on his heel.

"Hey—what's the rush?" She had to race to keep up with his long strides.

He turned and gave her a mysterious smile. "We're going to see the best show in town, and the curtain's about to go up."

12

"Look at that one." Matt pointed and Alex
laughed. "What a comedian."

They were perched on a big rock that jutted into the
ocean. Just a few feet away, fat sea lions barked and
frolicked in the surf. One clumsy old lion rolled con-
tentedly onto his back and drifted along with the current. Others chased after him, ducking and splashing
like children.

"Want to join them?"

"Won't they resent our intrusion?"

"Their playground's big enough for all of us."

Matt slid off the rock, then lifted Alex down to stand
beside him in the shallows. She gathered her skirt in
one hand, holding it above her knees. Beneath the clear
water, tiny anemones glowed with luminous color.
Schools of colorful fish darted among smooth pebbles.
The white sand was as soft as a carpet under their feet.

Alex watched a sailboat on the horizon. "Kip would love this. His dream is to live near the ocean." She turned to Matt. "You remember that school for gifted children he used to attend?"

Matt nodded. "Is he going to a special school in South Dakota?"

"My aunt and uncle don't believe in such things. They said they want him to have a normal education."

"What about his art?"

"When we talk, he never mentions it. But I think that's because he knows they're listening. In his letters he still reminds me about my promise."

"Your promise?"

She bent to retrieve a smooth rock that glinted beneath the water. "I promised him that one day we'd live in a big house in Malibu, where he could have his own studio overlooking the ocean."

"That's a pretty big promise to make to a kid."

She skipped the rock across the water and watched its progress, avoiding his eyes. "I know."

"Worried that you won't be able to keep it?"

"I'll keep it." She turned to him. "It may take me a while, but I'll keep my promise."

He chuckled, brushing his knuckles lightly over her cheek. "You know something, Alexandra?"

Alex pulled back to look into his eyes, suddenly afraid of the sensation that skittered along her spine. "What?"

"I don't doubt you for a minute." He tugged her hand. "Come on."

"Now where are you taking me?"

"Do you realize how many hours have passed since we ate?"

It seemed like only minutes ago, but when she glanced at her watch, she couldn't believe the time. It was nearly seven o'clock, and in two hours, it would be time to rehearse with the band.

They waded back to the beach, where they folded the blanket, put the remains of their nighttime picnic back into the hamper, and climbed into the golf cart. Matt drove along a gravel pathway that wound its way from the beach through a lush, flowery landscape. Alex breathed in the fragrance that was uniquely Carmel. The sweetness of flowers was laced with the tang of the ocean and the spice of pine.

When they reached a small outdoor café, Matt parked the cart and got out, but Alex hung back.

"I can't eat here dressed like this."

He laughed and caught her hand. "Who's going to see you? There isn't a soul around."

"But I feel so silly in an evening gown."

"Here then." He draped his suit jacket around her shoulders. "Now you look like one of the guys. Nobody will even give you a second glance." They both were still laughing when the tired-looking waitress approached their table. They shared an omelette filled with tomatoes fresh from the vine and helped themselves from a basket of biscuits still warm from the oven.

"Mmm. I can't remember anything that tasted this wonderful," Alex said with a sigh.

Matt leaned back, sipping strong hot coffee. "I was just thinking the same thing." But he knew it wasn't the food, or the café, or the glorious morning. "I can't remember when I've had a better time."

"It was . . ." She wanted to tell him how very special

the night had been, but she couldn't find the words. Instead, she finished lamely, "It was fun, Matt."

He was staring at her so intently, she knew her cheeks had grown flushed.

When the waitress returned, he paid the bill and stood up. "Let's not waste a minute of the hour we have left."

They drove the golf cart back to the beach, all the way to the water's edge.

"I'll race you to the rock," he said as he climbed out.

It was a struggle, but she managed to splash through the shallows, holding her skirt above her knees and barely keeping up with him. By the time they reached the rock, they were both out of breath.

Matt pointed toward the finger of land that stretched into the bay. "Want to go out to the light-house? The view from the top is fabulous."

Alex suddenly recoiled. "No, I'd better get back."

He glanced at his watch. "We still have plenty of time."

She shook her head. "It isn't that. I just don't want to waste your time going out there. I could never climb to the top. In fact, before I got even halfway up I'd be deathly sick. I have a terrible fear of heights."

"Hey, you're trembling. Let's get out of the water."

Matt lifted her up to sit on the sun-warmed rock and knelt behind her, all the while keeping his arms around her.

"I'm such a coward," she muttered. "Just thinking about the top of the lighthouse had me shaking."

"It isn't cowardly to harbor fears." He drew her back against him, letting his hands rest just beneath her breasts.

"You probably aren't afraid of anything," she muttered.

"Want to bet? I still have nightmares about the Jeep hitting the mine, and the explosion. I've gotten used to waking up in a cold sweat."

Alex found herself comforted by the knowledge that even this strong, independent man had demons of his own to fight.

The breeze lifted her hair, and Matt couldn't resist the urge to press his lips to her exposed shoulder. She shivered, and he moved his mouth upward along the sensitive column of her throat.

"Some people," he murmured against her skin, "are beaten down by the blows life deals them. Others are made even stronger by them. From what I know of you, Alexandra, you're a survivor. I don't believe anything could ever hold you back."

A survivor. If only he knew how afraid she felt at times. But whatever fears she harbored for herself, they were nothing compared with the fears she had for her little brother.

"I wish I knew what to do about Kip," she said bleakly, staring out to sea. "What can I do to help him survive when we're so far apart?"

"You can keep on doing what you're doing. Write him. Call him. Encourage him to keep on believing that one day soon you'll be together."

"He's so young," she said with a sigh.

Matt drew her closer. "But he has you."

"Matt Montrose." With a flicker of a smile she pushed free of his arms and slid from the rock, gathering her skirt in her hand. "Do you always have an answer for everything?" She walked through the shallow water to the sun-warmed sand.

She was startled when strong arms caught her and turned her around. She found herself staring into Matt's laughing eyes.

"Not always." He lifted a hand to brush the hair from her temple. Though his expression didn't change, she saw the sudden hunger in his eyes as he lowered his face to hers. "For instance, why can't I figure out what sort of magic spell kept me here all night? I should have been on the road hours ago. You've caused me to do something I've never done before: I'm late for an appointment. Whatever your magic is, woman, I've fallen for it."

He brushed his mouth over hers. He'd meant it only to be the lightest touch, but the moment he felt the warmth and tasted the sweetness of her lips, he was lost. It seemed the most natural thing in the world to gather her close and take the kiss deeper.

She shrank back, eyes wide. "I don't think . . ." The fear was back, triggered by thoughts of another time, another man.

"Don't think." He caught her by the shoulders and dragged her close. Against her mouth he muttered, "Just feel."

Pressing her hands to his chest, she tried to use them as a barrier to keep him at bay. But when his tongue eased between her parted lips, she found her arms wrapping around him, drawing him closer. Her mouth moved against his, searching, seeking.

She was shocked by her reaction. All of her instincts told her to be on guard. But she couldn't run. She couldn't even resist. She gave a murmur that could have been protest or pleasure.

No one had ever kissed her like this before, with lips

and teeth and tongue. Devouring. Seducing. Possessing. The taste of his lips was more potent than anything she'd ever sampled.

She'd never known a hunger as gnawing as this, or a thirst as great.

Overhead a gull cried, but neither of them heard it. A breeze feathered around them, carrying the tang of the ocean. It failed to cool their heated skin.

As Matt drew her closer, his fingers skimmed her back, which was exposed to the waist. At the intimate touch she reacted as if she'd been burned. Hot, sizzling sensations skittered along her spine. Sensing her fear, he quickly banked the fire that had begun raging. Taking a step back, he moved his hands slowly, lazily along her arms, allowing her time to take in several deep calming breaths.

Gradually she began to relax. But as she did, she felt herself responding to his tenderness in a most unexpected way. Instead of turning away, she actually stepped closer, causing his movements to freeze. The hands that had been stroking her arms became motionless. The look he gave her was one of bewilderment.

It was not forcefulness she craved; it was gentleness. The gentleness of his touch had her body humming with need. Her breasts tingled. Her thighs ached.

Without a thought to what she was doing, she wound her arms around his neck and drew herself against him. She heard his moan of pleasure as she brought her mouth to his.

Locked in an embrance, they dropped to their knees, feeling the sand shift beneath them.

She clung to him, experiencing a rush of heat that had her palms sweating, her heart pounding. Sunlight

played over her half-closed lids, creating a kaleido-
scope of light and darkness until she was seeing him
through a fiery mist.

His hands left her shoulders to roam her naked
back. With every movement of his fingertips she felt
her resolve weaken. She sighed and tightened her grip,
holding on as if she feared falling.

He was aware of nothing except his need for this
woman. Running kisses across her shoulder, he
brought his hands up her sides until his thumbs found
the gentle swell of her breasts.

"Matt . . ."

He covered her mouth before she could say more.
Need consumed them both. Impulses too strong to
deny seemed to propel them over the edge of reason.

Her body begged to be touched. Somewhere in the
back of her mind a warning sounded, but she could no
longer fight the feelings he'd aroused in her. His
thumbs teased, tormented, until she could no longer
think, only feel. She gasped and arched against him, as
wave after wave of pure pleasure surged through her.

In some small corner of her mind she knew that she
had to find the strength to resist what he was offering,
but though her mind resisted, her body betrayed her.
As long as he would go on touching her like this, kissing
her like this, she couldn't muster the willpower to
refuse him anything. Combing her fingers through his
hair, she dragged his head closer and offered him her
lips.

Matt tore his mouth from hers and pressed it to her
throat. The scent of jasmine was stronger here, cloud-
ing his mind, arousing him as he'd never been aroused
before. He heard her little gasp as her hands moved

along his arms. At first she seemed about to push him
away, but almost at once her fingertips began to knead
the muscles of his shoulders.

Dear God, how he wanted her. Wanted her naked
and warm beneath him. Wanted to feel her skin grow
hot and moist beneath his touch. Wanted to see her
lose control and soar with him.

He'd known desire before, but he'd never before
known such need. Desperate, driving need, a need that
clawed at him, seeking release.

No woman had ever taken him so far, so fast. With
only a kiss she'd brought him to the very edge of an
abyss. One more step and they would both tumble into
a pool of dark, sensual pleasure.

A short distance away he heard the voices of children. Their unexpected presence brought him back to
reality. What was happening to him? He'd almost taken
her here, in public, like a savage. Struggling to cling to
the last thread of sanity, he held her a little away, looking at her as he held her in his arms. Her long hair was
tousled, her eyes too bright.

"Matt." Alex's heart was pounding so loudly she
could do no more than whisper his name. She saw the
way he was studying her. "What's wrong?"

"Come on," he said, more roughly than he'd
intended. "We'd better get back. You'll miss your
rehearsal."

"Yes. The rehearsal . . ." She nervously tugged at her
skirt as he helped her to her feet. The flash of vulnerability only made him want her more.

In a gentler tone he said, "I don't want to get you
back late—I wouldn't want to have to fight all five guys
at once."

He laced his fingers through hers and led her back toward the golf cart. He'd bent the rules as far as he could. Now it was time to get back to reality. He had business commitments, as did she. Only the gods knew if or when they would ever meet again.

When they reached the cottage, he lifted a hand to her face tracing the outline of her lips with his thumb. His eyes darkened with desire. "It's a good thing I'm leaving."

Her heart tumbled. "Do you have to?"

He nodded. "I've neglected my business as long as I can. Besides," he added with a wry smile, "I don't think I would have the strength to walk away a second time. If I don't leave now, you won't be safe." He lowered his head and brushed her lips with his. "Good-bye, Alexandra," he murmured against her mouth.

Feeling again the rush of heat, he had to force himself to break contact. He took a step back, turned, and left without another word.

"Nice of you to show up," Gary called irritably when Alex entered the club.

"What do you mean? I made it with five minutes to spare." She went to stand behind Len and began reading the sheet music over his shoulder. He turned and winked at her, handing her a half empty mug of steaming coffee.

Except for her hair, which was still damp from the quick shower, she looked as fresh as if she'd slept for eight hours. She was dressed in a red halter top and a long, gauzy skirt in shades of red, black, and white, which she'd picked up in a secondhand shop in L.A.

"Thanks, Len." She drained the mug, then turned to Gary, who was still scowling. "What do you want to start with?"

"This." He shoved the music into her hands and began to tune his guitar.

She had sung no more than a dozen notes when Gary shouted, "Hold it. Alex, where's your head, anyway?"

She gave him a puzzled frown. "What do you mean?"

"I mean," he said through gritted teeth, "we'd agreed to do it slower. Like this." He strummed a chord and began to sing the song himself.

"But we've never done it like that before."

He swore, loudly, viciously. "Are you questioning me?"

"Yes."

"Just do it, Alex. Okay?"

"Sure." She started over, only to have him interrupt again and again.

For the next four hours the rehearsal went from bad to worse, with a snarling, surly Gary continuing to interrupt Alex.

Finally Bear lifted his hands in a gesture of defeat. "Look, man, I don't know about the rest of you, but I need a break." He pointed at the view of sand and sea beyond the wall of windows. "That's sunlight out there. And a surf just begging to be enjoyed. Now if you don't mind, I'd like an hour or two to get out of here before we have to get back to work."

Gary ran a hand through his hair and nodded. "Yeah. Sorry. Why don't you all clear out until show-time."

Len put an arm around Alex's shoulders and walked out of the room with her.

"What's wrong with Gary today?" she asked him. "I've never seen him in such a foul temper."

Len gave her a sideways glance. "Maybe he didn't get enough sleep last night. How about you?"

She grinned. "I didn't get any. But I think I'd better grab some now, or I might not make it through the first set."

"Good idea, bright eyes. It looks like it's going to be a long night."

When they entered the cottage, Alex headed straight for her room. Within minutes she heard the front door close. The voices of the band members drifted through her open window as they made their way to the beach.

There was a single knock on the door of her room before the door was thrown open and Gary strode in. The frown was still on his face, and his voice was heavy with anger. "Where the hell did you go last night with that Hollywood stud?"

Stunned at his unexpected outburst, she snapped, "Where I go, and with whom, is none of your concern. Now if you don't mind, I'd like to take a nap."

"I do mind." Gary stomped across the room to her. "I worry about you. You're like some damn babe in the woods."

Alex was outraged. With her hands on her hips, she faced him. "I am not a baby. I can take care of myself."

"Yeah. Sure. I've seen how you handle men."

"And what is that supposed to mean?"

He knew he was saying too much. But for every hour she'd been gone, his temper had gone up a notch, until it had slipped way beyond his control. He needed the release of a good fight. "Don't think I haven't noticed your reaction to every guy who's ever made a pass at you. You ignore them, hoping they'll go away. Only that never works, Alex. Don't you know men just can't resist that kind of challenge? The more you run away, the faster they chase you."

"Thank you for that brilliant lesson in life. Now if you'll excuse me . . ." She turned away, but he caught her by the arm.

"We're a team, Alex. What happens to one of us affects all of us. We've got a chance for something big here. I don't want to see you blow it for all of us by falling for some rich guy's line."

She shook off his hand. "I see. First you say you're worried about me," she said, her words tinged with sarcasm, "and now you admit you're really worried about *your* chances for success."

"No—I mean yes. I'm worried about you and us. Alex, listen—"

But she'd lost the last thread of patience. "No, Gary. *You* listen." She poked a finger at his chest, causing him to back away. "We work together. And right now we're forced to live together. But that doesn't give you the right to pry into my life. I'll go where I please, with whomever I please. And I won't allow you to interfere. Do you understand?"

At the harshness of her tone he realized he'd been out of line. Running a hand through his hair, he muttered, "I don't know what the hell came over me. I'm behaving like a goddamn Neanderthal." Or a jealous lover. The thought jolted him. "Sorry, Alex. I guess I acted like a jerk."

He went to the door, then turned. "No hard feelings?" he asked softly.

Alex hesitated a moment, allowing her anger to dis-
sipate as quickly as it had materialized. She nodded.
"No hard feelings."

Gary cleared his throat. "Will he be there again
tonight?"

"You can stop worrying, Gary. He's gone." She was
surprised at how painful it was to admit out loud.

He hoped he didn't look too relieved. With a quick
smile he said, "Better catch that nap now. I'll see you
later."

When he was gone Alex stared at the closed door for
long minutes before slipping out of her clothes and
pulling on an oversize football jersey. A few minutes
later, her face bare of makeup, the shades drawn
against the sunlight, she climbed between the covers
and lay in the dimness of her room. But sleep eluded
her.

She found herself wishing Tina could be there. It
would have been so easy to talk to her roommate. She
frowned, thinking that Tina probably would have
reacted exactly the way Gary had. What had she been
thinking of, going off to a deserted stretch of beach for
the night with a man like Matt Montrose?

She rolled onto her side, eyes wide open. The hours
spent with Matt had raced by. He was so easy to talk to.
She'd had the almost overpowering desire to confide
things to him that she'd never told anyone else.

She lay awake, reliving every word, every touch,
every second of the time spent with Matt. She shivered
as she suddenly recalled the taste of his lips on hers.
When he held her, she felt safe. Safe and sheltered.

Safe. What an odd thing to feel with the brother of Dirk Montrose. Where Dirk's touch had repelled her, Matt's excited her. She recalled how confused she'd felt when he'd kissed her.

The thought of his lips pressed to hers caused her heart to beat erratically. It was the last thing she remembered before she drifted off to sleep.

13

Kip raced to the mailbox and tore open the envelope. He read the letter hungrily, then carefully folded it and jammed it into his pocket before going back to his chores. Once he'd finished he ran to the barn and climbed up into the hay, where he was certain no one could see him. There he read the letter over and over until he had consigned every word to memory.

Dear Kip,
  How I miss you. I wish you could be here with me. From my room there's a view of the sand and surf that just begs to be painted. I keep thinking how much you'd love it here. The ocean is the clearest blue I've ever seen. And the town itself is so unique. There are no traffic lights or parking meters, no billboards or neon signs or tall buildings. I've been thinking maybe we should build our house in Carmel instead of Malibu.

I guess our band is doing something right, because the crowds are growing. Lately they're standing in line every night, and our contract has been renewed for another month.

When I phoned last week, Aunt Bernice said you were out doing chores. I'll try to call you Sunday afternoon, around five o'clock your time. Please ask Uncle Vince to let you stay near the phone. I miss hearing your voice.

I guess that's all for now. I love you, Kip. Hang on to the thought that someday soon we'll be together again.

Alex

The little boy brushed the tears from his eyes and wished that someday would come sooner.

Zane Christy stood near the back of the room, his eyes blinking furiously behind his thick glasses. Unknown to Alex and the band, two of the actors who owned the club were seated in the audience. They had surprised Zane with an unannounced visit to see for themselves what all the fuss was about.

The room was packed, as it had been every night lately.

Zane really had no reason to linger. Everything was running smoothly. But though he told himself he just wanted to see to last-minute details, the truth was that he stole every opportunity he could to observe Alex. Moondog hadn't had an entertainer this exciting in years.

At exactly nine o'clock the musicians started their first set.

As soon as Alex began to sing, an expectant hush settled over the audience. When she drew out the last
note of the song, the crowd was on its feet, shouting
and cheering. Each new song was received in the same
manner. Without even trying, it seemed, she held them
in the palm of her hand. Every upbeat song had them
nodding and tapping their toes, every sad, haunting
melody left them breathless.

Gary flashed a grin at Bear. Alex was in rare form
tonight, and her energy infused all of them with new
life.

He hadn't bothered to tell the others that he'd spotted the owners in the crowd. No sense spooking everyone. Nerves were always just below the surface until
they finished their first set. Then they usually settled
down, so that by the last set of the night, they could
really kick back and play with abandon.

He glanced at Alex. Tonight she was wearing a
clingy black crepe gown that fell in soft swirls to her
ankles. The dress looked like something Katharine
Hepburn might have worn in one of her early movies.
To complete the costume, she wore strappy black sandals tied with silk ribbons and black gloves that buttoned above her elbows. Her long hair was loose, cas-
cading over one shoulder. The effect was unique and
unquestionably sexy.

Gary watched as one of the owners, who'd made a
fortune in action movies, leaned toward the other one,
a hotshot leading man who had a long-running part in a
soap opera. The two whispered, nodded, then continued watching Alex. At that moment he knew. Alex had
done it, he thought with a growing sense of elation. He
could tell by the expression on their faces.

The guitar strings sang beneath his fingers. This was the moment he'd been waiting for. With the owners' connections in show business, doors that had been closed to the band would now open. The future was whatever they chose to make it.

"We're going to change the lineup for the last set," Gary announced during their break. "Alex, I want to do only the songs you wrote."

"Fine with me. But why?"

"We've got a great audience tonight. The place is usually crowded, but tonight they're extra attentive. I don't know if you've noticed, but nobody's left since we started playing. There isn't an empty table in the room. I figure it's a good time to introduce them to more of your talent."

"Okay. Len, do you have all the music?"

The piano player was already shuffling through the pages. "Yeah. What'll we start with?"

"How about 'Missing Him'?"

Alex almost protested. She'd written the song after Matt had appeared in her life and then disappeared so abruptly. It was still a raw wound. Still, she always felt better, cleansed somehow, after singing it.

"Okay," she said. "Then what?"

With the others looking on, Gary listed the songs he wanted performed. When they had enough to fill the last hour, Alex went to freshen her makeup. A few minutes later she was waiting in the darkness beyond the stage. On cue, she stepped out to face the spotlight. For the next hour she held the audience spellbound.

"The owners have another club in San Francisco." Zane Christy spread the contracts in front of Gary. "They'd like you to perform there when your contract is up here."

Gary studied the terms, then looked up. "I don't see a length of time listed on this contract."

Zane laced his fingers across his chest and leaned back in his chair. "It's open-ended. They thought they might renew on a month-to-month basis."

That suited Gary. He saw San Francisco as a stepping-stone to bigger things. "And the pay?"

"It's negotiable."

Gary hoped the greed wasn't apparent in his eyes. "We have to take a lot into consideration. There's the cost of relocating. And the wear and tear on our instruments. And Alex's costumes."

Zane nodded.

Watching his eyes for a reaction Gary said, "Five thousand a week."

The manager didn't flinch.

"For my band and singer," Gary quickly amended. "And another thousand a week for me."

"So you're asking six thousand a week total?"

"Yeah."

"Done. I'll have my secretary fill in the numbers and you can sign the contracts right away."

As Zane left the room Gary cursed himself. He should have held out for more. But what the hell did he know about business? All he cared about was getting another gig in a better club. In fact, the money was way down on his list of priorities. What mattered was that they were on their way to the big time.

*   *   *

Later, when the whole group had gotten the exciting news, Gary poked his head around Alex's open door. "Going to join us for a little celebration on our night off?"

She looked up from the letter she was writing. "I don't think so."

"Come on," he coaxed. "Bear knows a place where the food's spicy and the music's loud."

"You can tell me about it tomorrow."

"Alex. How many times have we been offered a fat contract like this?"

"Not nearly often enough," she said with a laugh.

"Then don't you think that justifies a little celebration?"

She grinned. "Okay. You're right. It sounds like fun. Just give me a minute." She finished the letter, folded it, and sealed the envelope, then stuffed it into her pocket to be mailed in town.

When Alex came out of her room a few minutes later wearing white shorts and a white silk shirt tied at her midriff and with her hair in a long fat braid, the band was waiting for her.

"Come on," Bear called, leading the way. "Wait till you taste the chili."

They spent the next several hours in a crowded, noisy little bar where people crammed onto a tiny dance floor and gyrated to the loudest music Alex had ever heard. Everyone seemed to know everyone else, and after the first drink, Casey, Bear, Jeremy and Len had all found willing partners on the dance floor. Between dances they wolfed down bowls of chili and platters of nachos, washing it all down with mugs of foaming beer.

"Come on." Gary dragged Alex to her feet. "You can't just sit here looking so calm when there's music like that."

"You're right." She smiled. "It's impossible to sit still."

The music pulsated, and in the crush of bodies, they were pressed tightly together.

"Isn't this better than sitting alone in your room?"

"Much better."

Gary looked down at her flushed face and felt pleased with himself. It was the first time he'd managed to drag her out of her self-imposed reclusiveness.

Someone bumped him, and he brought his arms protectively around Alex to keep her from being crushed. "I didn't know you were such a good dancer," he said.

She shot him a grin. "In this crowd, anyone who manages to remain vertical is a good dancer."

He laughed. The tempo slowed and he drew her closer. "But you're really good."

"So are you."

"Back in school, I rarely had the chance to dance with a girl. I was usually up on the bandstand playing. Of course," he murmured against her temple, "if I'd known how good it felt, I'd have probably given up music a long time ago in favor of this."

"I'm glad you stuck to music."

"I'm not so sure." He stopped dancing and stood very still, staring down into her eyes. After a moment's hesitation he said, "Had enough chili and nachos?"

She nodded.

"Me too. Come on. Let's get out of here."

"What about the others?"

"Look at them," he said, pointing. "Do you think they'll miss us?"

She caught a glimpse of Casey and a pretty blonde locked in each other's arms. Bear was nuzzling the neck of a busty waitress. Jeremy was trying to dance with two girls at once, and Len had found a soul mate, judging by the look in his eyes.

She laughed. "Not a chance."

Taking her hand, Gary led her across the crowded room.

Outside, the silence was broken only by the occasional cry of a gull, and the night air was perfumed with the fragrance of wildflowers. Forsaking the gravel path that led back to the inn, they walked along the beach, stopping occasionally to skip stones across the moonlit waves.

"Who do you write all those letters to?" Gary asked, bending to retrieve another stone.

"My little brother, Kip."

"Brother?" He hoped the relief wasn't too evident in his tone. All this time, he'd assumed she was writing to that Hollywood stud. He skipped the stone and watched it bounce from wave to wave before it dropped out of sight.

"Do you know anybody in San Francisco, Alex?"

She shook her head. "You?"

"No." He caught her hand and dragged her back from an incoming wave seconds before she would have been soaked. Glancing at their linked hands he added, "But what the hell. What do we need with other people? There are enough of us to look out for one another." He glanced at her. "Don't you agree?"

She shrugged and removed her hand from his grasp. "I guess so."

"What I mean is, we're family. The guys and I are always here for you, Alex, if you need us."

"Thanks." She wondered why he was acting so strangely.

A moment later another wave rolled in, and Gary caught her by the shoulders, propelling her out of the way. He kept his arm around her shoulders as they continued walking.

"I have a feeling about us," he said, glancing at the canopy of stars. "I've had it since you first joined the group."

She waited, puzzled by the tone of his voice.

"We're going to go far, Alex. Clear to the top, in fact. Nothing can stand in our way." He paused and turned her to face him. "And do you know why?"

She shook her head.

"Because we're a perfect team. You've got the talent and I've got the drive." His voice grew low. "I knew it the moment I heard you sing. You were the one I've been waiting for all my life." He drew her close and brushed his lips over hers.

Surprised, she pulled back, her eyes wide.

He didn't rush her. He didn't need to. He had all the time in the world now. With his fingers lightly touching her face he pressed his forehead to hers and muttered thickly, "It gets damn lonely on the road, Alex." He brushed his lips over hers again and took a step back. "Just remember. Whenever the loneliness gets to be too much, I'm here."

∘   ∘   ∘

Later, alone in her room, Alex went over the events of the night. As she lay in her bed she pondered all Gary had said and done. Had she given him any reason to believe that she was interested in anything more than friendship?

She tried to dissect what had transpired between them. Was she reading more into it than he intended? The truth was, he'd done nothing wrong. He certainly hadn't pushed for more when she didn't respond.

Why then was she feeling uncomfortable about it?

She pulled the covers over her head, determined to put an end to the questions that plagued her. She'd always been cursed with a wild imagination.

14

Alex and the band walked out of the club on Fisherman's Wharf in San Francisco. Their job had been extended to ten weeks. After a shaky start, the crowd had begun to discover them. Tonight they'd played to a full house, and their energy was high.

"I'm ready for Italian food," Bear announced.

"Me too," Casey called.

The others echoed their agreement.

They passed dozens of restaurants along the wharf before reaching the one Bear had chosen.

"How come you always get to choose the places we eat?" Alex asked.

"Who better to judge food?" Bear patted his ample stomach, and the others laughed.

Len's dark eyes scanned the menu. "Maybe we ought to let you order for all of us."

"Good idea." Before they could stop him Bear ordered a family-size platter of pasta topped with fresh seafood, an enormous salad, and a basket of garlic bread. "And two bottles of Chianti," he added as the waiter began to walk away.

Their dinner conversation was always lively, but tonight they seemed even more animated than usual as the waiter filled their wineglasses.

"Did you see that dude at the front table?" Len asked.

"You mean the one who practically drooled every time Alex came onstage?" Jeremy chuckled. "I thought his girlfriend was going to clobber him with her bottle of Perrier."

The others joined in the laughter.

"I never noticed," Alex said.

That only made them laugh harder.

"That's the trouble," Casey told her. "You're so into your music, you're never even aware of the effect you have on those poor slobs in the audience."

"Those poor slobs?" Gary said, joining in the teasing. "What about *us* poor slobs? All we are now is a showcase for Alex's talents."

Alex drained her glass of wine and giggled. "I'm glad you finally realized it."

Five pairs of hands reached for her throat. Laughing she held up her hands in defeat. "All right, all right. You guys know better. I'd be the first to admit that without your music, I'd still be waiting tables."

"Just keep remembering that," Len said, topping off her glass. "If your head starts to get too big, we'll bring you down to earth real fast by playing the wrong notes."

"I always wondered what you guys would do if some night I walked up to the microphone and start singing off-key."

"See that fishing boat out there?" Gary pointed his fork at the boats in the harbor. "They'll use you for bait."

They all roared.

After dinner they left the restaurant and Bear signaled for a cab. The driver, seeing six people, insisted that only four could ride.

"Go ahead, Alex," Bear said. "Me and Gary will flag down a second one."

Alex shook her head. "All I've done since we got here is eat. I need the exercise. If you guys don't mind, I'd like to walk."

Gary stepped back. "Sounds good. I think I need a walk too. I'll see you guys back at the apartment."

The others exchanged knowing looks, then climbed into the cab.

Despite the late hour, crowds of tourists still clogged the sidewalks. When a noisy cluster of college students headed toward them, Gary moved closer to Alex and led her across the street.

"They treat this city like one big fraternity party," he muttered.

"Maybe it is," Alex said with a giggle.

She filled her lungs with fresh air, hoping to clear her head. She knew she'd had too much wine, but she didn't care. All she wanted to do was savor the moment.

Gary paused beside a street vendor. "How about a lemon ice?"

"None for me."

"One." He dug into his pocket for the money. When he offered Alex a taste, she accepted it.

"Mmm. That's wonderful," she said, licking her lips.

"There goes my dessert," he muttered with a smile. "I knew I should have bought you your own."

"You mean you won't share?"

His smile grew. "Do I have a choice?"

"No." She took another taste, then handed it back to him.

They stopped and sat on a park bench beneath a streetlamp to finish the ice.

"I love this city," Alex said with a sigh.

Gary nodded. "It's a hell of a long way from Cleveland." He threw the paper cup in a trash can, and they walked home in companionable silence.

Though it wasn't nearly as luxurious as the cottage in Carmel, they considered themselves lucky to have found anything at all. The rooms were clean and the rent was reasonable. Gary and Len shared one room, Casey, Bear and Jeremy the other. Alex was the only one to have a room of her own, and the guys loved teasing her about it. At least once a day one of them threatened to move in with her because of a roommate's snoring.

There was a cramped kitchen and a small sitting room that barely accommodated all of them.

"Do you miss your home in Cleveland, Gary?" Alex asked when they were inside.

He shook his head. "I've been having too much fun to even think about it. Do you miss L.A.?"

She nodded. "Sometimes I miss it so much."

"You can always go back for a visit. It's not that far."

She grew quiet. How could she explain that the things she missed were gone for good. There was no way to visit Nanna's, or to recapture the love and laughter she'd shared with her brother and grandmother in that little house.

"What's wrong, Alex?" He caught her by the chin, lifting her face for his inspection. "What did I say to make you sad?"

"Nothing. Really," she insisted when he continued to study her. Turning away she said, "I'm really tired, Gary. The walk helped me unwind. I guess I'll turn in. See you in the morning."

As she started to open her door he drew her back against him, putting his hands on her shoulders. He kept his voice low. "I'm here if you'd like to talk."

"Thanks." She took a deep breath, and for the first time considered it carefully. She needed a friend. And all he seemed to be offering was friendship. Still, she hesitated, afraid that he might intend more than she desired. "Good night, Gary."

He pressed a hand against the door to keep her from opening it. When she looked at him in alarm he brushed her lips with a quick kiss. "Anytime, Alex. Keep it in mind. We'd be good for each other."

Was it the wine, or the loneliness? Whatever the reason, she found his offer so tempting.

With considerable effort she went by him into the darkness of her room, closing the door firmly behind her. But as she undressed and climbed into bed, she was aware of the sound of Gary's movements next door.

She shivered. It would be so easy to take what he offered. After all, they were both lonely. And through their music they did share a special bond.

She curled up in bed, agitated at the direction her thoughts were taking. But a nagging voice kept calling her back from sleep. It was Gary's voice, soothing, coaxing: *Anytime, Alex. . . . We'd be good for each other.*

And then she heard another another voice. Matt's voice, low, teasing. His was the one she longed to hear.

"Guess what?" Gary said as he burst through the door of the apartment. "We've had another job offer."

Jeremy and Casey looked up from the cartoons they were watching on TV. Bear, shaving in the bathroom, threw open the door to hear, and Len and Alex, who were at the table going over some music, turned toward him.

"Cliff Carlson caught our act and wants us to open his show in Reno."

"Cliff Carlson?" Bear dropped his razor in the sink and hurried out of the bathroom, wearing only a towel. "The comedian?"

"That's the one."

"Reno? All right!" Jeremy and Casey exchanged high fives.

"How soon?" Len asked.

"Next week. As soon as our contract here in San Francisco is up. He said he especially liked the new stuff that Alex had written and would like to hear more of it."

"When did you talk to him?" Bear asked.

"I didn't exactly talk to him. His manager called and arranged this meeting. He admitted that he hasn't caught our act yet, but he's heard good things about us, and Cliff needs a fresh new opening act and told him to call. I was hoping for Vegas, but Reno's a step in the right direction."

"How much are we getting for this gig?" Jeremy asked.

"Two thousand a week each plus room, food, and beverage while we're guests of the Sierra Casino."

"Wow! Have you already signed a contract?"

Gary nodded. "Less than an hour ago. It's a done deal."

While the others were busy congratulating each other, Len turned to Alex. "Looks like we'd better get busy on these new songs. Think you can have them ready in time?"

She shot him a wide smile. "Even if I have to give up sleeping." She thought of the letter she'd started to Kip. Now she would have even more good news to share with him.

"Hey, Alex. You've got company." Len shouted.

Alex looked up from the trunk she was packing. She couldn't believe how many costumes she'd acquired. To think she'd left L.A. with one small suitcase.

"Who is it?" she called irritably.

"Me," came a familiar voice. "Get out here and let me see what you've been doing to your hair."

"Tina!" Alex raced to the open doorway to hug her old roommate. "Oh, I've missed you. I'm so glad to see you."

"Well, after getting your last letter, I figured I'd better get my butt up here before you move on again. When do you leave?"

"Day after tomorrow."

"I can't keep up with your crazy schedule."

"I know. I'm a little breathless myself. Let me look at you."

Holding her a little away, Alex studied the woman,

whose close-cropped hair was now bleached white. She wore a black spandex jumpsuit and black platform boots, a red and white baseball jacket, and six earrings in one ear.

"Is this what hairdressers to the stars are wearing this year?"

"Hey, when the field is this crowded, I need a trademark look. I've got to find a way to get noticed, you know."

"This ought to do it," Alex said with a laugh. She glanced at the huge leather duffle bag slung over her friend's shoulder. "How long can you stay?"

"Just tonight. I'll have to drive back tomorrow if I'm going to make it to work on Monday."

"Got your own shop yet?"

"No, but I'm working on it." Tina glanced at the open trunk. "I still can't believe you're going to be the opening act for Cliff Carlson. He's just about the biggest comedian around."

"Yeah." Alex sank down on the edge of her bed while Tina continued prowling the room. She stopped and picked up a photograph from Alex's night table. "Is this new?"

Alex nodded. "Kip sent it to me a few days ago. He's grown so much."

"How's he doing?"

After a moment of silence, Alex said, "Okay."

Tina turned. "Hey. This is me, remember? Now, how's he really doing?"

Alex dropped her hands into her lap and clenched them tightly together. "I wish I knew," she said. "I can't tell. When I talk to him on the phone, he seems so far away. And even his letters don't say much. Just that he's doing fine in school, the farm chores are getting easier. That's about all."

"Maybe he's happy," Tina remarked.

"I wish I could believe that. But there's something sad in his voice. Something . . . lifeless. Like he's given up hope of ever seeing me again."

"Hey. Come on. Lighten up." Tina dropped her duffle on the bed and rummaged through it until she found a brush and comb. "Go wash your hair. I'm going to make you glamorous for tonight's show."

A short time later, as Alex sat on a low stool and allowed Tina to fuss with her hair, she found herself grinning in spite of herself at Tina's outrageous stories. She realized again how much she missed her old roommate.

"I almost forgot." Tina dug in her purse and removed a packet of letters. "Most of these are bills. Since I didn't know where to forward them, I've just been holding on to them until I could see you."

Alex tore open the envelopes and began piling up the unpaid bills. "So much for the money I'd been setting aside for a visit with Kip in South Dakota."

"So," Tina said, hoping to lift her friend's spirits. "How's your love life?"

"What love life? Haven't you heard? When you live out of a suitcase, you don't have time for anything as dumb as romance."

"Dumb? You think romance is dumb?"

"I think it takes entirely too much energy. I'd rather be singing."

"The woman is impossible," Tina said to her reflection in the mirror. "And some day, when a guy comes along who knocks her off her feet, she'll eat those words." She twisted Alex's hair into a knot on top of her head, pulling out little wisps to let them drift around her face. "I've always heard about the groupies and wild parties. What happened to sex, drugs, and rock and roll?"

"AIDS, rehab, and retro. Welcome to the nineties."

The club was filled to capacity. Word had already gotten out that this was their last night in San Francisco. The crowd was noisy and enthusiastic. After the last set, Alex and the band received a standing ovation that lasted a solid five minutes. Tina, watching from the wings, thought she might burst from excitement. As soon as the band came offstage for the last time she flung herself into Alex's arms and hugged her until they were both breathless.

"God, that was wonderful. I mean, I knew you were good, but until tonight I had no idea just how good." She turned to Gary, who was grinning from ear to ear. "You realize she's going to be a superstar, don't you?"

"There was never a doubt." Gary put an arm possessively around Alex's shoulders and drew her close.

Caught up in the moment, Alex wrapped her own arm around his waist and pressed her cheek to his. "Then you know something I don't."

"We all know it," Bear said as he began to put away his sax. "We've got something special going."

The rest of the band nodded in agreement as they went about putting their instruments in cases.

"It's a feeling," Len said, carefully stacking his sheet music. "We're headed right to the top. Unless we do something really stupid, nothing can stop us."

Tina's smile froze when she caught sight of Gary nibbling the corner of Alex's ear. He whispered something that made Alex blush and turn away.

"Let's go eat." Bear caught Tina's hand and dragged her toward the exit, preventing her from seeing any more of her friend and the band leader. "If I don't get some food in the next five minutes, my body will be forced to begin living on its own fat."

15

It was almost dawn before they returned to their apartment.

Bear pressed a hand to his stomach. "I didn't think it was humanly possible to consume that much seafood and still walk."

"Or drink that much wine," Casey said, heading directly to the bathroom.

Tina turned toward Gary and Alex, who trailed the others. Gary had his arm around Alex's shoulders, and he pressed a kiss to her temple before he caught sight of Tina watching them.

"I'll see you in the morning," he told Alex. He squeezed her hand and headed toward the bedroom he shared with Len.

"I suppose you two are going to spend the night catching up on old times." Bear tugged on one of Tina's many earrings, causing the smile to return to her eyes.

She gave him a lopsided grin. "You bet. Who knows when we'll have another chance?"

"I'll leave you two alone then. Besides," he added, "if I don't go to bed this minute, I'll fall asleep right here on the floor."

Alone in Alex's room, the two friends got undressed. Alex pulled on a baggy T-shirt and went to the kitchen, returning a short time later with two steaming mugs of coffee. Tina sat cross-legged on the bed wearing one of Alex's faded football jerseys.

"Now," Alex said, handing Tina a mug, "tell me everything that's happened since I left."

"Everything? Okay." Tina brought her up to date on all the waitresses and busboys they'd known at Kisses. Then, for the next several hours, she regaled her with hilarious stories about the customers at the Hair Emporium.

"Sounds like you like your work, even though the place is a zoo."

Tina sipped at her third mug of coffee. "It is a zoo. And I love it."

"Have you had any celebrities as customers?"

"You know Deanna Kendrick, the actress in that new sitcom, *Housesitter?*"

Alex nodded.

"She's a regular. She liked my work so much, she asked the director to hire me."

"Oh, my gosh." Alex's eyes were wide with surprise. "What a compliment. What did he say?"

Tina shrugged. "He said they have enough hairdressers on the set already, but if they need another, he'll keep me in mind."

"Oh, Tina, that's wonderful! I just know the word will get around about you."

"Yeah, well. It's a start." She hesitated for a

moment, "Now tell me what's going on with you and Gary Hampstead."

"There's nothing going on. Gary's a friend."

"Tell that to someone else."

Alex looked offended. "No, really, Tina. He's just a friend."

"Yeah? Well, while I was standing in the wings tonight, watching your act, your 'friend' couldn't keep his eyes off you."

Alex blushed. "So far, there's nothing more than friendship between us. But I have to admit that he's been—offering more if I'm interested."

Tina studied her. "And are you? Interested?"

Alex stared into her mug. "I don't know. It's lonely on the road. There's no time to meet anybody, or do things with other people. We're a tightly knit group, and it just seems easier to stick together than to try to meet anyone new. You saw what it was like tonight: we perform, we go out after the show together, we come back and sleep. Every day, it's the same thing."

"And what about the photographer you wrote about? You know, the one who's going to direct a movie? Matt Montrose."

Alex shrugged, but Tina caught the quick light that came into her eyes before she looked away. "I never heard from him again. But why should I? We spent a few hours together. We had a few laughs."

"It sounded like a whole lot more than that in your letter."

"Well, maybe it seemed that way to me at the time. But in the morning he was gone. He has his career; I have mine. He has a new movie to direct, which will probably take months of his time. And who knows where I'll be next week, or next month? We'll probably never see each other again." She avoided her friend's eyes. "I guess that's one more reason why Gary's offer keeps looking better and better."

"So you haven't taken Gary up on this offer of 'more than friendship' yet?"

"Like I said, so far, we're just friends, Tina."

For a moment Tina seemed about to say something more, but she just drank her coffee instead.

"What do you think about Bear?" Alex asked.

Tina glanced at her. "Why do you ask?"

"I think he's sweet on you."

Tina looked pleased. "What makes you think that?"

Alex stretched her legs, flexing her toes, and glanced sideways at her friend. "Just the way he treated you tonight. He kept filling your plate and watching you eat."

"So you mean he's in love with my appetite?"

They both laughed.

"I just thought he paid a lot of attention to you, that's all."

"Well he was just being nice. It's natural enough; I'm your friend. He wanted me to feel comfortable."

"Maybe," Alex said, getting up. She drained her cup and crossed the room to set it on the dresser.

Tina glanced at the morning sunlight that streamed through the windows and stifled a yawn. The drive from Los Angeles in Alex's little car had been an exhausting one, and after the night they'd put in, she was running out of steam. "If I don't get a couple hours sleep, I'll never make it home."

"Come on. I've been selfish," Alex said, turning

down the bed. "But it's been so long since I've had any-one I could really talk to."

"We'll talk again in a few hours. As soon as my brain's had a chance to rest. I promise."

"I wish there were some other women in the band," Alex said as she climbed into bed and made room for Tina. "There are some things that are just easier to talk about with a woman, you know?"

"Yeah." Tina stifled a yawn. "Like guys."

They were both asleep in a matter of minutes.

"That's everything." Alex closed the lid of her trunk and watched as Bear and Casey struggled to haul it outside to Bear's van.

"And that's everything I brought," Tina said with a throaty laugh as she dropped her comb and brush into her duffle bag. "I believe in packing light."

Alex stood beside the bed and watched as Tina slung the bag over her shoulder. "I wish you were going to Reno with us," she said.

"Yeah. Me too. But then what would all those stars do without their hairdresser?"

"Let them do their own hair."

"Hey, don't say that out loud. You're talking about my bread and butter."

They both grinned, then grew quiet, knowing the time had come to say good-bye.

"Come here," Tina said, "and give me a hug. I've got to get on the road." They wrapped their arms around each other.

"I'm going to miss you more than ever," Alex whis-pered.

"Yeah. Don't forget to write."

"You too."

Tina pulled away. "You riding in Bear's van?"

"No. He has all the instruments in the back. I'll probably ride with Gary."

"What about the rest of the band?"

"They'll ride with Bear."

"Come on, Alex," came Gary's muffled voice from the other side of the closed door. "Time to get moving."

Tina started toward the door, then paused and turned back. This was much worse than the first time, when she'd thought Alex would only be gone for a few weeks. Now the truth had hit her: life on the road was going to be a reality for her friend for a long time to come.

"Alex, I didn't want to have to tell you this. In fact, I was hoping I could just get out of here and mind my own business. But you don't seem to be a very good judge of guys. And there's something I think you should know."

"What is it?"

Tina licked her lips, hesitating. Then before she could lose her nerve again, she said quickly, "Gary's married."

If Alex had taken a blow from a sledgehammer, she would have been less stunned. For long moments she could merely stare at her friend. Then she slumped onto the edge of the bed.

"What?" Alex barely managed to whisper.

"So I was right," Tina said angrily. "Gary didn't even have the decency to tell you the truth."

"He's never given me a single hint. Are you sure, Tina?" But Alex knew the answer before the words were out of her mouth.

Tina shrugged. "All I know is, when I first started working at Kisses, he introduced someone as his wife. A pretty thing. Blond, blue eyes. And as big as a house—she was expecting his baby within a matter of weeks."

His baby. He was a husband and a father. Alex felt numb. "But why didn't he tell me?"

Tina's eyes narrowed. "I guess you'll have to ask him." She went to Alex and laid a hand on her shoulder. "Are you okay?"

"Yeah." Taking a deep breath Alex slowly got to her feet.

"You're not mad that I told you?"

"I'm grateful, Tina. You saved me from making a fool of myself. I can see I still have a lot to learn."

"What are you going to do about it?"

"I don't know. Yet. But I'll think of something."

Despite the shock her friend had just absorbed, Tina thought she detected a new toughness in Alex; a hint of a growing determination.

The two walked together to the waiting vehicles. As they shared a last hug, Tina whispered, "Take care, Alex."

"You too. Remember your goal."

"Hairdresser to the stars," Tina whispered. "How about your goal?"

"Superstar," she replied without hesitation.

"Atta girl. Knock 'em dead in Reno. See you soon."

*   *   *

Gary glanced at Alex, who kept her face averted, watching as the scenery sped by. She hadn't spoken a word since they left. It was because of Tina, he figured. Though he couldn't imagine two more dissimilar women, it was obvious they'd become close friends. Now that they'd had to say good-bye again, Alex was probably feeling a little stab of homesickness. He thought it wise to hold his silence until she indicated she was ready to speak. And tonight he'd make a special effort to be nice to her. She looked like she needed a little tenderness.

"When were you going to tell me?"

He took his gaze from the traffic long enough to see that she was still staring out the window. "Tell you what?"

"About your wife."

The cars up ahead began to slow, and Gary automatically jammed his foot on the brake. The car made a screeching protest before he managed to bring it under control.

Up ahead there was a small diner; he maneuvered the car into the far right lane, and they lurched into the parking lot. Coming to a grinding stop, he said, "Let's get some coffee."

"I don't need coffee."

"I do." He got out, slamming the car door, and didn't speak again until they were seated in a booth with steaming cups of coffee in front of them.

"Sara and I got married two years ago."

"Sara." Alex stared daggers at him. "And the baby?"

"I see you know everything." He stirred sugar into his coffee and drank. "A little girl. Corey's ten months old."

"Where are they, Sara and Corey?"

"In Cleveland. With my folks."

"Why?"

"Why are they in Cleveland?" He shrugged. "Sara didn't like the idea of raising a baby on the road. And my folks thought it would be fun to have a granddaughter in the house."

"And you, Gary? What do you think about it?"

"God damm it, Alex! I'm doing the best I can for everybody. I want Sara and Corey to have a home. I want my folks to see their grandchild. And more than anything, I want the pot of gold at the end of the rainbow. I want it all. I want fame and fortune."

"Regardless of the cost?" she asked softly.

"What the hell does that mean?"

"Are you willing to sacrifice Sara and Corey for fame and fortune?"

"I'm not sacrificing them, Alex. They're fine. They've got a home with my folks."

"And if Sara found that life was a little too lonely and decided to replace you with someone else, what would you think?"

His eyes narrowed. She'd just struck a nerve he hadn't even known was exposed. "Sara wouldn't do that. She's a terrific person. Besides, she's too busy being a new mom."

"You mean you believe only men get lonely, or think about cheating on their spouses, is that it?" When he said nothing she asked, "Do you really think Sara and Corey are better off in Cleveland while you're here chasing your dream?"

"Yes, damn it, I do." He shoved aside his cup and glared at her.

"And what about me? Did you think I'd never find out about them?"

He shook his head. "I guess I didn't think at all. I could see that you were lonely."

"I see." Her tone hardened with sarcasm. "You were willing to make the supreme sacrifice for my sake."

He swore under his breath. "I was lonely too. And tempted. You don't make it easy for a guy to ignore you, Alex. You're beautiful, and fun to be with, and talented. Hell, every time I hear you sing, it tears my guts out. So I thought . . ." He paused. "It was Tina who told you, wasn't it?"

"Tina's not the issue here. If it hadn't been Tina, it would have been someone else. There's no way you can keep a thing like a wife and daughter a secret forever. The important thing is, what do you intend to do about it?"

"What the hell can I do?"

"This is your life, Gary. Yours and Sara's and Corey's. You should be sharing it with them."

"A life on the road?"

"Why not? Is it so bad?" She was silent while the waitress poured more coffee. When they were alone again Alex said softly, "If you love each other, a life apart is no life at all."

Gary sat awhile, deep in thought. When at last he looked up and met her gaze he said, "If I were to ask her, and if she were to agree, what would that do to the relationship between you and me?"

She gave him a gentle smile and placed her hand over his. "Gary, our only relationship is a professional one. And nothing will change that. But I think it's pretty plain that if you don't use me to ease your loneliness, you'll end up using someone else. Gary, you need your wife with you."

"And what do you need, Alex?" He placed his other hand over hers.

She glanced at their hands, then lifted her gaze to his. Instead of uncertainty, he caught the hard glint of steel in her eyes. "I haven't figured that out yet. But when I do, I'll let you know."

16

"*Wow!*" Len stacked his music on top of the white grand piano and ran his fingers tentatively over the keys. "Can you believe this suite? It looks like something they'd save for royalty."

"Well, what are we?" Casey demanded, turning on the giant-screen TV. "Chopped liver?"

"Last time I looked you weren't wearing a crown," Len said with a laugh.

"You haven't heard of the king of rhythm?" Casey drummed his fingers across the glass coffee table, keeping time to the music of the soft drink commercial on the screen.

Bear, wearing a terry robe with the hotel logo, stepped in from the balcony, where he'd been enjoying the hot tub. "Can you believe we're opening tonight for Cliff Carlson? I heard that a planeload of his Hollywood cronies came in for the show."

Alex looked up from the orange juice she was sipping and felt the first twinge of stage fright. "Where did you hear that?"

"From the bellman. He said he hadn't seen this many celebrities since Elvis used to play here."

"Great." Alex pushed aside the half empty glass and pressed a hand to her stomach. "Now I have the rest of the day to get sick."

"Don't let 'em rattle you, Alex," Jeremy said. "Those Hollywood types are just ordinary people."

"Who make millions of dollars and jet around the world to play tennis and have lunch with presidents and kings," Bear added dryly.

"Thanks, I needed that," Alex said with a laugh. "You guys have really put my mind at ease."

They were still laughing when Gary rushed out of his room headed for the door.

"Where're you off to in such a hurry?" Len asked.

"Airport. I'm late." He pulled the door open. It closed behind him with a slam.

"He's meeting someone at the airport?" Jeremy asked.

Bear shrugged. "He didn't say a thing to me. Probably another big deal in the works. You know Gary."

"It's his wife and daughter," Alex said.

They all turned to stare at her.

"You know about them?" Len asked.

She nodded. "We talked about it on the way here from San Francisco, and I suggested they might enjoy Reno." She got to her feet. "I think I'll go take a walk around the casino. Maybe it'll calm my nerves."

As she crossed the room, Bear watched her with a look of admiration. After the door closed behind her he said to no one in particular, "Well what do you know? Damned if Alex Corday isn't one hell of a woman."

"Honey, you know the guys. And this is Alex, our singer." Gary turned to Alex almost hesitantly. "My wife, Sara."

Alex smiled at a slender woman in jeans and sweater who looked no older than a teenager. Wisps of curly blond hair framed a freckled face, which was bare of makeup.

"It's nice to have another female around." Alex extended her hand. "Now I won't feel so outnumbered."

"And this is our daughter, Corey," Gary said, indicating the chubby infant in his wife's arms.

The little girl, a mirror image of her father, had fine blond hair and big blue eyes rimmed with long lashes.

Alex's smile grew. "Hi, Corey."

At once the baby began wailing and clung more tightly to her mother.

"I'm sorry," Sara explained shyly. "She's just not used to so many strangers. For so long now there's just been me and her grandparents."

"Come on." Gary's tone was a little too abrupt. "I'll show you our room and help you get settled before I have to go downstairs for rehearsal."

Sara held back. "So soon?"

Gary placed a hand beneath her elbow, guiding her across the room. "It's just for a couple of hours," he could be heard explaining as he led her into their room and shut the door behind him.

Even with the door closed, the sound of the baby's

crying and Sara's voice raised in protest could be heard by everyone in the suite.

"Maybe we should go down to the showroom and check out the sound system," Bear said.

In unison everyone made a dash for the elevators.

"Everybody ready?"

Leaving his wife and baby standing in the wings, Gary joined his musicians onstage and looked them over with a critical eye. Dressed in matching black tuxedos as stipulated in the contract, they all appeared a little stiff and awkward.

"Where's Alex?"

"Don't worry. I haven't run out on you. Although I must confess, the thought did cross my mind."

They looked up as she came toward them from the opposite side of the stage. For a moment none of them said a word. As usual, it was Bear who finally expressed what all of them were thinking.

"Bright eyes, you are a knockout."

She grinned. "I splurged in a little junk shop in San Francisco."

"Pretty terrific junk," Casey said dryly.

"You like it?" She twirled, giving them a good look at the red sequined gown that fitted her like a second skin. The long skirt was slit to the thigh. On her feet were red sequined pumps.

"If you walked the streets in that, you'd get arrested." Jeremy tugged on a lock of her hair and she shot him a brilliant smile.

"Thank you. That's the effect I was hoping for. Glitz and sleaze."

"On you, bright eyes, nothing could ever look sleazy. In rags you'd still manage to look elegant."

They all started at the sound of the announcer's voice.

"This is it," Gary said, feeling the tension that always gripped them just going on. "Post time, everybody. Let's show 'em what we've got."

The musicians took their places. As the announcer's voice faded, the curtain began ascending. The men in the band hardly even blinked when the spotlight blinded them. They had already slipped under the spell of performing.

Matt sank back into the softness of the booth and sipped his drink. With the filming of his first project completed and the tedious job of editing about to begin, he was glad for the brief respite.

He had come to Reno at the request of his father, who was taking a much needed break from the pressures of business. The condo in Aspen had been taken over by Elyse and her friends. The chalet in Gstaad, which Sidney Montrose would have preferred, was being occupied these days by Dirk and an army of European ski bums who had attached themselves to him since his hurried departure from the U.S.

Spending the weekend as guests of Cliff Carlson gave father and son the chance to escape. They had been skiing in Tahoe the last two days. In the morning they intended to leave and return to the grind of business as usual. Matt told himself he was here to show support for Cliff, an old friend who had just made an appearance in his father's newest movie. The success of that film had boosted Cliff's already brilliant career. He reported that he was now being inundated with scripts and had begun sifting through them for his next project.

The lights of the showroom dimmed. As Matt listened to the voice of the offstage announcer, he found himself tensing with anticipation. He could list any number of reasons why he was here.

The simple truth was up on that stage.

He'd come because Cliff had mentioned the name of his new warm-up act. Whispers—with vocals by Alex.

Alex stood in the darkness and pressed a hand to her stomach, which was flittering nervously. To her left she heard a child's whimper and saw Sara lift Corey high so she could see her father. The little girl waved, but Gary was too engrossed in the music to notice.

Alex saw the child look toward her, and she waggled her fingers in salute. The little girl waved back and began to smile. Just then Alex heard her cue and took a deep breath.

Her nerves were forgotten. She caught the note, high and pure, and held it, then plunged heart and soul into the music. She sang the entire song in darkness, completely unaware of the way the audience craned and shifted to catch a glimpse of the woman in the shadows. It wasn't until the very end of the song that the spotlight caught her in its glare. As always, her hands came up, as if to shield her from the glare. Her eyes were wide, like those of a frightened doe. She continued to hold the note, sweet and pure, until a violin from the orchestra pit picked it up. The music soared.

The audience gave an audible gasp and leaned forward for a better view of the beautiful creature onstage who seemed to shimmer in the glow of light. She was unaware of their reaction.

Gary and the other musicians settled down to enjoy themselves. There was no longer any reason to worry. Once Alex began to weave her spell, all they had to do was go along for the ride.

Buddy Holbrook sipped Mountain Valley spring water. It was the first of many the former child star, now a successful talent agent, would drink this night.

Five years ago, after four weeks at the Betty Ford Clinic and a succession of therapists, he'd turned his life around. Now it pained him to look back at fuzzy memories of his wasted youth. Five ex-wives had made a fortune on books about him; his assorted children neither knew him nor wanted to. To pay off mounting debts from booze and drug addictions, he'd been forced to make a string of B movies, most of which were still playing on late night TV, much to his embarrassment. But from all the pain had come new strengths he'd never even known existed within himself. He'd paid his debts and mended fences with people he'd offended while under the influence.

Having spent more years in Hollywood than most people, there was nothing about the town Buddy didn't understand. And there was no one in a position of power that he didn't know intimately.

Power. He grinned. He had it. In spades. And he knew how to wield it.

Buddy had flown in as a favor to his client, Cliff Carlson. Cliff had been a small-time comedian until Buddy had taken him under his wing. What a lot of people didn't know was that very little of Cliff's success was due to his talent, great as it was. In Hollywood, as in the rest of the world, talent alone wasn't enough. Connections, Buddy thought with a smile of satisfaction. It was all a case of collecting life's markers. The truth was, a lot of people of influence in Hollywood owed Buddy Holbrook. And he was very good at collecting what was due him.

When the music started he sat back, intending to enjoy a relaxing evening among friends, but when he heard the singer's first note, he felt a shiver along his spine. Before he had time to react, the spotlights found her. The effect was dazzling.

Buddy's hand tightened around his glass, and for the first time in years, he found himself wishing he was drinking something more potent than water, to counter the electricity that was sizzling through his system.

By the time her first song had ended, Buddy had forgotten everything except the woman onstage. It seemed to him that all his life he'd been looking for someone with her potential. Either she was the most dynamic bundle of raw talent he'd ever witnessed, or he was hallucinating.

When the warm-up act finished its last song, Buddy was on his feet cheering, along with everyone else in the room.

°   °   °

"What the hell was that? Is she for real, or did some artist just design a hologram of the perfect dream woman?"

To the delight of the audience, Cliff Carlson ambled onstage, carrying his trademark soccer ball. He dropped it to the stage, where he would manipulate it throughout his act for punctuation.

"I've seen singers before, but this one is a dream weaver." He paused for comic effect. "Or was I back-stage having a wet dream?"

While the audience laughed, he kicked the ball against the curtain; it bounced back, stopping directly at his feet. At the same time his drummer gave him a thundering *ba-da-boom ba-da-boom.*

"And how about that guitar player? A surfer in a tux. Go figure. Why is it that all the studs today have more hair than most women?" He touched a hand to his own close-cropped, thinning hair and kicked the ball again. Again it hit the curtain, bounced back, and stopped at his feet. Again the familiar drumroll.

Cliff was amiable, laid-back, irreverent. A lot of his jokes were aimed at himself and his inadequacies. Though they were often silly or tasteless, they were never cruel. A slight, good-looking thirty-eight-year-old who still had the fresh face of a college youth, he embodied everyone's brother, neighbor, friend.

At the age of sixteen he'd played off Broadway. By eighteen he had gotten a bit part in a popular TV sit-com and parlayed it into a successful career as stand-up comedian, actor, and master of ceremonies for every award show in Hollywood and New York. He'd acquitted himself well in several movies and was basking in the praise for his role in Sidney Montrose's latest film.

Once the public had decided they loved him, the critics had latched on to him as the latest golden goose of Hollywood.

But despite his success, Cliff honored his commitments. The Sierra had given him his first job as a comedian: every year he paid them back by bringing his sold-out review to their club. A grateful management would have given him the moon if he asked.

He went on for five more minutes, milking the jokes about the musicians until he could sense the audience's flagging interest. Instantly he turned up the wattage behind his smile and said, "Let's bring out our band for another round of applause. Ladies and gentlemen, Whispers."

As the band members made their way onstage, the audience applauded enthusiastically.

"And their singer, Alex."

The whistles and applause were deafening as Alex came out and caught Bear's hand, bowing slightly.

Seeing the reaction, Cliff decided he could use this girl to hold the audience's attention a while longer. He'd been too busy to come to the band's rehearsal, and there had been no time to meet them before the show. He'd just have to hope the singer had enough brains to string two words together.

He held out his hand. "Come here, honey. Let's give the audience a chance to get to know you."

Alex accepted his outstretched hand while keeping a grip on Bear's.

"Your bodyguard?" Cliff asked, positioning himself next to Bear so the audience could see the contrast in their sizes. Beside Cliff, small, slight, and balding, Bear looked like King Kong, a point Cliff was quick to make.

After several jokes about Bear's girth, he dismissed him and turned to Alex again.

"That's some voice," Cliff said.

"Thank you." She gave him a shy smile.

"Are you married?"

She shook her head. "No."

He arched a brow and mugged for the audience. "Want to be? At least for tonight?"

Alex didn't know what came over her. Maybe it was the fact that she felt so comfortable in his presence. After all, she'd practically grown up watching him in all those reruns.

"Is this a proposal?" she asked coyly.

He did a double-take. The audience roared. He stepped back, then gave an exaggerated appraisal of her from head to toe and began a barrage of questions, each of which brought a delightful, unexpected reply from her.

He kept her onstage for a full five minutes more before allowing her to make a graceful exit. "Let's have a nice round of applause for the lovely Alex."

She floated off on a cloud.

Alex wiped off her stage makeup and changed into simple slacks and a baggy sweater. Then she went to the dressing room next door, where she could hear the sounds of celebration from the rest of the band.

When she opened the door they all fell silent.

"Well?" She paused in the doorway looking bewildered. "What did you think? Was I that terrible?"

"Terrible?" Gary crossed the room and stood in front of her. "Bright eyes, you were absolutely brilliant!

Where have you been hiding that wicked sense of humor?"

While her mouth dropped open in astonishment, they all burst into applause. Len pressed a kiss to her cheek. Casey thrust a beer into her hand.

At a knock on the door they looked up to see Cliff Carlson's manager.

"Cliff would like to see all of you in his dressing room," he announced.

"Now?" Gary asked.

The manager nodded. The expression on his face was unreadable, and a feeling of gloom descended on the group. They had the distinct feeling that their celebration had been a little premature.

Alex's self-doubt grew with each step she took toward the comedian's suite of rooms. What if he had resented the way she'd entered into his routine? What if he publicly humiliated her for daring to make a joke during his show?

The manager led the way to the suite, opened the door, and gestured them inside.

The first room was a large sitting room overflowing with people. Many of the guests were easily recognizable actors or comedians. Others, though not well known, appeared to be Cliff's old friends. In one corner of the room was a bar, where a uniformed waiter was dispensing drinks. A waitress offered canapés and picked up empty glasses as quickly as they were set down.

The mood was upbeat. From the easy laughter and flow of conversation, it was obvious that the audience was happy with Cliff's first night.

As the manager ushered them through the throng, several of the guests recognized Alex and the musicians and offered their congratulations. Each time, the manager hurried them on, giving them little chance to mingle.

Alex's fears multiplied. She felt as if she were going to her own execution.

When they reached the door to the next room, the burly man guarding it knocked once, then opened it to admit them.

"Cliff," his manager called, "they're here." He stood aside to admit Alex and the others.

As she stepped into the comedian's dressing room, Alex had a quick impression of him buttoning a clean shirt and tucking it into the waistband of his trousers. His hair was still damp from the shower. Her gaze was riveted on him; she was aware of nothing else. This little man could make or break them.

"Hello again. It's Alex Corday, isn't it?"

She nodded.

He took her hand and continued to hold it as he looked beyond her to the band members. "Tell me your names again."

As each one introduced himself, Cliff shook their hands. "You guys were terrific tonight. And this one . . ." He swung his gaze back to Alex. "You ever done comedy before?" he asked.

Aware of his intense scrutiny, she shook her head, still too afraid to speak.

"You're a natural. Your timing was perfect. Where'd you learn that?"

She shrugged, feeling uncomfortable beneath that piercing gaze. "I—I don't know. It just . . . happened."

"Nothing just happens. It was chemistry. Didn't you feel it?"

She swallowed, then nodded.

"Damn right. Chemistry. It broke the ice, sweetheart. Got the audience rolling. After that, I could do no wrong." He turned to the musicians. "Did you hear the ovations? They loved me."

The guys in the band nodded and wisely kept silent, waiting for the star to show them where all this was leading. They still harbored the fear that he was going to chastise them for something they'd done wrong.

"I want you to do that schtick with me every night, sweetheart. Got it?"

Alex nodded, afraid that she hadn't quite understood. "Schtick?"

"The jokes, the teasing, even the flirting. Let it be spontaneous, you know? Let me lead the way, and you just follow. Like you did tonight?"

"I . . . sure."

"Good." He patted her hand, which he still held in both of his. "Good."

Then he flashed one of his famous smiles. "Excuse me. I got so excited, I forgot my manners. Alex, Gary, Casey, Bear, Len, and Jeremy." He looked distinctly pleased with himself for remembering every name correctly. It was one of his many talents. "I'd like you to meet some very good friends of mine."

For the first time Alex realized there were others in the room. Until this moment, she'd been so overwhelmed by the mere fact of meeting Cliff Carlson, she hadn't been aware of anyone or anything else.

She turned at the precise moment that Cliff said, "This is Sidney Montrose and his son Matt."

17

"*Sidney Montrose. Wow!*" Bear said excitedly, pumping the director's hand up and down. "I can't believe I'm meeting you. Loved your new flick."

"Nice to meet you." Sidney was charming and gracious as he shook each hand. After so many years in show business, it was always refreshing to meet new, unpretentious people.

When he came to Alex, he said, "There's something very familiar about you, young lady. Have we met before?"

Alex realized she hadn't moved. From the first moment she'd spotted Matt, she'd been paralyzed. Now, with her hand in Sidney's, she heard Matt say, "In a manner of speaking, you've met her, Dad."

"I . . ." It was difficult to speak around the lump in her throat. She licked her lips nervously and tried again. "For one thing, I was a waitress at one of your parties last year."

"Oh God. Only in Hollywood," Cliff Carlson said with a laugh. "One day a waitress; the next playing Reno. Someday, Alex, when you're being interviewed by Barbara Walters, you'll be able to tell everyone that you once worked as a waitress to the rich and powerful. Come on," he said with an easy laugh. "I want all of you to meet the rest of my friends."

Alex glanced over her shoulder at Matt, but she had no chance to speak to him. Cliff was already herding her and the others into the next room, where they were soon swallowed up by the crowd.

For the next hour Alex found herself being introduced to so many celebrities, her head was swimming. There were actors, actresses, directors, comedians, all of them famous. A few of them even took the time to be charming. As she stood amid a cluster of laughing, chatting guests, she heard someone speak her name.

"It's Alex, isn't it?"

A big hand closed around her fingers. She looked up into a face she'd seen in movies since her childhood. Though his hair was now steel gray and the famous baby blue eyes required bifocals, his face was remarkably unlined and little changed from that of the childish cherub who had charmed generations of audiences.

A little gasp escaped her lips. "Buddy Holbrook?"

He smiled. "Nice of you to remember."

"Remember? Why, how could anyone not know you?"

"Yeah." He gave a rumble of laughter. "Me and Lassie. We have the most recognizable faces in the history of film."

"I must have watched your old movies a hundred times."

"That's nice, sweet lips. Just don't mention how young you were when you first saw them."

He maneuvered her away from the crowd until they were standing just inside the doorway. It was cooler here, and quiet.

Up close, without the stage makeup, without the dazzling gown, she was even more of a knockout. He liked that. It hadn't been just illusion. There was something fresh about her, an innocence that would appeal to a wide audience.

"I'm a talent agent now," he said, taking a card from his jacket pocket. "Do you have an agent?"

"No, Mr. Holbrook."

"It's Buddy," he said matter-of-factly. "I'm Cliff Carlson's agent. That's why I'm here. I liked what I saw onstage tonight. I'd like to handle you. That is, if you're interested in making show business a career."

"Interested? I'm determined to."

He saw the look that came into her eyes and knew he'd made a wise decision to keep this low-key. He wouldn't have to do much selling at all. This little fish was leaping toward the hook before it was even baited.

"Look, I don't want to lay too much on you too fast. I'll be here for two days. Room eleven seventy-eight." He wrote it on the card, though he doubted she'd need any reminder. "Call me. We'll talk business."

As he turned away she touched his arm. "Mr. Hol— Buddy?"

He turned.

"What about the guys in the band?"

He shrugged. "What about them?"

"Would you represent them, too?"

"Are you a package deal?" he asked.

She nodded emphatically. "Absolutely. If it weren't for them, I wouldn't be here."

Loyalty. He liked that too. It was a rare commodity in the shark tank he operated in. "Okay. Why not. Talk it over with them and get back to me, sweet lips."

Alex leaned weakly against the wall, watching him walk away. Buddy Holbrook. She must be dreaming. In Hollywood, he was known as a starmaker. And he wanted to represent her and the band.

"Have you had enough yet?"

At the sound of Matt's deep voice beside her, Alex slowly turned. Cliff was in the middle of a hilarious story that had everyone in stitches, but all she could think of was the way the corners of Matt's eyes crinkled when he smiled.

"Enough what?"

"Enough praise, adulation, and Hollywood small talk."

She grinned. "I don't think I'll ever get tired of the praise and adulation. But as for the small talk, my head's swimming. Is that a sign I've had enough?"

He leaned closer, and his warm breath feathered over her cheek. "It may be a sign of overdose."

Steeling herself against the shock, she tried to keep her tone light. "What should I do about it?"

"Escape," he muttered, catching her hand. "Or you'll wake up with the worst hangover of your life."

With a laugh she allowed him to drag her away from Cliff's suite. They walked down a dim hallway, littered with wires and cables, and crossed the back end of the darkened stage, where tables of props had been hastily covered with canvas.

"Where are we going?"

"I hope someplace where no one will call me 'Matt baby,' or slip me a business card while detailing the high concept of his latest script."

He led her along another hallway, opening a door at the far end, and they stepped out into the predawn darkness, breathing deeply, filling their lungs with crisp, clean air.

"I feel like I've just escaped from a tomb," he muttered.

"I suppose for anyone who's spent a lifetime around this, it could prove to be tiresome. For me, on the other hand, it's been one of the most exhilarating nights of my life."

"I'm sorry, Alexandra." He lit a cigarette, reflecting ruefully that he'd been intending to quit again. He took two drags and then tossed it aside in disgust. "It never occurred to me that anyone actually enjoyed those parties. Would you like to go back?"

And miss being alone with this man? Alex shook her head. "No. Really. I've had enough for one night. Any more and I'd probably start believing all the flattery."

"Believe it." He pinned her with his gaze. "In case you're not convinced yet, let me add my voice to the chorus: you were wonderful tonight."

"Thanks. I'm beginning to feel like Cinderella."

A gravel path led to a fountain ringed by stone benches. They walked slowly along the path and sat down side by side, each taking care not to touch.

"I saw you talking to Buddy Holbrook," Matt said.

She watched the soothing play of colored lights on the tumbling water. "He offered to be my agent."

Matt thought about the warnings that ought to

come with every Hollywood offer. Maybe someday the government would demand them. They would probably read like the warnings on a pack of cigarettes: hazardous to your health.

"They say he's one of the best."

"Do you know him?"

"Have all my life," Matt said simply. "Through the good times and bad. And with Buddy, there were a lot of bad times. Let's hope he's put them all behind him."

Alex got up and started to pace nervously. "Do you think I should sign with him?"

He watched her for long silent moments before getting to his feet. Reaching for her hand, he stared at the long, slender fingers. "I can't tell you what you should do, Alexandra. Only you know where you want to go, what you want."

At this moment there was only one thing she wanted. She felt her heartbeat begin to accelerate as he encircled her slender wrist with his thumb and fingers.

"I'm confused," she whispered.

"Yeah. Life's confusing." His other hand cupped the back of her head, and he drew her fractionally closer. "In the last months I've thought about you so many times." He bent his head and brushed his lips over hers. "But I was in the middle of filming and couldn't get away, even for a day."

She felt the heat rise in her and started to back away, but his hand was there at the back of her head, holding her still.

"I even called the Cypress, and they said you'd left."

"You—were looking for me?"

He nodded. Against her mouth he whispered, "I

couldn't get you out of my mind. The taste of you." He pressed his lips to her temple, breathing in her scent. "The way you smell." He wrapped his arms around her and dragged her against him. "The way you feel." Finally his lips covered hers in a savage kiss.

The feeling shocked her, trickling along her spine, leaving her trembling. It jolted her as it skittered over nerves strung as tight as guitar strings.

She sighed, and he took the kiss deeper. Instantly she felt the rush of flame. She was on fire, a fire that heated her blood and seared her skin until, despite the coolness of the air, she was engulfed by it, tasting it on her lips, breathing it into her burning lungs.

He lifted his head and studied her, tracing her lips, her cheek, the sweep of her brow with his fingertips. "Why do we never meet until it's time for me to leave?" he muttered.

"It's a game the fates play on us."

When he shot her a puzzled glance she explained, "My father used to say that in Greek mythology, the fates always liked to trick mortals into believing they were actually in control of their destiny. So they would dangle tempting little morsels in front of humans and lead them into all kinds of troublesome places, just to prove that mere mortals, left to their own devices, would always get lost. Then the fates would step in and save them, to prove their power."

"Fascinating. Come on." With a laugh he grabbed her hand and started leading her away.

"Where are we going?"

"To thumb our noses at the fates."

o   o   o

"The filming is completed. But when I get back tomorrow—" Matt glanced out the window at the rising sun. "I mean today," he corrected himself, "I'll start editing."

"When does your plane leave?"

"In a couple of hours."

At his words her heart fell. They had so little time. She pushed aside such gloomy thoughts. At least for now, they were together. And for now, that was enough.

They sat across from each other in a booth in a little diner tucked away between two towering hotels. At the moment the smell of onions on the grill and the hiss of hot grease as the cook slapped two more burgers down was more tempting than the trays of hors d'oeuvres in Cliff Carlson's suite.

They both seemed determined not to think about the fact that they would soon be parting once more. Instead, they focused on safe, impersonal subjects.

"When will your movie be released?"

"I guess it depends on how much editing I have to do. It's scheduled for next spring."

"You must be so excited."

He nodded, and she loved the way a lock of his dark, shaggy hair drifted over his forehead. She had the urge to reach out and brush it back. Instead, she curled her hand around the handle of her coffee cup.

"I have a lot more respect for my father's work now that I've taken on this project," Matt said. "I'm worried about him," he added, more to himself than to her.

"Why?"

He shrugged. "Just a feeling I have. He looks tired. I sense there's something he isn't telling me."

"About his work?"

"Maybe." He waited while the waitress came over to top off his cup. "Or it could be personal," he went on when she was gone. Matt thought about all the problems his father had had through the years. In almost every instance they'd been somehow connected with Dirk. "Whatever it is, it's got him down."

"Maybe he'll confide in you on the flight home."

"I hope so. I've waited all these days for him to say something. I guess the time was never right."

"You could be imagining trouble that doesn't exist."

"I hope you're right." His smile returned, and he reached across the table to take her hand. "Where will you be after Reno?"

She shook her head. "In this crazy business, who knows?"

"If you sign with Buddy, there's no telling where you'll end up." He laced his fingers through hers and stared at their joined hands. "I know one thing; Buddy wouldn't even consider signing you unless he believed in you. So if it's fame and fortune you want, I think it's a safe bet that your wish will come true."

The waitress returned with their burgers, and Matt watched as Alex disposed of hers within minutes, along with a chocolate shake and an order of fries.

He shook his head in disbelief. "How can someone so thin put away so much food?"

"One of my many talents," she said with a laugh. "Do you want those fries?"

He passed her his plate, and she smothered the fries in ketchup and devoured every one.

"Want another order?"

She considered for a minute, then decided against

it. "It'll be time for breakfast in a few hours. I guess I can wait."

He was still laughing when the waitress cleared their table, but his laughter died as he caught sight of the clock on the wall.

"Come on," he said, grabbing her hand.

"Where to now?"

"It's time to get back. I still have to pack."

Outside, he put an arm around her shoulder and drew her close. They walked slowly, as if to hold on to the time left to them.

The sky was alight with ribbons of pink and scarlet. The air was scented with the roses that formed a hedge around the entrance to the sprawling casino-hotel. The last of the fading stars in the heavens looked so incredibly close. For one strange moment it seemed they were the only two people in the world. Then they entered the hotel lobby and caught sight of the sleepy clerks who had survived the night shift.

"What floor are you on?" Matt asked as they stepped into the elevator.

"Two. I like to be close to the ground."

He pushed the button and they rode in silence, watching the number flash on the panel above the door. When they reached the second floor, Alex led him along the silent corridor until they reached the door to the band's suite. Before she could reach for her key he hauled her into his arms and covered her mouth with his.

She had no thought of resisting. It felt so good to be held against him, his thundering heartbeat keeping time with her own. She sighed and moved in his arms, welcoming the sensations that seemed to pour through her each time he touched her.

His hands slipped beneath her sweater, and he moved his fingers across her naked flesh. When his hand cupped her breast, he swallowed the little moan that escaped her lips.

She felt a wave of incredible heat. Needs swamped her, needs she hadn't even known she possessed.

With a ragged breath he lifted his head and pressed his mouth to the tangle of hair at her temple. "It seems like all we do is say hurried good-byes," he murmured.

"We have no choice."

He swore and dragged her roughly to him. Against her mouth he breathed, "The hell we don't. I can't just walk away again."

He savaged her mouth, kissing her until thought and reason fled.

"Give me your key, Alexandra," he muttered against her lips.

When she handed him the key he managed to unlock the door while still pressing her against it. His lips continued weaving their magic as he muttered against her mouth, "Let's get to your room." He nudged the door open and lifted her in his arms.

She wrapped her arms around his neck, unable to think of anything except the pleasure his touch brought. She could no more resist what he offered than she could hold back the dawn. The needs that trembled through her had stripped her of any coherent thought. Wherever he led, she was compelled to follow. She would accept the consequences of their actions later, when her will was restored to her.

As he carried her through the door, the stillness of the room was shattered by the cry of a baby.

Across the room Sara, wearing a faded robe and a look of surprise, stood holding her wailing infant.

Matt hastily set Alex on her feet. Feeling completely disoriented, she smoothed down her sweater and struggled to find her voice.

"Sara, this is Matt Montrose. Matt, Sara. Gary's wife," she added softly.

Matt nodded toward the young woman, then turned to Alex. "Not such a good idea," he mumbled. "I guess I'd better get to my room and pack."

They stood uncertainly, staring at each other with naked hunger. Then Matt touched a finger to her swollen lips and murmured, "Next time, Alexandra, I promise, we won't say good-bye."

She watched as he strode down the hall to the elevators. When he disappeared inside, she softly closed the door to the suite, turning to find Sara and Corey watching her with wide, curious stares.

18

"*I'm sorry,*" Sara mumbled, her face flushed with embarrassment. "Looks like Corey picked a bad time to cry." She began to change the infant's diaper. To fill the awkward silence she added, "She usually sleeps a lot later than this."

"It isn't her fault. This is all new to her." Alex battled a wave of disappointment and fought to calm her unsteady breathing. There was no sense dwelling on what might have been. Matt was gone—again. Nothing would change that. And maybe she should be grateful that circumstances had saved her from her own foolish desires. Now that she was beginning to think more rationally, she realized she'd been in over her head. What she felt for Matt Montrose was a lot more powerful than any emotion she'd ever experienced before. She needed time and space to sort through it.

"Can I get you anything?" she asked when the baby continued fussing.

Sara pointed to the bar. "There's a bottle in the fridge."

Alex retrieved the bottle and placed it in the microwave oven. "How long should I heat it?" she asked.

"Forty seconds ought to do it."

When it was warmed, she handed the botttle to Sara, watching as Corey sucked greedily. Despite the overwhelming emotions she'd just fought, the sight of the baby brought a smile to Alex's lips.

"She's really beautiful," she murmured, taking a seat across from them.

Sara tried to return her smile but her lips trembled. "She's a good baby. But all of this is so confusing for her. From the time she was born she's only known one house and one routine. Now, finding herself among all these awful strangers—" She sniffled. "I don't mean awful. I mean strangers."

Alex realized the young mother was on the verge of tears. "Give it a couple of days, Sara. Then it won't seem so strange."

Sara blinked furiously, avoiding Alex's eyes. "I just can't figure out why Gary suddenly sent for us. Everything was going well."

"Don't you want to be with him?"

"I suppose. But his parents . . ." She shrugged. "It was nice having them around to help while Gary was so far away."

"Didn't you hate the long separations? Didn't you miss him?" Alex asked.

"Of course. But—"

"He probably missed you the same way," Alex went on. "Maybe this is best for both of you. For all three of you," she added, watching as the baby's eyes closed in contentment. "Won't it be nice for Corey to get to know her father?"

Sara studied the infant in her arms. "Maybe. But I'm not sure this is the kind of life I want her exposed to."

"Don't be too quick to condemn it before you've given it a fair chance. It's true there are no houses with picket fences, and we never eat breakfast until well past noon," Alex added with a laugh, "but despite what other people think, we live fairly normal lives."

There was no corresponding smile on Sara's lips as she lifted accusing eyes to Alex. "You mean you think it's normal to stay out all night and bring strange men back to your room at five in the morning?"

Stung, Alex opened her mouth to argue, then realized she had nothing to say in her own behalf. She knew how it must have looked to Sara. And if Sara chose to believe the worst about her, she had no defense. She had, in fact, stayed out all night with Matt, and if Sara and the baby hadn't interrupted, Alex knew in her heart that she and Matt would be in her room right now, lost in a world of passion.

Feeling her cheeks redden, she stood. "I guess I'd better get some sleep. Gary called a rehearsal at three." She paused at the door to her room, about to say more. Then, thinking better of it, she turned away without another word.

A few minutes later as she climbed into bed, she thought about the high hopes she'd had for Gary's wife. It would have been so comforting to have another female around to confide in, to laugh with, to commiserate with when things went wrong. Instead, she had the feeling she'd just invited an enemy into camp.

Pounding the pillow, she drew the covers over her head to blot out the morning sunshine that peeked through the gap in the drapes.

"Hey, Alex. Where'd you disappear to last night?"

The guys were seated around an oval table tucked into a corner of the suite. Room service had just delivered a combination breakfast-lunch, and plates and serving trays crowded the lazy susan in the middle of the table.

Bear was busy sorting through the food.

"Who ordered the omelette?" he asked.

"I did." Len reached out and took the hot platter.

"Burger and fries?"

"Mine," Jeremy said.

"Soup and a club sandwich?"

Casey drummed his knife and fork on the tabletop before accepting his plate.

"Mine's the hash and poached eggs," Bear said, reaching for a steaming platter. "And the chocolate shake." He looked up as Alex poured herself a cup of coffee and picked at a bowl of strawberries. "So? Where'd you go? One minute I saw you talking to Cliff Carlson, the next minute you'd disappeared."

"I got hungry." She dipped a ripe berry into a dish of powdered sugar and bit into it. "I got tired of liver pâté and fish eggs. I had a craving for a greasy hamburger and fries smothered in ketchup."

"It isn't called fish eggs, it's called caviar," Bear corrected her. "I ate a whole jar of it."

She gave him an affectionate smile. "Two jars. I was watching."

"So who'd you go with?"

"Matt Montrose."

Gary, who'd been silent, turned to stare at her. "Pulling another all-nighter with the Hollywood stud, Alex?"

"Yes." Her chin came up, and she felt the color rush to her cheeks. "As a matter of fact, we did stay out all night. Talking."

"Must have been a fascinating conversation," Gary muttered.

"It was."

"Care to share any of it?"

She bristled. "No, I don't. But there is one thing I'd like to tell you. All of you," she added, as the others looked up from their food. "Buddy Holbrook wants to be our agent."

For a minute everyone around the table looked thunderstruck. Then they all started shouting at once.

"Buddy Holbrook? He's just about the most famous name in Hollywood," Len said with awe.

"I can't believe it!" Casey bellowed. "Record contract, here we come. We're going to be rich and famous."

"I saw you talking to him last night at Cliff Carlson's party," Jeremy said. "But I figured he was probably just making a pass . . ." He trailed off when he caught sight of a frowning Sara entering the room carrying the baby.

"Sorry," Gary said when he saw the look on his wife's face. "Did we wake her?"

"All I asked was that you keep it down while she took her nap." Sara glowered at all of them, saving her most ferocious look for Alex. "And instead you're out here shouting like kids in a schoolyard. It's bad enough she missed her sleep last night. Now you've spoiled her nap as well."

"Here," Gary said awkwardly. "Give Corey to me and you grab a cup of coffee."

"No," she said when he stretched out his arms to her. "I don't want any coffee. And I don't need your help. Besides, you don't even know how to hold a baby properly. At least your father knew how to cuddle her."

She turned away, missing the look of pain and anger that crossed Gary's face, and stormed back into their room, slamming the door for emphasis.

There was an awkward silence. To break the tension, Bear lifted his shake aloft and whispered, "Sorry about waking the kid, Gary. Here's to Buddy Holbrook. May he get us a million-dollar recording contract to make up for it."

"The sooner the better," Gary added with a wry smile. "Although I'm not sure at this point that even a million dollars would make my wife happy."

"Give her time," Alex said. But when she glanced at the closed door, she was plagued with doubts. Maybe her advice to Gary had been all wrong. With a gig at the biggest hotel in Reno and Buddy Holbrook offering to handle their career, the last thing the group needed was to have their leader distracted by domestic discord.

"When are we supposed to meet with Holbrook?" Bear asked.

Alex fished his business card from her pocket and went to the phone. "He's in room eleven seventy-eight. I'll call now and set up an appointment."

°   °   °

Buddy's suite was identical to theirs—except that it was on the eleventh floor. All the way up in the elevator, Alex felt her stomach lurch. By the time they walked through his doorway, her pulse was racing.

"Something wrong?" he asked as he shook her hand and took note of her damp palm.

"Just a fear of heights," she said a little breathlessly. "I should have arranged for us to meet in the first-floor lounge."

It was the perfect excuse he needed to shepherd them out of his suite.

Across the room, Alex caught sight of a stunning blonde in silk and lace who moved past the open door of the bedroom.

"Come on." With his hand under Alex's elbow, Buddy turned her toward the elevators, and the others followed. "Can't have our star getting sick before we even get a chance to discuss business."

Star. If the others hadn't caught it, Gary had. He bit his lip as he stepped into the elevator. If Buddy thought of Alex as the star, he'd have to find a way to set him straight.

"Here's a quiet place." Buddy led them to a pair of sofas and several high-backed chairs clustered around a square, glass-topped table.

He made small talk while a waitress brought tea, coffee, and assorted soft drinks. When everyone had been served he said, "I liked what I saw and heard last night. And when I see potential, I don't wait around or play any mind games. As I told Alex, I'd like the chance to represent you. I have a strong client list, and I know my way around this business. And I know what musicians dream of. I'm sure you'd like to cut an album, and do a string of concerts while you climb the charts."

"Wouldn't everybody?" Casey said with a laugh.

The others nodded.

"Exactly," Buddy said. "But you have to start somewhere. For openers, this is what I can offer you: Cliff Carlson is also my client; so this gig here is over next week, and then he returns to Hollywood to start reading scripts. I have another client who opens in Vegas in two weeks. He still doesn't have an opening act, and I think you guys would be perfect."

"How much?" Gary asked.

Buddy shot him a sideways glance. "You don't let any moss grow under your feet, do you?"

"It's my band; Alex is my singer. Since I'm responsible for seeing that all our bills get paid, I have a right to know if we're going to make a living wage."

"Fair enough." Buddy recognized the not so subtle message he'd just been given. The blond surfer, as Cliff had jokingly referred to the guitarist last night, was warning him that he resented being shoved aside in favor of his singer. From now on, Buddy would be careful to direct his words to Gary. Buddy Holbrook had written the book on massaging entertainers' overblown egos. "How does ten thousand a week sound?"

With a look of disgust Gary started to rise. "That won't even cover our expenses."

Buddy's hand shot out, stopping him. "I meant each."

"Ten thousand apiece?" Gary sank back down.

Buddy nodded. "Plus expenses. First-class airfare,

and a limousine at your disposal. Individual rooms. All your meals, of course." He saw the glances exchanged by Len and Jeremy and knew he'd added the right perks. "Deal?"

Gary didn't want to look too eager. To draw out the moment he asked, "You didn't say who we'd be opening for."

"I didn't?" Buddy gave a self-deprecating smile. "How could I forget the most important item of all. You'll be opening for Dwayne Secord."

"Dwayne Secord? But he's country," Gary protested. "Granted, he's the biggest seller out there, but we don't play his kind of music."

"He's the hottest act in the country. His latest album was number one on both the country and pop music charts," Buddy said. "That's why he doesn't have an opening act yet. He told me he doesn't want a country band, and he doesn't want a strictly rock group. He's looking for something different. Something that will appeal to the widest possible audience. The minute I heard you last night, I thought of Dwayne. When I phoned him this morning, I told him I had found the perfect opening act for his Vegas show."

Gary considered for a moment longer. Dwayne Secord had just won every music award in both the country and pop fields. His act was so unique it couldn't be pigeonholed, and he had the kind of raw energy that would pack a Las Vegas showroom every single night. It was impossible to put a price on the kind of exposure this gig would bring them.

He saw the pleading look in Alex's eyes, though she managed to hold her silence.

Buddy saw it too and realized that the young woman

was aware of Gary's need to make the decisions for the others. No matter how she felt, she would accede to Gary's wishes out of a sense of loyalty.

"Well," Buddy said. "What do you think?"

Gary stuck out his hand. "I think you've got yourself a deal, Buddy."

"I'll have my secretary draw up the papers. She can fax them to me this afternoon. Why don't we arrange to meet in my suite around five. That is," he added with a smile, "if Alex thinks she can face up to the eleventh floor for a few minutes."

Alex nodded. If she had to, she'd take some Dramamine. There was no way she'd miss this opportunity.

Buddy shook hands with the rest of the band members, then turned to Alex. "I'm betting that when Dwayne gets a look at your act, he's going to want you to sing with him. Got any problem with that?"

Alex shook her head. "I love his style. I think we could work well together. What do you think, Gary?"

He shrugged. "I think we're jumping the gun. He may not like our music at all."

"You're forgetting something," Buddy put in smoothly. When they looked at him he removed his glasses, to give them the full effect of his direct stare. "I'm the one who got Dwayne Secord to the top of the charts. He has complete confidence in my instincts."

"Then we do, too." Alex offered her hand, and it was engulfed in Buddy's huge one.

"That's my girl."

As she walked away with the musicians, Buddy leaned back in his chair and pulled a cigar from his pocket. Holding a lighter to the tip, he watched the curl of smoke through narrowed eyes. To his way of thinking, musicians were a dime a dozen. But these musicians were obviously important to Alex, so he'd keep them around. It was a small price to pay. After all, he'd found his golden goose. He would, by God, earn her trust and keep her happy at any cost.

19

There was a thud on the door of the suite, as if someone had kicked it. Bear opened it to find Alex nearly staggering under the weight of the bags and boxes in her arms.

"Looks like you've been shopping."

Flushed with excitement, Alex deposited everything on the sofa. "I found the most wonderful secondhand shop in town."

"When are you going to give up hunting for bargains, Alex? Didn't you hear Buddy the other day when we signed that contract? We're going to be rich."

"Uh-huh." She dropped into a nearby chair and kicked off her shoes. "I'll believe it when I see it. Besides, I've got better things to do with my money than waste it on clothes."

"What could be more important than clothes?" In a pair of faded shorts and a T-shirt, Sara looked up from where she sat feeding Corey. "I'm so sick and tired of wearing these old things. If Gary ever makes it big, I'll put all those Hollywood fashion plates to shame. I'd give anything to have money to waste on clothes."

"You think fancy clothes will change you?"

"Maybe not. But they'll change the way Gary looks at me."

It was obvious to Alex that Sara needed a healthy dose of self-esteem. But she was making a big mistake if she thought that clothes would make her more important in the eyes of others.

"What are you saving for, Alex?" Bear tore open a bag of Oreos and popped two into his mouth, washing them down with a glass of milk.

She shrugged, thinking about her promise to Kip. The first thing she intended to do was save enough money to support her little brother. And send him to special art classes. And, of course, there was the matter of the house in Malibu. "Just—things."

Despite the closeness she felt with the guys in the band, Alex had never allowed them to glimpse her personal problems. The thought of sharing the intimate details of her life with them was too upsetting, the pain of her separation from Kip still too close to the surface. She was afraid she might embarrass herself by bursting into tears if she tried to talk about it.

"I'm going to join the others outside at the pool," Bear said. "Want to come with me, Alex?"

"No, thanks. I'm going to put these things away and figure out what I'm wearing tonight."

When he left, she glanced at Sara, who set the bottle aside and held the sleeping infant on her shoulder as she got up and strolled to the door of the balcony that overlooked the pool.

Gathering up her purchases, Alex headed toward her room, pausing as a thought struck her.

"Sara, would you like to join the guys at the pool?"

"I can't," the young woman said with a trace of impatience. "Corey's asleep. She'll probably sleep for another hour or more, and by then it'll be time for Gary to come up and dress for the show." She couldn't keep the bitterness from her tone. "Ever since I got here, Gary and I seem to spend all our time apart. He has rehearsals and shows, I have Corey. So much for family togetherness."

"Go ahead and enjoy yourself," Alex said. "I'll be here. I'll look in on Corey while she sleeps."

Sara seemed tempted for a moment. Then she turned away dejectedly. "I'd better not. She might wake up."

"That's not a problem. If she wakes up early, I'll watch her until you come back."

"She'll need changing," Sara said hesitantly.

With a laugh Alex said, "I know how to change a diaper. Go on. Grab a little sun while you have the chance."

Sara seemed to weigh the offer carefully, and Alex realized that she was debating leaving her baby in the hands of a woman of dubious morals.

With a sudden burst of enthusiasm Sara went to settle the sleeping baby in her crib and change into her bathing suit. As she headed toward the door she said, "You're sure you don't mind?"

"Not in the least. Enjoy yourself."

"Okay." Sara hurried out.

It was nearly two hours later when Sara and Gary returned to the suite, laughing easily together. Gary caught his wife's hand. "I'd forgotten how good you look in a bikini."

She blushed like a schoolgirl. "And I'd forgotten how much you like to tease." She tossed her head, sending her wet hair dancing around her shoulders. "I think I swallowed half the pool when you pushed me under."

"You got your revenge." He rubbed his arm. "I didn't think you were strong enough to drag me down."

"Believe me, it wasn't easy." She gave a low, throaty laugh. "But it was worth it to see the look on your face when I managed to dunk you."

They were both still laughing when they caught sight of the empty crib. Instantly Sara's smile fled. "I knew I stayed away too long. What was I thinking of?"

With a cry of distress she ran and pounded on the door between their room and Alex's. "What have you done with Corey?"

Alex opened the door and gave them both a curious look. "What in the world is wrong?"

"What's wrong? The crib is empty, that's what's wrong. I should have known better than to trust someone like you. Where is Corey?" Sara demanded.

"Right here." Alex stepped aside, allowing them to enter her room. Corey was sitting on a quilt on the bedroom floor. In front of her was a music box with a twirling ballerina on top. On the infant's face was a look of pure enchantment.

When she caught sight of her parents, she clapped her hands.

"Where'd she learn that?" Gary asked.

"I taught her. See?" Alex clapped her hands together and the little girl mimicked her.

Frowning, Sara bent and gathered the baby into her arms. Corey immediately started to howl and reached out her hands for the music box.

"Why don't you let her stay a while longer?" Alex said. "Just until you two have had time to change."

"We've imposed long enough. She can play in our room while we dress." Sara turned away. Her words were stiff and formal. "Thanks for your help."

"You're welcome. I think I enjoyed myself more than she did. I'd be happy to watch her anytime you want."

When Corey continued to cry, Alex thrust the music box into Gary's hands. "Maybe this will soothe her."

"Thanks." Gary followed his wife from the room. "I'll see that you get it back later."

"There's no rush. I'm just glad I was able to amuse her."

Alex could hear Sara murmuring words to soothe her crying daughter. As she closed her door it occurred to her that she had just spent two very enjoyable hours. For two hours she hadn't given a single thought to Kip. For two hours she had completely lost herself in the joy of a child's laughter.

Maybe, if Sara would loosen up a little, Alex could persuade her to leave Corey with her again sometime.

The week spent as the warm-up act for Cliff Carlson was like a week in the classroom. Every day Alex and the members of the band learned something new. From his years of playing small clubs around the country, Cliff had learned how to use the audience to his advantage. Within minutes of stepping out onstage, he was able to gauge their moods.

"It's not so hard," he explained to Alex after the last show. He'd changed their act drastically after getting no response to his first jokes. And though Alex had been forced to pay close attention, she'd managed to keep up with the changes and roll with them.

"I could see that they weren't interested in the band members; only you. So I had to scramble to get the guys off the stage and keep you there a little longer than we'd planned."

"But how did you know what the people out there wanted?"

"It's a gut feeling," he said, staring off into the now deserted rows of seats. "An extra sense I get when I step onstage. You can have that same sense, if you learn to open yourself to it."

"How?"

"There's a moment when you walk on and the spotlight momentarily blinds you, and you feel all alone in the universe. Then, as your eyes adjust and you begin to see those people setting out there in the dark, you become connected. When you see them watching, nodding, smiling, you have a glimpse into their souls. In that moment," he said softly, "you sense exactly where they want you to take them."

His eyes looked glazed with passion. This was clearly something he could talk about for hours.

"You have power over the audience, Alex. Even though you haven't sorted it all out, you've already been using it. I've seen you."

"But I don't even see my audience," she protested. "Sometimes when the song ends and they applaud, I find myself surprised that they're still there."

"That's your style. That's what sets you apart. But don't you see? Even lost in the music, you're connecting with your audience. They feel the pain of loss, or the frustrations of love or whatever else you sing about, through you. And you, in turn, absorb their emotions and translate them into song."

She nodded. Though she'd never heard it verbalized before, she knew it was true. The bond between herself and the audience was a vibrant, living thing. It was the thing that drove her to perform.

"Thanks, Cliff. I've learned so much this week."

"So have I. You're going to be big, Alex. I think the day will come when the whole world will know your name. Come on." He caught her hand and led her through the maze of cables and curtains backstage toward his dressing room. "I'm throwing a little party before I head back to L.A."

"You're back early." Sara was sprawled on the sofa in the living room, flipping through the TV channels. Through the open doorway to the bedroom Alex could see Corey asleep in her crib.

"I have a lot of packing to do before we leave in the morning for Vegas," she said. "Thought I'd get started now."

"Is Gary still at Cliff's party?"

"Yes. Would you like to join him?"

Sara's eyes lit up for a moment, but then she nodded toward the bedroom. "I can't. Corey's sleeping."

"I'll watch her. I can leave the doors open between our rooms."

"She might wake up. She's been doing that since we came here."

"It's no problem. I'll change her and rock her until she falls back to sleep."

Sara looked down at her faded jeans and T-shirt. "I don't have anything to wear."

"Everybody's dressed just like you are. You don't think the dancers and the guys in the orchestra get all dressed up after a night in costume, do you?"

Sara shrugged. "I guess I thought they'd all look glamorous."

"They've all creamed off their makeup and let down their hair," Alex said with a laugh. "The last thing they care about now is glamour. Go on, Sara. You'll have a good time."

For the first time Sara smiled. "I'd really like to. That is, if you really don't mind staying with Corey."

"Of course not. You go enjoy yourself. And don't worry about Corey."

With a little laugh Sara went to touch up her makeup and run a brush through her hair. She dropped a kiss on her daughter's forehead and was gone.

About an hour later, the door to the suite opened and Gary and Sara walked in, wearing identical smiles. Gary's arm was around his wife's waist. Her head was snuggled against his shoulder.

"Is the party over so soon?" Alex called.

They seemed surprised to see her.

"No," Gary said, pressing a kiss to Sara's temple. "We just thought we'd come up to bed."

Sara asked dreamily, "Did Corey wake up?"

"No. She's been sleeping like an angel."

"Great. Well—thanks, Alex." The door to their room closed.

Alex heard the sounds of muted voices and laughter. With a knowing smile she returned to her packing.

"Are all the instruments loaded into the van?" Bear asked the next morning, snapping his suitcase shut and pouring himself a tall glass of orange juice. His red eyes bore testament to how late it was when the party broke up the night before.

Jeremy nodded and set his luggage beside the door. Six other pieces of luggage were already awaiting the hotel bellman. "I took care of our instruments an hour ago."

"Man, I'm not looking forward to spending all day on the road," Bear said as he began methodically eating scrambled eggs.

Gary surprised them all by saying, "Why don't you fly and let me drive your van to Vegas? I'll take Sara and Corey with me, and we'll make a two-day trip out of it."

"What about your car?" Bear asked.

"I think the old clunker has had its last run. Buddy offered to sell it for scrap and send us to Vegas by plane. But to tell you the truth, I'd rather drive with Sara and Corey."

"You mean it?" Sara asked with a sudden laugh. "Don't you have to be in Las Vegas right away?"

"We have a week before we open with Dwayne Secord. I was planning a couple of long rehearsals before we open, but we could still get them in at the end of the week. What do you say, Bear?"

The sax man shrugged. "I'd much rather hop on a plane and be in my hotel room in a matter of hours, as long as you don't mind driving the van all that way."

"I think Sara and I could use some time alone."
Gary took his little daughter from his wife's arms and
settled her on his lap. Pressing a kiss to the infant's
cheek he added, "And it would give me some time with
Corey too."

"This will be our first family vacation," Sara said
solemnly.

"Don't go getting your hopes up," Gary warned.
"It's a long dull drive from Reno to Las Vegas."

"Not for me," Sara reminded him. "I've never seen
this part of the country before."

"Good. It's agreed then." Handing the baby back to
his wife, Gary took the keys from Bear and began passing out the airline tickets. "Buddy said you're all flying
first class. Enjoy."

There was a knock on the door, and Alex opened it
to admit the bellman. "Looks like it's time to go," she
said as she picked up her purse.

To her surprise, Sara was right behind her, with
Corey in her arms. "I never properly thanked you for
last night," the young woman said earnestly.

"You're welcome, Sara. I didn't mind. It was no
trouble at all. I hope when we all settle in in Las Vegas
you'll let me watch Corey again. She's great company—when she's awake," Alex added with a laugh.

Sara gave her a warm smile. "I think you mean it."

"I do."

Alex leaned close to give the infant a hug. Then, following the bellman out, she called to Gary, "See you in
Las Vegas."

He nodded vaguely. Before the door even closed, he
had pulled his wife into his arms like an impatient lover.

20

If working with Cliff Carlson had been an education, the two weeks spent with Dwayne Secord was an introduction to a way of life Alex had never even imagined.

Dwayne Secord's fans packed every concert. It was impossible to walk through the casino before showtime. Long lines of patrons snaked slowly through the rows of slot machines and gaming tables, waiting patiently for hours each evening until the doors to the showroom were opened.

Dwayne received a standing ovation just for walking onstage, and with each song the screams grew higher in pitch until the sound was deafening. He seemed to feed on the enthusiasm of his frenzied audience, gaining strength as the show went on. When he took his final curtain call, the audience was left drained, while he seemed even more energized than when he'd started.

"Come on, Al." He'd given her the nickname at their first meeting. The chemistry between them was perfect. Each had discovered the quirky sense of humor in the other. Though sparks flew when they sang together, they were content to be nothing more than friends when the curtain came down.

Dwayne dragged her out to a thundering ovation. "They love you," he muttered as the crowd leapt to its feet.

"It's you they're cheering."

"Want to bet?" He blew kisses to a girl in the front row who was crying and walked with Alex to the far side of the stage where a little girl thrust a bouquet of roses into her arms.

Dwayne shot her his famous grin, half lip-curling sneer, half country-boy charm. "See the guy in the black turtleneck? He got so hot after your last song I thought he was goin' to jump up here and attack you."

"Uh-huh. Dwayne, you've got them so excited right now, you could bring a trained elephant out and they'd applaud."

He broke into gales of laughter as the curtain descended for the final time. "Now there's one I hadn't thought of. How'd you like to be replaced by a singin' elephant?"

"Just go ahead and try," she said with a laugh. "It won't look nearly as good in this gown as I do."

"And you do look good. I've been meanin' to tell you." He caught her hand. "What've you got planned for tonight?" he asked, shifting directions so suddenly she had no time to stop and think.

"You mean besides sleep?"

She could feel the energy pulsing through him. It

was always the same. After each show he was restless, edgy, always wanting to plunge into something that would consume him until morning, when he would at last be able to settle down and sleep. Most of his band refused to even try to keep up with him. They much preferred private parties in their suite, where they wouldn't have to deal with hoards of fawning fans. Casey, Bear, Jeremy, and Len were still more interested in eating than in anything Dwayne might suggest. As for Gary, he had discovered the joys of family life. Ever since the drive from Reno, he and Sara had formed a special bond. After the show he made it a point to go straight back to his room, where he and his wife enjoyed a romantic dinner while the baby slept.

"You know you're not ready to sleep, Al. What would you like to do?"

"I don't know." Ever since she'd started this engagement in Las Vegas, she'd been running as if constantly on a high. "What have you got in mind?"

"Meet me in my dressin' room in half an hour," he said with a mysterious smile.

A short time later, wearing faded jeans and her favorite old blazer, she knocked on his door. He looked the same as he did onstage. His long legs were encased in slim-fitting jeans. The western-style shirt was silk. The black wide-brimmed hat was one of more than a dozen he'd had custom-made. His smile was easy, and his Oklahoma drawl authentic.

"Ever gambled, Al?"

Alex shook her head.

"Lord," he called to his band members and the eager girls they'd invited up to their suite, "I've got me a virgin. Come on, Al. Time to get your feet wet. Let's get to those tables."

"I don't want to lose my money."

"Hell, we'll use mine. I've got jillions."

"What about your fans?" she asked as he led her toward a private elevator.

"What about them?"

"Won't they mob you out in the casino?"

"I pay him to worry about those things," he said, nodding toward the burly bodyguard who trailed two paces behind.

As they walked through the crowded casino, Alex was amazed by the transformation in the crowd. Dwayne Secord's face was instantly identifiable. Jaws dropped; conversations stopped in mid sentence. People stared. But no one violated Dwayne's privacy. The few who dared to approach him were quickly deterred by his bodyguard.

"We'll start slow, Al." Dwayne stopped beside a twenty-five-dollar slot machine and pulled a hundred-dollar bill from his pocket. An employee exchanged his money for four tokens, which he handed to Alex.

"Drop two of them in," he said.

"Two?" She lowered her voice . "Dwayne, that's fifty dollars."

He grinned. "Why are we whisperin'?"

"Because I don't want anyone else to overhear us and know how foolish we're being."

"Come on, Al," he muttered against her ear. "There's a jackpot just waitin' for someone to claim it."

Reluctantly she deposited two tokens in the machine and looked for a handle to pull. There was none.

"Just press this knob." He indicated the spin button.

She pressed it and watched as wheels spun and various pictures flashed by. When the wheels stopped spinning, she turned to Dwayne.

"I don't hear any sirens. I guess we lost."

"Right, Al. Put in two more."

"That's a hundred dollars."

He gave her his famous smile. "Uh-huh. You goin' to play or run scared?"

She dropped in the last two tokens and pressed the knob. Again the machine took their money and gave nothing back.

She looked at him in alarm. "What happened to the fortune waiting for someone to claim it?"

"It's still waitin'. We just fattened the pot. Let's try again." He signaled a change person, who handed him more tokens in exchange for more bills.

The machine ate up five hundred dollars before they gave up.

"Come on." Dwayne put his arm around her waist and escorted her toward an empty blackjack table.

"We can't play here," she said as he pulled out a chair for her.

"Why not?"

"There's no one else playing."

"Then I guess they're holdin' it just for us." He took the seat beside her and signaled to a dealer, who immediately took Dwayne's money and exchanged it for chips.

With a floor boss watching, the dealer shuffled the cards and the game began. When they walked away an hour later, Alex had won fifty dollars. Dwayne had won thirty thousand.

"I got so nervous when you doubled that bet," she said with a shaky laugh.

"And drew a ten," he added.

"Yes. To your eleven. I never would have had the nerve, knowing I had two thousand dollars riding on the turn of a single card."

"It's only money," he said. "Come on. Your education isn't complete yet. It's time you learned how to shoot craps."

He ushered her to a table and dropped several hundred-dollar bills, which were immediately changed to chips. While a man at the other end of the table tossed the dice, Dwayne explained the game to Alex. By the time the dice had come around to their side of the table, they had lost several hundred dollars.

"I don't like this game," she said.

"You just don't like losin'."

"And you do?"

He shot her a lazy smile. "Nobody likes losin'. Here. Roll the dice."

She did as she was told, and a joyful shout went up when they landed. She continued to toss the dice for half an hour and had the other players at the table cheering for her each time she made her point. When Dwayne finally cashed out, he folded another ten thousand dollars into his pocket.

"I've decided not to replace you with a trained elephant," he said, putting an arm around her shoulder. "I haven't scored so much in years. Must be your beginner's luck. Come on, little rabbit's foot. I hope you've worked up an appetite. I'm starvin'."

Despite their casual garb, they were seated in a quiet booth in the elegant gourmet dining room, where a waiter and maître d' hovered over them to see to their every need. By the time they took their leave, all the other patrons had left. Dwayne left the staff, who had been forced to work overtime to accommodate him, a generous tip.

With the ever present bodyguard behind them, they strolled outside past the pool. To the east, the sky was already streaked with dawn light. Within a few hours the pool area would be swarming with hundreds of tanned bodies.

Their private suites were situated in a separate section of the hotel. Security was so strict in this area that it could only be entered with a special key. Two guards nodded a greeting as Alex and Dwayne entered, followed by their own man.

Dwayne escorted her to her room and waited until she'd opened the door and switched on the light.

"Did you enjoy your first lesson in gamblin'?"

She laughed. "I enjoyed it a whole lot more knowing it was your money we were risking. Thanks, Dwayne. It was a lot of fun."

"Yeah, it was. Just be careful," he said, brushing a kiss over her cheek. "Don't go thinkin' you can win a couple thousand every time you walk up to a table."

"You don't need to worry. I don't think I'm going to get hooked on gambling."

"You got any vices?" he asked with a grin.

"None I'm going to tell you about."

"Hell, you can't blame a guy for tryin'."

They shared an easy laugh.

Dwayne turned away. "See you tomorrow, Al. And in case I forgot to mention it earlier, you put on one hell of a great show tonight. I already told my orchestra leader I'd like to add a couple more duets to the act tomorrow. I mean, tonight."

"A couple more? When were you going to tell me?"

"I just did."

"But when are we going to rehearse them?"

"Hell, I was afraid you'd want to rehearse." He yawned. "How about three o'clock?"

Dazed by the sudden turn of events, she simply nodded.

"Night, Al. See you in a few hours."

"Sure." She closed the door and leaned weakly against it. How would she ever be able to fall asleep now? She'd just been invited to share even more of the spotlight with one of the most famous singers in the country.

Her palms were sweating as she slipped out of her clothes. She'd been with him all night, and he'd kept the surprise from her until now.

Alex settled Corey into the high chair and began spooning food into the little girl's mouth, all the while carrying on a lively conversation.

Now that she had begun spending a few hours each afternoon with the infant, the two had formed a bond. The little girl laughed at Alex's silly chatter and the funny faces he made, and she seemed to enjoy the songs Alex sang to her.

When the door opened and Gary and Sara walked in, Corey clapped her hands and smiled.

"How was the pool?" Alex asked.

"Refreshing," Sara responded cheerfully.

"If you like your water as warm as bathwater," Gary added.

"I should know," Sara said playfully. "I think I swallowed half the pool from all the dunkings."

"Sounds like you had a good time."

"We did. Thanks, Alex," Gary called before disappearing into the bedroom.

"Yes. Thank you, Alex." Sara bent to press a kiss to Corey's soft, warm cheek. "I can finish feeding her if you're in a hurry to go."

"No problem." Alex spooned more food into the baby's mouth and said, "Why don't you change first?"

"Okay." With her hand on the doorknob, Sara turned back. In a low voice she said, "Gary told me you were the one who suggested that he send for Corey and me."

Alex dabbed at the baby's chin with a napkin and said nothing.

"I know I was pretty awful when I first arrived. I was scared, and homesick, but that doesn't excuse my behavior. I'd like you to know that I'm sorry for the way I acted. And I'm grateful that you were willing to give me another chance. What I'm trying to say," she muttered, feeling her cheeks growing hot, "is thanks, Alex." She moved closer and grasped Alex's free hand between both of hers. "Thanks for the time you spend with Corey. And thanks for helping Gary and me find the love again."

"Wow." Alex gave an embarrassed little laugh. "You make me sound like some kind of saint or something."

"You're better than that," Sara said, drawing Alex close and hugging her. The flush on her cheeks deepened. "You're a friend. I just hope I can be the same for you."

○   ○   ○

Alex felt the adrenaline pumping. She'd taken great pains with her appearance for this, their last show in Las Vegas. She wore her hair pulled to one side with silver beaded combs. The silver beaded gown she wore had a plunging neckline that revealed more cleavage than usual.

Dwayne had added so many duets that she was joining him onstage for nearly half his act. He loved the chemistry between them. More than that, he loved the way his fans reacted to Alex. A beautiful woman in a seductive pose only seemed to add to the rugged cowboy mystique he'd created for himself.

Earlier in the day Buddy had flown into Las Vegas to present his latest plans to the band. He'd proudly announced that he'd booked them into the very prestigious Rainbow Room at the top of Rockefeller Center for a two-week run.

"Who are we opening for?" Bear asked.

"You're not the opening act this time," Buddy said with a wide smile. "You're the main attraction."

"In the Rainbow Room?"

Buddy nodded. "While you're playing Rainbow and Stars, I've booked Alex into every morning show and daytime talk show I could fit into the schedule. Want to hear something funny?" he asked.

They stared at him, too surprised at his news to do more than nod their heads.

"Ever since Dwayne and Alex started those duets, the press has decided it's a hot romance." He passed around a copy of the latest gossip magazines, showing pictures of Dwayne and Alex at the pool, Dwayne and Alex at a dice table, Dwayne and Alex singing, soulfully gazing into each other's eyes. "As soon as the talk shows found out that Alex was going to be singing in Manhattan, my phone started ringing off the hook. I didn't even have to hire any PR people. These rags are giving us more publicity than money could ever buy."

"But when they interview me, they'll find out that there isn't any romance," Alex protested.

"We'll talk about it when you get to New York," Buddy said with a wave of his hand. "Which reminds me. You leave tomorrow morning, a day ahead of the band, so you can do an interview with *This Is Entertainment.*" He handed her an airline ticket. "We've got a couple of important things to talk about," he said, turning to the others. "I think it's time you hired a road manager and a business manager."

"What's that going to cost us?" Gary asked.

"Whatever it costs, it'll be worth it. I've brought along a list of professionals that I can recommend. If none of them suits you, I'll have my secretary put together another list. Right now, I suggest you guys do whatever it takes to lighten your load. The way your career is taking off, you don't need to be worrying about all these minor details. I intend to keep you on such a fast treadmill, you'll need all the help you can get just to travel from one gig to another."

Remembering his words now, Alex stood in the wings, preparing to take her final bow. When Dwayne took her hand and led her to the center of the stage, she rewarded him with a dazzling smile before bowing to the wildly cheering audience.

"Because it's our last night," he shouted above the din, "I think we'll give you one more song."

The crowd was on their feet, roaring, but when the

music started, an eerie sort of expectant, hushed silence settled over them.

Dwayne and Alex launched into a song they'd only rehearsed once, but the words and music were a perfect blend of drama and beauty that was enhanced by their voices. When the last note died away, the crowd erupted once more into a frenzy of cheering.

Swept up by the emotions of performing, Dwayne took Alex into his arms and kissed her, to the delight of his fans.

Then the curtain descended, and though the audience continued applauding and shouting for more, Dwayne ordered that it remain down.

"That was the ultimate," Dwayne said, spinning her around and around. "Put on your dancin' duds, Al. We're goin' to party till dawn."

When he released her, she felt as if she were still spinning. She hurried to her dressing room and dropped into a chair. Staring at her reflection in the mirror, she heard again the adulation of the audience. It was more intoxicating than any wine.

A celebration was exactly what she wanted.

21

"*I've never seen* the casino this crowded."

"There's a fight tomorrow night. Title fights always bring in the high-rollers. Give me your hand so we don't get separated."

Alex clung tightly to Dwayne's hand as he followed his bodyguard, who cut a path through the crush of people all the way to the gourmet dining room. Dwayne had lost at least twenty-five thousand dollars at the dice tables, but his mood was as upbeat as if he'd won a fortune.

They entered the dining room, where they had to wait behind another couple for the maître d'. Alex's attention was caught by the woman's profile as she smiled up into the man's face: it was Lauren Keller, the hottest young actress in Hollywood. She had starred in two of the year's top movies, and her face had appeared on every notable magazine. Everyone agreed that if her career continued on course, she had every-thing it took to become a Hollywood legend.

Dwayne bent close to Alex and muttered, "We'll get a table tucked away in some small, secluded corner and drink gallons of champagne. Then we're goin' dancin'."

"If I'm going to dance the night away, I'm afraid my gallons of champagne may have to be reduced to a glasss or two," she said with a laugh.

At the sound of her voice, the man in front of her stiffened slightly, then glanced over his shoulder. When their gazes met and held, she felt the jolt of recognition clear to her toes.

Why was it that the fates seemed to enjoy shocking her? Why was she always so stunned by these chance encounters?

She was once again face to face with Matt Montrose.

Seeing the look on her face, Dwayne turned to study the man ahead of him. He looked back at Alex and whispered, "Friend of yours?"

She nodded, afraid for a moment to trust her voice.

"Hello, Alexandra." The familiar deep tone never failed to send a shiver along her spine.

"Matt." She inclined her head slightly.

Alex was aware that the woman with Matt had turned and was studying her with avid interest.

Matt smoothly handled the introductions. "Alexan-dra Corday, I'd like you to meet Lauren Keller."

Alex hoped her smile didn't waver as she offered her hand. "Lauren. It's a pleasure to meet you. This is Dwayne Secord. Dwayne, Lauren Keller—and Matt Montrose."

Each man seemed to take the measure of the other before they shook hands.

Dwayne turned toward the actress. "Why I just saw you in *Stormwatch*, Miss Keller," he said, pouring on his charm.

"It's Lauren," she corrected him with a smile.

"You were wonderful, Lauren. When will you have another movie out?"

She placed a hand possessively over Matt's sleeve. The calculated movement wasn't lost on Alex.

"That's what Matt and I have just been discussing. Now that he's the hottest director in town, I think it might be fun to work with him."

Alex couldn't tear her gaze from Matt. Despite the elegantly tailored cashmere suit and proper tie, there was about him that same air of rugged independence that she'd first admired. He looked tanned and fit. And wonderful.

He stood very still, content to watch her while Dwayne and Lauren carried the conversation.

"I wish we could have caught your concert. The critics raved about you. Both of you," Lauren added politely, nodding at Alex, though it was clear that her attention was riveted on Dwayne. She said it with such sincerity, Alex was almost inclined to believe her. "But we just got in," she continued, wrapping both arms around Matt's arm and drawing herself close. "I was very disappointed when I learned that we'd missed your last show."

"I'll have to send you front row seats for my next concert." The words rolled as smoothly from Dwayne's tongue as warm honey. "Are you down here for the fights?"

Lauren nodded. "I had to coax Matt to bring me. I've never seen a championship fight." She tossed her head slightly, aware that many of the room's patrons were staring and clearly enjoying the fact that she was recognized. "I think it will be exciting to see the world's only remaining gladiators, don't you?"

Dwayne chuckled. "Now that's one I hadn't heard before. What do you think, Al? Want to stay over and catch those sexy gladiators?"

Alex had to pull herself back from the thoughts that kept crowding her mind. "I'm afraid I can't. Buddy arranged some New York bookings."

"Oh yeah. Too bad," Dwayne muttered. "It would have been fun."

The maître d' approached Matt. "I have your table ready, sir."

"Thank you." Matt shook hands with Dwayne. "It was nice meeting you."

He didn't offer his hand to Alex. The thought of touching her was far too tempting—and too painful. Instead he merely said, "It was good seeing you again, Alexandra. I wish you success in New York."

"Thank you."

She watched as he and Lauren followed the maître d'. When she turned to Dwayne, he was looking at her closely.

It wasn't until they were seated in a private booth that Dwayne said, "So. What's between you and the tall, dark, silent one?"

She busied herself with her napkin, avoiding his eyes. "I don't know what you mean."

Dwayne placed a hand over hers, stilling her movements. "I may be a big ol' country hick, Al, but I'm not blind. Whatever is between you and Matt Montrose, it's thick enough to cut with a carvin' knife. Now tell me what gives."

"It's . . . true that we've met before."

A waiter opened a bottle of champagne and poured some into Dwayne's glass. When he'd tasted it, Dwayne nodded his approval and the waiter filled their glasses.

When they were once more alone Dwayne said, "And?"

Alex looked up. "We went out once or twice."

"Un-huh. And?"

She shrugged. "That's all, Dwayne."

"Honey," he said, "that may be all you did, but that sure as hell ain't all you want. Him either," he added, nodding toward the table where Matt and Lauren were sitting.

"Well . . ." She lifted the tulip glass and sipped the champagne. The last time she'd had champagne had been with Matt in Carmel. The thought brought a twinge of pain before she pushed it aside. "That's all it's ever going to be."

Dwayne lifted his glass and touched it lightly to hers. "You're one hell of a bad liar, Al," he said with a grin. "But you're the best singer I've ever worked with. Here's to all the things we're still hopin' for. I don't know about you, but I want 'em all."

In spite of herself Alex found herself laughing. "Oh, Dwayne. You're so good for me."

"You'd better believe it, honey. And don't you ever forget it."

Still laughing, she happened to glance toward Matt's table. At that moment his gaze met hers. She turned away and drained her glass.

It was almost two hours later when she and Dwayne left the dining room. As they passed Matt's table, she put on her best smile, and she and Dwayne bade Matt and Lauren a polite good night.

Alex stumbled off the elevator and headed for the coffee shop, while the bellman hauled her luggage to the waiting limousine. She and Dwayne had danced the night away in the Starlight Lounge. Whatever worries had plagued her, they were soon forgotten as she gave herself up to the pulsating beat. It had been more fun than she'd expected. Dwayne was funny and relaxed, and he'd kept her laughing all night.

Now she was paying the price for such pleasure. She had returned to her room with just enough time to pack. Her body was crying out for sleep. Instead, she intended to ply it with caffeine.

"Alexandra."

Matt appeared from behind her, causing her to shrink back for a moment. He reached out a hand to steady her and felt the current that always flowed between them at the simplest touch.

"Sorry. I didn't mean to startle you."

Alex held herself stiffly, resenting the feelings that his touch awakened.

He nodded toward the coffee shop. "Having breakfast?"

"There isn't time. My bags are already being loaded into a limo. I just thought I'd grab a cup of coffee."

"How many are riding to the airport with you?" he asked as they went into the coffee shop.

"Just me. The guys in the band aren't leaving until tomorrow." She fumbled for her sunglasses, wishing she'd taken more time with her appearance. For the early morning flight to New York she'd decided to opt for comfort instead of fashion. She was dressed in a pair of faded jeans and a simple ivory silk shirt.

"Two coffees to go," Matt told the waitress.

After he and Alex paid for the coffee, they strolled across the lobby and through the front doors.

"Where are you headed so early in the morning?" she asked him, getting into the limo.

He took a sip of his coffee to hide the smile that touched his lips. "I thought I'd ride along with you as far as the airport."

Before she could argue he had climbed in beside her. Had he been waiting for her? she wondered. Or had they merely met by accident?

"How long will you be in New York?" he asked.

"Two weeks."

"And then where?"

"I never know. We have Buddy to take care of all the arrangements. I just go where I'm told."

Through the windows of the limousine, the hotels and casinos sped past in a blur of neon. Early morning traffic was already beginning to clog Tropicana Boulevard. Alex glanced at the driver, noting the closed glass partition that sealed off their conversation from him.

"Are you happy, Alexandra?" Matt asked.

"I'm doing what I always dreamed of."

His voice lowered. "I asked you if you're happy."

"Of course." She was glad for the sunglasses that hid her eyes from his scrutiny. "Why shouldn't I be?"

"No reason. You just seem to be pushing yourself to the limit."

"Isn't that how you get to the top?"

He leaned forward to set his cup on the silver tray before them and turned to her. "Is it?"

The limousine swung smoothly into the airport and came to a stop at the curb. Alex placed her empty cup beside Matt's. "I'll let you know when I get there."

Matt watched as the driver got out and went to the rear of the vehicle to remove the luggage from the trunk. Passing a hand over his eyes he said, "I wish we had more time. Seems to be the story of our lives. We pass each other on our way to the next stop, but there's never any time for the things that matter."

Out of the corner of her eye Alex saw the driver place her luggage outside the ticketing agent's. "I have to go, Matt."

"I know." He swore, then dragged her against him and kissed her, lingering over the kiss until she thought her heart would explode. "Dwayne Secord. Is he . . . important to you?"

"He's a friend, Matt. Just a good friend."

That was all he'd needed to hear. "Someday," he muttered against her lips, "we're going to find ourselves in the right place at the right time."

The door was abruptly opened by the driver, who helped Alex from the vehicle.

"Good-bye, Matt," she called breathlessly.

She allowed herself one final, quick glimpse of his handsome face before she disappeared inside the terminal.

"Morning, sweet lips." Buddy stepped through the doorway of Alex's suite at the Carlyle, then stopped short. "What's that you're wearing?"

Alex glanced down at the navy blazer and long navy skirt she'd chosen. "I thought you'd want me to look professional."

"Don't think," Buddy snapped. "Just do as you're told." He held up a plastic garment bag. "I had this made for you. I had to guess at your size. Let's see how it looks."

In her bedroom Alex stripped off her clothes and opened the garment bag, letting out a sigh of pleasure. For a moment she'd feared that Buddy might have been trying to change her image with a modern designer suit. Instead, the dress was a perfect replica of a forties gown. It was made of shimmering red crepe with a strapless top overlaid with red netting that buttoned to her throat. The sheer sleeves were long, with buttons at each cuff, and the long slender skirt fell to her ankles. The costume came complete with red strappy sandals and glittering red earrings that dangled just above her shoulders.

When she stepped out of her bedroom, she twirled around for Buddy's inspection.

"Well?"

"Now that, sweet lips, is high voltage." He helped her into a long hooded red velvet cape. "Let's go knock 'em dead."

As they settled themselves in the back seat of the limousine Alex said, "I've never worn anything this fine before. It feels so good next to my skin."

"Get used to the good life," Buddy said with a laugh. "From now on, all your stage costumes are going to be custom made. Now." Instantly the smile was gone; he was all business. "Let's talk about what you want to reveal in this interview."

"What do you mean?"

"I mean that you have to control the flow of information, sweet lips. Let's set some goals."

While Alex listened, Buddy outlined what he wanted her to say and how he wanted it said.

"The most important fact is your two-week engagement. You reveal where, when, for how long. And you insert that information into every sentence possible, so the locals know where they can see you. Got it?"

She nodded.

He withdrew a slip of paper from a folder and handed it to her. "This is the introduction they'll give you."

"You wrote this?"

He nodded.

"But how do you know they'll use it?"

"Because I'm a personal friend of the man who will be doing the interview."

She arched a brow. "Do you also know what he'll ask me?"

Buddy grinned. "Of course. I passed along a couple of things I thought the audience might like to know."

"Such as?"

"The sold-out concerts in Vegas. The chemistry between you and Dwayne Secord."

"But I—"

He held up a hand. "I've decided that you should refuse to answer anything at all about your relationship with Dwayne except to say that you're good friends."

"We are, but if I say that, they'll think I'm hiding something. Maybe I ought to—"

"I told you, sweet lips." His smile was still in place, but Alex had the distinct impression that Buddy was holding on to his temper by a thread. "Don't think. Just do as you're told. When he asks you about your relationship with Dwayne, just smile and say you're friends. If he asks you more than once, you say it more than once. Can you remember that?"

Alex nodded.

"Good." Buddy patted her hand as the limousine pulled up to the curb. As they walked into the studio, Alex found herself in a whole new world of hairdressers, makeup artists, TV technicians—and instant headlines.

"New York audiences are unlike anything else in the world." Dressed in a custom-tailored tuxedo, Gary handed his guitar to a stagehand and mopped his brow.

"Especially when they love you," Bear said with a grin. He loosened his bow tie and removed the restrictive cummerbund. "And bright eyes, they really love you."

Alex tilted up the bottle of Evian water and drained it. "I guess all those interviews are beginning to pay off. Did you notice there wasn't an empty seat in the house?"

"Come on," Casey said, nervously drumming his fingers on a backstage light panel, "Let's get out of these monkey suits and go eat. I'm starving."

"I wish I could join you." Alex trailed behind them toward their dressing rooms.

"Why can't you?"

"I have to be at the TV studio at six for a morning interview."

"Lucky you." Len ruffled her hair and gave her a

mock pained expression. "I'll think about you when I'm waking up around noon."

"Thanks, pal. Don't choke on all that good food."

Alone in her dressing room, Alex hung up her beaded gown and pulled on a robe. Looking in the mirror, she began to cream off her stage makeup. At a knock on the door she called, "Come in."

"You made Liz's column again," Buddy said, tossing down a newspaper.

Alex glanced at the article, which hinted at a sizzling romance between Dwayne Secord and the "hot new singer whose fabulous voice matches her fabulous face and has New Yorkers standing in line for hours." It was accompanied by a small photo of Alex.

"I told you a simple denial wouldn't work," Alex said as she stepped behind a screen to change into a sweater and jeans.

"Like hell it didn't work."

At Buddy's remark she straightened to stare at him over the screen.

"If I'd wanted to get out the truth, sweet lips, I would have issued a statement through my office."

"You mean you *wanted* them to believe all that stuff about a romance?"

"Exactly. Nothing like a few hot rumors to sell tickets."

"So what do I do about tomorrow's interview? Buddy, they won't even want to talk about my show. All they'll care about is Dwayne."

"Come on. Quit your worrying. That's my job." He grinned. "Like I keep telling you, don't think. Just do what I tell you. Let old Buddy run the show. I'm going to take you straight to the top, sweet lips."

22

"*The Rainbow Room* wants to hold you over for another two weeks."

At Buddy's announcement, Gary started to cheer, but he froze when Buddy added, "But I told them they were too late."

Alex and the band members were seated in Buddy's suite. The weekly meetings had become almost routine. Buddy had taken over every facet of their career, from costumes to interviews to hiring a road manager. Their money was handled by a team of financial advisors. No one made a decision without getting approval from Buddy.

"Did you line up another gig for us?" Gary asked.

"First things first." Buddy took a sip of Perrier and lime, clearly enjoying the bit of drama. "We're heading to Nashville next week, as soon as this thing's over."

"Where are we playing?" Bear asked.

"You're not. You're recording." He chuckled at the expressions on their faces. "Got your attention, huh?"

"What do you mean, we're recording?" Gary sat on the edge of his seat. "Recording what?"

"The California songs Alex wrote."

The group turned to Alex to find that she looked as surprised as they were.

"You didn't know about this?" Gary asked suspiciously.

"Not a thing." She turned to Buddy. "Do we have enough material for an album?"

"More than enough. I thought we'd do one side of your original tunes, and the flip side would be the classic oldies that have become your trademark."

"What about backup musicians?" Gary asked.

"Already got 'em. Some of the best in the business."

As he ticked off their names, Gary rose and began to prowl the room, mentally going over the enormity of the task before them. The others swiveled their heads from him to Buddy.

"How long do we have in the studio? This can't be hurried, Buddy. I want our first album to be perfect," Gary said.

"Take as long as you need. We all want it to be perfect," Buddy told him.

"Who's going to produce it?"

"Aaron Simons."

For a minute Gary couldn't find his voice. When he finally could speak he sputtered, "He's—he's the best there is. How'd you get him?"

"Connections," Buddy said simply. "He owes me."

"Whose label are we recording for?"

"We'll have our own label."

"Then who's going to distribute it?"

"Classic Records."

"My God. Video?"

"I'm negotiating with Howard Seal."

Gary found himself speechless. The names Buddy tossed out so casually were those of people at the very top of their field. Howard Seal had just directed the award-winning video for Dwayne Secord's last album.

"Publicity?" Gary demanded.

"I've already got people cranking up for publicity. Would you stop worrying, Gary? I'm on top of it. Here's the recording contract, with all the *i*'s dotted and the *t*'s crossed. All it needs now is your signatures."

Gary finally stopped his pacing. For the briefest moment he continued to frown. Then the frown turned into a wide smile, and he extended his hand to Buddy.

"Did you hear the man? He said he'd do it and he did. A recording contract, with Aaron Simons producing and Howard Seal directing the video." He took the contract from Buddy's hand and held it in the air. "This is what we dreamed about. He negotiated us a goddamn recording contract."

While Buddy watched, they crowded around Gary and exchanged high fives. Gary picked up Alex and swung her around until she was dizzy.

"I always knew the day we found you was the luckiest day of our lives," he cried.

When he set her on her feet, the others crowded around to hug her.

"What about the day you found me?" Buddy asked with a laugh.

"The second luckiest day. Buddy, you're a genius." Gary quickly read the documents and affixed his signature to them. Then he handed the contracts to the others to sign. "Where's your phone, Buddy? I have to call my wife with this news."

It occurred to Alex that Gary and Sara had come a long way in their relationship in the last few months. There had been a time when he wouldn't have even considered sharing such news with his wife until after he'd celebrated with the band. Now, thankfully, Sara was uppermost in his mind.

Everyone recognized the change in him. He'd mellowed. And his love for his wife was reflected in the glow in Sara's eyes these days. Clearly she'd never been happier.

In fact, none of them had ever known such happiness. Success was only a heartbeat away.

"Hold it, Alex. Take it again from the top."

Gary's command from the control room brought a moan from Alex in the studio. The musicians had spent weeks laying down the tracks; now it was time for her to record the vocals. Her frustration was growing with each interruption.

"Now what?" she demanded into the microphone.

"Your phrasing was garbled on that last one. Let's try it again. This time hold the note a beat longer, then slide into the chorus. One two, one two three," he said for emphasis.

Despite her frustration she nodded, sensing instinctively that Gary was right.

"On the count of three, Alex."

The music played through her headphones again and she began to sing. This time her phrasing was perfect, and she completed the song without interruption.

"That's it," Gary's voice boomed over the speaker. "Grab some tea and honey, and we'll try one more before we call it a night."

"No more," Alex protested. "I need some sleep."

"The tea will revive you. Let's go for one more."

She paused a moment, then gave a reluctant nod of her head.

Len came into the studio and handed her a steaming cup of tea. "That was great, Alex." He perched on the stool opposite hers. "Your voice has never sounded better."

"Thanks, Len. I hope you're right. This means so much to all of us. I don't want to let anybody down."

"You won't."

They looked up as Gary's voice came over the speakers.

"Alex, on this next song, I've been going over the words you wrote. When you sing 'never again, never lonely again,' I want to hear tears in your voice. Can you give me tears?"

Alex glanced at Len and the two of them exchanged a quick smile. Len remembered well the way the words had affected her the first time she'd ever sung them. She'd actually had to stop and pull herself together before going on.

"I think I can manage tears, Gary."

"Good girl. If you're ready, let's start."

She handed the empty cup to Len. He squeezed her hand before walking to the door.

Alex took her place at the microphone and waited while the music swelled through her earphones. Then she began to sing. As always, she forgot about everything except the haunting words she'd written, which had come from the darkest recesses of her heart.

Two hours later, as the Nashville skyline bled with a spectacular sunrise, she was still singing, and there was no sign of fatigue in her voice.

"God. I can't believe her face. It's so expressive. Look at this shot. And this one. The camera loves her."

Howard Seal watched the images with a critical eye. He was a small intense man of forty-eight who was never without his trademark baseball cap. After directing two successful feature-length movies, he'd agreed to direct a music video as a favor to Buddy Holbrook. That video had won a prestigious American Music Award, and overnight his focus had shifted. Now he was in such demand as a video director, he had to turn down more offers than he could accept.

"I like this one." Buddy squinted at the screen. "Can you hold it a minute?"

At a signal from Howard the film was halted, freezing the image on screen. Alex, in a sheer white gown, stood beside a sagging wood fence. In her hand was a wide-brimmed picture hat with streamers flying in the breeze.

"That's it," Buddy murmured. "That's the image we want to project. Soft, romantic. Everybody's fantasy woman. Okay, let's see more."

Howard signaled and the film began rolling. While she sang of lost love and a broken heart, she walked across a rolling meadow alive with wildflowers toward a half burned farmhouse, and beyond, a grave on a windswept hill. As the music swelled to its conclusion, she knelt and touched a finger to the simple wooden cross, then placed a bouquet of wildflowers on the grave. A close-up revealed a single tear rolling down her cheek.

Then she turned, and a handsome man could be seen crossing the meadow. Her face was alive with emotion as she flew into his arms and was lifted high, then brought down for a long, passionate kiss.

After the screen went blank, the two men continued to sit and stare.

At last Buddy got to his feet and extended his hand to the director. "You've done it, Howard. I've got that tingling I always get when I've just seen something special. It's a winner."

"I hope so," Howard said with a laugh. "I worked Alex and the band members until I thought they'd drop. They deserve an award just for putting up with my temper."

"Don't worry. I've got a feeling they're going to go right to the top of the charts with this."

"When is the release date?"

Buddy smiled. "Two weeks. But the buildup starts now."

"I think you've earned a break." Buddy made the announcement over dinner. "The album's ready to be released. The video is complete. The P.R. Firm is geared up for a barrage of publicity. This will be your last chance to cut loose before you start the big European tour."

Alex secretly rejoiced, thinking about the letter in her pocket. In his latest missive, Kip had sounded especially lonely and blue. She'd been hoping for a chance to visit him in South Dakota. All she wanted to do was hold him and hug him and see for herself that he was all right.

Her thoughts were interrupted by Buddy's voice. "Alex, you and I have to leave for New York in the morning."

"New York. Why?"

"Remember the designer who made your gowns for your gig at the Rainbow Room, and the costumes for the videos?"

She nodded.

"She's designed your whole wardrobe for Europe. Everything's ready. But she's been working with a dressmaker's form. Now she needs you to go through final fittings."

"I need a couple of days first."

"Why? Where do you want to go?"

"South Dakota."

He looked at her like she'd just said she wanted to go to the moon. "What's in South Dakota?"

"My little brother."

"Is that all? I'll fly him up to be with you in New York."

"It's not that simple."

"Why?"

Alex's mind raced. "He's—in school."

"So tell your folks to let him miss a couple of days."

"My folks are . . . I don't have any folks. He lives with an aunt and uncle. And they wouldn't understand or approve."

"Neither do I. You can't spare a couple of days right now. If he can't come up to New York, you'll just have to leave for Europe without seeing him."

"Buddy, I haven't seen him in almost a year."

"So ask him to send a picture."

"I miss him. I need to see him. And he needs to see me."

He was about to argue but the look in her eyes stopped him. Damned if she didn't look like she was going to break down and cry. It wasn't that he had a soft heart, he told himself. He just didn't want to see her use up so much emotion. She needed to save it for the tour.

"One day," he growled.

She shook her head. "Two."

"Two days, one night. That's it. You can leave in the morning. I'll expect you in Manhattan by Wednesday night. I'll have my secretary make all the arrangements."

Alex went around the table and leaned down to kiss his cheek. "Thanks, Buddy. You won't regret letting me go to see my brother."

"I already do."

He watched glumly as she hurried off to pack.

$\overline{23}$

From the air the land looked forbidding, uninhabitable. Alex shivered. Badlands National Park looked like a view of another world. The mighty Missouri River cut across the land like a jagged scar.

As the plane dropped lower, Alex could make out lone farms, small towns, and gradually, wide highways, church steeples, here and there a cluster of houses. Though it seemed so far removed from the life they'd shared, this was where Kip lived now. She was determined to spend this brief time learning to love and accept it.

By the time the plane had landed at the Sioux Falls airport and the passengers were departing, her palms were sweating. She made her way through the terminal, peering around expectantly. And then she saw him. Her heart began beating wildly.

"Kip! Oh, Kip."

They fell into each other's arms and clung tightly to each other.

"Oh, let me look at you," she murmured, holding him a little away. "You've grown so tall. Why, you must have grown a foot since I saw you."

"Two inches. I know 'cause Aunt Bernice had to let down my jeans as far as they'd go."

They were still too short. His clothes looked threadbare and shabby. She touched a hand to his fiery hair, which badly needed trimming, and traced a finger over the freckles that dusted his nose. He was so thin. But maybe that was part of growing up. Maybe she was looking for things that weren't there. She would concentrate, instead, on everything positive.

"Oh, it's so good to finally see you."

She hugged him fiercely, and he returned the embrace.

"Let's go, girl," Uncle Vince said, standing to one side to allow people to pass. "Your aunt stayed home so there'd be supper ready when we got there. Let's not keep her waiting."

With one arm still around Kip, she extended her hand to her uncle. "Hello, Uncle Vince."

Vince shook her hand, then turned away to pick up her overnight bag. He walked on ahead with it, and she and Kip followed, their fingers linked.

"I'm so glad you were able to miss school to meet me," Alex muttered.

"Me too. It caused an awful fight," Kip whispered.

She shot him a worried look. "I'm sorry, Kip. I didn't want you to get into any trouble on my account."

"It doesn't matter." He squeezed her hand hard. "They're always fighting about something anyway. And when they're not fighting with each other, they're fighting with me."

Vince turned around to scowl at Alex. "What are you two whispering about?"

"Just catching up. We've missed so much," Alex said, drawing her little brother close.

They stowed Alex's bag on the front seat of Vince's car and she and Kip climbed into the back. Soon they had left the city behind. The car sped past mile after mile of farmland; nearly two hours had passed before they turned up a wide dirt lane and pulled up in front of an old two-story frame house.

"This is it," Vince announced. "What do you think of our neck of the woods?"

"It's—so much bigger than I'd expected. There's so much land."

Despite the fact that the house was square and ugly, with peeling paint and shingles missing from the roof, the fields around it were vast and beautiful. It looked like something from a picture postcard, with snow dusting the neatly laid out fields and the big modern barns and outbuildings which looked as if they'd been added recently. "You must be a very successful farmer, Uncle Vince."

He gave a rumble of laughter. "That's what my neighbors have been saying lately." Then he seemed to catch himself and the smile disappeared, replaced by a frown. "I do all right," he muttered before getting out of the car.

Alex retrieved her bag from the front seat, then caught Kip's arm. "Wait," she said. Slipping a camera from her purse she said, "I'd like to take some pictures."

She snapped several photographs of Kip standing beside the car, then several more of him on the front porch.

"Are you coming?" her uncle said.

"Would you mind taking a picture of the two of us?" She handed the camera to her uncle.

He snapped several pictures of her and Kip standing together, their arms linked.

"That's enough," he said. "Let's get in out of the cold."

Inside, the smell of a roast in the oven mingled with the scent of the freshly baked cherry pies that had been left to cool on the kitchen counter. Aunt Bernice came through the doorway, wiping her hands on her apron.

"You're late," she said accusingly.

"Plane was delayed," her husband said. "Girl, come greet your aunt."

"Hello, Aunt Bernice." Alex crossed the room to kiss her.

The woman stiffly offered her cheek, then stepped back. "You'll sleep in the spare room tonight." She pointed to the stairway and added, "Kip will show you the way. We'll eat in an hour. That probably seems early to you, but here on a farm we eat at five and turn out the lights by nine."

"And we're up with the chickens," Uncle Vince added.

"Come on." Kip started up the stairs, and Alex followed. "There aren't any chickens," he said as he led the way. "Uncle Vince just likes to say things like that to impress people."

"Impress them?"

"That he's a farmer."

He opened a door and turned on the light. Though the room was sparsely furnished with an ancient four-poster bed and an old dresser with an oval mirror, it was made warmer by the rag rug on the hardwood floor.

"He isn't, you know."

Alex dropped her bag onto the bed. "Isn't what?"

"A farmer."

"What do you mean?" She crossed the room to stare out the window. For as far as she could see, there were only the snow-dusted fields, and far off in the distance, a small house. "Isn't all this land Uncle Vince's?"

Kip came to stand beside her. "It is now. But my friend Paul told me that Uncle Vince had the poorest farm around these parts until this year, when he started buying up all the land around him. Then he hired a tenant farmer to do the work. Uncle Vince doesn't do anything except run to the mailbox every day and study the papers his lawyer sends."

Her brother lowered his voice. "Paul said Uncle Vince boasted to his dad that he'd found a little gold mine, and as long as it keeps on producing gold, he'll never have to lift a finger again."

Alex remained very still for several moments, digesting what Kip had told her. It made sense, of course. The sale of Nanna's land, and the insurance benefits for a ten-year-old boy. Still, as long as her aunt and uncle were providing a home for Kip, they deserved the money. She had no right to argue with the way they invested it.

"Come here," she said, drawing her little brother close for another hug. "Oh," she whispered against his hair, "you feel so good, Kip. I've missed you so much."

"You have? You really miss me?"

His question was so earnest she drew him away to stare into his eyes. "Why would you even have to ask such a thing?"

"'Cause Aunt Bernice and Uncle Vince said you were having too much fun to bother writing or calling."

"But I write you every week. And I phone every Sunday night." She saw the disbelief in his eyes. "Haven't you received my letters?"

He shrugged. "I got one a month ago."

A month. And she had written faithfully every week. "And the phone calls? Didn't they tell you about them either?"

He shook his head.

"Oh Kip. I missed you every day that we've been apart. Sometimes I missed you so much I cried."

"Yeah. Me too," he admitted sheepishly. "But Aunt Bernice said if she caught me ever crying again, she'd give me something to really cry about."

Alex felt a ferocious anger slice through her like a knife. But, she cautioned herself, she had to be careful. Though she could escape Vince and Bernice's hostility tomorrow, Kip would be forced to remain and endure.

"You listen to me," she said, drawing him down to sit next to her on the edge of the bed. "No matter what I do or where I go, I will write you every week. And even if I don't manage to reach you, I'll keep on trying to call. No matter what they tell you, you have to remember that I love you, Kip. And that is never going to change. As soon as I'm of age, you're coming to live with me. That's a solemn promise."

They looked up as Uncle Vince's voice bellowed from the bottom of the stairway, "Chow time. Come and eat."

She took her brother's hand, and they went slowly down the stairs.

"I don't suppose you get much chance to eat good

home cooking," Uncle Vince said as he carved the roast.

"No." Alex sipped her water.

"Ask your brother what a good cook your Aunt Bernice is."

Kip dutifully nodded. "She makes good food, Alex."

"It's plain," Aunt Bernice said, her mouth pursed into a pout. "Probably not what you're used to in those places you work."

"You wear one of those skimpy costumes?" Uncle Vince asked as he dropped a slice of beef on Alex's plate.

"I wear dresses."

"Like that thing you wore to your grandmother's funeral?" Aunt Bernice seemed suddenly animated. She clearly enjoyed herself when she had the chance to attack.

"Uncle Vince said you were singing in a bar," Kip said, his food forgotten.

"I'm singing with a band. We just recorded our first album, in Nashville."

"Really?" Her little brother's eyes lit with new enthusiasm.

Alex nodded. "It'll be released in another week. At the same time we start our European tour."

His voice took on a worried note. "You're going to Europe?"

Alex saw a look pass between her aunt and uncle.

"How long will you be gone?" Kip asked anxiously.

"Six months."

"How will you be able to call me from there?"

"They have telephones, just like here. Don't worry. I'll still be able to call you."

"Won't that cost a lot of money?" Bernice asked.

"I'll manage."

"If you're making enough money to waste it on phone calls from Europe, I think you ought to contribute something to your brother's keep. For your information, missy, it costs a lot of money these days to raise a boy."

Alex bit back the angry words that she longed to hurl at her aunt. When she thought about the sale of Nanna's beloved property, and the insurance benefits they were receiving, as Kip's guardians, from her father's death, she wanted to cry out at the injustice of it. It was obvious that the money wasn't going for the care of her little brother. She came to an abrupt decision. As soon as she left here, she would call her uncle's lawyer. In order to avoid suspicion she merely took a deep breath and said, "I'll see what I can manage."

Bernice pushed herself away from the table and returned with slices of cherry pie topped with ice cream. She saved the biggest pieces for herself and her husband.

"Bet you won't taste anything as good as this over on the other side of the world," Uncle Vince boasted.

Alex took a bite and forced a smile to her lips. "It's wonderful, Aunt Bernice."

The woman gave no sign that she'd heard the compliment.

When supper was finished, Bernice shoved back her chair. "I hope now that you're a big-deal singer you don't think you've become too important to wash dishes and clean up after a meal."

"Of course not. Kip and I will do the dishes."

Without another word Bernice followed her husband to the living room, where they turned on the TV to watch the news.

"I always do the dishes," Kip said when they were in the kitchen. "It's one of my chores."

"What are some of your other chores?" Alex filled the sink with soap and hot water and began to stack the dishes.

"I have to milk the cows before I go to school, but that's not hard. There are only two dozen, and I like the cows." He lowered his voice. "I talk to them sometimes. I think they like it when I do."

Alex smiled as she washed the dishes and handed them to him to dry.

"This isn't a dairy farm." Kip seemed proud of his newly acquired knowledge. "It's a wheat farm. So Uncle Vince says we'll be a lot busier in the spring, when we'll be plowing and planting. The truth is, Uncle Vince won't be doing any of that. The tenant farmer does everything, and Uncle Vince said I'd be helping him in the spring. But for now, I just have to help Aunt Bernice around the house."

"I'm glad. When we finally get a house together, Squirt, you'll be able to lend a hand in the kitchen. The truth is," Alex added with a laugh, "I'll need all the help I can get. Since I've been on the road, I think I've forgotten how to boil water."

"What's it like on the road, Alex?"

She told him about the hotels and casinos where they'd stayed, and about the guys in the band, and about Sara and little Corey. Long after the kitchen had been cleaned and the dishes put away, she continued to regale him with stories about all she'd seen and done.

They were both surprised to see Vince standing in the doorway. "We're going to bed now," he announced. "I think you'd better do the same. We start morning chores early here." He started to leave but then turned back. "What time is your plane tomorrow?"

"Three o'clock."

He studied Kip, seated beside his sister, and said, "Your aunt and I still think you ought to go to school in the morning. But against our better judgment, we've decided to allow you to miss another day so you can see your sister off."

"Thanks, Uncle Vince," Alex said through gritted teeth. Her uncle was making no attempt to hide his true feelings about her visit. Nor was Aunt Bernice. But for Kip's sake, she had to keep a lid on her anger.

Still Vince remained in the doorway. "Are you going up to bed now?"

"We'll go up in a little while," Alex said. "There's so much to catch up on, we'd like a little more time."

"We don't take kindly to having our sleep disturbed."

"We'll be quiet."

Alex waited until he'd left before glancing at her brother. "Is he always so grumpy?"

"Sometimes he isn't so bad," Kip whispered. "Especially if he's just talked to his lawyer. But most of the time he's mean."

Alex felt a rush of fear. "Has he ever hurt you?"

Kip looked away, but not before she saw the anguish in his eyes. "I can take care of myself," he said. After a moment he caught her hand. "I know that Uncle Vince and Aunt Bernice don't really want me. So why did they insist on bringing me here?"

"I don't know. Maybe Uncle Vince thought it was his duty to his dead brother. Or maybe they just feel guilty about the way they treated Nanna for all those years."

But in the back of her mind was a nagging doubt. Why had they brought Kip here? And what did the California lawyer have to do with their acquisition of new land?

Determined to put the smile back on her little brother's face, Alex again started telling Kip stories about her journeys with the band. They remained at the kitchen table, whispering and giggling, until nearly midnight. At last, when they were both yawning, they made their way upstairs.

Outside his room she drew her brother close and whispered, "Good night, Kip. I'll see you in the morning. Remember, I want you to wake me in time to help you with your chores."

As she climbed into her bed, Alex knew that her uncle would be only too happy to sound the wake-up call at dawn. She regretted that she'd kept her little brother up so late. But though he'd probably have to struggle through his morning chores, it was worth it just to see the smile on his face while they'd been together.

Holding on to the thought, she drifted off to sleep.

It wasn't Kip who suffered through the dawn chores, it was Alex. In the past year, the only chance she'd had to see this time of the day was when she was going to bed. The thought of getting dressed in the chilly darkness and making her way to the barn with her brother was pure punishment. But, she told herself, if a ten-year-old could do it, so could she.

She stood with her hands in her pockets while Kip hooked up the milking machines. It made her smile to watch her little brother call the cows by name and talk to them. Was it her imagination, or did the cows actually respond to his voice? When the milking was over, she helped Kip wash the machinery.

"If this were spring," Uncle Vince explained over a breakfast of eggs, potatoes, and hearty slabs of beef, "we'd be out in the fields by this time, getting ready for planting."

Under his breath, Kip whispered, "He means I'd be out in the fields. He's still be in his robe and slippers."

The two shared a grin.

"So," their uncle continued, unaware of their private joke, "it's lucky you came when there wasn't much to do."

She wanted to ask him why he never helped a little boy with the chores, but she held her silence and watched as her aunt removed a batch of biscuits from the oven. The aroma of cinnamon filled the air.

"Nanna used to bake these," Alex said as she broke one open and spread it with butter. "Remember, Kip?"

"Yeah." He drained his milk. "Whenever I smell this I think of Christmas at Nanna's."

"You drew a picture of her baking. I still have it," Alex said. "I wish you'd draw something for me before I leave."

Kip ducked his head but was unable to hide the pain in his eyes.

"He doesn't have time for such nonsense anymore," Aunt Bernice said quickly. "We're plain people. We don't have to put on airs and pretend to be something we're not."

Alex stared at her aunt in surprise. "How can you say such a thing? Kip is an artist."

"Don't fill his head with nonsense. He's not an artist. He's not going to get any special favors around here. We're simple people. And we won't allow him to start thinking of himself as anything special." Her gaze pinned the little boy. "Since you aren't going to school today, you can get busy on the rest of your chores."

"Yes, ma'am." Kip stood up, went to the closet for his jacket, and fled.

When Alex made a move to follow, her aunt said, "Just a minute, young lady. Your uncle and I would like a word with you."

She sat back down, glancing from one to the other.

"I don't know why you came here, girl," Uncle Vince said. He sipped his coffee. His tone was casual, as if he were discussing the weather. "Your aunt and I have already informed our lawyer about your visit, just in case you have any bright ideas about grabbing the boy."

Grabbing Kip? She couldn't hide her astonishment.

"I came for a visit," Alex said. Her hands were curled into such tight fists in her lap, her nails were biting into her palms. "I miss my little brother. He's all the family I have left. I didn't come to stir up trouble."

"That's good. Just remember it for the future. Because if you do intend to stir up trouble, girl, you'll discover that you've picked up a hornet's nest. Remember that paper you signed at the motel? It was a document waiving all rights to guardianship."

"That's a lie. I never would have signed such a thing. I read it. It declared you executor of Nanna's will."

"Not the second page," Vince said smugly. Seeing her shocked look he added with mock sorrow, "Oh, did I tell you they were both copies of the same document? Sorry. I lied." Alex saw something dark and feral glitter in her uncle's eyes. "My lawyer has those documents, with your valid signatures, in a safe place."

Abruptly he shoved back his chair. Bernice's eyes gleamed with undisguised hostility as she too rose, and without another word they left Alex alone in the room.

If she had expected a truce, she'd been wrong. By their words and actions, her aunt and uncle had made it perfectly clear that they considered themselves at war—and Alex was the enemy.

On the ride to the airport Kip was silent, though he sat as close to his sister as he could. She draped an arm protectively around his shoulders and drew him to her. "I didn't realize how hard it would be to leave," she murmured.

"Maybe you could stay a few more days."

She shook her head. "I have my work. Besides, you have to get back to school. Have you made many friends here?"

"A couple. There's Paul. He's got six sisters. He's the only boy, so he and his father do a lot of things together. His folks are nice to me."

Alex shuddered. Her little brother was crying out for affection, for the warmth of a family. She closed her eyes and drew the boy even closer. In the front seat, Vince and Bernice had given up all pretence at civility.

"Here we are." It was the first time either her aunt or uncle had spoken a word to Alex since their discussion at breakfast, and for the first time since her arrival, Vince sounded almost cheerful.

Alex and her little brother got out and walked slowly toward the airport terminal. The closer they got, the slower they walked.

"I love you, Kip." Alex touched a hand to his hair, loving the silky softness of it against her palm.

"I love you, too, Alex."

"Remember. No matter what, I'll write every week and call every Sunday."

He nodded, fighting tears. "Will it be a year until I see you again?"

"Don't be silly." She bit her lip to keep it from quivering. "But however long we're apart, know that I love you."

"I love you too, Alex," he said again.

"And you mustn't believe what Aunt Bernice and Uncle Vince are telling you. You are special. And someday, when we're together again, I'm going to prove it to you. Do you believe me?"

The little boy nodded tentatively.

The boarding announcement for Alex's flight was made. Drawing Kip into her arms, she hugged him fiercely. Vince and Bernice stood together, their eyes hard, their arms crossed over their chests, watching as she released him and picked up her bag.

A wall, Alex thought. A solid wall, built of their hatred, which they intended to use to keep her and her brother apart. But why?

Vince offered a smug smile. "Good-bye, girl."

She chanced a last glance at Kip, then turned quickly away.

As the plane lifted off the runway, Alex peered through her window. Blinking back the tears she'd been fighting, she watched a car move along the highway and wondered if it was Uncle Vince's.

When she thought about the farmhouse surrounded by vast expanses of wheat fields, she should experience a sense of relief that Kip was safe. It should have been the perfect place to raise a frightened boy who'd lost so many loved ones in his young life. But she had come away with a feeling of desperation. There was something sinister about how determined Vince and Bernice were to have Kip at any cost. Why? They were completely incapable of giving him the things that mattered most. There was no warmth, no love in their house. And without those things, a sensitive boy like Kip would wither and die. How much longer could he endure?

She renewed her vow, more fervently than ever: on the day she turned twenty-one, she would be back to claim her brother. Nothing would ever keep them apart again. For now, she would contact her uncle's lawyer and let him know that she was aware of the documents she'd been tricked into signing, and that she intended to regain custody of Kip.

24

Alex's visit to New York was a whirlwind of interviews, public appearances, and costume fittings. From the moment she stepped off the plane, she was thrust into the glare of publicity. Buddy had very carefully laid the groundwork for the kind of media frenzy that would promote both their album and their international tour.

What he hadn't counted on was the controversy.

A young backup singer in Dwayne Secord's band had announced publicly that she was carrying his baby. And then she'd dropped the bombshell: they'd talked of marriage until Alex had come between them. Now, she claimed, Dwayne was denying any knowledge of her or the baby because of his obsessive attraction to Alex.

Alex's photo appeared on the front page of every tabloid and magazine, and the gossip was repeated on every radio and TV news program and talk show. The whole world was reading about Alexandra Corday, who, along with her band, Whispers, was thought to be the brightest new star on the horizon.

"Oh, Buddy. Why did this have to happen now?"

Buddy patted her hand. "That's the way life is, sweet lips. Always throwing us a curve when we least expect it." He helped her from the limousine and walked with her into the television studios where she was to tape another interview.

"You know what they'll want to talk about. How can I steer the conversation away from Dwayne?"

"You can't. I've told you before. Simply tell the truth. Tell them that you didn't know anything about this relationship between Dwayne and his backup singer, and then go on to other topics. Talk about the album, about the European tour, about the songs you're working on for your second album."

They entered the green room, where Alex began to pace back and forth. "But I feel like I'm letting you and the guys in the band down."

He put his hands on her shoulders, stilling her movements, and turned her to face him. "You could never let us down, sweet lips. You've done nothing wrong. You've got nothing to hide. You know it and I know it. But you have to develop the attitude that you don't care what the rest of the world thinks, as long as you know you're right."

He could see that she was mulling over his words.

"You're right, Buddy. And that's just what I'm going to do. I'm just going to have to develop a thicker skin."

"Good girl." Lifting her chin he murmured, "Now let me see that thousand-watt smile."

An assistant producer entered and summoned Alex to makeup.

"Thanks, Buddy." She brushed his cheek with her lips. "I needed that little pep talk." With her smile in place she walked away.

When he was alone, Buddy chose the most comfortable chair in the room. He removed a cigar from his pocket and held a lighter to the tip. Leaning back, he started to chuckle.

When Dwayne had come to him with his little problem, Buddy had agreed to handle it. But what had begun as a simple one-night stand between a famous singer and a member of his band had snowballed into angry words and a need for revenge. When the backup singer had hurled Alex's name in her angry tirade, Buddy's antennae had picked it up immediately.

"What's Alex got to do with this thing between you and Dwayne?" Buddy had asked her.

"After she came along, Dwayne never looked at me again," the singer had sniffed. "But I know how to fix them both. I'm going public with my story. I'll ruin both their reputations."

Buddy knew he could have bought her silence. For almost sixty seconds, he'd even considered it. But all his years in the public eye had taught him the cardinal rule of advertising: it doesn't matter what they say about you, as long as they spell your name correctly.

He was sorry that Alex and Dwayne had to suffer such notoriety, but the truth was, they were enjoying the kind of publicity no amount of money could have bought.

How much luckier could he get? With the media leaping on every rumor, he had no doubt that the album would go double platinum. And the tour was a guaranteed sellout.

Just as Buddy had predicted, as the time for the tour drew near, the album was selling out all across the country, and the ticket sales for their concerts had sky-rocketed.

"You're going to need an assistant," Buddy remarked casually to Alex. "We're doing dozens of cities in six different countries. You'll need someone to pack, to keep your wardrobe in good repair between shows, someone who can even help with your hair and makeup. I've asked my secretary to supply you with a list of women we've worked with in the past."

As he handed Alex the list he saw the way her eyes lit up. "What is it, sweet lips?"

"I think I know the perfect person. How much can we pay her?"

"Two hundred dollars a day. But she has to guarantee us the full six months of the tour," he cautioned. "We don't want someone taking off in the middle of an important gig and leaving us to scramble for a replacement."

Glancing at her watch, Alex mentally calculated the time difference and rushed to the phone to dial her old number in L.A. After six rings a sleepy voice answered. "Yeah? Hello?"

"Tina?"

"Un-huh." Unable to recognize the voice through the fog that still clouded her brain, she muttered, "This had better be important enough for you to wake me at five in the morning."

"Well," Alex said, laughing, "if this is Christina Theopholis, hairdresser to the stars, then it may be the most important call you'll get all year."

"Alex? Is that you? What's wrong? What's happened? Oh my God! It's about that singer, Dwayne Secord, isn't it? I've been reading all about you and him. Alex, you can tell me. Are you all right?"

"Yes, it's me. And nothing's wrong. This isn't about Dwayne, although I'll tell you all about him when I see you. Right now, my agent wants to hire an assistant for me, someone who can pack between shows, keep my wardrobe in good repair, and"—she couldn't control the laughter that bubbled in her throat—"do my hair and makeup."

"Holy shit. Are you offering me a job?"

"Why else would I call you at this time of the morning? Buddy says he'll pay you two hundred dollars a day for six months."

"That's . . . wait, let me find a pen and some paper." After a minute she yelled into the phone, "That's thirty-six thousand dollars! Alex, I don't even make that for a whole year."

"So is that a yes?"

"Yes, yes, *yes!*" She was screaming so loud Alex had to hold the phone away from her ear. "When do you want me?"

"How soon can you be in New York?"

"How about this weekend?"

"Perfect. We leave for Europe early next week. I'll have Buddy's secretary call you with the information about all the documents you'll need. What'll you do about the apartment?"

"Looks like my roommate will finally be able to let

her boyfriend move in. We've been fighting about it for months. Now the problem is solved peacefully." There was a pause. Then Tina said softly, "God, Alex. I can't believe this is happening."

"I know. Neither can I. See you this weekend."

"Yeah. 'Bye."

Alex hung up the phone and turned to Buddy. "Looks like I've just hired an assistant."

Alex and Tina enjoyed a warm reunion, staying up all night to laugh, cry, and exchange gossip. Tina had a million questions about Alex's heartthrob, Dwayne Secord, and dozens of hilarious stories about the rich and famous who had begun to visit the salon where she worked.

"This job will put me over the top," she said, drinking her fourth cup of coffee. "When we get back from Europe, I'll have enough money saved to open my own shop. And the publicity should have them standing in line to see Alex Corday's hairdresser."

"I thought you were going to be known as hairdresser to the stars."

"I was. But I have a feeling your name is going to be so big, it will open all the doors I need opened."

Alex glanced at the clock on her night table. "Speaking of doors, you do realize Buddy will be knocking on ours very soon now. How are we ever going to face that plane ride in a few hours?"

"Don't worry. You can sleep all the way to London."

"I'm too keyed up."

Tina laughed. "Yeah. Me too. Want to try to grab a few hours of sleep, or should we start packing?"

Alex grinned. "Let's pack. I couldn't even think about sleeping right now."

They were running on pure adrenaline. Alex was amazed by the enormity of their undertaking, but while she fretted over costumes, music, and the vitamins she would need to sustain her energy through the strenuous tour, Tina calmly took control and organized everything.

"Great costumes." Tina secured the gowns and matching accessories in plastic bags, then tagged each one so that they could be easily identified.

Alex shot her friend a smile. "It's a long way from the secondhand shop where I used to buy my clothes in L.A. Buddy hired a seamstress who's worked for him before."

"I'm impressed. She's almost as good as me."

At a rap on the door Alex hurried across the room to admit Buddy, followed by a uniformed bellman.

"Everything ready to go?" Buddy asked.

Tina nodded and indicated the six enormous upright suitcases on wheels that held everything they would need for the tour.

"You two look like you didn't get much sleep."

Tina and Alex exchanged grins.

"We had a lot of catching up to do," Alex explained.

"Come on." Buddy steered them from the room and ushered them down to the waiting limousine. "It's a good thing I booked everybody first class. Once we take off, I think it's going to be lights out."

On the plane, Alex buckled her seat belt and settled back. The thought of what awaited her at the end of the journey had her heart racing. She knew she was far too excited to ever be able to sleep, but at least she wasn't the only one. Gary and Sara were trying to amuse Corey, who was uncharacteristically silent. Casey was drumming his fingers on the tray table. Bear was devouring a bag of doughnuts. Jeremy had been staring at a page in the airline magazine for ten minutes without turning the page, and Len had opened his briefcase and was busy arranging and rearranging his sheet music. All were clearly fighting nerves. It was the last coherent thought Alex had before sleep overtook her.

The customs officials at Gatwick were polite and efficient. The weary travelers were quickly whisked away by train and deposited at a plush hotel in the heart of London.

After only a few hours of rest, Buddy accompanied them to their first interview, during which Alex found herself once more answering questions about her romance with Dwayne Secord. Standing off to one side, Buddy could hardly contain his smile. As he'd hoped, news of the scandal had preceded them, assuring that the concert would be a sellout.

When the interview ended, Buddy took Alex's arm. "Come on, sweet lips. We'll pick up the others and spend the rest of the day taking in the sights."

That night, as the lights of London came on, they retired to their rooms, content to order room service and retire early. They had managed to take in Big Ben, Westminster Abbey, the changing of the guard at Buckingham Palace, and the Crown Jewels in the Tower of London.

Too tired to even finish her meal, Alex shook her

head in wonder. She was actually in London. And tomorrow night, she would be performing in front of a sold-out house. If the rumors were to be believed, several members of royalty would be in attendance.

She went to the window of her hotel room to stare at the scene below. None of this seemed real. Maybe it was the fact that she was so far from home, or maybe it was just the exhaustion of the trip. For whatever reason, she found herself thinking about the tiny house in L.A., and Nanna and Kip.

"Oh Nanna," she whispered, feeling the sting of tears. "Sometimes it's so overwhelming. I wish you could be here, just to get me over the first-night jitters. And more important, to share all this with me."

Almost at once she experienced a feeling of peace. Her nerves were forgotten. They were all sharing this with her—not only Nanna, but her father and mother too. And she had no doubt that soon Kip would be sharing her life as well. Her conversation with her uncle's lawyer had calmed her. He'd promised full cooperation. Climbing into bed, she fell into a peaceful, dreamless sleep.

"I understand you have received dozens of marriage proposals since the start of your tour." The pretty German journalist thrust a microphone in front of Alex's face as she passed through customs.

"That's right."

"Will you consider any of them?"

Alex merely smiled. She had learned the art of dealing with such questions. They really required no response.

"What do you think of our country?"

It was another absurd question, since she'd just stepped off a plane. But she gave the requisite answer: "It's so beautiful from the air. I can't wait to see everything."

"Did you know that Gunther Mueller, the handsome star of our most popular soap opera, has offered to give you a guided tour?"

"How wonderful. I can't wait to meet him." Alex felt Buddy's tug on her elbow and kept her smile in place. "Excuse me. I'm afraid I must be going."

"Our camera crew is going along. Your fans are hungry for every detail of the time you spend here with us."

With a sigh Alex allowed herself to be led away to a limousine, where more reporters were waiting.

It was the same in Ireland and Scotland, the Netherlands and France. Though the languages were different, the enthusiasm and warm welcome were the same everywhere they went.

With each stop along the tour, Alex felt the outpouring of love, of friendship. For the first time she realized that there were no barriers in music. It was the bridge between cultures, between languages, between people. When she sang, she touched the hearts of everyone. When they cheered her, they touched her in the same way.

"I can't believe how much you've all grown and changed in this business," Buddy said as they met in his suite. "You've learned how to relate to each individual audience, how to handle a difficult interview, how to reach out to the whole world. In just six months you've come so far."

"And I can't believe this is the end of our tour." Alex stood by the window, staring at the Paris street scene far below. "When do we leave for home?"

"That's why I called you here," Buddy said.

Alex turned. Everyone sat up a little straighter.

"Don't tell us you've added a couple more cities to the tour," Gary said. He thought of the promise he'd made to Sara to look for a house with a yard for Corey. As the group had matured as entertainers, he and Sara had matured in their relationship. They'd learned how to make concessions, how to deal with the stress of a baby in their lives and the demands of the road. Where once he'd only been playing house, leaving the vexing problems behind while he pursued his goals, now Gary felt totally committed to the woman he'd married. He was finally learning how to merge his professional and personal lives.

"No. No more cities. You'll be going home in the morning, just like you'd planned." Buddy sipped his Perrier and lime and glanced at Alex. "But I thought you and I could make a little detour."

She waited, knowing how Buddy loved adding his little touch of drama to every announcement.

"How would you like to see the South of France before you fly home?" he asked.

"Buddy, the only thing I want to see is *home*."

"But Cannes is swarming with famous actors, actresses, directors, and producers right now. It's the Cannes Film Festival, sweet lips. And several of those directors, who happen to be personal friends of mine, have asked to meet you."

He saw the light that came into her eyes and quickly pressed his advantage. "I don't think you want to pass up an opportunity like this—unless, of course, you're so homesick you can't put off seeing the good old U.S. of A. for another minute."

"How long?" she asked.

"A couple of days. A week at the most."

"You promise no more than a week?"

"Or two."

She thought about protesting, but the chance to meet famous actors and actresses at the Cannes Film Festival was too great a temptation to pass up.

"Okay." She turned back to the window and gazed out. "I guess I can force myself to enjoy all this a little while longer."

Alex stood inside the airport terminal, watching her fellow musicians mill about waiting for their boarding announcement. She'd planned to say her good-byes at the hotel, but when the time had come she found she couldn't bear to be separated from them yet, so at the last minute she'd changed her mind and accompanied them to the airport.

Giggling, Corey raced from the stroller she'd been busy pushing to her father, who scooped her up in his arms.

"It seems like only yesterday that she was barely toddling," Alex said.

"And look at her now." Gary settled the little girl on his shoulders, to her delight. "Do you realize how much I would have missed if she and Sara were still living with my parents?"

"I'll always be grateful to you, Alex, " Sara said, and squeezed her hand. "If it weren't for you, Gary and I would be strangers. Instead, we've grown closer than ever."

"Why are you thanking me?"

"In a moment of truth, Gary told me everything. How he'd almost—turned to you in his loneliness. And how you'd suggested that he needed Corey and me with him, even though it might be difficult raising a baby on the road."

Alex shrugged off a twinge of embarrassment. "I'm just glad it's all worked out for you."

"There were times I had my doubts." Gary put his arm around his wife's shoulders, and Sara hugged him. "But we both figured if it didn't work out, we'd just blame it all on you."

They all laughed, and Alex hugged them before turning toward the others.

Len's dark eyes peered at her through his thick glasses. On his freshly shaved head was a French beret.

"I'm going to miss you, Alex. You watch out for those French dudes, hear?"

"I will." She hugged him hard.

"And try to finish the last song, so that when you get back, we can start our next recording session."

"Don't worry. I'll have it ready or die trying."

"Don't go dying, either, Alex," Jeremy said, coming up behind her to tug a lock of her hair.

"You mean you'd miss me?"

"Uh-uh. I mean you're our meal ticket," he said, to the laughter of everyone.

Casey drummed his fingers nervously on the ticket

counter, then drew her close for a quick hug. "Take care," he whispered.

"Yeah. You too."

"I don't know what I'll do until our next gig."

"You could always fill in as a backup at the recording studio."

"Not a bad idea. Thanks, Alex."

She turned to Bear and Tina, who stood close together, wearing identical smiles.

"You two look like the fat cats that ate the canary."

"We did. Feathers and all," Tina said.

Seeing the glint of laughter in her eyes, Alex said, "What are you hiding?"

The two gathered her close. "We're going to make the announcement on the plane, but we want you to be the first to know. We're getting married when we get back home."

"Oh Tina! Bear!" She felt the sudden sting of tears as she hugged each of them. "I knew it. I just knew it."

"How could you know it when we didn't even guess?" Bear's smile grew. "All of a sudden last night, while we were sharing a brioche and a crème caramel, I realized I couldn't live without this woman."

"See," Tina added with a laugh. "I was right. The man's in love with my appetite."

The boarding announcement boomed over the loudspeaker. There was a sudden rush of activity as everyone scooped up their bags and duffels and embraced Alex and Buddy for the last time. Alex waved as they made their way to the plane. When she turned to leave, she was forced to take Buddy's arm, because she couldn't see through the blur of tears in her eyes.

25

Cannes was unlike anything Alex had ever seen before. There was none of the greenery of Ireland, or the rugged beauty of Scotland; it had none of the sophistication of Paris, or the urbane charm of London. But it had a style of its own. It was flanked by mountains, the sky was unmarred by clouds and white sand beaches were dotted with colorful umbrellas.

Cannes was garbed for a festive party. The narrow streets were lined with limousines and Rolls-Royces. Tourists stood in line for hours outside the Palais for a glimpse of the celebrities who had come for the annual film festival. Directors and their stars made grand entrances up the staircase in front of the Palais before the start of each showing. Afterward critics smugly pronounced winners and losers, dashing hopes and breaking hearts or creating instant, overnight superstars.

Thrust into this media circus, Alex felt completely

out of her element as she followed her agent into the elevator of the Carlton Hotel.

Buddy nodded his approval of the scarlet silk off-the-shoulder gown that fell in simple fluid lines to her ankles. "Good choice. Red is your color."

They headed for a hotel cocktail party, the first of at least half a dozen they planned to attend that night. At the door they were stopped by a uniformed guard who demanded to see an invitation. Buddy reached into the breast pocket of his tuxedo and presented it. They were admitted at once, and the maître d' greeted them warmly and a waiter offered them drinks from a silver tray.

Alex glanced around at the sea of beautiful people, all engaged in animated conversation. "I don't think this was such a good idea, Buddy."

"Trust me, sweet lips. You see all these fine people?" He threw an arm around her shoulders and leaned close to whisper in her ear. "These people are my family. I grew up with the hustlers and dreamers and con artists. I understand what makes them tick."

"Is it the same thing that makes you tick, Buddy?"

He chuckled. "You're catching on, aren't you?"

"I'm a quick study."

"Yeah. You sure are." He caught her hand and led her into the midst of the throng. "Come on, sweet lips. There's someone I'd like you to meet. Luis, I thought I'd find you here."

A darkly handsome man, wearing his coat across his shoulders like a cape and his long silver hair pulled back in a ponytail, was holding court for a cluster of reporters. He embraced Buddy, then fixed Alex with a penetrating stare. "So. You are Buddy's new songbird."

"Alex Corday, Luis Perez."

"Mr. Perez. I can't tell you how much I admire your work. It's a pleasure to meet you."

"Call me Luis, my dear. And the pleasure is mine. I am very much impressed with your new album. You have an exceptional voice and range. And your videos . . ." He turned to the journalists, who hung on every word spoken by this highly acclaimed director, whose films had won every award in the history of the film industry. "I am jealous that Howard Seal was permitted to direct this young woman's first videos. His work is inspired, though I think some of the credit should go to the one who inspired him." He seemed to come to a sudden conclusion. Very theatrically he announced, "A prediction, ladies and gentlemen. This young lady has only given us a glimmer of her talent thus far. I believe she will one day return to Cannes as an enduring star, a force to be reckoned with not only in the field of music, but also in films."

Suddenly the focus of all the lights and cameras shifted. Alex found herself barraged with questions from the press.

"Miss Corday, what is your background?"

"I was studying at UCLA when I started singing with Whispers. Since then our first album has gone double platinum, and we've just completed a six-month tour of Europe."

"Playing to sold-out houses in six countries," Buddy added proudly.

"Alex. Is that short for Alexis?"

"Alexandra," she said, trying to remain calm while flashbulbs exploded and the glare of TV lights nearly blinded her.

"Are you a native Californian?"

She nodded.

"How old are you?"

"Almost twenty." She had decided during this tour that it sounded so much more sophisticated than nineteen.

"Tell us about Dwayne Secord," one of the reporters shouted. "Have you seen him since you went on tour?"

"No, I haven't."

"Does that mean your hot romance has cooled?"

Buddy immediately interrupted. "Thank you for your attention, ladies and gentlemen. If you have any further questions, we'd be happy to schedule individual interviews." He handed out business cards with the name of his hotel written on them.

"Just tell us if you and Dwayne Secord are still 'good friends,'" the reporter persisted.

Everyone laughed.

Alex smiled. "Yes."

"You may say that Alex and Dwayne are very good friends," Buddy added. As more questions were shouted he drew Alex close and shouldered his way through the crowd, with Luis trailing.

When they reached a quiet corner, Buddy released Alex and turned to his old friend. "That was brilliant, Luis. Thank you."

Alex was stunned. "You mean you didn't just happen to run into each other? This was all planned?"

"My dear." Luis took her hand and lifted it to his lips in a courtly gesture. "In this circus, everything must be carefully choreographed; no one does anything spontaneously. Except, perhaps, for the drunks, who will be forced to see the proof of their rude or bizarre behavior in the photos taken by the paparazzi and smeared across the pages of the scandal sheets." He turned to Buddy. "Is that not so, my friend?"

Buddy nodded. "Ah yes. I remember it all too well. It got to the point where I hated waking up and looking at the newspapers, because I knew I'd find out what I'd done the night before." He shook his head. "At least they told me I had a good time."

Alex recalled the numerous stories about Buddy Holbrook's escapades in his younger days.

"Where are we headed now?" Buddy asked.

Luis reached into his pocket and withdrew two envelopes. "You have your choice. There is a party on the rooftop of this hotel, and another on the beach, both guaranteed to be star-studded."

"I'd rather not take my chances on the security along the beach. There's a full moon out there. Brings out the nut cases hoping to rub elbows with celebrities. I think we'll try the rooftop. How about you, Luis?"

"A good choice. I will join you."

"But Buddy." Alex grabbed his arm. "You know I can't go up to the roof."

"Of course you can. Just don't think about where you are."

"But—"

"Come on."

It took them almost an hour just to make their way to the door. With each step they were stopped either by old friends who wished to chat or by business associates who wanted to boast about their latest deals. In each instance, Buddy took the time to introduce Alex, after which he expounded on the band's successful album and European tour.

"I'll never remember all these names," she whispered to Buddy.

"Don't worry. You'll remember the most important ones—and best of all, they'll remember you. That's all that counts, sweet lips. In the world of entertainment, it's not what you can do, it's who remembers your name when he's casting a new flick."

They took the elevator to the roof. All the way up, Alex breathed deeply, fighting the waves of fear that were starting to well up inside her and threatening to overwhelm her. When they stepped out of the elevator, Buddy took her arm.

"There's a table," Alex said, hoping the chance to take a seat for a few minutes might restore the strength to her knees.

"Rule number one at a party like this, sweet lips: never sit. Mingle. If you sit, you'll be branded a wallflower. Just move along at my side," he said, steering her around a cluster of unfamiliar faces. "Ah. Here we are." He handed her a glass of champagne from the tray of a passing waiter and plucked a glass of Perrier for himself.

Flowers grew in profusion in huge pots around the three-foot wall that surrounded the rooftop garden. The air was perfumed with their fragrance. Colored lights had been strung in some of the plants to add a festive touch. Uniformed maids carried trays of appetizers and drinks.

Alex tried to ignore the lights of the city twinkling so far below her.

"Buddy. Buddy Holbrook."

Alex felt Buddy stiffen, even as his smile remained in place.

"Hello, Rudy."

"Good to see you back. Talking to any directors about a possible movie?"

"For myself?" Buddy laughed. "Sorry, Rudy. I'm through with that end of the business for good."

"Yeah. I heard you were an agent now, handling all kinds of hot new talent."

"Speaking of hot new talent, Rudy Silk, meet Alex Corday."

"I've heard of you." The man's jowls jiggled as he shook Alex's hand. "Great album. Terrific videos."

"Thank you."

"Film is my medium. Buddy and I go back a long way—I probably remember more about his life than he does. I was in on every one of his capers. But since I was only half as drunk as he was, my memories are sharper."

"Why don't you just forget about it, Rudy." Buddy's tone remained light, but it was edged with a hint of temper. "I have."

"Sure. Sure." Rudy turned away. "Catch you later."

"Hey, Buddy, Buddy Holbrook," a handsome, white-haired man shouted from across the room, causing heads to turn in Buddy's direction. Soon he was the center of attention, surrounded by old friends and well-wishers. As more and more of them crowded around him, Alex found herself being pushed toward the wall.

"Excuse me." She tried to push her way toward him, but the crush of bodies was too great.

"Buddy." She heard the way her voice trembled and hated herself for her weakness. "Buddy, please. Give me your hand."

The voices around her had swelled to such a volume

that no one except those closest to her even heard. No one took any notice of her distress.

She felt the back of her knees pressed against the wall and tried not to think about where she was. At the very top of the building. Oh God, she thought, the top of the building. Why had she allowed herself to be manipulated like this?

It was too late. She was losing control. Fear, like an evil genie, had been unleashed, rushing through her system. A trickle of sweat inched along her spine. She could feel the panic that clogged her throat, threatening to choke her. Her breath was coming in short painful gasps. She couldn't breathe. She could feel the bile rising in her throat. She was going to be sick right here in front of hundreds of important people, and the most humiliating thing about it was that there was nothing she could do to fight the feeling. She was going to embarrass herself in front of everyone.

There was a buzzing in her ears, a clear indication that she was going to faint. She felt her knees begin to buckle.

And then she felt strong arms lifting her and heard a deep voice saying, "Breathe deeply, in and out, Alexandra. Just keep breathing deeply. I'm getting you out of here."

"Matt. Oh, thank God. Matt."

It was the last thing she remembered before blackness overtook her.

She was floating, drifting. A not altogether unpleasant sensation, except that she couldn't seem to see anything.

Music was playing, a familiar melody. Gary's guitar. Len's piano. It was playing so softly, she thought at first it might be only in her mind. Then she heard her own voice singing and knew that it was the album playing somewhere nearby.

She put a hand to her forehead and discovered a damp cloth across the upper part of her face. No wonder she couldn't see.

When she started to pull the cloth away, strong gentle fingers closed over hers.

"Maybe you'd better give yourself a few more minutes."

She knew his touch, his voice. "Matt."

She tore away the cloth. She was lying on a sofa in a dimly lit room. He'd draped a towel over the lamp to keep the light from hurting her eyes.

"Then I wasn't hallucinating. I thought . . ." She reached out a finger to touch the little frown line that furrowed his brow. "I thought maybe I'd dreamed it all."

He steeled himself to show no emotion at the touch of her fingers against his flesh. "No dream. I'm real."

He'd removed his jacket and loosened his tie. She was uncomfortably aware of the width of his shoulders, the muscles of his upper arms. She shivered. Instantly his arms were around her.

"Here. Drink this." With his arm around her shoulders he raised her to a sitting position and held a tumbler of whiskey to her lips.

His face was close, so close she could feel the warmth of his breath against her cheek. She drank, feeling the fire begin in her throat and spread through her insides.

"A little more," he urged when she tried to stop.

She drank, then indicated that she'd had enough. He lowered her to the pillows, and she watched him drink the remaining whiskey and refill the glass. She found it odd that his hands were as unsteady as her own.

"Did I make a scene?"

He shook his head. "I don't think more than a handful of people even noticed. Those who did probably thought you'd had a little too much to drink."

"Buddy . . ."

"I told someone to tell your agent that you'd become indisposed and had retired for the night." He could see her relax at that.

"How did you happen to be there, Matt?" she asked him.

"I saw you across the room and had started toward you when I noticed the crowd pushing you against the wall. At first, when I saw how pale you were, I thought you were ill. Then I remembered your fear of heights. I caught you just as you were slipping to the floor." He dragged a hand through his hair. "I wasn't sure I'd make it in time."

"Thank God you did." She sat up and waited for the dizzyness to pass. Pressing the back of her hand to her forehead, she said, "It's such a terrible feeling. I knew it was happening, but I was powerless to stop it. All I could think of was the embarrassment I would cause myself and Buddy in front of all those people."

"Does this happen often?"

She shook her head. "It isn't usually this severe. I was feeling uncomfortable about being on the roof, but I thought I had it under control. Then the crowd shoved me toward the wall. When I realized I couldn't get away, I lost it. God, I hate this weakness."

"You aren't weak, Alexandra," he told her, his tone gruff. "You're a strong, capable woman. This fear of heights is not a weakness. It's not something you can control." He paused. "How long has it been since you ate?"

She thought about it. "Since this morning, I guess. Buddy has kept me too busy running around town to think about food."

"That probably added to your problem." He went to the phone. "I haven't eaten either, but I'm going to remedy that right now."

She listened to the sound of his deep voice as he picked up the phone and ordered in fluent French. A short time later two uniformed waiters entered the suite and proceeded to set a table for two with fine linen, crystal, and silver. When they left, there was wine chilling in a bucket of ice and gardenias floating in a small, shallow bowl in the center of the table. Their perfume filled the room.

Matt turned off the lamp so that the only light came from the candles on the table and several more in sconces along the walls. He held her chair for her.

"Something smells wonderful," Alex said as he lifted the silver dome from a tray and began to fill her plate.

"I ordered medallions of veal with mushrooms Provençal, and new spring potatoes." He uncovered a basket of freshly baked rolls, thick and crusty on the outside, hot and steaming inside. "And for dessert, crème caramel drizzled with raspberry liqueur."

"It sounded so much more exotic in French. What other languages do you speak?"

"I picked up some Spanish on my trips to Latin America. A smattering of Arabic. A few other dialects."

"I'm impressed."

"Don't be. It was all part of the job."

They ate in silence for several minutes, savoring the delicious meal.

"This is wonderful," Alex said.

"You see. You needed food."

"But this isn't mere food. This is . . . heavenly."

"And this is the nectar of heaven." He filled her glass with the pale gold wine and said, "Try it."

She sipped the wine and leaned back, her spirits restored. After the babble of so many voices and the crush of so many bodies, the peace and serenity of this place was a soothing balm.

"I'm so glad Buddy isn't expecting me to return. I don't think I could bear any more of that scene tonight."

"I know what you mean. It's like being trapped in a zoo."

"So what are you doing here in Cannes, Matt?"

"My film is being considered for an award."

"Oh, Matt!" She caught his hand. "That's wonderful."

He closed his other hand over hers. "I'm not sure how wonderful it is. I was advised not to take the risk. The critics here can be brutal." His tone lightened. "There's no need to ask why you're here. I'm sure an aggressive agent like Buddy Holbrook has begun to realize that the next logical step for you is film. He's probably not going to leave here until he has a deal for you."

She shrugged, feeling the warmth of his touch surging through her veins. At this moment, Buddy's film deal was the furthest thing from her mind. "When will they be showing your film, Matt?"

"Tomorrow night. I'll have to deal with the requisite news conference and photo session tomorrow afternoon."

"Then I should go now. You probably have a million last-minute details to take care of." She tried to draw her hand away, but he continued to hold it.

He stood, drawing her up and around the table to him. His voice was low, barely more than a whisper. "Don't go, Alexandra." He loved the color that flooded her cheeks. "I told you one day we would find ourselves in the right place at the right time."

He thought about crushing her against him and kissing her until she was breathless. He wanted to seduce her with soft words and impassioned promises. But he knew in his heart that the decision had to be hers, and hers alone. And so he merely held her hand and stared into her eyes, and said, in a voice husky with feeling, "I don't want you to leave, Alexandra. Not now, not later. I'd like you to stay the night."

26

Was this what she wanted? She thought it was, and yet, if he hadn't been holding her hand she would have backed away and run like a frightened deer.

On that rooftop she had allowed him to glimpse her weakness, her vulnerability. The shame of it still festered in her. Now she wanted him to see her strength, her control.

"If I stay," she said softly, "it will be because it's what I want."

He saw the confusion in her eyes and thought of the moment of terror he'd experienced when he'd seen her going into a faint. He'd known in that instant that he would do anything to keep her safe from harm. But right now, holding herself stiffly, struggling with her pride, he knew that what he felt for this tough, tender woman was much more than a simple desire to keep her from being hurt. But he didn't want to give this feeling a name. Not yet. Not when it was so new and fragile.

He wouldn't call it love. That was too strange a concept for a man who was alone by choice. But if he wouldn't admit to loving her, he would at least acknowledge that he would do all he could to persuade her to stay. Even beg, if he had to.

"Then tell me what you want." His eyes narrowed slightly. He moved his thumb across her wrist and felt her pulse leap.

"I want . . ." Her throat was suddenly dry. With an effort she managed to whisper, "Oh Matt, how can I go on pretending? I want you."

For a moment he couldn't speak. Her simple words affected him as nothing else could. Feelings he'd never even known existed suddenly blossomed within him.

He'd expected her to put up a fight, or at least to deny her true feelings. Instead, she'd given him honesty. He would give her at least as much. With his gaze locked on hers he lifted her hand to his lips and pressed a kiss to her palm.

"Alexandra, since the first time I saw you I've wanted you. Wanted this."

At the intensity of his words, she felt a tiny thrill.

He ran his hands along her arms and across her shoulders, bringing them up to frame her face.

She saw herself reflected in his eyes, eyes that she had once thought dark and mysterious. Now she could see only warmth in them, and dark, desperate desire.

He plunged his hands into her hair, combing his fingers through it, until his hands suddenly fisted, drawing her head back. The need for her was so sharp, so unexpected, he let out a savage oath before lowering his mouth to hers.

There was no warmth, no tenderness in the kiss. Instead there was hunger. A hunger so great, a need so deep, they were both rocked by it.

"Dear God," he murmured against her throat. "I want you, Alexandra. Now."

His hands reached for the ruffle of scarlet silk at her shoulders. He wanted to be gentle, but the time for gentleness had passed. He knew he was tearing the delicate fabric, but he no longer cared. His lips followed his fingertips as he tugged the dress lower, revealing pale, creamy flesh.

He heard her gasp as her fingers fumbled with the buttons of his shirt. She was trembling with need by the time her dress floated to the floor at her feet.

In the flickering light of the candles she was so beautiful he felt his breath catch in his throat. He ran hot, nibbling kisses over her upturned face and heard her little moan of frustration as she struggled to finish undressing him. His fingers closed over hers as they fumbled with his clothes until they joined hers at their feet.

His lips moved lower, to follow the curve of her shoulder, and then lower still, to find her breast. Desperately clinging to him, she felt her legs weaken, and they dropped to their knees.

His lips moved over hers, demanding, possessing. With each kiss he felt her gradual surrender as she gave herself up to the pleasure of his touch.

With a moan she whispered his name. He lowered her to the rug and lay beside her. He felt a sudden thrill, knowing it was his name she whispered, his touch she craved. The need to take her here, now, was like a fever in his blood. It took all his willpower to step back from the brink. As she lifted her lips to his, he vowed to go more slowly, to savor each taste, each moment of this precious time with her.

With lips and fingertips he began to explore her body as she lay, soft and pliant, beneath him. Steeped in pleasure, she sighed as he lazily traced her collarbone with his fingers and followed the trail with his lips. Moving lower, he circled her breast, cupping it in his palm before taking it into his mouth.

Like a starving man at a banquet he feasted on her, yet the more he tasted, the more he wanted. He knew now that he would never have enough of her.

Her body was on fire. With each touch, each movement of his tongue, she felt the flame leap higher, the need grow, until she was being consumed by flame.

He heard her little gasp and moved his mouth lower, then lower still, until, with lips and tongue and fingertips he brought her to the first peak.

She arched, her hands fisting into the clothes that lay crumpled beneath her, her eyes glazed with passion. Heat consumed her. Her body was a mass of nerve endings, as hundreds of unexpected sensations ripped through her. These feelings were so new, so unexpected. He gave her no time to recover before he took her on another dizzying ride.

She had no guidelines now, no notes to follow, no rules. In his arms she experienced a symphony of pleasures she'd never even imagined.

He covered her mouth with his, her body with his own, smothering the shudders that rippled through her.

Struggling for breath, Alex arched against him, her body begging for release. But still he waited, determined to drive her to the same madness that consumed him.

"Please Matt," she managed to whisper. "Love me. Now."

But he was beyond hearing as he drove her even higher. It was no longer enough to have release—he wanted her to lose the last vestige of control. He needed to make her his completely.

Her hands clutched his back, her nails gently raking his flesh as she opened to him. And still he drove her closer and closer to the edge of madness, without granting her the release she sought.

Her skin was damp with a sheen of sweat. Heat poured from her body to his. He heard her plea, though the words were no longer coherent.

She was his, he thought as he raised himself above her. His. And he knew no other man had ever taken her to such a place before.

"Tell me, Alexandra. Tell me that you want me."

In the flickering light of the candles, her face was shrouded in shadows. Her eyes opened. They were glazed with passion, heavy-lidded with desire. "I do, Matt. I want you. Only you. Always you."

Needs clawed at him. Desperate for release, he could wait no longer. He breathed in the fragrance of gardenias and knew that from this moment on, their perfume would always remind him of her.

As he took her, he was surprised by her strength. She wrapped herself around him, moving with him, climbing with him, higher, then higher still, until they seemed to touch the stars, which shattered into a million glittering fragments.

❖   ❖   ❖

They lay, still joined, their breath coming in short rasps. His face was buried against her neck. Her fingers had gone slack on his shoulders. Lifting his head, he pressed his lips to the sheen of sweat on her forehead.

"Am I too heavy for you?"

"Mm-hm."

"Would you like me to move?"

"No." She could barely get the word out. Her throat felt clogged with unshed tears, though she didn't understand why. "Not yet."

He rolled onto one side and drew her into his arms. "Better?"

"Much."

She felt so good here in his arms, as though she'd been made for him alone. He brushed a kiss over the corner of her mouth and muttered, "The next time I seduce you, remind me to carry you to the bed first."

"Absolutely. It would have been much more comfortable." She nibbled his lips. "And would you mind scattering rose petals over the sheets?"

"Only in your dreams," he said with a laugh.

She snuggled closer, loving the way they fit together. "Your arms around me are just about the best thing I've ever felt."

He was still smiling as he stared down at her, but she saw something flicker in his eyes. Something that made her feel . . . treasured.

"And you're the best thing they've ever held." He traced a finger along the curve of her eyebrow, across her nose, around the outline of her lips, all the while studying her as if memorizing every feature. "I don't ever want to let you go."

"That's good." She smoothed a lock of hair back from his forehead. "Because there's nowhere else I want to be."

Seeming to come to a sudden decision, he asked, "How much longer are you in Cannes?"

"Buddy said a week, maybe two."

"Whatever time you have left, spend it with me."

"But your film, your interviews, your news conference . . ."

"I want you with me."

"There will be talk."

"I don't give a damn about gossip. Alexandra, we've finally found the time to be with each other. I don't want to waste a single minute."

She knew that what he was offering was a rare and special gift. It was what she wanted more than anything. But seeing the intense look on his face, she couldn't resist drawing out the moment.

"I don't know, Matt. I might have to be persuaded."

He heard the hint of laughter that warmed her words. Getting to his knees, he lifted her in his arms, rose, and carried her to the bedroom.

"Maybe a soft bed will persuade you."

"I don't think it's enough," she said, chuckling as he deposited her in the middle of the bed. "I don't see any rose petals."

"Will this do?" He caressed her with exquisite care, pressing nibbling kisses across her face, her neck, her shoulders. It was a tender, playful side of him she'd never seen before.

"Mmm. I'm beginning to weaken."

"Don't go getting weak on me now." He couldn't believe he could want her again so soon, but he was already fully aroused.

"Oh. You like your women strong?" She surprised him by rolling over and straddling him. As she bent to kiss him, her hair spilled forward, tickling his chest. He caught a handful and dragged her closer. She saw the way his pupils darkened with desire.

"Woman, do you know what you're doing to me?"

She kissed him and murmured against his mouth, "I hope it's the same thing you're doing to me."

"I was wrong about you, Alexandra," he muttered as she rained kisses upon his face, then lower, across his chest and stomach. "You're not some sweet-eyed innocent. You're a seductress."

"Good. That's exactly what I had in mind." She brought her mouth still lower and heard his gasp of surprise.

"Now I know I'm not going to let you leave. In fact, we may never leave this bed."

He rolled her over, and with sighs and whispered words of love, they tumbled into a world of dark, mysterious pleasures.

Matt studied the woman asleep beside him. She had abandoned her pillow in favor of his.

He itched for a camera. There was something so appealing, so vulnerable about her at rest. One arm was under the pillow, the other rested lightly at his waist. Her hair spilled across her face. She slept as peacefully as a baby, her chest rising and falling in silent rhythm.

There had been little time for sleep. All night they had explored each other with a freedom, an abandon known only to truly passionate lovers. They had been by turns rough, then gentle, as they discovered each new hidden pleasure. Once he had found her weeping, and his alarm had turned to relief when she told him that she was simply overwhelmed by all the strange new feelings she was experiencing.

He felt a surge of protectiveness toward this woman that left him shaken. He would do anything within his power to keep her safe from all harm.

At a knock on the door he saw her stir. Annoyed, he whispered, "Go back to sleep. It's a standing order with room service. I forgot to cancel it."

He slipped on a pair of jeans and hurried to the door, where he accepted a tray from the waiter and nudged the door shut.

"Is there coffee?" she asked, sitting up.

"Yes. But only one cup." He brought the tray to the night table and poured from a silver carafe. "We'll share."

She accepted the cup from him and sipped, then handed it back.

"What else is there?"

"A basket of freshly baked croissants." He buttered one and offered her a bite.

"Mmm." When she licked a crumb from her lip she saw him staring at her with a strange look on his face.

"What's wrong?"

"I think you'd better put something on." He crossed the room and returned with his shirt, then quickly went to the glass door that opened onto a small, private courtyard. Over his shoulder he said, "Otherwise, I'm going to find myself right back in that bed."

Laughing, she pulled on the shirt and followed him out into the courtyard. Despite the number of people walking nearby, Alex and Matt were completely hidden from view by a riot of plants and pots of flowers that grew in profusion.

"What a wonderful little garden," she said.

He turned and, seeing the way his shirt displayed her long legs to perfection, muttered, "Maybe that wasn't such a good idea after all. I may have to wrap you in a couple of blankets if I'm going to last through breakfast.

They shared a laugh as they sat together at a little table, her long bare legs resting on his denim-clad ones. They lifted their faces to the sunshine and sipped from the coffee cup.

Finally Alex stood. "I'm going to shower."

"Don't be long. I miss you already." Brushing his lips over hers, he stretched and followed her back inside.

When Matt picked up the morning newspaper from the breakfast tray, he caught sight of a photo of Alex on the front page. The bold French headline leapt out at him, proclaiming that a new singing sensation was on her way to stardom.

Matt read quickly through the article describing Alex and the band's latest sold-out tour and going over the details of her hot romance with Dwayne Secord. Since Alexandra had already explained how Buddy had fueled the rumors about her and Dwayne to grab attention for his new client, Matt paid scant attention to that part of the article.

It was an article on the second page that held Matt's attention.

Our research has uncovered the fact that Alexandra Corday is the daughter of Marney Corday, whose fame as a singer flared briefly before her untimely death of cancer, and famed stuntman William "Wild Bill" Corday, who fell to his death in a freak accident during the filming of the movie, *Code of Honor*. Little Alexandra, nine years old at the time, witnessed the bloody accident. When contacted, director Hunt Worthington admitted that he still has nightmares about that fateful day and wondered what effect it might have had on Corday's daughter.

When Alex walked in after her shower wrapped in Matt's robe, she found him clutching the paper and staring into space, deep in thought. "What's wrong, Matt?" she asked.

He seemed to mentally shake himself before handing her the paper without a word. She read the entire account. When she looked up, he could read the pain in her eyes.

"I should have known someone would dig this up," she said.

"Why didn't you tell me?"

"I've never talked about it. I wouldn't know where to begin."

He sat down on the edge of the bed and drew her down beside him. "Why not start at the beginning."

"I couldn't, Matt. It's too painful."

"If we're going to share everything, we need to share the bad as well as the good. Trust me, Alexandra. I need to know."

She took a deep breath. He was right, of course. But

how to begin? At first her words were awkward, halting.

"Looking back on it, it didn't seem like a day for tragedy. It was one of those glorious California days that the travel ads rave about. There was a hint of a breeze."

She clasped her hands in her lap, determined to tell him everything with as little emotion as possible. "I was nine years old. I remember I was dresssed in jeans and brand new gym shoes. This was the first time my father had ever allowed me to come along to watch him work, and he had explained in detail what would be happening. It was a simple stunt, according to my dad. I remember shielding my eyes from the sun and watching the action above."

Matt saw the way her hands suddenly clenched as the memory washed over her.

"It was perfectly quiet on the set. Then suddenly I heard the sharp crack of gunfire. At the top of the twenty-story office building, my dad climbed through an open window and pulled himself to the roof. A minute later a second man followed. Dad began what was to be a perilous escape along the narrow ledge that rimmed the building." Alex touched a hand to her heart. "I was so caught up in the drama that for a minute I forgot that it was pretend. I saw the second man take careful aim before he fired. The sound was very loud. My dad executed a half turn, clutched his chest, then pitched forward."

She swallowed, and Matt held his silence, giving her time to collect her thoughts.

"In my excitement I started clapping my hands and dancing up and down as my father hurtled toward the net. He'd promised that the first thing he'd do after the fall would be to blow me a kiss."

Her words were barely a whisper now; she seemed to be speaking more to herself than to Matt. "What must he have thought when he plummeted over the edge of the building and realized that the net had been strung too far to the right? The reports said that he'd missed it by only a few feet. I don't think his last thoughts as he sped toward the pavement were for himself. He had to know that I was standing below with the crew, watching him fall to certain death."

She seemed to catch herself. Her voice grew stronger for a moment as she turned to Matt. "I was straining to watch every single movement. As my father dropped toward the net I raised a hand in greeting, as we'd planned. I wanted him to know how proud I was of him."

She got to her feet, suddenly too agitated to sit, and crossed the room. "I waited to see the net sag with his weight. My laughter died on my lips as Dad sped past the net and continued hurtling through the air. It occurred to me, for just a moment, that something had gone terribly wrong. Then my childish mind rejected that thought. This was, after all, my daddy. He could do anything."

She lowered her head so that Matt couldn't see her eyes.

"I remember staring transfixed at my father hurtling through space. This wasn't happening, I thought. It wasn't. It couldn't be. I tried to cover my eyes, but my hands remained paralyzed at my sides. Someone was screaming. I didn't realize at first that it was my own voice I heard. I couldn't move, couldn't stop watching my father."

She licked her lips and swallowed. "All around me

the director, the crew, the extras, seemed frozen. I realize now that they were incapable of moving. Their worst nightmare was happening before their eyes. I kept thinking, why doesn't someone run over and save him? Then, just before he hit the ground, one of the crew thought to grab me, burying my face against his shoulder. Though he pressed his hand against my ear, the sound seemed to shudder through me when my father's body hit the pavement."

"Dear God." Matt started to go to her but she lifted a hand. She had to get through this quickly, before she lost her courage.

"I remember pushing myself free and racing toward my father. Everyone started forward, then suddenly drew back. Grown men were sobbing. Women were shrieking hysterically. Someone was yelling for an ambulance. The director ordered the set cleared immediately. But for all those long, agonizing minutes, there was such confusion, no one noticed me. I just stood there, seeing my father's shattered body."

She wrapped her arms around herself and, despite the already warm morning, shivered. "I remember being cold, so cold. There was no feeling in my arms or legs. My father lay face down, one arm bent beneath him, as if cradling his head. And I kept remembering the silly song he used to sing to me and my baby brother, Kip. I don't know why the silly Popeye words kept playing in my head." On a shaky breath she began to sing, "'I'm strong to the finish, 'cause I . . .'"

She shook her head. "Someone shouted, and a studio limousine screeched to a halt. The security guard thrust me into the back seat and barked orders at the driver. I was whisked away and rushed to my grand-

mother's, where she had to shield me from the flashbulbs and microphones of a hundred reporters who
swarmed around her house. Though her own heart
must have been broken, Nanna kept me safe in her little upstairs bedroom and tended to Kip, who was still a
baby in a crib."

Alex was silent for a moment, hugging herself. "I
remember huddling beneath Nanna's blankets, knowing I musn't cry," she all but whispered. "You see, in
our house there had been so many tears. My mother
had died less than a year before that. But her death had
been a silent one, in the sterile, antiseptic halls of a
hospital. Nanna and Dad had shed a thousand tears for
her. And now, my brave, strong father had died too.
But his death . . ." She swallowed and went on. "His
death had been violent, and bloody, and replayed on
the front pages of newspapers and on TV screens
across the nation. Nanna told me I musn't turn on the
TV, but I was little, and I forgot, and when I turned it
on I was forced to relive the horror all over again, on
every channel. And as I saw my father falling, I remember hearing those words in my head, 'I'm strong to the
finish 'cause I eat my spinach. . . .'"

She suddenly found herself sobbing against Matt's
shoulder.

He'd never loved her so much, wanted so desperately to protect her from any further pain. He'd die
rather than see her hurt again.

"Go ahead, Alexandra. Let it out. Let it all out."

The tears came freely now; she'd stopped trying to
hold them back. She'd spent a lifetime trying to hold
them back. They stung her eyes and burned her throat,
and her body shook as Matt gently held her. But when

the tears had run their course, she felt cleansed. And when Matt carried her to bed and comforted her the only way he knew how, she was grateful for his tenderness. She clung to him, eager to absorb some of his strength. For just a little while, until she was back in control again, she would allow him to be strong for both of them.

27

Knowing how vulnerable Alex was at this time, Matt personally took care of checking her out of her room at the Majestic and into his at the old, elegant Carlton. It was a simple matter. For a generous tip, a maid packed her things; a bellman carried her luggage to a waiting limousine. Her bill was settled. But when Matt turned away from the hotel desk, Buddy was waiting, fangs bared.

"Where the hell did you take Alex?"

"Alexandra is going to stay with me," Matt said calmly. "Why don't we talk over here, Buddy?" He led the way to a quiet corner of the lobby and sat down.

Buddy took the chair opposite him, perching on the edge of his seat, and looking ready to do battle. "Why the hell did you two sneak off when my back was turned last night? I figure, if you're man enough to shack up with my client, you ought to be man enough to face me first."

Matt's hand shot out, grabbing Buddy by the front of his shirt. Though his voice was so low no one nearby could hear a word, Buddy knew by the fire in his eyes that he was struggling to control a murderous rage.

"If you hadn't been so busy with your bullshit games last night, you might have noticed that Alexandra was in trouble. And if you'd read the newspapers this morning, you'd have discovered why she has a fear of heights. Last night you deserted her on a crowded rooftop. I got her out of there just before she fainted in front of the very people you wanted to impress. As for the rest of your accusation . . ." His eyes narrowed fractionally, and Buddy sucked in a breath, anticipating a blow. "Call it what you will. The fact remains, Alexandra will stay with me until she leaves Cannes. And you have nothing to say about it." With great effort he released his hold on Buddy.

Buddy rose and took several steps backward, straightening his tie. He could see that Matt Montrose was not a man to be crossed. He dug a hand in his pocket and pulled out several slips of paper. "You'll give her these messages?"

Matt nodded, taking the notes and stuffing them into his pocket. When he stood and started to walk away, Buddy caught his arm. Matt glared at him, the fire back in his eyes.

Buddy held up his hands in a gesture of surrender. "Hey. I just wanted to say . . ." He cleared his throat and offered his hand. "Tell Alex I want whatever she wants. Tell her to call me whenever she wants to talk to me."

Matt stared at the hand for a moment, then took it. "Sure."

°   °   °

As he dressed for the viewing of his movie, Matt kept an eye on Alexandra, who was busy carefully applying makeup to her pale face.

"I almost forgot." He handed her the messages Buddy had given him.

Alexandra read them, then tossed them aside. "Parties Buddy wants me to attend with him tonight."

"Do you want to go?"

She shrugged. "Only if we happen to cross paths."

"We're bound to. Don't be too hard on him, Alexandra. He's doing what you hired him to do. He probably has made some good contacts for you."

"Then I don't mind. At least I'll have you to hang on to."

He came up behind her and lifted her hair out of the way to press a kiss to her shoulder. "That's right. And don't you forget it."

They studied each other's reflection in the mirror.

"You look stunning," he murmured.

"You mean despite the red eyes?"

"There isn't even a trace of those tears. Come on. Time to face the world."

Matt walked into the room and was instantly surrounded by photographers and reporters.

"What message are you hoping to convey with this movie?" one of the reporters shouted.

Though Alex had tried to remain in the background, Matt drew her toward him, wrapping an arm around her waist. It sent a clear message to all that they were together. And though the reporters were dying to probe into their personal affairs, they knew better than to try with a man like Matt Montrose.

Matt handled the press with the same ease with which he seemed to handle everything. "It's a universal message, I think. No matter who you are, no matter what you make of your life, you yearn for understanding, acceptance, love."

"Speaking of love . . ." another reporter called out, but Matt cut him off.

"I think we should view the movie first. I'll answer your questions afterward."

They stepped into the waiting limousine and were driven a scant half block to the front of the Palais. As their names were announced, Matt and Alex began to climb the wide red-carpeted stairs, pausing after a dozen steps to turn and face the screaming crowd. The sound of the mob was deafening. With a quick wave, they ascended the rest of the stairs and disappeared inside.

A host of celebrities followed. There was the usual babble of voices until the lights were dimmed. Then the credits began to roll and the crowd in the theater became silent.

Like the others, Alex was instantly spellbound by the haunting faces that filled the screen. Every scene, every word of dialogue, touched a nerve. As the film ended, the audience was on its feet cheering the director. The lights came up. Matt, seated beside Alex, seemed stunned by the reaction.

Alex brushed tears from her eyes and joined the others in their salute to his talent, swallowing the lump in her throat that threatened to choke her. Matt's film had been one of the most uplifting movies she had ever seen. It left her with a good feeling, and it was obvious that it had affected everyone else in the same way.

When they stepped outside, the critics were already holding sway with the press.

"Without a doubt the finest . . ."

". . . has done a superb job directing his first . . ."

". . . look for the name Matt Montrose to grace the screen for many years to come."

". . . will surpass even his famous father."

They broke off to applaud Matt as he walked down the steps and approached the bank of microphones, keeping a firm grasp on Alex's hand as he began answering the questions being hurled at him.

"Did you hear them, Matt? One of them actually called you a genius," Alex said warmly an hour later as they strolled down the street, basking in the glow of his success.

He chuckled. "That's this year. Next year they may call me a bum. It's the nature of this business."

She stopped, turning him to face her. "Stop being so modest. Admit it, Matt. You loved hearing the applause."

He dropped his hands to her shoulders. "Of course I did. And I hope they keep on applauding my work. But I can't work merely to please them. I have to have enough integrity to do what I think best, regardless of what the audience and critics think."

A breeze caught Alex hair, and he reached out to catch the strands, tugging on them. "You and I both know how fickle the public is. It isn't logical to expect them to love everything we do. This film will now become the yardstick by which they measure my next work." He caught her hand and resumed walking. "If it doesn't measure up, they'll be just as eager to boo me as they were to applaud today."

"I'll never boo you."

He threw back his head and laughed. "Promise?"

"Cross my heart."

She was so serious he couldn't resist teasing her. As he studied their linked hands he said, "Well, you might not applaud every movie I make through the years, but I bet there's one performance you definitely won't find fault with."

She turned to study his handsome profile. "I don't believe this. Did the humble director, Matt Montrose, just turn into a bedroom braggart?"

"Is that what I am?"

She saw the laughter lurking in his eyes. "Is this to be a private performance?"

"For your eyes only."

"Just when did you want to present this performance?"

"I thought we could slip away to my room right now."

"Now? Before the big cocktail party?"

"Mm-hmm. Come on. We won't even be missed." He grabbed her hand, and the two of them began running, chuckling like two conspirators.

"How is Kip doing?" Matt picked up the photograph that Alex had set on the night table.

She shook her head. "I'm so worried about him. Ever since my visit to my uncle's farm in South Dakota, I've been even more concerned."

While Matt listened quietly, she told him everything she had learned about the recently purchased land surrounding her uncle's farm, and about his California lawyer, who had offered to cooperate with her. She clutched her arms and began to pace. "I have such disturbing feelings about my aunt and uncle, Matt. I know that any boy Kip's age would be given chores to do on a farm, but I have the feeling that they keep giving him more and more to do while they do less and less. I discovered that they won't even allow him to draw or paint. It's as though they enjoy making him feel worthless."

Matt offered her the comfort of his arms.

"Oh, Matt," she cried, "do you think I'm just being silly and overprotective?"

"Not at all. I think you ought to trust your own instincts about such things." He held her a little away. "Would you like me to contact my lawyer?"

She shook her head. "Let me try to work it out first with their lawyer. I don't want to anger them more; I'm afraid they'll take it out on Kip." She drew in a shuddering breath. "But it helps just knowing you care."

"I do care. And I promise you, Alexandra, if there's anything you ask me to do about it, it will be done."

She remembered Nanna's old saying that a problem shared with a friend was lighter by half. She suddenly felt as if the weight of the world had been lifted from her shoulders. Her heart told her that Matt was as good as his word.

"Bad news?" Matt saw the look in Alex's eyes as she replaced the telephone.

"Buddy has a series of concerts finalized back in the

States. He said advance ticket sales have been so strong, we may have to add more cities."

"That's wonderful news." He regarded her closely. "So why aren't you smiling?"

"Oh, Matt." She crossed her arms over her chest and looked at the floor, avoiding his eyes. "Buddy said we have to leave in the morning."

Matt went to her and drew her into his arms. "You knew the day would come when we'd have to say good-bye."

"I know. But I just didn't expect it to be so soon."

Nor had he. It hurt even more than he'd thought it would. "Let's cancel our plans for tonight," he murmured against her temple.

"I'd like that. I can't bear the thought of having to share our last night with strangers."

She kissed him lightly, but as she drew away he pulled her back roughly and kissed her until she was breathless. When they finally stepped apart, he picked up the phone and ordered a special dinner.

"The waiters will be here in a little while. In the meantime, I have a favor to ask," he said solemnly.

Alex looked at him in surprise. In the two weeks they'd been together, this was the first time he'd asked anything of her.

"What is it, Matt?"

She saw the warmth of laughter in his eyes, and something else. Something deeper.

"Would you mind putting on that black beaded gown you wore in Carmel?"

"No, I don't mind. It's one of my favorites."

"Good. Because I'd like to satisfy a fantasy that was uppermost in my mind that whole long night in Carmel."

Despite the intimacies they'd shared, she found herself blushing when he said, "Tonight, after dinner, I'd like the privilege of taking it off you before we make love."

Matt and Alex lay with their arms around each other. All night they had made love frantically, as though by loving they could somehow hold back the inevitable dawn.

They had talked long into the night about where their busy schedules would take them, and how they could steal time together.

"I give you my word," Matt whispered. "We'll find ways to be together."

As long as the darkness held, Alex could believe, but with each passing hour, her hopes faded. Was this the price she had to pay for the success she'd craved? Would she have to deny her heart in order to pursue her dream?

A stray sunbeam found its way through the shutters, and Alex closed her eyes against the pain. Not yet, she prayed. Just a little while longer in his arms. She couldn't bear the thought of leaving him.

Her suitcases were packed; her traveling clothes were carefully laid out. Yet, she felt no joy at the antici-pation of going home.

The bedside phone shrilled, and Matt's hand shot out, catching it before the second ring. He listened, mumbled something, and then hung up.

"Your wake-up call," he whispered against her lips.

She nodded, too bereft to attempt to speak, and dragged herself out of bed to shower. As she mechanically pulled on her clothes, she heard Matt open the door to admit the bellman. When she came out of the bathroom her luggage was gone.

She studied her reflection in the mirror, then went into the bedroom. It was empty. Matt was in the small courtyard. For a minute she drank in the sight of him. Shirtless, barefoot, wearing only a pair of jeans, he stood with his hands jammed into his pockets, his head down.

He hadn't expected it to be this painful. All night he'd had to fight the temptation to beg her to stay with him. But he knew he had no right. Within days he would be back in Los Angeles, preparing for his next film, which would take place in Fiji. They would be a world apart. He wanted her with him, but talent like Alexandra's deserved to be showcased all over the world. Only a fool would ask her to throw it all away for the sake of love.

Love. There were no more doubts in his mind. He loved her, loved her as he'd never loved anyone before. But what could he offer, except the life of a gypsy, as he traveled the world in search of his own dream? That wasn't the life he wanted to offer the woman he loved. And until he could offer her more, he would settle for this. He had to direct; she had to make music. For now, they would have to be content to grab what little time they could together. As for the loneliness, he'd experienced it before; at least now he'd be warmed by the thought of what they had shared, and the hope that they would share more in the future.

As if sensing her presence, he turned, and for a long moment held her gaze. Then, forcing a smile to his lips, he said, "There's still time for me to dress and go with you to the airport. At least I could make things easier until your departure."

"No. Buddy is outside in the limo. He'll take care of everything. Besides, I don't think I could bear a public good-bye."

Nor could he.

He went to her and gathered her close. Framing her face with his hands, he kissed her, slowly, thoroughly.

She knew that at this moment, if he asked her to stay, she would, without even weighing the consequences.

"We'll find a way, Alexandra," he told her.

"A way?"

"To steal time for each other. You'll see. We'll make time."

She nodded and hugged him fiercely, squeezing her eyes shut to block the tears that threatened.

Then she turned and left without looking back.

28

"Do you, Christina Theopholis . . ."

Alex, still wearing her stage costume, stood beside her best friend in a gaudy wedding chapel just off the Strip in Las Vegas. Casey, dressed in a black tuxedo, stood beside Bear.

Despite the solemnity of the occasion, everyone gasped when the preacher, dressed in a white spangled jumpsuit, continued in his best Elvis voice, ". . . take this man, Prentice Worthington the Third, to be your husband?"

"Prentice Worthington the Third?" Alex whispered.

"Yeah. Isn't that a stitch? I almost refused to marry him when I found out what his real name was. I wasn't sure I could handle being Mrs. Prentice Worthington the Third."

"It's better than being Mrs. Bear," Alex said, giggling.

"It turns out his father is the multimillionaire developer, Prentice Worthington, Jr."

"You're kidding."

They realized the preacher was staring at them.

"I do," Tina said quickly.

"And do you, Prentice Worthington, take Christina Theopholis to be your wife?"

"I do."

As the preacher spoke about the love, the sacrifice, the commitment, Alex's laughter faded. She felt her eyes fill with tears. It didn't matter if the ceremony took place in a small-town church or a world renowned cathedral, a picturesque meadow or a gaudy tourist attraction, the result was the same: two people pledged their love for a lifetime.

"You may kiss the bride."

Tina and Bear turned toward each other with radiant smiles and sealed their vows with a kiss.

"Oh, Tina." Alex wiped away her tears as she hugged her friend. "I'm so happy for you. For both of you," she added as she kissed Bear.

The band members gathered around to congratulate the bride and groom. As they started down the aisle, the preacher picked up his guitar and began to serenade them with an off-key rendition of "Love Me Tender."

Outside, the party climbed into waiting limousines. Buddy announced, "I made dinner reservations in a private suite at Caesar's."

When they arrived at the suite, they were surprised to find Dwayne Secord and his band, who were appearing in town at a nearby casino, already celebrating.

"Congratulations on your second album," Dwayne bellowed as they entered. "Only out a couple of months, and it's already double platinum." He shook

Buddy's hand, then added, "Congratulations, newly-weds." He hugged Tina and pumped Bear's hand. Turning to Alex he drawled, "Hell, Al, you just keep on gettin' prettier all the time. You've got such a bloom on your cheeks, if I didn't know better, I'd think you were the blushin' bride."

"Just a bridesmaid," she said with a laugh.

He clasped her to him in a great bear hug, then plucked a glass of champagne from a tray and handed it to her. "According to the gossip rags, you and that director have finally given up staring at each other with big calf eyes and progressed to the heavy breathing stage." He saw the smile that touched her lips. "Does this mean the romance between you and me is over?"

"I certainly hope not." Relaxed and happy to be with her old friend, she brushed his cheek with a kiss. "What would those scandal sheets do if they didn't have us to write about?"

"And what would we do if they ever stop writin' about us?"

"I don't know." She glanced at him. "Would it be so bad?"

"Sweet lips," Buddy said, putting an arm around each of them, "it's the kiss of death for an entertainer. When they stop writing about you, you're all washed up."

"There. You see?" Dwayne led Alex to a seat at the banquet table. "Let's hurry and toast the newlyweds before they manage to duck out of here."

"You think they'll want to leave so soon?"

He nodded toward Tina and Bear, who seemed oblivious of the celebration going on around them.

"Al, take a look at them. If this was your weddin' night, would you want to spend it with a bunch of noisy musicians?"

She thought of Matt, back in L.A. When they'd talked on the phone the night before, he'd been preparing to leave for Fiji for the preproduction work for his next movie.

"Where'd you just go to, Al?"

She shook her head and forced a smile to her lips. "I was just thinking. You're right, Dwayne. If this was my wedding night, I'd want to spend it alone with my husband. On a tropical island."

"Speaking of tropical islands." He gave her a probing stare. "I dropped by your dressing room and it looked like a jungle and smelled like a funeral parlor. Where'd all those gardenias come from?"

"Her Hollywood stud," Gary said. "Since we started back on the road, every one of her dressing rooms has been filled with gardenias. I think he must own stock in a florist supplier."

Sara put her hand on her husband's sleeve. "I think it's sweet. It looks like he bought up every gardenia in the state of California and shipped them to Alex."

"I hope he owns stock in the phone companies," Gary said as he filled Alex's glass, "because it seems like he's managed to interrupt every rehearsal this week with a phone call." He added in a whisper, "I bet he doesn't call daily after he gets to Bali Ha'i."

Dwayne turned to Alex. "What does he mean?"

"Matt is flying to the Fiji Islands to prepare for his next film project."

"Some guys have all the luck." Dwayne said. "*Our* next gig is the Palace of Auburn Hills in Michigan. I hear they had ten inches of snow on the ground there last night."

"Better pack your long underwear," Alex said with a laugh.

"Thanks. I needed that." Still grinning, Dwayne put an arm around her shoulders and proposed a bawdy toast to the bride and groom.

It was nearly eight in the morning when Alex returned to her suite. After a night of talking and laughing with Dwayne, she was feeling pleasantly tired. They had offered dozens of toasts to the happy couple and then had spent some time at a blackjack table, where Dwayne had turned two thousand dollars into twenty thousand.

"Night, Al." Dwayne pressed a kiss to her cheek and waited until she was inside and he'd heard her turn the lock in the door before walking away, followed by his ever present bodyguard.

Inside her room, Alex carefully unpinned her corsage and hung up her gown. As she turned toward the bed she caught sight of the blinking red light on her phone, indicating a message. She pressed the button and waited until the voice mail was activated.

"Miss Corday, this is Annie at your Los Angeles answering service. I was told that this was an emergency. You are to phone your uncle in South Dakota at once."

She felt the first faint stirrings of fear. Something must have happened to Kip. Why else would her uncle phone? With trembling fingers she dialed the number and listened to the distant ringing. At last she heard her uncle's voice.

"Vince Corday here."

"Uncle Vince, this is Alex. I was told you wanted me to call."

"Where the hell have you been, girl? I left that message with your service hours ago."

She swallowed back the sharp retort that sprang to her lips. She would not bother to explain herself to him. Where she went and what she did was none of his business. "Why did you call, Uncle Vince? Has something happened to Kip?"

"I thought maybe you could tell me."

She slumped down on the edge of the bed. "I don't understand," she said, her voice trembling.

"Kip's gone. Run away. I've had the state police looking for him for hours, but so far, there's not a trace of him. We thought he might be on his way to find you."

Matt carried the last of the suitcases out to the Bronco and returned to his bedroom for a final check. Spotting his favorite camera lying on a chaise, he picked it up and put the strap around his neck.

He'd made arrangements for a couple to drop by his Malibu beachfront house once a week to pick up the mail and keep everything in good repair until he returned.

On the table beside his bed he caught sight of the professional portfolio his mother had personally delivered four days ago, along with a stern lecture.

"I know that you're looking for a leading man for

your next film," Elyse had begun after only a few brief moments of small talk. "I want you to remember that Dirk is family."

"Dirk is in Europe," he'd said tiredly. "And according to his letters to you, he's working regularly in films there." He didn't bother to add that he'd heard rumors that Dirk's "art films" were little more than pornography.

"He wants to come home," Elyse had said, walking around Matt's bright, airy room, touching the art objects he'd collected on his travels around the world. Expensive crystal shared a shelf with a simple handwoven basket from a small village in Honduras. A priceless sculpture stood beside an earthenware bowl made by a child in Mexico.

"All he needs is one good role, and then Hollywood will have to pay attention to him." When she had turned to face her stepson, Matt had seen the tired lines around her eyes and mouth. She'd fought so long and hard for Dirk, she didn't know how to stop, even though it was exacting a terrible toll on her health and her marriage. She had clutched Matt's hand. "Winning the award at Cannes has made you the most talked-about director in Hollywood, Matt. Everyone is waiting for your next film. All I ask is that you look at Dirk's portfolio, and watch the video he sent me. If you think he might be right for the lead in *Pacific Love,* I expect you to be man enough to say so. If not, I'll respect your judgment."

Matt had closed his hands over hers and kissed her cheek. "All right. I can't make any promises but I'll consider Dirk."

"That's all I ask. Thank you, Matt."

He'd spent the rest of the evening going over the pictures in the portfolio and studying the video. He had to admit that Dirk had matured as an actor, and his golden-boy looks were perfect for the lead in Matt's next film. Still, Matt couldn't bring himself to forget all the times Dirk had twisted a good thing into a complete mess. How many times had Dirk taken handouts from Sidney and Elyse, only to turn up broke and desperate again? Matt couldn't afford to have anyone in this movie who wasn't willing to give one hundred percent.

He picked up the portfolio, finding the photos beneath it. Buddy Holbrook had sent them by messenger, along with a note saying he'd done this without Alex's knowledge or permission. He'd sent them to Matt because he wanted his client to be considered for the lead in *Pacific Love*.

Matt had seen the way she'd immersed herself in her work. Her looks and her talent were more than adequate for the challenging role, but he wondered how he could remain objective if he were to direct her in the film. Both of them would be living under a microscope until the project was completed. He wasn't sure that would be fair to a woman like Alexandra, who was still squirming under the glare of so much publicity.

Leaning a hip against the table, Matt stared down at the photographs. Just seeing her picture made him realize how unsatisfying his life was now that they were apart. God, he missed her. When he called it only served to sharpen the edge of his loneliness.

The ringing of the phone interrupted his musings. He frowned, hoping it wasn't Elyse again. She'd phoned every day since their meeting.

Glancing at his watch, he was tempted to let it ring. He had barely enough time to get to the airport. Still . . .

"Hello."

"Matt?" The sound of that breathy voice had his pulse racing.

"Alexandra, what's wrong?"

"Oh, Matt. I don't what to do. I just spoke with my uncle. He said Kip's run away."

"The police . . ."

He could hear the tremendous effort she was making to hold back the panic. "They've been searching. So far, nothing."

Without a pause he said, "I was just on my way to the airport. I can be in Vegas in an hour or two. Until then, hold on, Alexandra. We'll find him."

Even after she replaced the receiver, she continued to cling to it as though it were a lifeline. Matt had been so calm, so sure. For now, she would hold fast to his words to give her strength.

The minute Matt stepped through the doorway Alex rushed into his arms. "Oh, I'm so glad you're here. I know it was selfish of me to lay this burden on you just when you were about to start such an important project, but I—"

"Shhh." He touched a finger to her lips to silence her. "There's nowhere else I want to be at a time like this. Now," he said, leading her to the sofa and sitting down beside her, "tell me everything you know."

"According to my uncle, Kip went to bed around five o'clock."

"Isn't that awfully early for a boy of Kip's age?"

Alex nodded her head. "When I questioned it, my uncle said that Kip had been sent to his room without supper as a punishment for breaking a rule." Her eyes were troubled. "I think there's more to the story, but that's all he would say. He claims that neither he nor Bernice looked in on Kip until morning. And that's when they discovered that his bed hadn't been slept in, and he was gone." She grasped Matt's hand. "I can't stand not knowing more. I've already booked a flight to South Dakota. It leaves in an hour."

"Cancel it. You need to be right here, where the authorities can reach you by phone."

"And what if they don't phone?" She got to her feet and began pacing. "I have to go there. What if Kip is lost out there somewhere, cold and frightened? Or worse, what if he's in danger?"

Matt longed to pull her into his arms and offer her comfort, but he knew she was going on pure adrenaline.

"When is the last time you slept?"

She stopped her pacing to turn to him. "You don't think I could sleep at a time like this?"

"All right. We'll rule out sleep. When is the last time you ate?"

She shrugged. "Some time last night."

He went to the phone and ordered room service. Then he said, "Have you told the others about this?"

"I couldn't. I knew if I tried, I'd break down."

"What's Buddy's room number?"

When she told him, Matt dialed the number and informed him as simply as possible about Kip's disappearance. Buddy assured him that the others in the band would be notified.

Room service delivered their order, and Matt insisted that Alex eat. She did so mechanically, not even tasting the food.

When she'd finished and was sipping hot tea, Matt asked, "Have you spoken with the South Dakota authorities?"

"Yes. But that was more than two hours ago. They should have called again by now."

Matt calmly called the state police in South Dakota and spoke with someone in charge of the investigation. When he was finished he turned to Alex. "A little boy answering Kip's description was seen hitchhiking along the highway a few miles from your uncle's farm."

"And that's all they've learned?"

"It's a big interstate. The police theorize that a trucker might have picked him up. They're attempting to notify some of the known trucking companies in the area. Does Kip know the name of your hotel here?"

She nodded. "I mentioned it when I phoned him last Sunday."

"When you spoke with him, did he seem troubled about anything?"

She thought a minute. "No more than usual. He's become very quiet and withdrawn since going to live with my aunt and uncle. It's almost as though he's too afraid to cry or complain. He just seems . . . hurt."

Matt saw the way she turned away to hide the pain. He went to her and gathered her close. Against her temple he murmured, "Don't give up on him now, Alexandra. He's a smart boy. He's going to come through this just fine. You'll see."

She touched a hand to his cheek, needing to feel the warmth of human contact. "Do you really believe that, Matt?"

He placed his hand over hers. "I do. Now, if you don't mind, I'm going to make a few more calls. I have some friends on the force in L.A. Maybe they can help."

"I need to do something. I've never been very good at feeling helpless."

"Just keep thinking good thoughts." He picked up the phone, then added, "And Alexandra . . ."

"Yes?"

"Pray," he whispered.

29

Buddy and the members of the band rallied around Alex, keeping a vigil in her room. She wept in Tina's arms, and when Sara and little Corey entered her suite, she clung to them for long, tense minutes, taking comfort when the little girl snuggled against her. Soon, Corey had everyone laughing at her antics. Even Alex was able to forget, for a little while, the fears that tormented her.

"I'm going to cancel tonight's show," Buddy announced.

"No," Alex, who was seated on the sofa playing with the baby, said immediately. All heads swiveled toward her. "It's too close to showtime to refund all those tickets. Besides, it's the only thing that will get me through the night. I can't imagine sitting here staring at the phone all those long hours, waiting for it to ring."

Matt came up behind her and put a hand on her

shoulder. "You think it's possible to go on at a time like this?"

"I don't know. But I think I should try."

"Hell yes. That's my girl. What a trouper," Buddy said proudly. "You might break down a couple of times, but the audience won't know why. They'll just assume you're caught up in the music. I think you can do it, sweet lips."

Gary ran a hand through his hair. "For God's sake, Buddy. Don't let her do this. Cancel the show."

"You know the score, Gary. The show must go on." Buddy's voice took on a brisk tone. "I think that except for Tina and Matt, we should clear out of here and let Alex get some rest. She's going to need it to get through tonight. Okay, sweet lips?"

Alex nodded, feeling the effects of the hours of tension. After they'd gone, Tina and Matt watched helplessly as Alex struggled with her private demons. She paced the floor; she stared out the windows. Finally she began sorting through her photographs of Kip, and it was the only thing that seemed to give her any small measure of comfort.

After hours of waiting by the phone, she at last gave in to the need for sleep. Matt carried a blanket from the bedroom and tucked it around her as she lay curled up at one end of the sofa.

Tina stood by the window, studying the man who had stolen her best friend's heart. Now that she'd had a chance to observe him, she could understand why. He was quiet, competent, self-assured.

"I thought you were headed for Fiji." Tina's words were whispered out of deference to Alex.

"I was. I got the phone call just in time. A few min-

utes more and I would have been on my way to L.A.
International."

"How long can you stay?"

"For as long as Alex needs me."

Tina smiled. "You're good for her."

He didn't return the smile. She could see his tension in the frown line between his brows, in the way he
clenched his hands at his sides. "Not nearly good
enough." He ran a hand through his hair and turned
away. "Right now I'd give up everything—my dreams,
my photography, the chance to direct this next picture—if I could just see Kip walk through that door.
He's the only thing that will ever put the smile back in
Alexandra's eyes."

Just then there was a knock on the door. Matt and
Tina exchanged a look, and Matt opened it to find a
well-dressed young man holding up a badge.

"Detective Clayton Potts, Nevada State Police," he
said. "I was told this was the suite of Alexandra
Corday."

Alex was awake instantly. She sat up, throwing off
the blanket. "What is it? Where is he?"

The detective stepped inside, and Matt closed the
door behind him. "I'm sorry, Miss Corday. We haven't
found him yet. But our office was contacted by the
South Dakota State Police and asked to stay close to
you. They're pretty certain the boy is heading for
Nevada. And we've located a trucker who gave your
brother a ride as far as Casper, Wyoming."

Alex's eyes were wide with concern. "How long do
you think it will be before he gets here?"

The detective shook his head sadly. "It all depends
on how many rides he's able to get, and how much

time he wastes between rides. He could be asleep somewhere. He could be stopping to eat." He looked up. "Do you know if the boy had any money?"

"I made it a point to send him some in every letter, but when I asked him about it, he said he rarely got it. I guess my aunt and uncle open most of his mail before he ever sees it. When they do, they must keep the money for themselves." Alex lowered her voice. "I doubt if they've given him a penny since he went to live with them. And certainly not enough to buy a decent meal."

The young man had deceptively old, tired eyes. His demeanor was surprisingly gentle. "Every police force between South Dakota and Nevada has been notified. Believe me, when they locate him, they'll see that he's well fed."

Alex crossed to the window. Just beyond the glittering town with its patchwork of hotels and casinos loomed hundreds of miles of uninhabited desert and mountains. And somewhere out there was a little boy, hungry, frightened, and desperately alone.

Oh, Nanna, she thought, pressing her forehead to the cool windowpane. Please watch over Kip and guide him safely to me.

Matt watched Alex struggle to pull herself together for the show. There'd been no time alone to offer her the comfort of his arms. All day she'd been forced to endure the presence of the detective, who reported regularly to the police in South Dakota.

There had been calls from reporters who had picked up the story from the police. So far, Buddy had managed to hold them at bay, but Matt knew that at any minute it could turn into a media circus.

There had been one hopeful sign: a trucker in Salt Lake City had admitted giving a ride to a boy who answered Kip's description. But that had been nearly eight hours earlier, and there had been no further word.

Alex's fingers fumbled with the zipper on the back of her gown.

"Here. Let me do that." Matt finished zipping it up for her. He wrapped his arms around her, drawing her back against him.

"Oh, Matt." She lifted troubled eyes to meet his in the mirror. "How will I go on if Kip doesn't—"

"Shhh." He pressed his lips to her temple. "You'll hear from him. Soon. I know it."

"I want to believe that."

"Then believe it. Hold on to it."

They turned as Buddy hurried into the room. "Come on, Alex. Showtime. Are you going to wait here by the phone?" he asked the detective.

Detective Potts nodded.

"If you hear anything," Alex said, "I want to know immediately."

"Yes, ma'am."

Walking between Matt and Buddy, Alex headed down to the showroom.

Alex stood bathed in the glow of the spotlight, her eyes shining with tears she couldn't hold back. Every love song, every verse about a broken heart, exposed a raw nerve. The audience, sensing her pain, seemed caught

up in the drama, applauding wildly after each song,
sometimes giving her standing ovations. Each time, she
seemed stunned by their reaction. But a glance at Gary
reassured her.

"They love you, Alex. Listen to them. They're with
you."

She returned their affection by giving them the performance of a lifetime.

Matt, watching from the wings, saw the fatigue that
was slowly overtaking her after more than two hours
onstage. "Here." He handed a stool to a stagehand and
ordered, "Take this out to her. Now."

Alex's eyes widened in surprise when the stagehand
approached. She glanced offstage and saw Matt's
thumbs-up. Smiling, she seated herself and gave him a
smile of gratitude.

The spotlight narrowed on the slender figure in the
beaded gown, her long hair falling over one shoulder as
she bowed her head in a moment of quiet contempla-
tion.

"I'd like to sing you the first song I ever wrote," she
told her audience. "I was nine years old, and as I
watched my baby brother asleep in his crib, the words
just came to me."

Gary signaled to the band and they began the strains
of their first big hit, "Alone." An expectant hush settled
over the crowd.

As the familiar words poured from her, she experienced a strange feeling of serenity. This would always
be Kip's song. He was here with her; she could sense
his love, his strength, his determination. Nothing, no
distance, no adversity, could keep them apart. No one,
not her aunt and uncle, not even the law, would sepa-

rate them again. As the song built to a crescendo, the feeling grew stronger, until, unable to contain herself, she lifted her arms wide, then drew them close, imagining her little brother held firmly to her heart.

The spotlight shrank slowly until only her face was illuminated, tears glittering on her lashes. Then there was darkness, and the audience was on its feet once more, the cheers so thunderous they drowned out everything else.

In the darkness Alex heard the sound of Matt shouting from backstage. And then another voice broke through the din.

"Alex."

She turned, astonished to see the little boy who sped across the stage toward her. "Kip. Oh my God! Kip."

He hurled himself at her and they clung to each other, laughing, crying, hugging fiercely. When the spotlight came on again, brother and sister were lit up, locked in an embrace.

With tears streaming down her cheeks, Alex waited until she could control her churning emotions. Then she said breathlessly, "This is my brother, Kip. He's come a long way to be with me. And now, if you don't mind, we'll say good night."

Before the bewildered stagehands could lower the curtain, Alex and Kip walked off hand in hand, followed by the ecstatic band members.

"The first truck driver was nice. He offered to buy me a hamburger. But when I saw him go to the pay phone, I figured he was probably calling the police, so I ducked out and hitched another ride before he could turn me in."

Kip sat on the sofa, a blanket tucked around him. The remains of a chocolate shake, two hamburgers, and two orders of fries lay on a plate on the coffee table.

Alex sat beside him bundled in a terry robe, her face bare of makeup. Her need to touch him was so great that even while he ate, she kept her arm around him, as if afraid he might disappear if she let go.

Buddy and the members of the band had finally gone, leaving Matt and Detective Clayton Potts with Alex and Kip. When Kip had found out that the man in the business suit was a police officer, he'd become wary.

"Why didn't you want the trucker to call the police? Did somebody tell you to be afraid of police, Kip?" Detective Potts asked, watching him closely.

"I figured they'd take me back to my uncle's."

"Why don't you want to go back there?"

"I . . . miss Alex. She's my sister. We're family. We belong together."

She squeezed his hand and drew him close.

"But you understand that your sister waived her rights to be your guardian. In the eyes of the law, your aunt and uncle are your legal guardians."

"The law's wrong," Kip said softly.

"The law is there to protect your rights." Detective Potts cleared his throat. Though his eyes remained gentle, his words were firm. "I've been sent here to see that the law is carried out, Kip. My orders are to remain with you until you can be turned over to the South Dakota authorities."

Alex clutched her brother's arm. "Are you saying you're taking Kip away from me?"

"Those are my orders."

"But you can't. He's come so far. We've been apart such a long time."

"I was warned that you might try to stop me, Miss Corday. But my orders were very clear. The minute the boy shows up, I'm to take him into custody until he can be returned to his legal guardians."

"I'll run away again," Kip said defiantly.

Alex gathered him to her. Her eyes filled with tears. "We've both been through so much. At least let him stay the night."

"Sorry, Miss Corday. I have my orders. But if you'd like, I'll let him change." He indicated Kip's torn, dirty clothes. "That is, if you have something here that he can wear."

Alex kept her arm firmly around her little brother as she led him toward her bedroom. "Let's get you into a tub, Kip."

A few minutes later, Alex shouted, "Oh my God! Matt!"

At Alex's hysterical cry, Matt and the detective raced into her bedroom. Alex stood with Kip's shirt in her hands, staring in horror at her brother's back. From his shoulder to his waist there was a long, thin angry-looking welt.

"I can't let you take him. I can't bear to be separated from him again."

Alex, arms crossed over her chest, paced back and forth in the sitting room. Kip stood silently in the doorway, wearing one of his sister's T-shirts and a pair of her jeans rolled at the cuffs. The hotel doctor had made a visit to apply an antibacterial ointment to the boy's torn, puckered flesh.

"You have no say in this, Miss Corday. The courts will appoint a lawyer to represent the boy's rights."

"They can appoint a hundred. All I know is, Kip is my brother. You saw what they did to him."

"We heard the boy's version. We still haven't heard what your aunt and uncle have to say about this."

"Are you suggesting that Kip is lying?"

"I'm just saying that a boy might say anything necessary to be with a sister whose life-style seems so glamorous."

"It isn't the glamour that appeals to Kip. I'm the only one who can give him the love and protection he needs. And I'm not going to let him go again."

"The courts will—"

"Stop it." She pressed her hands over her ears and turned away in frustration. "Stop telling me that others will look out for us. All our lives we've heard that. But we know the truth: we're the only ones who care about each other."

Matt could see that the hours of tension and lack of sleep were taking their toll. Both Alexandra and her brother were on the verge of hysteria.

"Why can't Kip sleep here, Detective Potts?" he asked.

"Because I have my orders." The officer took a firm grasp of the boy's arm and led him toward the door.

Alex struggled not to cry in front of her little brother. She needed to be strong for both of them. "What will happen to him?"

"He'll be evaluated, and a judge will order a hearing to determine what is best for the boy."

"Where will he sleep tonight?" Alex asked through a mist of tears.

"In a youth shelter. A social worker will contact you tomorrow, Miss Corday, to give you all the necessary information."

As the detective and Kip walked out of the room, Alex leaned on Matt's arm to keep from falling. Her heart was racing, as though she'd just run up a flight of stairs, and there was a terrible buzzing in her head. Matt wrapped his arms around her and drew her against him. He could feel the shudders as she struggled to hold back the sobs that threatened.

"Come on, Alex. I want you to sleep."

She looked up at him. "How can I sleep when they've just taken Kip away?"

"Do it for Kip," Matt said as he led her into the bedroom. "You have to sleep so you can think clearly in the morning."

"Oh, Matt. I don't think I can bear being separated from him again. After all he's gone through, how can they be so cruel as to take him away from me?"

"They won't, Alexandra," Matt said and kissed her. "I promise you, they won't. We'll fight them. And we'll win."

We. She clung to the comfort of that word. Matt was here with her. And he'd just given her his promise. She let out a long, slow breath, then sat down on the edge of the bed.

"How will we fight them?"

"In the courts." Matt turned down the covers and helped her to lie down.

"But I signed a document—"

"Which you were tricked into signing," he said grimly. Rubbing the back of his neck tiredly, he went to the window. She'd been pushed to the limit. Now it was time for her to push back.

He picked up the phone.

"Who are you calling, Matt?"

"A friend. It's time to call in a few favors."

30

The hushed, expectant crowd in the courtroom hung on every word of Alex's cross-examination.

"You expect this court to believe that you signed a document without reading it?"

"My uncle deliberately led me to believe that both papers were copies of the same document declaring him executor of my grandmother's estate. There was no reason for me to believe that he was lying."

"Why did you wait so long to come forward and ask to be your brother's guardian?"

"My uncle told me I had to be twenty-one to assume guardianship. If I had known the legal age is eighteen—"

"You never questioned your uncle's word?"

"At that time I didn't think I had to."

"So you considered your uncle a reasonable, well-intentioned individual?"

"At first."

"Your answer is yes, Miss Corday?"

Alex said that it was.

"Could it be, Miss Corday, that you found it convenient to ignore the needs of an eleven-year-old while you pursued your own career?"

"That isn't true. I wanted Kip with me. But at first there was no way I could provide for him, or send him to school—"

"At first? Perhaps you could give the court some idea of what your life is like today. Tell me, Miss Corday, do you ever spend more than a week or two in any one place?"

Alex swallowed, trying to concentrate. Her attention was caught and held by Kip, who was seated between a social worker and a court-appointed lawyer. She hadn't seen him, or been allowed to visit with him since he'd been taken from her suite. He'd been interviewed by a battery of psychiatrists, psychologists, and pediatric health-care specialists, who had testified that the boy was by turns moody, apprehensive, shy, withdrawn, friendly, and sullen. Each gave a conflicting reason for his behavior, but none was willing to lay any blame on his current guardians.

She met Kip's steady, unblinking gaze and tried to smile, but she was too nervous. She returned her attention to the lawyer.

"I stay as long as our contract calls for. It could be a week, it could be a month."

She looked out over the sea of faces. Jason Tremont, a Harvard Law graduate and an old friend of Matt's, had been retained to represent her. He had requested a closed hearing, since it involved a juvenile. Because his request had been denied, the courtroom was overflowing with journalists, and as many curious onlookers as it would hold.

Vince and Bernice, along with their Los Angeles lawyer, seemed to be enjoying the public display. Vince had made it a point to smile and wave at friends and neighbors as the judge took her seat and called for order. Now he leaned back, his hands folded over his stomach, while his lawyer continued questioning Alex.

"But you have no place you call home, Miss Corday?"

She resented the question. She knew what her uncle's lawyer was trying to do: he wanted to show the judge that she couldn't make a home for her brother. "Our home, the home where Kip and I used to live with Nanna—our grandmother—"

"Spare us the endless details, Miss Corday. A simple yes or no will do. Do you have a place you call home?"

She looked down. "No."

Matt was seated in the front row, along with Buddy and the members of the band. He kept his gaze locked on Alex, willing her the strength to remain calm. He would have given anything to shield her from all of this, but all he could do was be here in this South Dakota courthouse to show his love and support.

He'd placed his trust in Jason Tremont. Jason was good, damn good. If anyone could persuade the judge to rule in her favor, he would.

"Would you tell this court, Miss Corday, what time you usually get home after a performance?"

"Usually around midnight."

"After the show do you go right to bed?"

"No. Not immediately."

"What do you usually do after a show?"

"Eat." She smiled, beginning to relax. "I'm always too nervous to eat before a performance, so I'm always hungry after a couple of hours onstage."

"So you eat. Is that your dinner?"

"Yes."

"So you eat your dinner around one or two o'clock in the morning?"

"Yes."

"And then what?"

She seemed puzzled. "Then I go to bed."

"Alone, Miss Corday?"

Her eyes narrowed. She should have known what he was getting at. "I live alone."

"I didn't ask if you lived alone, Miss Corday. I asked if you went to bed alone."

There was an audible gasp in the courtroom. Alex glanced at the judge, who in turn stared at the lawyer.

"Where is this leading, Counselor?" she asked.

"Miss Corday is an entertainer. Her life-style should be examined if she is to take on the care and responsibility of a minor ward of the court."

The judge nodded.

"I understand, Miss Corday, that there are five male members of your band, who travel with you."

"That's true."

"The leader of that group, Gary Hampstead; is he married?"

"He is."

"You know his wife?"

"I do."

"Did you ever engage in a sexual liaison with Mr. Hampstead?"

Jason Tremont was on his feet. "Objection, Your

Honor. This question has no place in these proceed-
ings."

"I'll allow it. But be warned, Counselor."

The lawyer looked triumphant. "I repeat, Miss
Corday. Did you ever engage in a sexual liaison with
Mr. Hampstead?"

"I did not."

For a moment the lawyer seemed deflated by her
response. His informant had made a mistake—or else
this woman was lying. No matter. There were bigger
fish to fry.

"Do you know Dwayne Secord?"

"I do."

He held up a series of photos of Alex and Dwayne
culled from various papers and magazines. "It would
seem, according to the press, that you and Mr. Secord
have spent a great deal of time together. Have you had
sexual relations with him?"

Again, tension rippled through the crowd as they
waited for her response. It was, after all, what they had
come for. For many, it was the most excitement they'd
ever known.

"I have not."

The crowd reacted with astonishment.

The lawyer's voice rose above the din. "Are you saying that all these reports are false?"

"I am."

He glanced toward Vince and Bernice and shot
them a smile before turning to Alex. "I suppose I could
ask Mr. Secord to testify, Miss Corday, but I won't
have to resort to such tactics. I'll simply remind you
that you are under oath. Are you familiar with a director named Matt Montrose?"

She swallowed, aware of what was coming. "I am."

"Is it true that you spent two weeks with him in Cannes, or are these reports also fabricated?" He held up a fistful of newspaper articles and glossy photos showing the two together.

When she didn't respond, he turned away and stared pointedly at Matt. Matt returned the stare. In his lap, his hands tightened into fists. How he'd love to wrap his fingers around the throat of this bastard.

"I'll ask you again, Miss Corday. Did you and Matt Montrose spend two weeks together in Cannes?"

"Yes." Her voice was barely a whisper.

"I'm sorry, Miss Corday. I didn't hear you. Was that a yes?"

"Yes," she said, lifting her chin.

The judge had to rap her gavel several times to silence the buzz among the crowd.

"Would you say you and Matt Montrose know each other . . . intimately?"

She blinked rapidly, fighting the sting of tears. She would not let them see her cry. She hated this man for taking something so rare and precious and cheapening it in front of the whole world. "Yes."

He smiled broadly at Vince and Bernice again, who this time returned the smile. "One more question, Miss Corday. You go to bed at two or three in the morning, whether alone or with Mr. Montrose—or others. What time do you wake up?"

She was openly glaring now. "It depends on whether or not I have an interview or rehearsal scheduled."

"Give me a time, Miss Corday. Eleven o'clock? Noon?"

"I suppose."

"And what do you propose to do about a little boy? Will he wake himself for school? Will he cramp your style when you want to entertain a—gentleman friend? Will he have to somehow make his life fit your rather unique schedule, Miss Corday? Do you consider this a loving, nurturing guardianship to provide a boy of eleven?"

"I love Kip," she said, praying her voice wouldn't tremble and betray her nerves. "And he loves me. That's all either of us wants or needs."

"Maybe all you want is love, Miss Corday—or so it would seem." With a leering smile he held up the photos showing her in the embrace of Dwayne Secord and Matt Montrose. "But a boy of this impressionable age needs much more." He turned, staring dramatically at Vince and Bernice, who couldn't hide their smiles of triumph. "He needs routine, discipline, order in his life. The sort of order that he knew on a clean, wholesome farm."

The courtroom was completely silent as he crossed the room and took his seat. "I see no need to question this witness further."

The judge glanced at her watch. "In view of the late hour, this court will adjourn until tomorrow morning, when I will accept closing arguments and render my decision."

The reporters were scrambling toward the exits, hoping to reach a phone in order to make their deadlines. Few in the courtroom took any notice of the little boy who pulled away from his lawyer and hurled himself into his sister's arms.

"Oh, Alex," he cried, tears streaming down his face. "They're going to force me to go back to Uncle Vince's. I just know they are!"

"Shhh." She hugged him fiercely, watching with a sinking heart as the bailiff started toward them. "You have to keep on hoping and praying that the judge will recognize the truth."

"I didn't mind when they were just hurting me, Alex. But now they're hurting you too."

"Don't worry about me, Kip. Just take care of you," she told him. The bailiff began prying them apart.

"I hate them for what they're doing to you, Alex."

"Don't let the hate eat away at you, Kip. Just think about all the love around you. Think about Mom and Dad and Nanna and me. We all love you. Don't let the hate crowd out all that love."

As the little boy was taken back to his lawyer and social worker, Alex felt as if her heart would break.

"I'm honestly worried." Jason Tremont paced back and forth in his hotel room, speaking in low tones to Matt, who stood by the window. "The press has latched on to this story about the tug-of-war between the superstar and her aunt and uncle over guardianship of a little boy. Too many in the media have painted Vince and Bernice as honest, upright people from a small town who are being railroaded by a shallow entertainer and her high-priced lawyer."

"I don't give a damn about the press." Matt shook a cigarette from the pack in his pocket and lit it, before remembering that he'd quit. The temptation was great, but he had a need to test his willpower. Crushing it into an ashtray, he exhaled a stream of smoke and said, "All I care about is what that judge is thinking."

"I'll tell you what she's thinking." Jason's voice

vibrated with anger. "Kip told the authorities that the welt on his back was made by a strap wielded by his enraged uncle. But he's just a kid. Nobody in that courtroom is listening to a kid. The doctor hired by Vince and Bernice testified that the welt on Kip's back could have been made by a leather strap that broke loose when the kid tried to load too many milk containers onto a cart. And even the hotel doctor, who examined Kip, couldn't refute that testimony. When he was cross-examined he admitted that although it looked like it had been inflicted with a heavy hand, it could have been caused in some other manner. Then their lawyer put sweet Aunt Bernice on the stand, and she said she and poor Uncle Vince hated to punish the kid by sending him to his room without supper, but they just had to teach him some responsibility, since he was a chronic liar who'd been spoiled rotten by his doting grandmother." Jason stopped his pacing to look at Matt. "Who do you think the judge is going to believe? A superstar and her Harvard lawyer, or poor, sweet farm folks saddled with a spoiled Hollywood brat?"

When Matt said nothing, Jason snapped open the locks on his briefcase and removed a sheaf of documents. "I'd better get to work. I don't think I'll get much sleep tonight. I have a feeling that judge has already made up her mind. And all I have is closing arguments tomorrow to change it."

Matt sat on the edge of the bed, studying Alex as she slept. He'd never loved her as much as he had this day, when she'd been forced to hold her head high and answer the most intimate questions about her life.

Vince's lawyer had tried everything he could to break her. But she was still intact.

He frowned. How would she withstand another separation from her brother? How much could one person possibly bear?

He rose and began to pace the darkened room. All his wealth, all his prestige, couldn't help her now. But he had to keep trying. It wasn't in him to give up without a fight. In all his life, he'd never accepted defeat. When his mother had died, he'd suffered the care of a succession of housekeepers until his father had brought home Elyse. He frowned. Elyse had tried to be a good mother. But her young son, Dirk, had a cruel streak in him that had forever shattered the peace of their home. Even so, Matt had learned to live with Dirk, or at least to separate himself enough from the trouble to survive.

Then there had been his photography. It had helped him escape—to the most dangerous places in the world: China, South Africa, the Middle East. Until the accident which had nearly taken his life. But he'd survived. He'd not only survived; he'd thrived. He'd learned that out of each adversity came new strength.

But this time, he was stumped. He didn't have a clue how to help Alexandra.

He stopped his pacing. A clue . . . Something nagged at the edges of his mind, but he couldn't put his finger on it. Something he'd overheard at the cemetery, that day they had buried Alexandra's grandmother. He paused by the window and watched a shooting star blaze a path across the night sky. What was it Vince had said?

The thought came to him in a flash: . . . *just like Vince junior. Before he joined the Marines, I always had to drag him away from his friends. Fool kid never knew what was good for him.*

Matt slipped into the other room and dialed Jason's number. Keeping his voice low, he told him what he wanted. Then he returned to bed.

Alex sighed, shoving the hair from her eyes. "Is it morning already?"

"No." Matt gathered her close. "Go back to sleep."

"I was dreaming," she murmured against his throat.

"I hope it was a good dream."

"It was very good. We were all together, you and I and Kip. And we were somewhere far away from all the trouble. Someplace where no one could ever hurt us again."

"Sounds wonderful. Now get some more sleep," he whispered. "And hold on to that dream."

He saw her eyes flutter closed. She pressed her lips to his throat and mumbled something before drifting back to sleep.

There were no empty seats left in the courtroom. Outside, news crews were assembling their cameras in anticipation of the judge's ruling.

When Matt caught up with Jason, the lawyer shook his head sadly. "Nothing yet," he muttered.

Vince and Bernice entered with their lawyer and took their seats. All three wore relaxed smiles. They could smell victory.

Alex, tense, edgy, sat beside her lawyer. She got to her feet when Kip entered the courtroom between the social worker and his lawyer. As they walked past, she caught Kip's hand and squeezed it.

They stood when the judge entered, then quickly resumed their seats.

"I will hear your closing arguments," the judge announced.

The lawyer for Vince and Bernice made an impassioned plea on behalf of his clients stating that they "should be permitted to continue the work of shaping and molding this fine boy who has for so long been spoiled and pampered." He finished, "I ask you not to consign this child to a life of neglect at the hands of someone who was only too willing to sign a document giving up all rights to him. Someone who has already admitted that her life-style is not capable of offering the loving, nurturing family life this boy deserves."

The crowd in the courtroom muttered their approval.

Jason Tremont made an equally impassioned plea. "In her grief, Miss Corday had no idea what was in that document she signed. We've seen evidence of the land acquisition by Mr. Corday since he assumed control of his mother's estate. We've heard the testimony of neighbors who claim that the man never showed affection toward the boy he called his 'little gold mine.' My client has agreed to hire a tutor for her brother, so that he will be free to travel with her and maintain his academic pursuits. In addition, she has agreed to search for a permanent home for the two of them, where they can put down roots in a community." Jason's voice rose dramatically. "This is a young woman who is driven to succeed in order to make a home for her brother. Throughout their lives these two young people have had to lose those they most loved: their mother and father, their beloved grandmother. I ask you not to cut this brother and sister off from each other. All they want is the right to be together. I believe they deserve that chance."

The next day, all eyes turned to the judge, who would at last render a decision. "Despite my misgivings about the manner in which the welt was inflicted upon this boy's back, I am inclined to believe that a man and woman in a solid, traditional community offer him the best hope for a stable homelife."

For Alex, time seemed to stop. She could feel her heart begin to break, piece by painful piece, as the horrible truth dawned: the judge, speaking for the court, was about to do the unthinkable. She clasped her hands together so tightly her nails dug into her palms, drawing blood. It couldn't be—dear God, it *couldn't* be happening.

"Furthermore, since I believe visitation by a woman of Ms. Corday's character could unduly influence . . ."

Alex realized that the court was moving to prevent her from even visiting Kip. Her aunt and uncle would have total control over Kip's life, and there'd be no one to know or care if he was abused. This was a nightmare that would never end.

"Therefore, this court grants . . ."

The judge hesitated as a young man in military uniform burst through the door of the courtroom. "Bailiff, you will remove—"

"Your Honor," the man said, striding toward the bench. "My name is Vincent Corday, Jr. Although it shames me to admit it, those people, Vince and Bernice Corday, are my parents. I haven't seen them since I ran away from home at the age of eighteen and entered the military to get away from them. I'm only here today to see that no one else ever has to go through the hell of physical and emotional abuse that I finally managed to escape."

The courtroom erupted into chaos. Some reporters raced toward the exits, hoping to scoop the other networks in breaking the scandalous news, while photographers jostled for the most dramatic pictures. Vince and Bernice engaged in a bitter argument with their lawyer, who finally stomped away. The judge rapped again and again for order, then in frustration instructed the bailiff to begin emptying the courtroom of all spectators.

Through it all, Alex and Kip stood locked in an embrace, tears streaming down their faces. Like a fierce protector, Matt stood beside them, holding the reporters and photographers at bay.

31

"I still can't believe it." Alex glanced at her little brother, who had finally fallen asleep in the plush leather seat of the private jet Buddy had hired to take them to Los Angeles.

"Believe it, sweet lips." Buddy lifted a glass of Perrier in a toast. "I'll never forget the look on their faces when Vince and Bernice's son stood up in that courtroom and accused them of a lifetime of abuse. That was a brilliant piece of work, Jason."

"It wasn't my idea." Sipping a drink, the laywer felt himself relaxing for the first time in days. "Matt phoned me in the middle of the night with the suggestion that the marines might be able to locate someone who would be able to corroborate Kip's accounts of abuse. The judge might not want to believe a little boy, but she could hardly ignore a marine lieutenant. His testimony changed everything."

"How did you know?" Alex asked.

"It was a gamble," Matt said. "We figured they wanted Kip for the insurance benefits. We had no way of knowing whether or not Vince, Junior, had been abused, though those things usually follow a pattern."

"Here's to gambling—and winning," Buddy said, lifting his Perrier. "Now, sweet lips, you can concentrate on your career."

"Wrong," Tina interjected. "I think Alex and Kip ought to go away somewhere and get reacquainted."

"I agree. Alex, how would you feel if you could do both?" Buddy asked. "Further your career and spend about six months with your brother on a faraway island?"

Alex smiled. "I'd have to think I just died and went to heaven."

Buddy turned to Matt. "Will you tell her, or will I?"

"It's all yours," Matt said.

Buddy clearly enjoyed being the center of everyone's attention. With more than a trace of his old theatrical style, he said, "I've just negotiated all of you a very sweet deal. As you know, Matt is going to begin filming in Fiji soon. Gary, he'd like you to write the score, and he wants you and the band to record the sound track."

Gary gave the rest of the band a thumbs-up. "I couldn't be happier, Buddy. I promised Sara we'd cut back on our road trips. This is the direction we'd like my career to take. It'll give us time to buy a house and make a home for Corey."

"Good. And as for you." Buddy turned to Alex, who was watching him in puzzled silence. "You'll sing the movie's theme song, of course. But the most important thing is, Matt would like you to star in the movie."

For a minute she was speechless. When she finally found her voice she said breathlessly, "I don't believe it."

"Well?" Buddy asked. "Is this a yes or a no?"

"Oh, Buddy. Matt." She hugged them both, then began hugging the members of the band. "How soon do we go?"

"It'll be a couple of months before we can begin the actual filming," Matt said. "But I'd like you and Kip to fly to Fiji as soon as you get your affairs in order. That'll give you the quiet time you both need to get over this ordeal."

The copilot announced it was time to prepare for the landing. Alex took her seat, reaching over to clasp Matt's hand.

"Thank you," she whispered. "For everything."

"Just happy to be of service, ma'am," he said with a smile. But he knew that he hadn't made the decision purely for her sake. The thought of being separated from her for months had been too painful. Now they could be together, and she and Kip could begin to heal.

"Kip and I have all his suitcases packed."

Alex looked up from her closet, where she was making her final selections before closing her own suitcase. "Thanks, Cassie."

Cassie Miller was proving to be the perfect tutor and companion for Kip. A twenty-two-year-old recent graduate of USC with a degree in education and a background in art, she'd been selected from more than twenty teachers they'd interviewed. The chance to work with a budding artist had intrigued her, and the thought of traveling with a celebrity had been a further inducement. Of course, the idea of spending six months in Fiji had cemented her desire for the job. She was every bit as excited about their trip as Alex and Kip.

There was a knock on the door, and Cassie hurried to admit the hotel bellman.

"Your limousine is ready downstairs," he announced as he began loading luggage onto a cart.

"Last chance," Alex called to her little brother. "If you haven't packed it by now, you'll have to do without it for a long time."

"Come on," Kip said, racing ahead to the elevators. "Matt said all we'll need in Fiji is our bathing suits."

"Sounds like my idea of heaven," Cassie called, hurrying to keep up with him.

Alex followed with the bellman, loving the sound of her little brother's laughter. She'd already found heaven, she realized. And once she joined Matt in Fiji, her life would be complete.

"Look, Alex. A sea of diamonds."

Alex steeled herself and leaned over her little brother to chance a quick peek out the plane's window. Far below, the blue sun-dazzled Pacific looked indeed like a sea of diamonds as they circled the airport on Viti Levu, the largest of the Fiji Islands and site of Suva, the capital. Alex closed her hands in a death grip over the arms of the seat and prayed they would soon be back on land.

"How much longer before we see Matt?" Kip asked when they had landed.

"If our charter plane is ready, we'll get there in an hour and a half."

Crossing the tarmac, they saw a man holding a sign bearing Alex's name. "I'm Alex Corday," she said as she approached.

"Miss Corday." He tipped his hat and nodded toward Kip and Cassie. "If you will follow me, please."

They were led to the small, private plane that would take them on the last leg of their journey. Kip was invited to sit up front with the pilot and copilot, who explained the various instruments and how they were used. The little boy was clearly delighted. Cassie joined him. Alex, on the other hand, sat in the rear of the plane with the shades drawn over the windows.

Once airborne, they flew over dozens of tiny islands that glittered in the Pacific like a string of jewels.

"There." The pilot pointed to the small patch of green below. "That's Thala, where you'll be staying."

Volcanic crags were feathered with the greenest vegetation they had ever seen.

"That's the rain forest," the pilot explained. "Look." He pointed to a rainbow, arching up from the mist of rain below into the brilliant sun above.

As they descended, they could make out white beaches and lush mangrove marshes girding the shore. When the plane rolled to a stop on the runway and the stairs were lowered, they stepped out into a world of vivid color and bright sunshine.

"Hello, Kip. Welcome to Thala," Matt called.

"Matt!" The boy raced to his side and hugged him, clearly overjoyed to be with him again. "Look, Alex bought me a camera. I was hoping you'd teach me how to use it."

"You've come to the right person," Matt said, returning the hug. "There's almost nothing I like better than teaching someone all about photography. It's still my first love."

"Matt, this is my tutor, Cassie Miller."

Matt shook her hand. "Hello, Cassie. I hope you enjoy yourself in Thala."

"From what I've seen so far, it's going to be quite an adventure."

"Look, Cassie." Kip pointed to a brightly colored bird that flitted past.

"That looks like a wild parakeet," she said in disbelief.

"There are whole flocks of them," Matt explained. "They thrive in the rain forest, sheltered by giant tree ferns."

"Will we be able to explore the rain forest?"

"I've already arranged a guide."

"Wonderful. This will be better than any textbook. Come on, Kip. Let's get a closer look at that bird." Cassie took Kip's hand and the two ran off.

Matt turned to Alex. Just seeing her made his heart lighter.

"It's a good thing you finally got here." He opened his arms and gathered her close. In that instant he felt a rush of love and longing for her that left him shaken. "It's been so long, I was beginning to think I'd just dreamed you."

"Oh, I'm real," she breathed against his lips. "And tonight, if Kip ever manages to settle down and fall asleep—I'll show you just how real."

"Why, Miss Corday. If only your uncle's lawyer could hear you now." He caught her hand and led her toward the Jeep parked beside the runway. Then he drew her close for a quick, hard kiss just as Kip and Cassie returned. "I can't wait to take you up on that offer," he muttered.

It was a measure of how relaxed she'd become that she merely laughed. But he detected a faint blush on her cheeks. And he loved her for it.

"The island is only a little over five square miles. We'll be staying here," Matt said, pulling up in front of a magnificent plantation house that commanded a splendid view. "The cast and crew will stay there." He pointed to a dozen native-style guesthouses arranged in a circle around a freshwater pool and waterfall. "They all have modern kitchens and baths and amply stocked bars."

As soon as he turned off the engine, Kip and Cassie leapt out and raced ahead to the house. Matt and Alex joined hands and followed at a more leisurely pace, strolling through the spectacular gardens.

"How many natives live here on the island?" Alex asked as they went up the steps and through the front door.

"There are almost a hundred."

"Don't they consider us intruders in their paradise?"

"Not at all. They're delighted for the opportunity to work. They've already been busy cooking, baking, and getting the guest houses ready, while some of the men have been working with my set director building a platform at the top of the volcano to accommodate our cameras and crew."

"*Top* of the Volcano?" Alex's heart did a flipflop.

"Don't worry. I won't make you spend days on some high peak. I'll film as much as I can around you. And when I need you to actually be there, I'll try to clear the set so you can take your time and work through your fear. All right?"

She nodded, unconvinced, but unwilling to do battle at the moment. She would deal with it later.

"Look at this, Alex!" Kip shouted from somewhere up above them.

Alex and Matt followed his voice up the stairs and found him in a bright airy room equipped with paints and easels, shelves of textbooks, and teaching aids, including a computer.

"I thought you might need a classroom," Matt said.

"Wow. This is the best classroom I've ever seen." Kip ran his hand lovingly over the easel, clearly eager to begin.

"Your bedroom is next door," Matt said, leading the way.

The bedroom was big and cheerful, with ceiling fans slowly rotating. Just beyond the shuttered doors was a balcony that offered an unrestricted view of the ocean and beach.

"Cassie, I put you on the other side of the classroom, so that you'd have easy access to your textbooks. And Alex," Matt went on, leading them along the hallway, "I put you in the room next to Kip's."

Alex looked inside and sighed at the room's beauty. A huge four-poster was hung with netting, and pastel rugs on the floor and pale watercolors on the walls gave the room a decidedly feminine flair.

They continued through the house, with Matt giving them a guided tour.

"This is the kitchen. And this is Mai." Matt indicated the tall, dark-haired woman in a long flowing gown who was checking something in the oven.

"Hello, Mai. Whatever you're cooking, it smells wonderful," Alex said as she offered her hand.

"We killed a wild turkey in honor of your arrival," the woman explained. "It will be ready soon."

As they made their way through the dining room and parlor, Alex and Cassie admired the bamboo furniture, handwoven rugs, and tapa wall hangings that decorated the elegant rooms.

"Until dinner we'll relax out here."

Matt took them out to a wide veranda that ran the length of the house. The colorful blinds were rolled up, and they gazed out at the spectacular view of the white sand beach and the swaying palm trees. A handsome man in a white uniform stood behind a bamboo bar.

"This is Mai's husband, Varra." Matt said. "Would you like lemonade, Kip?"

"Yes, please."

"Alex? Cassie?"

They both nodded.

Alex gave a deep, contented sigh. "The hours spent in the air were all worth it, Matt. I do believe you've found paradise. I can't imagine anything more wonderful than sipping lemonade while we sit and do nothing more strenuous than watch the sunset."

"Four lemonades please, Varra," Matt said.

Alex closed her eyes and let go of all the tension that had been building on the long journey.

"Make mine a Scotch, rocks, Varra. In fact, make it a double."

At the imperious tone, everyone turned.

Alex felt her heart leap to her throat and stay there. A tremor pulsed along her spine, leaving her suddenly chilled. Of all the people she'd ever known, this was the only one who could turn even paradise into a living hell.

"What's the matter, Alex?" The deeply tanned, golden-haired man crossed the veranda and took both her hands, forcing her to meet his cynical gaze. "Don't tell me you've forgotten me?"

She stifled the cry that sprang to her lips as she found herself looking into the ice blue eyes of Dirk Montrose.

32

For the space of several heartbeats, Alex couldn't seem to find her voice. Then, pulling her hands from Dirk's grasp, she took a step back.

"No. I haven't forgotten you, Dirk." She glanced at Matt, who was just turning away from the bar with a glass of lemonade. "You didn't mention that your brother was here."

"He didn't tell you? I'm to be your costar," Dirk said.

"Costar?"

As she accepted the glass of lemonade Matt offered her, she felt her hand shake. Some of the liquid spilled over the rim. She turned away quickly, hoping to hide her reaction.

"And unlike some people," Dirk said, keeping his most charming smile in place, "I didn't get the part because of my relationship to the director." He took a long pull on his drink. "I had to lower myself to do a screen test. I guess Matt liked what he saw, because here I am." He drained his glass and handed it back for a refill. He turned and pinned Alex with a boyish grin. "Now isn't this a cozy situation? Here we all are."

"Alex, are you all right?" Seeing her pallor, Cassie touched her arm.

"It's . . . the long flight. If you don't mind, I think I'll go to my room and freshen up before dinner."

Without waiting for a reply she turned away, but not before catching sight of Dirk's smug, satisfied smile. Hurrying from the veranda, she could feel Matt's puzzled stare boring into her back.

Dirk Montrose. Here in Fiji.

Alex paced her room, her arms crossed over her chest.

How could the fates have played such a cruel trick on her?

This was the first time she'd seen him since that night. The moment she'd looked into those cold eyes the memories had come crashing down on her—the way he'd cajoled her into his car, the way he'd changed from sweet, charming innocent to a foul-tempered, evil man bent on hurting her. The words he'd flung. The threats he'd made. And the horror of those moments when he'd lost control and hit that old man.

Hit-and-run.

The screech of tires echoed in her head. For so long now she'd been able to block it all. After the fire that killed Nanna and the challenges of her life since then, she'd been able to push the memory into the darkest recesses of her consciousness. But now she would have to live and work with a man she considered a monster.

"I was hoping dinner would help, Alexandra. But you still look pale." Matt took Alex's arm as she rose to go out to the veranda, where Varra was serving coffee and dessert.

"It's just the effects of the trip. I'll be fine after a good night's sleep."

"And here I was hoping you wouldn't want to get much sleep tonight." He smiled and touched her hair. "I had . . . other things in mind for your first night in Fiji."

She felt her tension begin to evaporate. Her lips curved into a smile. Matt was her strength, her rock, her anchor.

Across the room Dirk watched them with a strange, intense look on his face. Getting to his feet, he strolled out to the veranda after them. "Have you had time to read the script?"

Alex nodded, unwilling to look at him, as if somehow, by refusing to do so, she could make him disappear. Keeping her gaze on Matt she said, "I read it on the plane."

"Pretty hot stuff, don't you think?" If Dirk noticed that she was avoiding him, he chose to ignore it.

She closed a hand over Matt's. "I thought it was a beautiful love story."

"Love?" Dirk gave a short laugh. "It's so hot, I think we ought to call it 'Pacific Lust.'"

Cassie, clearly delighted to be in the company of such a handsome, fascinating movie actor, steered Kip closer so they could be included in the conversation.

"Will Kip and I be allowed to watch the filming?" she asked shyly.

"Some of the time." Matt accepted a cup from Varra. His brother refused the coffee in favor of another Scotch. Dirk had been drinking steadily since midafternoon, and by now his speech was slurred and his footsteps none too steady. "When it doesn't interfere with Kip's studies."

Kip and Cassie exchanged grins, and Alex realized that the two were eagerly awaiting the beginning of filming, while she was already dreading it. How in the world could she possibly play a love story with Dirk Montrose?

Matt felt the slight tensing of her fingers. With a look of concern he lifted her chin and studied her eyes. Fatigue? he wondered. Or was she worried about this new step in her career?

"Are you sure you're all right, Alexandra?"

"I'm fine. It's just jet lag. I think I'd better go to bed now."

She and Matt stood, and Matt pressed a kiss to her lips before she turned toward her little brother.

"Kip, it's your bedtime too."

Before the boy could argue, Cassie took his hand. "Come on. The sun and the sand and the ocean will still be here in the morning."

Matt watched them go. When he turned, he found his brother studying him. For a moment he thought he detected a glint of something dark and evil in Dirk's eyes. But in the next moment Dirk blinked and smiled.

"This is great," Dirk remarked with enthusiasm. "You and I finally working together. It's been a dream of mine for as long as I can remember."

"I'm glad too." Matt tried to push aside his uneasiness. Hadn't he given his word to Elyse that there was little trouble to be found on a tiny island like Thala? He hoped the worst thing Dirk could find to do in this place was drink a little too much.

At least for the few months they were filming, Elyse could be assured that her son would be able to put his past behind him and concentrate on a successful future. And maybe, just maybe, they could finally function as a real family.

"This is an excellent place to begin our studies of sea plants and animals." Cassie and Kip gathered shells along a stretch of deserted beach and placed them in a basket. "All of these shells were once living creatures, Kip. This one, for instance—"

"Was probably my dinner last night."

At the sound of Dirk's voice they both looked up.

Since his arrival on the island, he'd worked hard at perfecting his tan. Now, barefoot, wearing only a pair of white tennis shorts, he sauntered closer, aware of the effect his presence was having on the boy's young tutor.

"Hello." Cassie completely forgot what she'd been saying. This handsome movie star was better than any dream hero she could have invented. Tall, blond, muscular, and so comfortable with his blatant sexuality, he had her completely dazzled.

"Teacher, don't you ever take some time off to just play?"

"There's plenty of time to play after our lessons are over."

"Okay. The lessons are over. Let's call it a day." He took the shell from her hand and tossed it away. "Now I'd like to take you for a boat ride around the island."

"But I—" She stopped, unable to summon the nerve to argue with a man of his importance. He was, after all, not only the star of the movie but the brother of the director as well. Despite warnings from Alex to keep her distance from Dirk Montrose, Cassie couldn't ignore the attraction.

"Can I go too?" Kip asked.

"Hey, I'd really like that, kid. But you'd better not," Dirk put in smoothly. "Your sister is looking for you."

"Alex?" The boy brightened. "Is she through filming for the day?"

"Yeah." Dirk never took his eyes off Cassie. "You go find that sister of yours. Your teacher and I are going for a ride."

"Will you be back in time for supper?"

Dirk dropped an arm around Cassie's shoulders and started walking with her in the opposite direction. "Maybe," he called over his shoulder. "Or maybe we'll find something else to satisfy our hunger."

Kip watched them walk down the beach. He had a bad feeling about Dirk. There was something in those blue eyes that reminded him of Uncle Vince, something cruel and dark and frightening. But he would never speak of his fear. After all, Dirk was Matt's brother. And next to Alex, Matt Montrose was the most important person in Kip's life.

He turned and ran back toward the plantation house, eager to spend some time with his sister.

*   *   *

Alex's room was in semidarkness, the shutters closed to keep out the sunlight. She paced the length of the room and back, like a caged animal.

Each day, the sparring between herself and Dirk had escalated. He did everything he could to undermine her confidence, even attempting to ruin their scenes together. And each day she had to struggle to hold herself together, and her control was beginning to slip. She knew it, but she was unable to do anything about it.

Today had been the worst. Today she and Dirk had filmed their first love scenes.

The touch of his hand on her flesh had felt so repulsive, she had actually flinched. But instead of halting the action, Matt had ordered them to continue, saying the scene was perfect. With each touch, her reaction to Dirk had become more and more violent, until she wondered how she could possibly complete the scene. The first time they had kissed for the cameras, she felt a loathing that left her trembling.

And all the while, Matt had merely watched, in that cool, detatched way he had when he was directing.

In desperation, she had concocted a complaint about the effects of too much sun. Only then had Matt finally, mercifully, called a halt to the filming, and she'd fled to the sanctuary of her room.

Despite the heat, she was still trembling. She stopped her pacing and stood very still, willing her mind to empty. But it was impossible to stop the images that had been tormenting her from the first moment she had seen Dirk again, images of an old man, his eyes wide, his hands lifted as if to hold back the destruction that hurtled toward him like a fireball.

* * *

Matt sat alone in the small screening room, watching the daily rushes. He'd played them over and over, until he knew every frame by heart. Whatever flaws Dirk might possess—and they were many—Matt had to admit that there was one indisputable fact: Dirk had grown considerably as an actor. He was more than capable of carrying off this role. And Alexandra had proven herself to be a gifted actress.

But Matt had been around a camera too long to think it could lie. What he saw onscreen were a man and woman who sizzled in every encounter. There was no denying the very real tension between Dirk and Alexandra.

He froze the frame of their first onscreen kiss and sat back, making an effort to be objective, but the truth was, he couldn't be objective about Alexandra and his brother. Long ago, Dirk had planted the seed of suspicion in Matt's mind by suggesting that he and Alexandra had spent the night together after Sidney's party. Could there have been some grain of truth in what he'd said?

Jealousy. It was something so alien to him, Matt could hardly acknowledge it. But the truth was, it tore at his guts. He hated seeing the woman he loved in the arms of his brother.

Doubts nagged at him. He and Alexandra had spent every night together since her arrival. It was an accepted fact among the cast and crew that they were lovers. The feelings that poured between them were genuine. Such feelings couldn't be contrived.

Still, in every scene, Alexandra and Dirk made sparks fly.

As the film's director, he should be ecstatic. This kind of chemistry guaranteed box-office success. But where Alexandra was concerned, he wasn't just the director. He was the man who loved her. And right now, his thoughts were dark and tormented.

"Dirk." Alex knocked on the door of Dirk's hut, twisting her hands together nervously. Throughout the long weeks of filming, she'd agonized over this. Now that the film was wrapping, she had to confront him.

Though she had carefully thought through what she wanted to say, the butterflies in her stomach wouldn't be calmed.

Dirk opened the door. "Well." He studied her, then stepped back so she could enter. "What's up, Alex? Don't tell me you want to run through another love scene."

"I . . . need to talk to you."

"Okay. Talk." He took a seat and stretched out his long legs, crossing them at the ankles. It was a relaxed, careless pose that infuriated her. "Want a drink?" he asked, holding up a crystal tumbler filled with amber liquid. On the table beside him was a vial of tablets.

"No. I just . . ." She ran a tongue over her dry lips and went restlessly to the window, where she turned. "I want you to know that I've never forgotten about that night, when you forced me to go in your car."

"Oh?" He grinned and took a long drink. "Is that your story? I forced you?"

She clenched her fists. "You know what you did. What's more, you killed that old man. I read about it the next day in the paper. His name was Freddy Trilby. And he died."

"My, my." His smile grew. "And you never went to the authorities? I'd say that makes you an accessory to a crime. Now what do you have to say about that, Miss Goody Two Shoes?"

She turned away. "I intended to," she admitted, looking out the window. "And I would have, but something happened that day that made me forget about everything. There was a tragic fire at my home and my Nanna—"

He crossed the room so quickly she had no time to react. As he grabbed her arm she shrank back, but he drew her close and gripped her hair in his fist, pulling her head back sharply. The stench of liquor was strong on his breath as he hissed, "Don't bore me with all the details. I'm not interested in your sad stories. And I don't think the authorities would care about your puny excuses. The fact is, it's all in the past—and that's where it belongs. None of that has any place in my life now. And you have no right to jeopardize my future by bringing it up. So let it go, lady"—he yanked her hair so hard it brought tears to her eyes—"or I'll make you sorry you ever laid eyes on me."

"You can't frighten me, Dirk."

"Can't I?" He gave her a cruel, lazy smile. "You know that little brother of yours?"

Her eyes widened with fear, and he felt a rush of triumph. He's known that would be the right button to push.

"How'd you like to lose him?"

Alex tried to pull away, but he tightened his grasp. She forced herself to meet his gaze.

"The courts would never take him from me."

"I wasn't talking about the courts, lady. The kid told me he couldn't swim, so I've offered to teach him." He enjoyed the look of pure terror in her eyes. "But I've warned him he'll have to watch out for sharks. They've been known to come right up to shore and gobble up tasty little boys whose sisters have big mouths. Now, if you value that kid brother of yours, get out of here." He gave her a shove that sent her reeling. "And don't bother me again."

"You leave Kip alone or—"

"Or what? You'll cry?"

"I'll go to Matt," she said, driven by desperation. "I'll tell him everything."

Dirk had always had the ability to think quickly. Swallowing back his anger he shot her a smile of triumph.

"Go ahead. You think he doesn't know?"

She gave a little gasp. "I don't believe you."

He laughed, clearly on a roll now. "You know those strings he pulled to get your cousin to that custody hearing in time? He's had years of experience. He's pulled strings to save my ass dozens of times. When he found out about the hit-and-run, he pulled strings to get me out of the country. And now he's pulled some more to get me home. So if you're smart, lady, you'll shut your mouth and do the job you were brought here to do. But if you want to risk your relationship with Matt, go ahead and cry on his shoulder." He laughed again. "For all the good it'll do you."

Alex lifted a trembling hand to her mouth. Could it be? Could Matt have known all along? Had he kept in contact with Dirk all this time while he floated around

Europe? After all, it had been Matt who had brought Dirk back to star in his movie. Dear God. If Matt knew and had said nothing, it meant he would do nothing to bring the law down on his own family. Yet even hearing it from his brother's lips, she couldn't bring herself to believe it.

Feeling stunned and terrified, Alex yanked open the door and fled, desperate to escape Dirk's cruel laughter.

Cassie, walking through the gardens toward Dirk's cottage, was dismayed to see Alex running out his door. The young woman chewed on her lip. Just when she'd begun to think she had Dirk all to herself, Alexandra Corday was cutting herself in on the action. It wasn't fair. A star like Alex could have any man she wanted. It was obvious that she already had his brother. Why did she have to want Dirk, too? But at least now she knew why Alex had warned her away.

Someone else was watching as Alex exited Dirk's hut. Alone in his bedroom, Matt looked down and saw her make her way around the pool toward the plantation house. The more he brooded about it, the more his surprise turned to doubt. And the more the doubt turned to pain.

Dirk was smooth and charming as he led Cassie toward a lonely stretch of beach. He carried a blanket under one arm and kept the other around her waist. Today had been the last day of filming. The rest of the cast had been dismissed early, so that Matt could film the final scenes with Alex, at the top of the volcano.

"I—I can't keep quiet about this any longer." Cassie's

voice trembled with nervousness. "I saw Alex coming out of your hut yesterday."

Dirk enjoyed pouring on the charm. "Cassie, don't worry your pretty head about Alex. We had a one-night stand years ago, and she's never let me forget it. She's been doing everything she can to get me to pay attention to her again. I just can't get away from her. Can you imagine how my brother would react if he found out?" He shuddered. "Matt has a vicious temper." He drew Cassie into his arms and kissed her. "But let's not talk about Matt and Alex. Cassie, I swear, I never felt about her the way I feel about you. In fact, I've never felt this way about anybody before."

"I hope that's not just some Hollywood line."

"Hey." He caught her chin and stared deeply into her eyes, enjoying the role he was playing. "Look at me. Do you think I need to resort to phony lines?"

She smiled, showing her dimples. "Of course not. I'm sorry, Dirk. It's just—"

"Okay. That's better." He spread out the blanket and sat down. "You didn't say anything to Alex about me, did you?"

"Not a word."

"That's my girl." He drew her down to lie beside him on the blanket.

"But . . ."

"But what?"

"She said something about you."

His hand on her thigh stilled; his eyes narrowed. "What did she say?"

Cassie shrugged. "She didn't tell me why, but she said I wasn't supposed to let you spend any time alone with Kip, for any reason."

"The kid?" Dirk laughed, though the smile never reached his eyes. "It's not him I want to be alone with, honey, it's you." He slowly moved his hand upward, enjoying the sense of power it gave him to see how easily he could manipulate this girl. She was like putty in his hands. "What else did Alex say?"

"Nothing. I'm just worried about her. She was so tense this morning, she could hardly speak."

"She's probably just eaten up with jealousy about you and me."

"No. She was genuinely sick. I saw her in the bathroom. She was too sick to lift her head. She said it was because she knew she had to go to the top of the volcano."

"Why should that make her sick?"

"You don't know about her phobia? She's absolutely terrified of heights. She saw her father fall to his death, and ever since then, she becomes paralyzed whenever she has to climb higher than a story or two."

"A fear of heights? Now that's interesting." Dirk's eyes glinted with malice. It was so easy to get Cassie to betray a confidence. All he had to do was touch her . . .

He heard her sigh of pleasure and brought his lips to her throat. "Is there anything else I ought to know about my costar? Any more fears or phobias she'd hiding?"

Cassie boldly ran her hands through his blond hair and felt a tingle clear to her toes. She'd never been with anyone like Dirk before. He was the most skillful lover she'd ever known. She couldn't wait to tell her friends that she'd been in Fiji with Dirk Montrose. If she played her cards right, she and Dirk might even be engaged by the time they returned home—or at least have become an item in the tabloids.

"Well, she did try to put a call through to the Los Angeles Police Department, but I don't know what it was about."

His head came up. "When did she do that?"

"Before she left for today's shoot. But the lines were all jammed. I heard her say she'd try again tonight when she gets back to her room."

Dirk sucked air into his lungs. The damn bitch was going to do it. She was going to risk everything and turn him in. His mind raced. He had to stop her. He was on his way to stardom. He was so close he could taste it. Nothing and no one could be allowed to get in his way.

Cassie's eyes opened. Seeing the look on his face she said, "What's wrong?"

"Where'd you leave the kid?"

"Kip?"

"Yeah," he snarled. "Where is he?"

She shrugged, completely bewildered by his strange behavior. "Back in his room, I guess. He said he was going to try to paint a view of the ocean from his balcony. But why—"

He got to his feet. "I've got to go."

Scrambling up from the blanket, Cassie caught his arm. "Dirk, what's wrong? Aren't we going to . . .?"

He shook her off as if she were an annoying gnat. "I just remembered something important I have to do."

"Dirk!"

But he was already sprinting up the beach.

33

"*That's a wrap,*" Matt called to the technicians, who applauded vigorously before they began
packing away cameras and equipment. He turned to
Alexandra. "I know you're uncomfortable up here. If
you'd like, you can go down in the first Jeep that's
loaded."

"It's all right. I really don't mind, Matt, as long as I
don't have to move." She'd come to a decision. Once
the cast and crew had left them alone here, away from
any possible interruptions, she would tell him. She
knew now that he couldn't possibly have any knowledge of Dirk's crime, but she had to tell him she was
going to report it to the police.

"I'll just sit here in the middle of this platform and
wait to ride down with you."

He nodded and began giving orders to the technicians and drivers, who were piling the equipment into
vehicles.

Matt was pleased. His patience had paid off. The morning shoot had gone well, despite Alexendra's acute discomfort. In fact, he thought she looked better than she had in days.

Last night, after long hours studying the rushes, he'd found her asleep in his bed. Though she'd wanted to talk, passion had prevailed, and they'd made love with almost reckless abandon, falling asleep in each other's arms. This morning, knowing she had to film atop the volcano, she'd been back in her own room before he awoke.

But once they'd begun filming, she seemed more relaxed than she had at any time since her arrival. It was as though she had resolved some inner conflict and had found a measure of peace within herself.

Though she refused to glance up toward the rim of the volcano and sat without moving in the center of the platform they'd built, her color was good, and she'd even managed to joke with the crew.

"Where are you going with those?" She pointed to the cameras he'd slung over his shoulder.

"I thought I'd climb to the rim of the volcano and get a few pictures."

She looked alarmed. "You mean . . . you'd actually go inside?"

"Not very far," Matt explained. "Even though it hasn't erupted in many years, there's too much rock and ash to go more than a few hundred feet inside the crater. After that there's a steep drop. It shouldn't take me more than twenty minutes. Do you mind?"

She shook her head, swallowing her disappointment. "I guess I shouldn't mind." She managed a weak laugh. "As long as you don't expect me to go with you."

He brushed her lips with a kiss and felt the familiar rush of heat. God, he loved her. But he never seemed to find the right moment to tell her all that was in his heart. He hoped, with the filming completed, they'd have a chance to talk about a future together.

"Will you be all right?"

"I'll be fine." She gave him a warm smile. "I won't budge from this spot until you return." They both laughed at her joke, knowing she really would be too terrified to move from the safety of the platform.

As Matt started up the trail to the top of the volcano, Alex turned her back, too frightened to even watch. The mere thought of climbing higher made her weak.

The first Jeeps pulled away, carrying the equipment and technicians. She mulled over what she was about to do. It would hurt Matt, and it would drive a wedge between them. It might even drive him from her forever. The thought of losing the man she loved was too painful to contemplate. But she no longer had any choice. She knew that she had to go to the authorities with the truth and somehow deal with the consequences.

The press would have a field day with this one. She might even be prosecuted as an accessory to a homicide.

She shivered. No matter. Her mind was made up. Under no circumstances would she back down.

She watched the Jeeps as they followed the trail back down to the shore. Seeing the huts so far below caused her stomach to lurch. She closed her eyes and gripped the arms of her chair, waiting for the feeling to pass.

Minutes later she heard the crunch of wheels on gravel and was relieved that one of the Jeeps had returned so quickly. As soon as Matt finished photographing the volcano, they could have their private little talk and leave. She would be so grateful to be back on solid ground again.

She began speaking before she turned toward the sound of footsteps.

"Matt isn't back from the top yet, but—"

Her smile froze. It wasn't the Fijian driver walking toward her. It was Kip. His eyes were wide with fear. His arms were pinned behind him, making walking along the gravel path difficult.

The golden hair of the man who was shoving Kip toward her glinted. As they came closer, she saw Dirk's feral smile. In his hand was a very small, very lethal-looking gun.

Matt took the last of the photographs, then slowly climbed out of the crater. Standing at the very rim of the volcano, he lifted a hand to shield the sun from his eyes. He could see the Jeep just coming to a stop beside the platform. From this distance it was impossible to see the driver.

Knowing that Alexandra was eager to return to solid ground, he started down the trail.

Alex had started to rise when she'd heard the footsteps. Now she went around behind her chair and gripped it, staring unblinkingly as Dirk approached.

"Well, isn't this convenient? Nobody here but us."

The sight of her stricken face caused him to throw back his head and laugh. "Look who I brought to see the volcano."

"Why did you bring my brother up here?"

"I figured I might need a bargaining chip," Dirk said with a chilling smile. "In case you decided to try something stupid." He glanced around. "Did I hear you say Matt's up there?"

"No. He's . . ." She swallowed and tried to think. "He's gone down with the crew."

"Leave the lying to an expert, lady. Do you expect me to believe that he left you all alone up here?"

Feigning laughter, she said, "I wanted to stay a little longer. It's a pretty view, don't you think?"

His tone was icy. "Cut the crap, Alex. I know all about your secret phobia."

Seeing her look of astonishment, he gave a satisfied little cat smile. "Oh yeah. I know all about your fear of heights."

"How could you know that?"

"The same way I know that you ordered Cassie not to leave me alone with your precious little brother."

"Cassie . . ." Alex had seen all the signs. Despite repeated warnings, the innocent young teacher had obviously become deeply involved with this schemer.

He shrugged. "Can I help it if women find me irresistible?" Watching her eyes, he added, "Cassie told me something else, too."

He was enjoying himself. The sense of power was more compelling than any drug. "She said you tried to phone the L.A. police this morning. Fortunately, the lines were jammed, and you didn't get through."

Alex was horrified that Cassie had repeated something so private. "Why . . ." She licked her lips and tried again. "Why would Cassie tell you that?"

"Because she loves me." He gave a low, chilling laugh as he stepped up onto the platform, forcing Kip ahead of him, and approached her. "Didn't you know? I'm a real lovable guy, if you treat me right. But you just don't know how to treat a guy, Alex. You betray them. I'm not nice to people who betray me."

Hearing the crunch of footsteps his smile faded. He waved the gun and snarled, "Keep your mouth shut."

"No, Dirk. I know what you're planning. Go ahead and shoot me. I won't help you trick Matt."

As she opened her mouth to shout a warning, his arm swung out and he struck her on the side of the head with the pistol.

The blow sent her reeling. Dazed, she dropped to her knees and pressed a hand to the sticky warmth at her temple. Her fingers came away smeared with blood. As Kip tried to go to her, Dirk tightened his grip on the boy's shoulder.

"Aren't you the brave one?" he sneered. "But I won't have to shoot you, Alex; I'll just shoot the kid here."

He wrapped an arm around Kip's shoulders, then raised the gun and pointed it at his temple. He saw the fear that darkened her pupils.

Alex couldn't tear her gaze from the weapon that glinted in the sunlight.

"No." She lifted her arms imploringly. "Don't hurt my brother. I'll do whatever you ask," she whispered.

"That's better." Dirk took a step back, drawing himself and the boy into the shadows of the bushes alongside the platform.

Alex remained silent, powerless to prevent Matt from walking into Dirk's trap.

"Sorry, Alexandra. I didn't mean to keep you waiting so long, but the scenery inside the volcano is breathtaking. Kip would have loved . . ."

The words died on Matt's lips when he caught sight of Alex hunched over on her knees, looking like a small, wounded bird.

"My God. Alexandra." Matt knelt beside her and gathered her into his arms. "What happened?"

Dirk stepped out from the cover of the bushes. "Looks like your lover met with an accident."

Matt's eyes narrowed when he caught sight of the gun pressed to Kip's head. "What the hell is this about?"

"It's about my checkered past."

"Your past will have to wait." Matt turned to Kip. "Are you all right?"

The boy swallowed and nodded his head.

"Let him come here," Matt commanded. "I want to see for myself."

Dirk shoved the boy forward and he stumbled to his knees beside his sister. She gathered him close and hugged him fiercely.

Taking a handkerchief from his pocket, Matt touched it to the blood at Alex's forehead. When he was convinced that she was all right, he turned to Dirk.

"Explain yourself," he said.

"Don't take that tone with me, big brother. You're not the director of this scene. This gun says I'm the one in charge now."

"And what are you going to do, Dirk? Kill us all?"

Dirk smiled. "That's exactly what I'm going to do. Would you like to know why?"

When Matt remained silent, Dirk said, "It seems your girlfriend here has decided that it's her duty to expose an accident I was involved in."

"Accident?" Matt looked from Dirk to Alex. "I don't understand."

Alex felt a wave of relief that Matt knew nothing about the accident. "There was a hit-and-run accident," she said. "The night we met, after your father's party. Dirk killed an old man."

"Old man! Alexandra, tell me what this is about."

Struggling to keep the hysteria from her voice, she told him quickly about that night. "The next day, I read in the paper that the old man was dead."

"Why didn't you go to the police?"

"I intended to. That day you gave me a ride home from school."

Matt remembered how withdrawn she'd been, how frightened.

"But then, with the fire, and Nanna's death . . ." Her voice trailed off.

Matt turned to his brother. "So that's why you took off so quickly for Europe."

Dirk gave a slight nod. "Everything would have been fine if Alex had been home like I thought."

"Home?" Alex repeated.

"The day of the fire. Your car was parked out front. I figured since you were the only witness, all I needed to do was get rid of you and I'd be home free."

As the truth dawned, she looked at him with a growing sense of horror and revulsion. "Oh my God! The fire—you deliberately set it. You killed Nanna."

Matt stared at the gun in Dirk's hand. "And now he intends to kill us. How will you explain this one, Dirk?"

Dirk's smile was angelic. "It's simple. I'll tell the authorities you killed Alex in a jealous rage. Then you turned the gun on yourself."

"You think the police will buy that story?"

"Oh, did I forget to tell you? This isn't my gun." Dirk opened his palm and admired it, as if it were a beautiful woman. "It's yours, Matt. I took it from your room." He gave Alex another innocent smile. "The cast and crew have noticed how moody my big brother's been lately. Probably all those love scenes you and I had to do over and over, until we got them just right. And when I tell the police that you and I have been carrying on a torrid affair in secret, and about his jealous rages, they'll understand only too well how you happened to be murdered at the top of the volcano."

"No one will believe that," Alex sneered.

"Want to bet? I've already told Cassie we were lovers. That made her more than willing to spy on you. She'll be only too happy to repeat the story to the authorities."

"And Kip?" Matt asked calmly. "How will you explain his death?"

"In a panic, he's going to fall from the rim of the volcano, where he went to hide from his sister's murderer." Dirk motioned with the gun. "Let's go. We're climbing to the top."

"I can't, Matt," Alex whispered. "You know I can't climb to the top."

"You have to." He helped her to her feet and murmured against her ear, "If we can just buy some time, we might still be able to beat him."

She saw the fire in his eyes and remembered what he'd said about all those years of dangerous assignments. There was something about living on the edge that stirred the blood and brought out the best in a person.

She gritted her teeth and nodded. "I can do it."

"Good girl."

He kept an arm around her waist as they began to climb the steep slope. Kip clasped her hand and clung to it tightly, as if willing her his strength even as he tried to absorb hers.

The climb to the top of the volcano was the hardest thing Alex had ever done. All the way up she envisioned her father, climbing from a window to the top of the building, her father falling, falling through space, missing the net by no more than a few feet.

She stumbled and Matt held her tightly, murmuring words of encouragement, until she found her balance. With her breath coming in shallow gasps, she forced herself to put one foot in front of the other.

When they reached the pinnacle, Alex had to close her eyes against the dizziness that rose up in her. She knew that it was only a matter of minutes before she would be too sick to move. Sinking to her knees, she bowed her head.

With a look of contempt, Dirk turned to his brother. "Take a good look at the woman who thought she was strong enough to beat me. God, I hate having to deal with weaklings."

Matt's eyes narrowed on the gun. "Why don't you deal with me?"

Seeing the direction of Matt's gaze, Dirk taunted,

"Go ahead, big brother. Try to wrestle it away from me. It'll make it so much easier for me to kill you."

Matt gauged the distance between them. He knew it was impossible to dodge a bullet, but at least the distraction might be enough for Alexandra and Kip to escape into the surrounding brush.

"I wish there'd been time to tell you all the things in my heart, Alexandra."

Her head came up; her eyes widened with fear. She knew from the expression on Matt's face what he planned to do. Hadn't he always faced danger head on? "Please, Matt. Please don't risk it," she begged.

"Oh God," Dirk moaned. "Spare me the melodrama."

For one brief moment Matt thought about the searing pain when the land mine had exploded. Could a bullet be any worse? Steeling himself, he lunged.

There was the quick sound of a gunshot, and then the sound of Dirk's laughter, which was abruptly cut off when Matt continued coming at him despite the blood that spurted from his shoulder.

While the two men struggled for control of the gun, there was a second loud report. Matt's body jerked violently.

"You killed him!" Kip's voice was high-pitched with hysteria.

"Not . . . dead," Matt moaned as he dropped to his knees, fighting to hold on to the last thread of consciousness.

"Matt! Matt!" Kip's cries bounced off the rim of the volcano and echoed across the crater. He looked up at Dirk. "How could you kill your own brother?"

"Shut up, kid." Dirk's eyes were glazed with hatred.

"He was never my brother. He was Sidney Montrose's son. And I was always on the outside looking in."

"Your . . . choice," Matt barely got out. He could feel his life slipping away. He no longer had the strength to kneel and sprawled forward in the grass. "You spent . . . lifetime breaking the rules . . . crying when you got caught."

"Yeah? Well, who's crying now?" Dirk laughed, and the sound sent shivers down Alex's spine. "Don't you realize I'm about to make you immortal, Matt? The publicity about your murder-suicide will shoot your film to the top of the charts. And if you should follow in your father's footsteps and win an Academy Award for direction, I'll make such an emotional acceptance speech there won't be a dry eye in the house."

Alex realized that for this brief moment, Dirk had forgotten her, assuming that her fear had rendered her useless. She braced herself. Now, when everything depended upon being clearheaded, she couldn't afford to give in to the weakness that threatened her. If she had to die, she reasoned, she would do so without any sign of fear.

She closed her hand around a rock.

"The truth is," Dirk said, aiming the gun at Matt's temple, "I've discovered that I enjoy killing. The old man was a surprise. But when I watched that house burn with that old lady inside, I got a rush that was better than sex or drugs."

Alex felt a blaze of white-hot fury. Her fear was forgotten. There was no time left for any emotion except a burning, blinding rage.

"Who knows how high I'll get when—"

Dirk seemed genuinely surprised when the heavy

object struck the back of his head. He whirled, aiming the gun at Alex. "Do you really think you can win over this?"

Kip bent over and snatched up another rock, which he tossed with deadly accuracy. In a fury, Dirk turned and pointed the gun at the boy.

Without a thought for her own safety, Alex leapt between them, rushing at Dirk with all the ferocity of a wild creature. The two of them went tumbling down the hillside in a tangle of flailing arms and legs.

There was a single loud gunshot. Then nothing.

"Oh my God," Matt gasped. "Alexandra." Reaching beyond the pain, he forced himself to stand and stumble down the incline, with Kip following.

By the time Kip and Matt reached her side, Alex had disentangled herself from Dirk's grasp and lay gasping for breath. Dirk lay motionless beside her. A pool of blood made a widening circle on the front of his shirt.

Matt knelt and pressed his fingers to Dirk's throat. Finding no pulse, he turned to Alex. His hands were shaking as he gathered her close. "Are you hurt?"

Dazed, she shook her head. "I don't think so. What about you? Oh, Matt, are you all right? I thought—I thought you were dead." She touched his shoulder, where blood oozed from a raw, gaping wound.

"I'll live. Kip," he muttered, grasping the boy's hand. "Are you steady enough to go for help?"

The boy nodded and, assured that his sister and Matt were going to be all right, raced off.

Matt could feel the darkness starting to close in. Falling onto his side, he curled up on the grass. It had been the same after the Jeep hit the mine. First had been the pain, then the darkness.

Knowing he was close to losing consciousness, he muttered, "Too weak to get up."

"It's all right, Matt." she put her arms around him. "We'll just lie here together."

"You were so brave." He struggled to make his lips move. His words were slurred. "Where'd you learn that?"

She felt slightly drunk, and wondered if this was the sort of high her father used to feel after a particularly dangerous stunt. "Probably something in the genes." She stroked his hair and felt such a welling of love for this man whose eyes were slowly closing. "You weren't half bad yourself, Mr. Montrose."

His hand fisted in her hair and he dragged her face close. His mouth was moving, but no words came out.

Suddenly his hand went limp. She wrapped herself around him, willing him her strength. "Don't leave me, Matt. Stay. Live. There's so much I haven't told you yet. So much. I love you. Oh Matt, I love you."

She could no longer hold back the tears. With her face buried against his neck, she wept.

That was how Kip and the driver found them when the Jeep arrived to return them to the village below.

34

Alex closed the last of her suitcases and went to the window for a final look at the island. The drone of idling engines filled the air as the planes waited on the runway for their departure.

So much had happened. For days the little island had been overrun with swarms of reporters. The Fijian authorities had taken depositions from everyone involved and were now headed back to the mainland on the same plane that carried Dirk's body. Sidney Montrose had sent a team of medical specialists to tend to Matt's wounds, which were healing nicely.

Buddy had arrived to take charge of the media. At his insistence, no interviews were given unless he was present to direct the flow of information.

Gary, Sara, Bear, and Tina had made the long flight to offer their love and support. In just days their presence had brought a measure of normality to Kip's life, and Alex found herself relaxing in the knowledge that her little brother was surrounded by people who cared about him. Cassie, still reeling from the humiliation of having been duped by Dirk's smooth-talking charm, had tried to resign as Kip's tutor, but Alex had insisted that she stay on. In time, Alex assured her, she would be able to put this behind her and get on with her life.

It was still hard for any of them to believe that such horror could have occurred in this island paradise.

"Come on, sweet lips," Buddy called, interrupting her musings. "Time to board."

One of the natives picked up her suitcases and headed out the door. Alex took a last lingering look around the room. Then, taking Buddy's arm, she walked down the stairs and out into the blinding sunshine.

The islanders, wearing colorful, flowing ceremonial robes, stood in a half circle, calling out salutations as the cast and crew boarded the plane.

Alex looked around for Matt, who had been sequestered in the library with Buddy for the past few hours. She spotted him giving last-minute instructions to the technicians, who were loading equipment aboard the plane. Seeing her, he made his way across the tarmac.

"What was the doctor's verdict?" she asked.

"I'll be as good as new in a few weeks." He touched a finger to her cheek. "How about you?"

"I'm fine."

"Yes, you are." He lifted her chin and stared into her eyes. "In case I haven't told you lately, you are one hell of a woman, Alexandra Corday."

Seeing the two of them together Buddy hurried

over. It wouldn't do for them to get too cozy. He'd just spent the past couple of hours explaining to Matt how important it was for Alex to get back to civilization and do another tour as soon as possible.

"Come on, sweet lips," Buddy shouted. "Time to get aboard."

"Yes. I—I'm coming." She turned to Matt. "Is your luggage already on board?"

Matt ran a hand through his hair in a gesture of frustration. "Alexendra, there's so much I haven't . . . There are just so many damn loose ends. I wish . . ."

Kip raced up, slightly out of breath. "Matt, Buddy just told me that you aren't flying back with us."

Matt saw the shocked look on Alexandra's face and cursed his timing. He was surprised at how painful this was. "That's what I was trying to say. It looks like I'll have to be here for a few more days, maybe a week." He turned to the little boy and wondered why it was so hard to say good-bye. After all, the boy wasn't his little brother. But he found himself wishing . . . "I have a lot of things to do here before I can leave, Kip."

"Well," Kip said, looking a little defeated, "I hope I get to see your house in Malibu sometime."

"I'd like that." Matt gathered the boy close and enveloped him in an affectionate hug. "As soon as your sister and I can get our busy schedules together, I'll have you both come and visit. And you can show me what you've been doing with your camera. Okay?"

Kip's lower lip trembled. "Sure. I . . ." His eyes blurred with tears. Embarrassed, he wiped them away with the back of his hand. He seemed to have run out of words. "I guess I'll see you, then," he said finally.

He raced away and climbed the steps to the plane.

Stung by the unexpected turn of events, Alex turned away without a word.

Matt swore in frustration as he caught her arm. "I hope you'll believe me, Alexandra. This wasn't the way I'd planned it."

"Hey, Alex, come on," Buddy shouted. "We're going to be late. I've scheduled a news conference back in the States. You'll be the lead-in on the six o'clock news all around the country."

Alex started to walk away, but Matt put his hand on her arm, stopping her. He thought of all the things he wanted to tell her, but the time wasn't right. Maybe, the way their lives were going, the time would never be right.

"Good-bye, Alexandra," he said, holding her close. "Safe journey."

She clung to him for a moment, squeezing her eyes shut. One word, one hint that he wanted her to stay, and she would remain at his side forever. But when he remained silent, she drew away, fighting tears.

"Good-bye, Matt."

He felt a stab of pain as she walked across the tarmac and climbed the steps to the plane. Damn Buddy! he thought as he swore loudly, fiercely. And damn the fates that had just taken away the only woman he'd ever loved.

The thought of staying around to watch her departure was too painful. Turning away, he made his way back to the plantation house, where he went inside and slowly climbed the stairs. The sound of the plane's engines grew louder as the aircraft began racing along the runway.

Leaning a hip against the windowsill, Matt watched

from his bedroom window as the plane lifted into the air and slowly circled. The loneliness struck him like a blow.

He'd let her go, without telling her all the things he'd wanted to. He rubbed his shoulder, almost welcoming the pain. At least it would end. But what about the pain in his heart?

He thought about all the reasons why he should have begged her to stay. Then he thought about the reasons why he'd let her go without a word.

Buddy had argued vehemently that she go. She was so young; she had a right to taste life, all of it, without Matt's interference. Her career was so hot right now, she would find herself bombarded with movie and concert offers. And of course there was her brother, Kip. She had a right to spend some time alone with him. They had a need to build a life together, before she complicated her life with any other commitments.

Commitments. His hand clenched into a fist and he pounded it against the wall in frustration, turning away from the window.

It was then that he saw the vision standing in the doorway.

For a full minute he couldn't believe his eyes. He blinked.

"Alexandra?"

The vision smiled and floated toward him. He opened his arms, and she gave a delighted laugh as she pressed herself against him.

"My God. Are you real?"

"Maybe you'd better kiss me to find out." She lifted her face and offered him her lips.

His arms tightened, gathering her so close he

could feel her rapid heartbeat against his chest. He felt the familiar rush of heat as he pressed his lips to her hair.

Lifting his head a fraction he muttered, "But how did you . . . ? I saw you get on the plane."

She nodded and kissed his throat. "I tried to leave. But I just couldn't. So before the plane took off, I ran for the door, dragging Kip with me."

"Kip is here too?"

She laughed, a low husky sound that whispered over his senses. He was reminded of the first time he'd ever seen her. He'd known, even then, that one day he would have to make her his own.

"I hope you don't mind, Matt. I know you have the film to edit, and there are dozens of scripts you'll have to read before deciding on your next project. But I couldn't bear to be separated from—"

"Shhh." He plunged his hands into her hair, lifting her face to his. Slowly, lovingly, he pressed light kisses over her eyes, her cheeks, her nose, before once more claiming her lips.

Against her mouth he said softly, "I love you, Alexandra. I know all the reasons why I have no right to stand in the way of your career. I've been telling myself over and over that Buddy has a dozen contracts waiting for you back in L.A. There are record commitments, and concerts—"

"I told Buddy to put my career on hold."

"On hold? Are you sure?"

"I'm sure of only one thing. I don't want to be separated from you, Matt."

"If that's the case, Alexandra, I think you should know . . ."

She waited, afraid to move, afraid to even breathe until he spoke the words she most longed to hear.

"I love you, Alexandra. I love you so much I don't think I could stand it if we had to be apart again. I want you to marry me."

"Oh, Matt." She felt tears spring to her eyes and blinked them away. "Are you sure?"

"I've never been so sure of anything in my life," he whispered against her lips. "I want to marry you and be with you always."

"Marriage—you do like to live dangerously, don't you?"

Matt smiled. "I told you, Miss Corday. It's in my blood." After a long, leisurely kiss, he said, "You haven't given me an answer yet. Are you certain this is what you want, too?"

In reply she wrapped her arms around his neck and returned the kiss until they were both breathless.

"I'm going to take that for a yes," he muttered, taking the kiss deeper.

"Yes. Oh, yes, Matt," she breathed against his lips. "Let's go share the news with Kip."

"Where is he?"

"Downstairs with Mai and Varra."

As she started to go Matt dragged her back and buried his lips in the hollow of her neck. The flare of heat was instantaneous.

He brought his hands to the buttons of her silk blouse and nearly tore it in his eagerness to slip it from her shoulders. When she sighed in pleasure, he murmured against her heated flesh, "We'll tell him later. Right now, have mercy on a poor, wounded creature who hasn't had a moment alone with you in days. I'm starved for your love."

As they dropped to the floor, tangled in each other's arms, the sky outside opened up. The downpour beat a steady tattoo on the roof. Alex knew it was a good omen. All the really wonderful things in her life had happened on rainy days.

How lucky she was. All she'd ever wanted was to make a home for herself and her little brother. But she'd never dreamed she'd come so far.

The friendships she'd formed, the career she'd carved, were nothing compared to the love she felt for this man, a love that would last a lifetime and beyond. And that could be a very, very long time.

AVAILABLE NOW

FLAME LILY by Candace Camp
Continuing the saga of the Tyrells begun in *Rain Lily,* another heart-tugging, passionate tale of love from bestselling author Candace Camp. Returning home after years at war, Confederate officer Hunter Tyrell dreamed only of marrying his sweetheart, Linette Sanders, and settling down. But when he discovered that Linette had wed another, he vowed never to love again—until he found out her heartbreaking secret.

ALL THAT GLITTERS by Ruth Ryan Langan
From a humble singing job in a Los Angeles bar, Alexandra Corday is discovered and propelled into stardom. Along the way her path crosses that of rising young photographer Adam Montrose. Just when it seems that Alex will finally have it all—a man she loves, a home for herself and her brother, and the family she has always yearned for—buried secrets threaten to destroy her.

THE WIND CASTS NO SHADOW by Roslynn Griffith
With an incredibly deft hand, Roslynn Griffith has combined Indian mythology and historical flavor in this compelling tale of love, betrayal, and murder deep in the heart of New Mexico territory.

UNQUIET HEARTS by Kathy Lynn Emerson
Tudor England comes back to life in this richly detailed historical romance. With the death of her mother, Thomasine Strangeways had no choice but to return to Catsholme Manor, the home where her mother was once employed as governess. There she was reunited with Nick Carrier, her childhood hero who had become the manor's steward. Meeting now as adults, they found the attraction between them instant and undeniable, but they were both guarding dangerous secrets.

STOLEN TREASURE by Catriona Flynt
A madcap romantic adventure set in 19th-century Arizona gold country. Neel Blade was rich, handsome, lucky, and thoroughly bored, until he met Cate Stewart, a feisty chemist who was trying to hold her world together while her father was in prison. He instantly fell in love with her, but if only he could remember who he was . . .

WILD CARD by Nancy Hutchinson
It is a dream come true for writer Sarah MacDonald when movie idol Ian Wild miraculously appears on her doorstep. This just doesn't happen to a typical widow who lives a quiet, unexciting life in a small college town. But when Ian convinces Sarah to go with him to his remote Montana ranch, she comes face to face with not only a life and a love more exciting than anything in the pages of her novels, but a shocking murder.

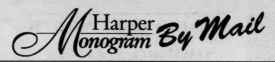

LORD OF THE NIGHT
by Susan Wiggs
A Venetian lord dedicated to justice suspects a lucious beauty of being involved in a scandalous plot.

ORCHIDS IN MOONLIGHT
by Patricia Hagan
Caught in a web of intrigue in the dangerous West, a man and a woman fight to regain their overpowering dream of love.

A SEASON OF ANGELS
by Debbie Macomber
Three willing but wacky angels must teach their charges a lesson before granting a Christmas wish.
National Bestseller